ECHOES OF SALEM

ECHOES OF SALEM

JOHN JENNETT

Contents

For my Mom, who chose me.

1

The Girl Who Vanished

The alarm didn't wake her. The cold did.

Maya Rodriguez surfaced from a shallow, dreamless sleep to find the heat had cut off again sometime before dawn. The apartment smelled faintly of old pipes and cheap coffee. She lay still for a few seconds, staring at the cracked ceiling and listening to the faint rattle of rain against the window.

Another morning in Salem. Another bill waiting for her.

She rolled out of bed and walked barefoot to the kitchenette. The digital clock on the stove blinked 7:38. Rent had cleared yesterday, taking with it what little breathing room she had. The electric company's notice was propped against the sugar jar; white paper, red letters. She avoided looking at it while she poured water into the coffee maker.

The machine gurgled to life, and for a moment the apartment felt less empty.

Maya wrapped herself in an oversized sweater and opened the blinds. The street outside glistened from an overnight drizzle, gray sky pressing low over the rooftops. The air smelled of salt and damp stone, the scent of Salem when the tourist crowds thinned and the ghosts were left alone again.

She liked this season best, the quiet weeks between Halloween hysteria and winter's deep freeze. When the town belonged to itself again.

Her phone buzzed on the counter. A payment reminder. Another from the gas company. She swiped it away and opened her banking app instead. The numbers didn't lie. They just stared back at her, indifferent.

$42.75 left until Friday.

She sighed and poured her coffee, black.

Bills could wait. They always did. The bookshop didn't pay much, but *The Wyrd Word* wasn't just a job, it was a refuge. A pocket of peace between the noise of everything else.

She pulled on jeans, boots, and her raincoat, tucking her hair into a loose braid. A few curls escaped anyway; they always did. Before leaving, she looked once at the old photograph on her fridge, a sepia image of her grandmother, back straight, eyes sharp. The family story was that one of their ancestors, Isabel de la Cruz, had been burned as a witch in 1693.

Growing up, her abuela used to whisper, *We were never witches, mija. Just women who remembered too much.*

Maya smiled faintly at the memory. Then she locked up and stepped into the rain.

The bus rumbled down Essex Street past shops that looked like they belonged in another century: brick façades, wrought iron, painted signs with names that traded on ghosts.

Hexed & Blessed Apothecary.

The Cauldron Café.

And her favorite: *The Wyrd Word Bookshop*, tucked between a candle store and an old church that still rang its bell on the hour.

The bell over the door chimed softly as she stepped inside, and the smell hit her, paper, dust, ink, and the faint trace of sandalwood incense that Gary burned when business was slow. It felt like breathing again after holding her breath all morning.

Rows of tall wooden shelves crowded the narrow aisles, each one crammed with stories: worn paperbacks, first editions, poetry collections nobody bought but Maya loved to touch anyway. There was a peace to it, the quiet companionship of words that had outlived their authors.

She hung her coat behind the counter and brushed a strand of wet hair from her cheek. The place was warm. Familiar. Her small slice of order in an otherwise indifferent world.

"Morning, Gary," she called toward the back office.

"Morning?" came the reply, muffled by a mouthful of bagel. "You mean *afternoon*, don't you?"

Maya smiled to herself. "It's eight-fifty."

"In retail time, that's practically noon."

Gary emerged from the doorway, a man in his late forties with thinning hair and the posture of someone who'd carried too many boxes of hardcovers in his life. His coffee mug read *Don't Talk To Me Until Page 100.*

He wasn't cruel, just perpetually inconvenienced by the existence of other humans. Maya had learned to take his sarcasm the way she took the creak of the floorboards: part of the building's character.

"I brought muffins," she said, lifting a paper bag from her purse.

Gary eyed it suspiciously. "Bribery?"

"Consider it preventive damage control."

He snorted but didn't argue, retreating behind the counter to unwrap one.

Maya turned toward the aisles, exhaling softly. The day hadn't even started, and she could already feel the static of exhaustion in her bones. But here, amid the smell of old paper and the whisper of turning pages, her pulse steadied.

This was her sanctuary.

Here, she wasn't the girl behind on rent or the daughter of ghosts. She was simply the keeper of stories.

By ten o'clock, the shop had settled into its rhythm: the murmur of customers, the occasional ring of the doorbell, the whisper of rain against the windows. Maya spent most of it reorganizing the mythology section, her favorite corner.

She traced a finger along spines she knew by heart: *Bulfinch's Mythology*, *The Mabinogion*, *The Book of the Dead*. And one thin volume bound in green leather that always drew her eye: *Arcana of the Weave*.

It was one of those rare acquisitions that came in unlabeled, slipped into a donation box months ago. No ISBN, no publisher. The text inside was dense, half in Latin, half in a language she couldn't place. She'd skimmed it a few times after closing, strange diagrams, runic sequences, and a phrase that lingered in her memory:
The song between worlds is never silent, only waiting for a voice to answer.

She'd never told Gary about it. He'd probably file it under "too weird to sell."

The doorbell chimed again.

A customer came in, tall, drenched, polite enough to wipe his shoes before browsing. Maya offered the usual greeting, then returned to her shelf. She liked people best when they left her alone among the books.

Still, she found herself glancing at the clock. 10:37. She was supposed to be unpacking a shipment in the back room. If Gary came out and saw her here again,

"Maya?"

Too late.

His voice carried from behind the counter, already edged with irritation.

She closed her eyes. "Coming."

The back room was colder than the front, lit by a single flickering fluorescent bulb that hummed like a trapped bee. Boxes lined the wall, each labeled in Gary's uneven handwriting. She grabbed a box cutter and started slicing tape, muttering to herself as she worked.

"History, mythology, self-help, *really bad romance novels...*"

It wasn't glamorous, but she didn't mind. The work was quiet, steady. The books didn't judge. They didn't demand explanations.

Another vibration buzzed in her pocket, this time an email alert from the power company. *URGENT: Service Interruption Notice.*

Her throat tightened. She opened it anyway.
Payment required within 24 hours to avoid disconnection.

She stared at the screen until the words blurred.

A floorboard creaked outside the door, Gary's steps, unmistakable.

She swore softly under her breath. Not now. Not again. She could already hear the tone he'd use: the sigh, the "you need to take this job seriously, Maya," as if she weren't already giving every frayed bit of herself just to keep the lights on.

The footsteps drew closer.

She pressed her palm against the nearest shelf and whispered, "Please, just... not right now."

It wasn't a prayer. More like a reflex. A plea to the universe to grant her one moment of invisibility.

And for reasons beyond reason, the universe listened.

The air thickened, heavy as a held breath. Light bent around her like heat rising from pavement. The buzzing of the bulb dimmed into a slow, underwater hum.

Maya froze.

Her heart kicked once, hard, then slowed. Her vision swam at the edges, the world folding in on itself.

Gary's voice came through the haze, muffled. "Maya? You in there?"

The door handle turned.

She stepped back, and vanished.

For one impossible heartbeat, Maya was nowhere.

The world didn't go dark or silent, it simply ceased to be a thing she could touch. The walls, the shelves, the floor beneath her feet, all of it dissolved into a shimmering absence. It felt like being pulled into a photograph just as the camera flash went off, caught between the blink and the burn.

Sound returned first, faint and distorted, as though carried through water.

"...Maya?"

Gary's voice. Faint. Far away.

The door creaked open, hinges crying out.

Maya tried to move. Her limbs obeyed, but she couldn't see them. Her hands, her *body*, were gone, or transparent, or something in between. She caught a glimpse of her sleeve against the boxes, and it wavered like heat above asphalt.

What the hell,

"Maya?" Gary stepped inside. His shoes scuffed against the concrete. He looked around, brow furrowed, irritation melting into confusion.

She could see him, but not the other way around. His gaze passed straight through her, searching shadows that didn't hold her shape.

Her breath quickened, but even that felt strange, like her lungs were trying to draw air from a world that wasn't hers.

Gary sighed, muttering under his breath. "Unbelievable. Probably outside on her phone again." He turned and left, the door swinging shut behind him.

The moment the latch clicked, the pressure broke.

The air rushed back in a single, violent pulse. Maya staggered forward, gasping, as her body flickered into solidity. Her hands, real again, braced against the table. The sudden weight of flesh felt almost unbearable. A warm trickle ran from her nose.

When she touched it, her fingers came away red.

The room was still spinning when Gary called from the front, "You all right back there? Sounded like something fell."

She wiped her face with the back of her sleeve. "Yeah," she managed. "Just, dropped a box."

"Try not to destroy inventory, okay?"

His voice was already distracted, lost to the rhythm of the cash register.

Maya pressed a trembling hand to her chest. Her heart raced so hard it hurt. Every nerve in her body felt alive, electric, wrong. The air buzzed faintly around her ears, a pitch just below hearing.

She stared down at her palms. They looked normal. *Perfectly normal.* But when she blinked, for half a second, they flickered, edges blurred, faint as mist.

Her stomach lurched.

She grabbed her coat, stumbled past the door, and out into the front of the store.

Gary looked up. "You okay? You look pale."

"I, I think I'm sick. Need some air."

"Fine, but, hey, we've got deliveries,"

The doorbell cut him off as she stepped outside into the rain.

The drizzle had turned to a cold, steady fall. Water spattered her cheeks, washing thin crimson streaks from her upper lip. She didn't care. Her whole body was trembling, not from cold but from the shock of what had just happened.

She crossed the street on instinct, boots splashing through puddles, until the noise of passing cars and church bells dulled to a hum behind her. She stopped beneath the overhang of an old brick building, pressed her hands flat against the wall, and closed her eyes.

The world felt thinner now, fragile, like something held together by breath and will alone. She could still feel the echo of that moment, the air folding, the weightlessness, the nothingness that had *felt like home.*

"Get a grip," she whispered. "You're not losing it."

But her reflection in the rain-streaked window disagreed.

She turned and froze.

The glass was fogged, yet her reflection stood sharp and clear for a heartbeat too long, even after she moved. Then it caught up, lagging by a fraction of a second.

She reached out, hand trembling. The reflection did the same, but again, late, like it was waiting for permission.

"Okay," she breathed. "That's... new."

The air around her prickled, the same low hum pressing at the edges of her hearing. The reflection shimmered faintly, the space behind it warping with a light that wasn't quite light, more like a pulse.

Then someone walked past behind her, and it snapped back to normal.

Maya stumbled back, heart racing.

She needed to sit down. To *think*.

The café down the street was half empty, the usual morning crowd of college students and retirees sipping their way through another gray Salem day. Maya took the back corner booth, still shaking as she wrapped her hands around a mug of coffee.

The warmth helped. So did the noise. The clatter of dishes, the hiss of the espresso machine, anchors to reality.

She kept glancing at her reflection in the window, half expecting it to vanish. It didn't.

Maybe she'd imagined it. Maybe the stress, the bills, the sleepless nights had finally caught up to her.

But deep down, she knew that wasn't true. She hadn't imagined the feeling of the air collapsing around her. Or the way Gary's voice had sounded, muted, distant, as though she were behind glass.

And that *sound*, that hum, she could still feel it if she focused. A vibration just below the surface of hearing, like something alive in the bones of the city.

Her phone buzzed on the table.

Lila.

You okay? Heard from Gary. Said you ran out mid-shift.

Maya hesitated, then typed back:

Felt sick. I'm fine.

A lie. Easier than the truth.

She locked the screen and stared out at the street. Salem looked normal, rain, gray sky, people hurrying under umbrellas. But underneath that, something pulsed. She could feel it now that she was aware of it. A rhythm that wasn't weather or traffic or nerves.

Like the whole town was breathing.

By the time she left the café, the rain had thinned to drizzle again. The clouds over the harbor hung low and heavy, their undersides streaked with dull silver.

She walked without plan or purpose, past the wrought-iron gates of the old cemetery, past the colonial houses leaning tiredly into the wind. The damp air smelled faintly of salt and iron.

Her phone buzzed again. The power company. She ignored it.

What did any of that matter now? She'd *disappeared*.

And yet, if she'd really done it, if it hadn't been some kind of stress-induced blackout, then how?

Her thoughts spiraled. Her grandmother's stories about their bloodline. The whispers of the women burned in 1693.
Just women who remembered too much.

Maybe this was what she'd remembered, something that wasn't supposed to be remembered at all.

She caught herself smiling faintly, despite everything. If Gary could see her now, he'd probably think she'd joined one of those witch tours the town lived on.

But the humor faded quickly. Her hand shook when she pushed it through her hair.

She didn't want this.

She just wanted the world to make sense again.

By late afternoon, the rain stopped. The sky over Salem turned a bruised shade of violet as dusk crept in. Maya found herself back near the bookshop, drawn there without thinking.

The Wyrd Word's windows glowed softly from within, casting stripes of amber across the wet sidewalk. For a moment, she stood across the street just watching. Her safe place. Her haven.

She wanted to go inside, to tell Gary she was fine, to lose herself in the smell of old paper and dust. But the thought of facing him made her stomach twist.

Instead, she walked to the side alley, the one that led to the delivery door.

The puddles there reflected the windows in fractured ripples. She caught her reflection again, broken across the water. It seemed to move before she did.

Her pulse quickened.

The hum returned.

It was stronger this time, not just in her ears but in her bones. The air grew thick, heavy with that same pressure she'd felt before she vanished.

"Maya," she whispered to herself, "don't."

But it was already happening.

The puddles stilled. The sounds of the city dulled to silence. The edges of the world blurred.

For a split second, she saw something move beneath the street, lines of faint blue light, like veins beneath the stone, converging somewhere deep below.

Then the vision was gone, and the rain started again.

Maya staggered back, heart hammering.

A man walking his dog passed her and gave a sideways look, but she barely noticed. Her hand was pressed to her chest, feeling that pulse again, not hers, not entirely.

Whatever this was, it wasn't done with her.

The Weave, the name surfaced in her mind like a memory she didn't know she had, was stirring. And it was calling her by blood and by name.

By the time Maya reached her apartment, the last light had drained from the sky.

The building loomed like a tired sentinel; three stories of red brick gone soft with rain. She took the stairs two at a time, keys jangling in her trembling hand. Every creak in the hallway sounded too loud.

Inside, the air was stale. She closed the door and leaned against it, letting her eyes adjust to the dark. Her pulse still hadn't slowed.

For the first time since morning, she allowed herself to whisper it out loud.

"I disappeared."

The words sounded absurd, small, and yet, true.
Her body remembered it. The pull, the hollow weightlessness, the hum that wasn't sound.

She kicked off her boots and flicked on the lamp beside the couch. The light buzzed once, twice, then steadied.

Her reflection in the window caught her eye.

It was there, normal, for the moment. She set her bag down and moved closer to it. The woman staring back looked pale, hair damp and tangled, eyes rimmed in fatigue. She looked like someone who'd seen something she shouldn't have.

She raised a hand. The reflection followed. Relief fluttered in her chest.

Then,

A heartbeat late.

Not much. Barely a blink. But it was wrong. The glass shivered faintly as though disturbed from the other side.

Maya stepped back, every muscle in her body tightening. The reflection didn't move.

The lamp flickered.

"Okay," she whispered. "No. Not this."

The reflection's mouth curved into a faint smile. Hers did not.

Maya stumbled backward, hit the edge of the coffee table. The mug she'd left there that morning toppled and shattered on the floor. The sound snapped the room back to normal.

Her reflection matched her again, same posture, same expression.

Maya pressed a hand to her face. She was shaking uncontrollably.

"What is happening to me?"

The lamp dimmed once more, as if the electricity had sighed.

She dropped to her knees and began gathering the shards of glass, each piece catching a sliver of her distorted face. The hum returned, soft, low, thrumming through the floorboards this time.

It wasn't in her head. It was *underneath*.

Later, after the pieces were swept away and the floor wiped clean, she tried to anchor herself in the ordinary: a hot shower, clean pajamas, a reheated container of noodles. But the world wouldn't settle. The TV remote clicked without effect; the signal kept cutting to static. Her phone refused to connect to Wi-Fi, spinning endlessly.

She sat on the couch with her knees drawn up, staring at the rain streaking the window.

Every time she blinked, she saw that after-image again. Herself, a heartbeat behind.

The clock ticked toward midnight. The hum deepened.

At first, she thought it was coming from the building, old pipes, maybe, or the heater finally giving up. But when she muted the room entirely, it was still there.

Not sound. Not exactly. More like a vibration inside her skull, a resonance she could *feel*. It pulsed in a rhythm that was too steady to be random, too alive to be mechanical.

Her fingers tingled. The lights dimmed again.

"No," she whispered, standing. "Not again."

But the air was already shifting.

A faint glow traced itself along the edges of the window, spiderweb-thin threads of light, blue and silver, weaving patterns that shimmered and then vanished. The apartment darkened until all that remained were those ghostly threads.

For a heartbeat, she saw something beyond them, lines converging far beneath the earth, like veins of light running deep under Salem's old foundations. The sight filled her chest with an ache that was equal parts wonder and terror.

Then, as suddenly as it came, it was gone.

The lights returned. The refrigerator hummed. The rain outside sounded like rain again.

Maya sank to the floor, shaking.

The apartment was exactly as it had been before, except for one thing.

The photograph on the fridge, her grandmother's picture, had fallen facedown.

She crawled over, picking it up carefully. The frame had cracked down the middle, splitting her grandmother's image in two.

Behind it, tucked into the magnet's corner, was a yellowed slip of paper she'd never noticed before. It was folded three times, edges brittle. She unfolded it carefully.

The handwriting was her grandmother's, neat, sharp.

The blood remembers what the world forgets.

If you hear the song, follow it home.

Her throat tightened. *Home.*

In her grandmother's stories, "home" never meant a house. It meant the old ground, the place where their ancestors had been buried, the Rodriguez family mausoleum on the edge of the old cemetery.

Maya closed her eyes. Her grandmother had always told her that the bloodline carried echoes, memories that sometimes whispered through dreams.

Maybe the whisper wasn't in her head. Maybe it was in her blood.

She looked at the cracked photograph again. Her grandmother's eyes, frozen in that half-smile, seemed to glint faintly in the lamplight.

The hum in the floor pulsed once more, soft, patient. Waiting.

She didn't sleep much that night. Every time she closed her eyes, she saw the blue threads under the city, winding like rivers of light through the dark.

Once, she dreamed she was standing on water, her reflection rippling beneath her, whispering something she couldn't quite make out.

When she woke, the clock read 4:12 a.m. The hum was gone. Only silence remained.

Outside, the rain had stopped. A thin fog crawled over the streetlamps, turning their light to gold.

She made coffee, though the smell alone turned her stomach. Her hands still trembled as she checked her phone, no new messages, no missed calls.

When she looked up, the kitchen light flickered again.

Something inside her snapped into focus.

This wasn't random. The pull she'd felt in the alley, the vision beneath the streets, the note, everything was converging. She didn't know what waited at the mausoleum, but she couldn't ignore it anymore.

She grabbed her jacket, shoved the note into her pocket, and glanced once more at the cracked photo. "If you're watching, Abuela," she murmured, "a little guidance would be nice."

The lamp flickered once, faint but distinct.

She smiled, a small, tired curve of her lips, and stepped outside into the fog.

Salem before dawn was another world entirely. The streets were empty, the air damp and heavy with salt. The old houses loomed like silhouettes in the mist. The town's famous history was quiet now, sleeping under layers of brick and centuries.

The gates of the old cemetery yawned open, the hinges whispering like breath drawn in. Fog coiled between the headstones, soft and luminous in the first edge of dawn.

Maya followed the gravel path by instinct more than memory, each step guided by that low vibration in her chest, the hum that had followed her from the city, down the alleys, into her dreams.

When she reached the mausoleum, the air grew still. The wrought-iron door bore the Rodriguez crest, but the pattern was deeper than she remembered, the serpent, yes, but around it now faintly glowed something else.

Lines of pale light traced themselves through the rust and age: a circle, perfectly inscribed, crossed by five slender spokes.

At the end of each line pulsed a rune, ancient and incomplete, one flickering faintly blue, another red, another gold, green, and white.

Maya's breath caught. The pattern was alive, responding to her nearness.

Her grandmother's note burned in her pocket as she reached out. "Follow it home," she whispered.

The iron was cold, but not dead. It thrummed under her palm. The lines brightened and spiraled inward, meeting at the center where the serpent's eye should have been.

The lock clicked open.

Inside, the mausoleum was small, stone walls, shelves of names, air dry as parchment. But the hum here was stronger, as though the ground itself was breathing through the floor.

Dust drifted in shafts of half-light. And on the altar at the far end, beneath the family seal carved into stone, something stirred.

At first she thought it was shadow. Then she saw the shape of it — a book, bound in dark leather that shimmered faintly like oil on water. It was half-embedded in the stone, as if the seal itself had grown around it.

The circle and five intersecting lines were engraved into the cover, their pattern matching the glowing sigil on the door. Tiny runes pulsed at the end of each spoke, beating softly like distant hearts.

Maya stepped closer, every nerve alive. Her reflection, faint, silver, impossible, shimmered across the leather, her face mirrored and fractured by the sigil's lines.

When her fingertips brushed the edge, the air rippled outward in silent rings.

The dust lifted. The runes flared. The faint scent of burning cedar filled the air.

The circle turned.

Five beams of light rose from the book, each color distinct — blue, red, gold, green, and white, and for a heartbeat, they hung there, crossing at a single radiant point above the seal.

A symbol older than language itself.

Maya felt it reach through her, through blood and memory and bone. The hum inside her chest answered, her heartbeat syncing to that pulse.

Then, just as suddenly, it ended. The lights folded inward. The stone beneath her feet cooled.

The book lay on the altar now, free from the seal, its edges smoking faintly. The runes along its spine faded to stillness.

Maya stared down at it, chest heaving. The world smelled of rain and ozone and something alive, something *awake*.

She reached out once more, fingertips trembling, and turned the cover.

The first page bore only five words, written in ink that shimmered faintly silver in the dawn's weak light:

The Covenant Was Never Broken.

The air stilled. Somewhere deep beneath Salem, the Weave shivered, as if recognizing the touch of one of its own.

Maya stood frozen, the dawn burning pale beyond the doorway, a relic older than sin cradled in her hands.

The hum returned, soft and steady. This time, it wasn't frightening.

It was familiar.

2

Bloodlines and Bones

Morning light broke thin and colorless through the blinds. For a long time, Maya lay still, unsure if she had actually slept. Her body ached as though she'd been running in her dreams. The taste of ash clung to the back of her throat.

The apartment was too quiet. No traffic yet, no neighbors slamming doors. Just the faint hum from somewhere, electric or alive, she couldn't tell anymore.

On the coffee table, the Codex waited. Its dark leather cover looked dull in daylight, ordinary even, but she could feel it humming in the air the way a heat source bends light.

Maya pushed herself upright, every movement slow, deliberate. Her head throbbed behind the eyes. A crust of dried blood ran from her nose to her lip, smudged from when she'd wiped it in the night.

Bills lay scattered across the kitchen counter: power, rent, overdue notice from her student loans. The real world still expected her to function.

She ran a hand through her tangled hair and laughed once, short, bitter. "Yeah, right."

The lamp by the couch flickered as if in answer.

Maya froze, watching it. The flicker steadied, then pulsed twice, faintly rhythmic.

"Don't start," she murmured. She unplugged the lamp. The hum didn't stop.

She turned to the Codex.

For a moment she considered wrapping it in cloth, hiding it under the floorboards. But her hand moved of its own accord, brushing the cover. The vibration changed, syncing with her pulse.

It felt almost... affectionate.

She jerked back, heart hammering. The hum dimmed, a small retreat.

Her phone buzzed, her landlord's number. She let it go to voicemail, rubbing the bridge of her nose until the pressure eased. Everything about the world felt thinner now, as though her apartment existed in a layer that could peel away at any moment.

She showered, dressed, made coffee she didn't drink. The steam rising from the mug looked wrong, its curls twisting in patterns too deliberate to be random.

When she reached for the Codex again, something new caught her eye.

The first page, *The Covenant Was Never Broken*, had faint impressions beneath the text, shadows of runes pressed into the fibers like the memory of writing. She tilted the book toward the window, and the marks caught the light: five tiny sigils, each one a point on an invisible circle.

Her breath shortened.

She traced them with one fingertip. The air prickled, and for a moment she thought she heard whispering just beyond the wall, no words, just tone, like distant chanting underwater.

The hum rose in her chest again, gentle but insistent, pulling her forward. Not metaphorically. Literally.

Her gaze drifted to the window. Outside, the fog over the city had thickened, rolling in off the harbor like milk poured through glass.

She knew where she had to go.

The streets were nearly empty when she reached the cemetery gate. The world felt muffled; even her footsteps made no sound.

The iron gate stood half-open. The frost on its hinges shimmered faintly in the fog's pale light. She hesitated only a heartbeat before stepping through.

The mausoleum waited at the far end, the shape of it ghosted by mist. Last night it had seemed vast; now it looked small, almost fragile.

The circle carved into its door no longer glowed. The runes at each spoke were dull gray, the serpent's eye cold. Yet she felt the hum vibrate through her ribs as soon as she touched the handle.

"Just checking something," she whispered to the fog.

The door groaned but yielded easily. Inside, the air smelled of old rain and cedar smoke. Dust motes floated in shafts of morning light.

The altar stood where she'd left it, the Codex's resting place now bare except for faint scorch marks on the stone.

She placed a hand on the surface and felt a faint heat, like a body's warmth long after death. Her fingers explored the carvings, finding shallow grooves that weren't part of the family crest. She pressed one absent-mindedly, and heard a click.

A section of the wall shifted. A whisper of displaced dust spiraled into the air.

Maya froze, then leaned closer. A narrow panel had opened beside the altar, no wider than a handspan. She slid her fingers into the crack and pulled. The stone moved easily, revealing a shallow niche.

Inside lay a small leather satchel wrapped in what looked like old linen.

Her pulse thudded in her throat as she lifted it free. The fabric disintegrated at her touch, leaving streaks of fine gray dust on her hands.

The satchel was supple, oiled to a deep brown, its flap fastened by a small bronze clasp in the shape of the five-spoke sigil. When she unfastened it, the air around her shifted, the pressure of a coming storm.

Inside were three objects: a bone stylus worn smooth from centuries of handling; a small pouch of black salt tied with red thread; and a brass tinderbox etched with the same circle-and-rune pattern she had seen on the Codex.

She set them carefully on the altar, each in a row. The stone beneath them vibrated faintly, and light, not bright but steady, began to gather along the engraved circle.

The Codex in her backpack stirred, a quiet heartbeat of energy that she felt through the straps against her shoulder.

"Okay," she whispered, "you're talking to each other. That's normal."

Her phone flashlight flickered. The beam shrank to a dim cone, then flared too bright, casting long shadows up the walls. The air pressed in, heavy and close, though not cold.

She heard it then, a sound like breath on glass. A single phrase formed out of it, soft as a sigh.

"Blood remembers song."

Her chest seized.

The words weren't in English. She shouldn't have understood them, yet meaning slid effortlessly into her mind.

Blood remembers song.

The hum deepened, vibrating through her bones.

Beneath her feet, lines of blue light traced through the floor, thin as veins, winding together until they formed a spiral beneath the altar. It wasn't light so much as motion made visible, threads rising like phosphorescent smoke to wrap around the book's edge poking from her pack.

The Codex drank the glow. Its cover shimmered once, then went still.

Maya stood rooted, pulse racing, every instinct screaming to run, but curiosity, stronger than fear, pinned her in place.

She knelt, brushing one hand across the glowing lines before they faded. The stone was warm. Alive.

The whisper came again, a tone rather than words this time, and the light ebbed away.

The silence left behind was immense.

When she stepped back into the fog, dawn had fully broken. The sky above the cemetery was a muted silver; frost clung to the grass like ash. Maya closed the mausoleum door gently, half-expecting it to resist. It didn't.

For the first time since the night she vanished, she didn't feel afraid of what she'd seen. The fear had transmuted into something quieter, respect, maybe, or belonging.

She slipped the satchel into her bag beside the Codex. The hum settled, low and content, like a cat purring against her ribs.

As she turned to leave, she noticed her breath rising in soft plumes. Five of them, each exhalation hanging in the air a little longer than the last.

The walk back to her apartment felt shorter than it should have. Maybe the fog disguised the distance, or maybe she was still walking in the echo of that hum. Her body felt tuned to something she couldn't name, as if she were hearing the world on a slightly different frequency.

By the time she reached her building, the sun had burned through the mist, leaving everything washed in pale gold. She kept expecting people to look at her differently, to sense it. But they passed without notice. Only one stray cat paused to stare at her from a fencepost, eyes like polished coins.

Inside, the apartment smelled of cold coffee and dust. The mundane details steadied her, the hum of the refrigerator, the drip of a faucet, the stack of unpaid bills mocking her from the counter. She set the satchel beside the Codex and exhaled.

"Let's see what secrets you've got," she said softly, not expecting an answer.

The Codex didn't glow this time. It sat silent, a presence rather than an object.

She cleared the kitchen table, laid out the reliquary's contents: bone stylus, salt pouch, tinderbox. The air felt faintly charged, like the moment before lightning.

Each piece was worn smooth from use, old, but not dead. The tinderbox had a delicate seam around its lid etched with runes she didn't recognize. She brushed away a layer of soot. Inside lay a small flint and a strip of oilcloth stained with something dark, maybe resin. It smelled of burnt cedar and iron.

The stylus was stranger, bone, ivory perhaps, capped with bronze at one end. When she lifted it, it vibrated faintly, responding to her heartbeat.

Maya set the stylus on the open Codex. The book responded immediately, not light this time, but movement. The pages rippled as though touched by wind, though the air was still. Symbols shimmered faintly along the margins, rearranging themselves into patterns she didn't understand.

"Oh, you're awake again," she murmured, leaning closer. "Great."

When she touched one of the shifting runes, it steadied under her fingertip. It felt warm, like skin.

Five faint outlines appeared across the page, matching the circle from the cover. At the tip of each line, a rune pulsed, red, blue, gold, green, white.
The same colors she'd seen in the mausoleum.

She stared, transfixed. The light was soft, almost tender. Her reflection in the window shimmered again, faint double-image, but this time she didn't look away.

Her pulse steadied. The Codex hummed quietly, matching her breath.

Without quite realizing it, she picked up a pencil and began sketching. She drew the circle first, then the lines, then the runes as best she could recall. Each one left a different weight on the paper, the red one felt heavier, the green almost cool.

Halfway through the last spoke, her pencil snapped. The sound broke the trance.

The light vanished.

Maya blinked and found herself sitting in dim afternoon light, hand cramped, heart pounding. The Codex lay inert again, the bone stylus still across its page.

She laughed softly, shaking her head. "Sure. Because that's normal."

Her stomach growled. She hadn't eaten since yesterday morning. She ordered cheap takeout and paced the kitchen until it arrived, every creak in the apartment making her flinch.

When she finally sat down to eat, the Codex seemed to watch her. She couldn't explain it, the feeling of being observed, not maliciously but attentively, like something curious about her in return.

After dinner, she sat back down with the sketch and studied it under the lamplight. Her fingers tingled when she traced the lines she'd drawn.

The hum returned, faint and familiar. It settled her like a heartbeat.

Sometime after midnight, exhaustion caught her. She folded her arms on the table and let her head rest against them. The lamplight swam in her peripheral vision, blurring into gold haze.

She didn't mean to fall asleep.

When she opened her eyes again, she was standing in a courtyard lit by fire.

The smell hit first, pitch, smoke, and iron. The air was thick with the heat of burning wood. Around her rose the outlines of a crowd: shadowed faces, torches raised.

At the center of the square stood a wooden stake. A woman was bound to it, her dark hair tangled and soaked with sweat. The fire hadn't yet reached her, but the crackle of kindling was close.

Maya's heart lurched.

She knew that face.

Isabel de la Cruz.

The resemblance was impossible to miss, same eyes, same jawline. Her ancestor's face, seen in yellowed portraits and family stories, now alive and breathing in front of her.

The crowd chanted something in low rhythm. The words meant nothing; yet carried weight.

But Isabel wasn't pleading.

She was singing.

Her voice rose above the noise, thin but pure, carrying through smoke and flame. A single note that built in strength until it vibrated in Maya's bones. The fire wavered, as if uncertain whether to burn.

The song changed key, a harmony of grief and defiance. Around the stake, air shimmered like heat distortion. Symbols flared at her feet, lines crossing and forming the fivefold circle.

Light burst from it.

The crowd stumbled back, shouting.

Maya lifted her hands to shield her face, but she couldn't look away. The circle burned upward, fire turning white, spinning into the sky.

The light struck her palm like a brand.

Pain seared through her.

She screamed, and woke with her hand pressed to the table, the room dark except for the faint glow of the Codex.

Her palm burned, not painfully but with deep warmth that pulsed in rhythm with her heart.

When she lifted it to the light, she saw it: the faint outline of the circle with five spokes, etched into her skin like a scar seen through glass.

Not deep. Not angry red. Just luminous, like the trace left by heat on metal.

She touched it. The warmth steadied, and the Codex hummed in response.

For a long time she sat there, staring at the mark. Her breath shook.

The dream, no, the vision, still clung to her senses: the smell of pitch, the sound of singing, the look in Isabel's eyes as the light consumed her.

Isabel hadn't been killed by the fire. She had become it.

Maya whispered into the dark, "You weren't afraid, were you?"

The hum pulsed once, as if answering.

She laughed softly, tears stinging her eyes. "You're insane," she told herself. "Talking to a book."

But the mark on her hand kept glowing, and the air carried that faint trace of cedar and smoke.

She woke late the next morning, still sitting at the table, the coffee cold beside her. The mark on her palm had faded to a faint blush, but she could still feel it when she pressed her thumb against it.

The Codex was open to a new page she didn't remember turning.

Lines of script she couldn't read covered it, looping symbols that shimmered faintly silver when the light hit. At the bottom, one sentence stood out in English, written in the same hand as *The Covenant Was Never Broken*:

The blood remembers what the flame cannot burn.

Maya stared at the words until they blurred.

She closed the Codex, fingers trembling, and sat back in the chair. The room smelled faintly of smoke again, though the windows were shut.

For most of the day, Maya drifted between doing and not doing, the state of someone moving through a world that no longer felt entirely solid.

She tried normal; laundry, cleaning, a walk to the corner store for milk and aspirin. People smiled, nodded. They saw her.

But the hum followed. Soft. Persistent. Sometimes she caught it under the electric buzz of streetlamps or in the whisper of her shoes on pavement. A pulse at the edge of hearing, syncing with her heartbeat.

By afternoon, she'd given up pretending she could ignore it. She came home, set the Codex on the table, and stared at her reflection in the dark screen of her laptop.

"You have to stop being afraid of it," she whispered. "You can't hide from something that's in you."

Her reflection blinked back with the faintest delay.

Maya exhaled slowly, grounding herself.

Then she opened her notebook and began to plan.

She'd spent enough nights watching training videos online, mindfulness, breathing control, focus techniques. The soldiers she'd once read about in old biographies swore by rhythm and repetition.

So she started simple: **breath control**.

In four, hold two, out six.

Every inhale she counted aloud, letting the rhythm settle her heartbeat until the hum inside her matched the cadence.

The Codex began to vibrate faintly on the table.

"Okay," she murmured. "We're listening to each other now."

She opened to a blank page in the back. When she wrote *Test 1* in pen, the ink shimmered faintly, silver thread woven into black.

She noted the date, time, physical condition.

Her handwriting felt steadier than she expected.

Then she added a final line: *Objective, controlled vanish for ten seconds.*

The words looked ridiculous on paper, but no more ridiculous than what she'd already lived.

She cleared a space in the living room, moving the coffee table aside. Laid a folded blanket on the floor in case she fell. Set the timer on her phone for ten seconds.

Her heart beat faster, but it wasn't fear this time. It was readiness.

She placed one hand over the Codex. The hum deepened, warm and familiar.

"Okay," she said aloud, "let's see if we can do this without passing out."

She closed her eyes. Focused on the breath.

In. Four beats.

Hold. Two.

Out. Six.

Her pulse slowed, syncing with the rhythm. The air around her thickened, not like fog this time, but like water, heavy, supportive, alive.

She felt the shift just before it happened, the faint vibration of her skin, the world drawing in around her, sound folding into itself.

Then she was gone.

Not gone the way she'd been before, not panicked, not flung into nothingness. This was clean. Smooth. The hum became a tone, and the tone became silence.

She couldn't see, exactly, but she could *feel* the space around her. Every object in the room hummed with its own frequency, the chair, the table, even the cooling cup of coffee. The air vibrated like threads of a vast unseen web, and she could sense each one's tension.

It wasn't emptiness. It was connection.

Ten seconds felt eternal.

The timer beeped faintly from somewhere far away, and she let go.

The world snapped back.

Sound, light, weight, all at once.

Maya dropped to her knees, gasping. The air tasted metallic. Her nose started bleeding immediately. She grabbed a towel, pressing it hard, but the bleeding was light, more like the body reminding her of its limits.

Her hands shook violently. Her vision swam in pulses. But she was grinning.

She'd done it.

Not by accident. Not by fear.

By *choice.*

When the trembling subsided, she crawled to the couch and collapsed onto it. The world flickered slightly at the edges, the way heat distorts air. The hum, still faintly audible, steadied into a slow, content rhythm.

Her phone screen glowed nearby. She picked it up with trembling fingers and recorded her notes:

"Duration ten seconds. Moderate nosebleed. Fatigue severe, but recovery... okay. The hum feels easier to follow this time. Less resistance."

She set the phone down, wiped the blood from her lip, and laughed weakly.

"You're learning," she told herself, or maybe the Codex.

The book sat open on the table. Its pages were motionless, yet she could feel it *listening*.

She took another slow breath. The hum responded, faint but certain.

The rest of the evening passed in fragments.
She drank water. Ate crackers without tasting them. Stared at the ceiling until it blurred.

Every time she closed her eyes, she saw light moving through the air, faint silver filaments tracing the shape of her apartment. Each time she focused, they vanished.

Sometime near midnight, the fatigue caught her fully. Her body wanted rest, but her mind buzzed.

She went back to the Codex. Opened to the same blank page where she'd written her notes. The ink shimmered again when she touched it.

"I know this isn't smart," she whispered, "but I need to understand what you are."

She dipped the bone stylus into her coffee, a ridiculous stand-in for ink, and began to write directly in the margin beside her test entry.

The words came without much thought:

When I listen, the world listens back.

She paused, staring at the sentence.

The Codex pulsed under her hand, soft and steady, and the ink shimmered brighter until the words looked alive.

A faint vibration rippled through the air, not sound, but resonance, like the low note of a tuning fork.

The silver glow spread along the margin, then faded.

Maya whispered, "You heard me."

Silence. Then a single, low hum rolled through the room, so subtle she might have imagined it.

But she didn't.

She closed the book gently, her fingers tracing the edge of the cover. The mark on her palm tingled, echoing the hum.

For the first time since this began, she didn't feel like something strange was happening *to* her.

She felt like part of it.

She cleaned up the living room, resetting the space to its normal order, the table back in place, the blanket folded, the lamp turned off. The air felt different somehow, quieter but not empty.

In the bathroom mirror, she studied herself.

The circles under her eyes were darker, but the expression was steadier. The faint warmth on her palm had cooled to a gentle throb, like an ember beneath skin.

She touched it lightly and whispered, "Grip stage, huh? Guess we're there."

Her reflection smiled half a second late. Then caught up.

She laughed, tired and unafraid.

That night she wrote again, not in the Codex but in her personal journal. Her handwriting wavered from exhaustion, but she didn't care.

There's a rhythm to it. Not a command, a conversation. Maybe it isn't about power at all, maybe it's about harmony. When I listen, it answers. The hum feels... alive. But not dangerous. Yet.

She closed the notebook, slid it under the couch cushion, and turned off the lights.

The room fell into perfect stillness.

Just before sleep took her, a faint hum stirred through the floor, so soft it could have been the building's pipes, or her own heartbeat, or something deeper.

Either way, she smiled.

"Goodnight," she whispered.

The Codex, closed on the table, pulsed once in answer.

3

The Flickering Veil

Maya woke to the hum again.

Not the refrigerator this time. Not even the traffic under her window. This was deeper, bone-deep, a low vibration that seemed to pulse from the floorboards through her ribs, syncing to her heartbeat.

The air felt heavier, faintly electric. When she sat up, her blanket slid from her shoulders in slow motion, like gravity had forgotten how to hurry.

She blinked hard. Everything snapped back into ordinary time.

Her phone buzzed on the nightstand. She reached for it and squinted at the clock, 7:18 a.m. No texts. No missed calls. Just the quiet knowledge that something had changed again overnight.

For a long minute, she stayed there, breathing carefully, letting the world reacclimate.

When she finally stood, the shadows followed a split second late.

She froze, watching the faint lag between movement and reflection. "Nope. Not doing this."

The shadows caught up, innocent once more.

Maya rubbed her temples, then made her way to the kitchen.

The light above the sink flickered when she sighed. Once, twice, in rhythm.

"Don't start," she warned it.

It flickered again anyway, as if testing boundaries.

She groaned, poured herself stale coffee from the pot, and grabbed the bills stacked beside the toaster, a depressing still life of envelopes and red warnings. Rent due next week. Utility reminder. Cell service overdue notice.

She flipped through each one, already knowing she couldn't pay them all. "Congratulations," she muttered. "You are the proud owner of thirty-seven dollars and forty-two cents."

The light dimmed, almost sympathetically.

"Great. Even my appliances pity me."

She stared at the glowing Codex on her kitchen table, closed but faintly warm. Since yesterday's discovery, it had refused to stay inert. She swore the runes on the cover shifted subtly every time she looked away, like the words rearranged themselves when unobserved.

"You're not helping either," she said.

But she sat down anyway.

The book's surface felt almost alive under her fingertips, cool at first touch, then warming to her skin like an exhale. The five-spoked circle on the cover pulsed once, faint silver veins flickering to life.

When she opened it, a shimmer of light ran between the pages, like static caught in paper.

She found herself flipping automatically to the section she'd stared at last night. The heading was still there:

Fragment of Passage, On Shadow Between Motions.

The text shifted as she read. The letters bent, reshaping themselves into words she could somehow understand without translation:

"Invisibility is not concealment, but displacement.
The Weave moves where the vessel does not.
To vanish is to begin travel.
The next breath carries you farther than sight."

Maya frowned. "Travel?"

She ran her thumb over the margin. Beneath her skin, faint indentations formed, runes pressed into the parchment long ago. A faint whisper followed, brushing her ear like a thought that wasn't hers:

The space between steps is not empty.

Her breath caught. She looked up. The light above the sink flickered again, then steadied.

"Okay," she said aloud, voice too loud in the silence. "Are you suggesting what I think you're suggesting? Because last time I disappeared, I wasn't exactly sightseeing."

No response. Only the soft hum returning, the rhythm of her pulse reflected back through the room.

She took a long swallow of coffee, grimacing. "Fine. You want data? Let's do data."

She cleared a section of the living room floor, dragging the coffee table aside. The space felt warmer than before, charged.

Her notepad lay nearby, still open to yesterday's log:

Test 1, Invisibility: spontaneous, 14 sec duration. Cost = moderate bleed, exhaustion. Recovery = 10 min.

She flipped to a new page.

Test 2, Controlled vanish, goal: voluntary fade, 5 sec. Observation: "space between steps", test hypothesis: partial displacement?

She wasn't sure why she wrote *displacement.* It just felt right.

The Codex sat on the couch, closed, but she could feel it humming through the air.

"Okay," she said, standing in the center of the room. "No drama this time. We vanish, we reappear. Five seconds. Easy."

She took a breath. In four, hold two, out six.

The lights dimmed slightly, shadows warping around her outline.

"Here we go."

Her heartbeat slowed. The hum deepened.

The edges of her body began to blur, the same sensation as before: skin dissolving into air, heartbeat stretching out of sync. She fought the panic, remembering the last time she'd vanished unplanned. This time, she clung to control.

Five seconds.

The hum swelled until it filled her skull. Her outline flickered, half visible, half gone. The world beyond shimmered, muted, translucent. Her reflection on the TV screen looked like smoke behind glass.

Then, for one terrible moment, she felt *motion*. Not a fall or drift, but *translation*. Like gravity had rotated ninety degrees and she was sliding along something invisible.

Then she was back.

Maya gasped. The lights flickered violently, then stabilized.

She stumbled to the couch, grabbing the towel she'd prepped, blood already warm under her nose. She wiped it away, heart racing, not from fear but exhilaration.

Her hands shook as she wrote:

Result: successful vanish (controlled). Duration 5 sec.
Phenomenon: felt "motion" though stationary. "Displacement" may be literal, not concealment but temporary shift.

The Codex vibrated faintly in approval.

She looked at it suspiciously. "You think you're clever."

The book didn't answer, but when she turned back to her notes, new faint script glimmered in the margin beneath her handwriting, not ink, but silver light spelling out words she hadn't written:

To vanish is to step between breaths.

Maya stared at it. "That's... not creepy at all."

She closed the Codex, half afraid of what else it might volunteer, and leaned back against the couch. The hum faded again, leaving a silence that was somehow thicker for having followed sound.

By late morning, curiosity had won over exhaustion.

She replayed the feeling in her head, that half-second glide, the subtle twist in reality. It hadn't felt like simple invisibility. It had felt like being somewhere else for a heartbeat. Not gone but *moved sideways*.

She picked up her notebook again and underlined *displacement*.

Then she drew a small diagram, two circles overlapping slightly, labeled *Here* and *Elsewhere*.

She stared at them, then added an arrow between: *Blink?*

When she looked up, the Codex's cover had shifted slightly, the five-spoked sigil now faintly glowing at the points.

"Yeah," she said softly. "I was afraid you were going to say that."

The apartment's air began to shimmer faintly as she stood again. She didn't know whether she was testing herself or being tested.

Her reflection in the window ghosted a second behind her.

"I'm not ready for this yet," she told it.

The hum that answered felt almost amused.

She tried another vanish, shorter, shallower, focusing not on disappearing but on the *moment before* she did, the way the air seemed to fold inward. For the briefest instant she felt herself lean into that fold, like walking into a gust of wind.

Everything warped.

The kitchen light brightened, then blew out with a pop.

When she opened her eyes, she was standing a half step to the left of where she'd started.

Maya stared down at the scuff marks on the floor. The shift wasn't large, inches, maybe, but it was *real*.

Her heart hammered. "Oh... oh no."

She stumbled backward and nearly tripped over the rug, breath coming too fast.

This wasn't invisibility anymore. This was movement, a *blink*, just as the Codex had whispered.

The hum around her deepened into something like a purr.

She whispered, "No. We're not skipping chapters here."

But even as she said it, she couldn't help smiling.

She felt it now, the subtle connection between her and the space she occupied. The Weave wasn't just showing her how to hide. It was showing her how to *travel through its skin*.

The air shimmered faintly again, as though in agreement.

Maya exhaled, dizzy but exhilarated. "All right, Weave. We'll take it slow."

She looked down at her notes and added one last line:

If invisibility is displacement, then Blink = deliberate crossing.
Conclusion: The door is opening.

The Codex pulsed once, silver light crawling along the edges of its pages.

Then the hum went silent.

And for the first time, Maya realized how loud silence could be.

By noon the apartment felt too small for her secret.

Maya couldn't stop replaying the morning's experiment, the pulse of space folding, the way she had felt both gone and *moving*. The Codex lay open on the couch, quiet now, but she could still feel its hum like phantom pressure in her chest.

She needed proof. Not for anyone else. For herself.

She set her phone on the counter and switched on the front camera, angling it toward the living room.

"Documenting," she said, voice low. "Controlled vanish, ten seconds. Observation only."

Her reflection on the screen looked absurdly normal, sweatshirt, messy bun, shadows under the eyes.

"Okay, girl," she muttered. "Five breaths."

In four.

Hold two.

Out six.

The air thickened, soft at first, then viscous as honey. The light from the window dimmed, colors leaching to gray. She closed her eyes and let the hum roll through her like a slow tide. When she opened them, the apartment looked slightly blurred, edges trembling as though viewed through heat.

She looked down. Her body was dissolving from the outside in, skin to fog to nothing.

She could still *feel* herself, but her limbs were suggestions of limbs. The phone screen flashed white, as if the lens couldn't decide what to capture.

Her heart stuttered.

Stay calm. Observe.

She counted to eight, then exhaled, and snapped back into solidity. Sound crashed in: the fridge, the ticking clock, the rain beyond the window. Her knees buckled; she caught herself on the counter, dizzy but alive.

Blood welled beneath her nose again, light but steady. She grabbed a tissue, laughing breathlessly through it.

"Still got it," she murmured. "Mostly."

The phone's recording light was still on. She stopped it, replayed the clip.

For eight seconds the image was pure white. No outline. No distortion. Just absence. Then, abruptly, she reappeared mid-frame, blinking at the camera like someone surfacing from water.

She froze the video on the white frame.

Her stomach dropped.

In the center of the blank image was a faint silhouette, an outline darker than light, a smear of shadow in the shape of a woman turned half away.

Her own reflection? Or something else caught between frames?

She stared until her eyes watered, then slammed the phone facedown.

When the phone rang again an hour later, she jumped.

GARY WORK flashed on the screen.

She hesitated, then answered.

"Maya! Finally." Gary's voice carried that mix of irritation and panic unique to middle management. "You're not gonna believe this, but the cameras are glitching again."

She swallowed. "Glitching how?"

"Same as last month, feed goes solid white for twelve seconds. The tech says it's an over-exposure error, but here's the thing." He lowered his voice. "It happened last night, and guess what? That's exactly when I texted you about inventory."

Her pulse quickened. "Coincidence."

"Sure," he said, not convinced. "Anyway, one of the customers swears he saw something, light flash in the stockroom. Says it looked like heat shimmer."

Maya forced a laugh. "Maybe the ghosts are unionizing."

"Ha-ha. Funny." He sighed. "Just... get in tomorrow. And if you're gonna quit, at least have the decency to give notice. I can't keep explaining 'white static' to the owner."

"Yeah," she said softly. "Got it."

He hung up.

Maya set the phone down, palms sweating. She looked toward the Codex; it sat innocently on the couch, as if it hadn't just invited her into an ethical crisis.

"Did you do that?" she asked.

Nothing. Just that faint hum, almost like laughter under her breath.

The afternoon dragged.

She ate crackers she didn't taste. Every few minutes she felt compelled to glance at the window, half-expecting the world outside to look subtly *off*, people moving too slowly, light bending wrong. Everything looked normal, which somehow felt worse.

By late day, she'd convinced herself she needed more data. Fear was manageable; uncertainty wasn't.

She set up the phone again, this time with a notebook beside it, and ran a smaller test, five seconds, focused breathing, eyes open.

The fade came faster now, smoother. A thin breeze rose from nowhere, carrying the scent of rain even though the windows were closed.

Through the thinning edges of her own body, she saw the room differently: glowing filaments of faint silver stretched through air and furniture like veins. Each one thrummed softly. The world wasn't empty; it was webbed, alive.

She tried to reach for a strand, and the whole network pulsed. Light, sound, texture collapsed inward.

Then she was solid again, heart hammering.

The clock on the wall read the same time.

Her phone timer read eight seconds.

She leaned against the counter, shaking with adrenaline. "You're learning," she told herself. "That's progress."

The Codex responded with a soft rustle of pages, though she hadn't touched it.

Twilight crept through the windows, turning everything silver-gray. Rain blurred the view of Salem's rooftops.

Maya made tea just to give her hands something normal to do. The act of stirring sugar into the cup felt anchoring, real.

When she carried it to the bathroom to wash her face, the mirror caught her mid-motion, and that was when she saw it.

The reflection blinked a half-beat late.

She froze, heart in her throat. The delay was subtle, barely perceptible, but unmistakable. When she tilted her head, the image followed after a breath's hesitation.

"Not funny," she whispered.

The reflection smiled back a fraction too soon.

Her mug hit the counter with a clatter, spilling tea across porcelain. She stared. The glass warped faintly, like water stirred by wind.

The edges of her reflection began to tremble, pixels in a film caught between frames. Behind that wavering image, darkness thickened, not the darkness of the room, but something deeper, without depth at all.

The overhead light dimmed, pulsing with her heartbeat.

She whispered, "No, no, not now,"

The hum returned, louder this time.

For an instant she felt the Weave again, the lattice of silver threads vibrating around her, but now something else moved among them, a static current dragging against the rhythm, fraying it.

The distortion in the mirror leaned forward.

Her breath caught; the room's air pressure dropped, ears popping. The shape behind her reflection, thin, eyeless, an echo of her own silhouette, tilted its head in perfect mimicry.

She lifted a trembling hand. Her reflection lifted too, but the echo behind it *lagged,* then caught up. The motion felt studied, like it had to think before copying.

"Stop," she whispered.

Her voice came back delayed, flattened, as if replayed from another room.

She backed away until her shoulder hit the doorframe. The mirror's surface rippled, one widening circle spreading from the center, distorting her face into waterlight.

A surge of nausea hit her. She clamped a hand to her mouth, staggering into the hallway.

The hum vanished. The lights steadied. The mirror was just glass again.

Her own wide-eyed reflection looked back, pale and shaking.

"Not... happening," she whispered, though her voice trembled.

She sat on the couch for a long time after, wrapped in a blanket, the Codex on her lap. The pages were cool to the touch now, silent. But when she opened it, her eyes fell on the margin beside last night's notes.

New lines had appeared, fine as hair, luminous silver pressed into the paper.

Reflection follows motion; residue follows creation.
Beware the echo between frames.

Maya shut the book and set it aside like something radioactive. Her pulse was still racing, her palms slick.

From the hallway, the mirror gave one soft tick, metal contracting in cooling air, but to her it sounded almost like breath.

She tried to distract herself with TV, then a shower, then pacing. None of it worked. The apartment felt crowded, as if the air carried more shapes than she could see.

Finally, near midnight, she returned to the Codex. The page was blank again, innocent. She took her pen and forced herself to write.

Observation: reflections delaying ~0.5 sec after vanish attempt. Possible cause: residual energy in local space ("Weave echo"). Alternate: contamination? parasitic current?

Conclusion: Need containment protocol before further tests.

She underlined *containment protocol* twice, though she had no idea what that meant.

When she capped the pen, the hum rose once more, quiet, steady, a heartbeat beneath her own.

Maya leaned back, eyes closed. The sound no longer frightened her, not completely. It was almost comforting.

The last thought she had before sleep found her on the couch was simple and half-terrifying:

The world isn't breaking.

It's waking up.

The next morning came without dreams.

Maya woke to light, not sunrise light, but something paler, flatter. The world outside the curtains looked washed clean, like color had been edited out. She sat up slowly, muscles tight from sleeping on the couch, and the blanket slid to the floor with a whisper that seemed too loud in the quiet.

The Codex was where she'd left it, closed and dark on the table. For a moment she hoped it might have stopped. But when her fingers brushed the cover, the faint hum answered back, steady as a heartbeat under the surface.

"Good morning to you, too," she muttered.

She started coffee, sat at the table, and opened her notebook. The page from last night stared back at her, messy handwriting, uneven lines. *Containment protocol.* The words looked like someone else's, scrawled in the dark.

She drew a slow breath and began a new entry.

Day 3.

Recurrent hum (auditory + tactile). Mirrors stable. No further lag observed overnight.

Hypothesis: resonance subsides when subject sleeps.

Possible correlation with emotional state (fear = amplification).

She paused, sipping bitter coffee.

Across the room, the Codex shifted, the faint rustle of pages turning by themselves. The sound prickled her skin.

"Don't start with me," she said without looking up.

The book ignored her.

Another page turned, softer this time, like the sigh of paper breathing. Then the hum rose, low and resonant, vibrating through the table and her ribs alike.

Maya closed her eyes, set down her pen, and listened. The sound wasn't mechanical. It was musical, almost, but with no melody, only pulse and tone. She realized her breath had synced to it again, the way it always did.

"Fine," she whispered. "Show me what you want me to see."

The Codex stilled.

She opened it slowly.

The page before her was blank except for faint impressions, indentations without ink, as if words had been pressed into the paper by invisible hands. When she traced them with her fingertips, they warmed under her touch.

Letters lifted out of the page in faint silver luminescence, forming a single line of text:

To write is to echo.

Her breath caught.

She reached for her pen out of reflex, but when the tip touched the paper, it moved on its own.

Her hand wasn't being forced; it was being guided.

The pen glided in looping arcs, her wrist loose as if she were following music. Lines spiraled across the page, forming symbols like runes, but smoother, more fluid, each stroke leaving a faint metallic sheen as though drawn with starlight instead of ink.

"Stop," she whispered. "I'm not,"

The pen kept moving.

Her heart pounded. She tried pulling her hand away, but the air around her fingers felt magnetic, caught in the same invisible current that always preceded her vanishings.

When the pen finally stilled, she dropped it. The hum cut off mid-beat, leaving silence so dense it pressed against her eardrums.

The room had changed.

The air looked denser, more *real* somehow, every dust mote suspended in bright suspension. The Codex sat open, the page gleaming faintly with what she'd written, or what had written through her.

Four lines, no more, each rune pulsing once before settling into stillness.

She didn't recognize the script, but she could feel its meaning, like memory half-remembered: not language, but concept.

Weave, Mirror, Thread, Echo.

The four words arrived not in her ears, but behind her eyes.

Her head throbbed.

She pressed the heel of her hand to her temple and whispered, "What are you trying to tell me?"

No voice answered. But the hum began again, fainter now, receding as if retreating into the floorboards.

Maya closed the Codex. "Okay. Okay, fine. We're communicating. Just, next time, maybe a memo instead of possession?"

The silence that followed felt amused.

The rest of the morning unfolded like a balancing act between two worlds. She forced herself through routine, laundry, dishes, bills, trying to keep the mundane alive. The motions helped until she caught herself humming the same low tone as the book.

She stopped immediately.

"Don't get in my head," she said. "Not unless you plan on helping pay rent."

The Codex said nothing, but she felt it listening.

By afternoon she had turned her living room into a lab: one table cleared for testing, a notebook for control variables, her phone camera set to record. Every detail mattered now.

Test 3 , Controlled vanish, static environment.
Objective: observe surrounding distortion vs. personal fade.
Tools: mirror (for reflection tracking), notebook, stopwatch.

She positioned the mirror opposite the table, just far enough to capture her full figure. The sight of her own face in that glass gave her a pulse of anxiety. She forced it down.

"Not today," she told the reflection. "You play nice."

She inhaled, eyes open this time and began to fade.

It happened faster now. The shimmer rolled over her like heat, limbs dissolving into translucent mist. But this time she stayed aware, *anchored*, watching the mirror as her image thinned.

Her reflection didn't vanish. It remained, faint but visible, a ghost made of static.

And behind that ghost, darker movement.

The echo again.

It was subtle at first, a ripple under the image. Then it leaned forward, matching her posture, but with a delay that made her stomach turn. The space between her and her reflection wasn't space at all, it was something *inhabited*.

The hum swelled.

"Not real," she whispered, though her voice didn't sound like hers anymore, it vibrated through the air like two voices overlapped. "Just an echo."

The echo in the mirror smiled.

Then she was solid again, gasping, back on the floor.

The mirror showed only her.

Her nose bled. Badly. She pressed the towel against it, hands trembling, head pounding so hard she could barely see.

After the shaking stopped, she crawled to her notebook and wrote anyway. She needed the words; they anchored her.

Test 3 Results:

Duration: ~6 sec.

Observation: mirror retained "after-image" during vanish. Possible interaction between Weave current and reflective surface.

Subjective sensation: observed secondary figure ("echo").

Emotional state: fear > awe.

She sat back, staring at the words. Then, out of the corner of her eye, she noticed new writing unfurling *underneath* her notes, delicate, silver, forming as if the paper itself were exhaling letters.

The mirror shows what the Weave remembers.

Silence follows recognition.

Maya's pen dropped from her hand. "No. No more of that."

She slammed the notebook shut.

Evening fell early, rain whispering against the glass. The city beyond her window blurred into watercolor shadows. The lamps flickered once, then steadied.

Maya curled up on the couch with the Codex on her lap. She hadn't meant to open it again, but the hum under the floor wouldn't stop until she did.

The pages glowed faintly, the runes from earlier pulsing like fireflies under skin. When she touched one, warmth bled through her fingertips, a pulse of reassurance, maybe apology.

She exhaled. "We're not enemies. I get it. But if you're going to keep doing this, you have to *warn* me."

A faint shift of air answered, like someone turning a page across the room.

She half-smiled despite herself. "Figures."

The hum deepened again, but softer this time, slower. Almost a lullaby.

She wrote one last line in her journal for the night:

If invisibility is displacement, and displacement is travel, then reflection must be residue, where the Weave fails to close behind.

The hum answered with a single pulse.

She took that as acknowledgment.

Near midnight, she woke with her cheek against the Codex. The air was cold; the hum was gone.

Completely gone.

The silence was so heavy it felt like pressure in her ears. Even the city outside seemed muted.

"Hey," she whispered, shaking the book gently. "You still there?"

Nothing.

She opened it. The pages were blank. Not white, *blank,* as though the ink had been erased from existence.

Then, across the first page, letters began to rise, not glowing this time, but dark, bruised purple.

All echoes end in silence.

Her heart kicked. She slammed the book shut, shoved it under a pillow, and sat rigid, staring at the ceiling.

The apartment was utterly still.

Then she realized she could hear something beneath the stillness, a low, irregular pulse like breathing through water. Not in the room. Beneath it. Beneath *everything.*

Her palm tingled, the same spot where the sigil had burned in her dream. She looked down. The faint pattern was glowing through her skin again, pulsing in time with that buried heartbeat.

She pressed her hand flat to the floor.

The vibration answered, faint but definite, as if something vast stirred beneath the city.

She whispered, "What are you?"

The floor answered with one long sigh, and the light in her palm went out.

The hum did not return.

She didn't sleep for the rest of the night. Instead, she sat by the window watching fog roll through the Salem streets, notebook open on her knees, coffee long gone cold.

Her final entry of the day filled half a page in cramped handwriting:

Summary:

1. Weave responsive to breath and thought.
2. Mirror interaction = residual echo ("shadow current").
3. Codex displays sentience. Communication = bidirectional.
4. Hum ceased 00:14 hrs. Unknown cause.
5. Silence heavy, structural, like something waiting to exhale.

She underlined the last sentence three times.

Outside, a car passed, its headlights cutting through the fog in thin, wavering lines. For a second, those beams looked like silver threads stretching through the night, vibrating faintly with the same rhythm as her pulse.

She watched them fade into distance and whispered, almost tenderly, "Listening lowers cost."

The words steadied her, even as unease lingered.

When she finally rose to turn off the lights, she caught her reflection in the window glass.

It didn't move.

4

⟨⟩

The Child and the Gun

Rain drew pale ladders down the kitchen window, the glass turning the street into a slow gray river. Maya ate standing up, a spoon in one hand and her phone in the other, cereal turning to paste because she kept forgetting to chew. The apartment had that morning hollowness she'd learned to stop fighting, no music yet, no traffic level with the windows, just plumbing somewhere in the building and the soft tick of the clock above the stove. The Codex watched from the bookshelf the way a cat does when it pretends to be indifferent.

She scrolled out of habit: headlines, a thread about some Salem tour guide dramatizing witch trials, a clip of rain on cobblestones. Bills sat under a magnet on the fridge, electric, rent, the red-letter one she kept moving to the back. She let the feed do what it always did, sand down the edges of her thoughts.

The buzz came as a hard sting in her palm, phone vibration doubled by something inside her. **AMBER ALERT** spilled across the screen in black and yellow. She tapped it open without thinking.

A girl stared up from the photo, school-picture careful, hair bowed back from her face. EMILY JAMESON, Seven, last seen in a blue jacket with stars. Missing since last night.

Maya felt the hum under her skin stir, first low, then rounding upward to meet her breath. She swallowed. The spoon hit the bowl with a small ceramic chime that sounded too bright in the gray morning.

She read the location. Three miles from here. Last seen near a convenience store whose video feed, the alert said, had corrupted into a white blur just past midnight.

Her thumb hovered over the screen. She could back out. She should back out. Instead she found herself pinching the photo to zoom, looking past the camera-ready stiffness into the part of the child's eyes that didn't know how to pose. The girl's smile didn't quite reach there. A little tremor of uncertainty. The kind you see on kids in big rooms with strangers.

The hum slid up her spine. She almost said no out loud, as if the sound were a hand on her shoulder she could shrug away.

She kept staring until her coffee went cold. The phone offered the number to call if she had information. Her pulse thumped in her hand, the same hand where the sigil had burned in her dream. The space under that skin grew warm, then hot like a coin left in sunlight. She flattened her palm on the table to take pressure off it; the heat pulsed anyway. Tiny filament flashes ran along the veins of her wrist, pale but visible, like someone shaking a glow stick that never quite breaks.

"Please," she whispered, to the rain or the room or the photo. "Somebody find her."

The apartment inhaled.

It was a small thing: the refrigerator hum drew back into itself, the pipes went still, the light in the fixture over the sink dimmed by a breath's worth of wattage. The Codex, quiet on the shelf since dawn, vibrated once, no rattle, just a thrum you feel with the bones of your teeth. The five-lined sigil on its spine shivered, silver in the gray.

Maya looked up just as the world tilted.

It wasn't a lurch or a drop. It was the subtle wrongness of a room turning half a degree under your feet while your eyes argue that everything's level. The rain on the window stuttered, magnified into thick, slow globes. For a heartbeat the kitchen felt like a photograph someone had pinched and pulled from the middle.

The hum spiked, and pain bloomed along her cheekbones behind the eyes, clean, bright pain, the kind that makes you understand the shape of your skull. She took a breath to steady and found there wasn't any air to catch. It had thinned to silk.

The photo on the phone filled her vision. Blue jacket. Star pattern. The scrim of something like fear held right behind lesson-smile. A mother's name. The number again, call if you know anything.

The sigil in her palm flared white-hot.

She dropped the spoon. Milk splashed. The bowl slipped in slow motion and shattered in ordinary time when it met the floor.

The Codex thrummed a second time, lower, like a note struck on a bigger instrument, and the kitchen folded along its corners.

Sound telescoped. The clock's tick stretched into a long string and snapped. The light went from gray to the blue-black of an unlit theater. The smell of rain cut out, replaced by something industrial and close: oil, old rubber, cold metal. The taste in her mouth went coppery. She tried to say no and heard the word arrive after she'd already thought it, as if sound had to climb a hill to reach her.

The floor was wrong under her feet. It had been vinyl, soft with decades of tenant scuffs. Now it was concrete, the kind poured with a careless sweep that leaves the vague memory of a hand's direction in the surface. Grit pressed through her socks. Somewhere water dripped with the quiet patience of dark places, every drop making a sound much too loud for its size.

Sound returned in fragments.

First the drip. Slow, patient, indifferent, water falling somewhere out of sight, measuring time in coins. Then the high, insect hum of fluorescents, a few bulbs failing in a rhythm that made the skin between her shoulders want to crawl. Farther off, metal ticked as it cooled, the settling clicks of a building that had learned to keep secrets.

Maya's cheek pressed to raw wood. Splinter. Dust. Pine resin gone sour with age. She straightened carefully and found herself tucked behind a wall of crates stacked four high, banded with steel. The air tasted of machine oil and old rubber, an industrial breath that clung to the back of the throat. Her socks registered grit through concrete, fine, sandy, ground from pallets and boot soles.

She didn't move for a heartbeat. Her body shook with a tremor that didn't read as fear so much as aftershock, as if the atoms of her had just remembered how to be together again. She breathed and the hum inside her ribs, hers, not the lights, turned to meet the breath, the way a sleeping animal lifts its head when you say its name.

She had teleported.

The word arrived like a thing she might break if she touched it wrong. She had been in her kitchen, rain, milk bowl, the phone with that photograph, and now she was here, wherever *here* was. The distance between those points stretched in her mind like a rubber band pulled to a squeal.

A voice echoed down the aisle between crate stacks. The language came at her on a slant, vowels elastic, consonants softened and smeared. Pashto? Dari? Or English kissed into unfamiliar shapes by a mouth that wasn't raised on it. She caught fragments when the speaker swung toward her side of the warehouse: "...no, not now... wait for him... I said wait,"

Another voice replied, lower, closer, on a phone. Footsteps paced, heel scuffing, toe dragging. A metal chair leg grated an impatient inch on concrete and stopped.

Maya swallowed. Her throat had gone dry in the displacement, as if her body had used up moisture to grease whatever impossible hinge she'd just swung through. The hum slid higher in her chest, warning or welcome she couldn't tell. She forced her breathing into the old pattern, four, hold two, out six, and the Weave tone joined her, a second pulse folded into the first.

She risked a look.

The aisle opened into a pocket of space lit by three long lights, two of them stuttering. The flicker made every shadow hesitate and lurch. A plastic folding table sat in the center, one leg shimmed with a paperback to keep it from wobbling. On it: a pistol laid carefully on a rag; a box of zip ties; a roll of duct tape half-used and torn crooked; a pack of cigarettes with one missing and the cellophane peeled back like a hangnail. Beside the table, at ankle height, a girl, blue jacket, white stars, sat on an upturned bucket, wrists bound behind her with plastic cuffs. Her ankles were cinched to a floor eye-bolt with another tie; someone had thought about leverage. A bandana gag cut white lines into her cheeks. He'd been neat with the knot. That made Maya hate him more.

A man paced with the phone pressed hard to his ear, back toward her, the cord of his neck taut. Early thirties maybe, dark hair shaved close, cheap jacket gone shiny at the elbows. His other hand worried a keyring like rosary beads. He moved like a trapped animal that refused to admit the trap.

"Tomorrow," he snapped into the phone, accent heavy but the words clean. "I said tomorrow. He doesn't, listen to me, you don't tell me," He turned, paused, breathed in through his nose. "Yes. Fine. Cash then. At least that."

Across from him, deeper in the gloom beyond the lights, a second man sat in a metal chair. He was only silhouette and cigarettes at first, the ember, the exhale, but when the stutter-bulb steadied, she saw a gaunt face, cheap mustache, eyes that sat too far back in his skull like someone had pushed them there. He watched the girl without watching her, the way men do when they don't see a person, only a thing they think they own.

Maya's hand found her mouth. She pressed hard to keep breath from becoming sound. Her palm burned under the pressure, the sigil heat, not pain exactly but announcement. She didn't dare look down at it. Everything that mattered was in front of her.

The hum behind her ribs lifted half a step, then another, until it felt like a string pulled tight. Move now.

She slid along the crates. The invisibility rose without permission, not a full vanish but a blurring, a pressure against the skin that made the warehouse's light slip past her the way water does around a stone. Edges softened. The eye loses patience for what is not insisting on itself. She let that happen. She didn't force. The hum rewarded that with steadier current. The air around her cooled as if apology for how hot her blood had gone.

She counted the steps between her and the girl. Eight? Less if she cut diagonally, if she trusted the strobe of the failing bulb to hide the movement. The phone man's pacing kept time with her breathing. The seated man didn't move at all, cigarette ash climbing, turning, breaking. He had the stillness of a snake in winter.

At step four, the hum changed: a lower harmonic rolling under the first. Warning.

She froze, one foot hovering over concrete. The sound came from behind her, no, not sound. Pressure. The particular attention the world pays you when a predator turns its head. She angled her eyes without moving her face.

A third figure stood at the mouth of the aisle she'd come through. He was a blockier shape than the other two, shoulders thick under a black coat too small across the back. He hadn't been there a moment ago. Or she hadn't seen him because the room had been a different equation then. He had a hand in his pocket, thumb dragging along the outside seam as if counting down a choice.

He took a step and the crate at Maya's hip whispered, wood against wood. She didn't breathe.

Phone man said, "Hold on," to whoever lived in his ear and set the phone on the table with the care you use for things you're pretending not to throw. His fingers hovered over the pistol but didn't touch it. He turned toward the seated man and said, in a language Maya didn't know, something that sounded like *watch her*. The seated man did not answer. He did not need to. The cigarette ember brightened.

The girl in the blue jacket coughed behind the gag. It wasn't a sound of airway; it was a sound of a child trying to be brave for an audience that doesn't deserve it. Tears had dried into salt constellations on her cheeks. She lifted her face toward the light, not to plead, but the way a plant will do in a cellar as long as it can remember the idea of sun.

Maya moved on the exhale, the only beat available. Her body learned this in another life, sneaking past curfew, slipping through a caution tape she'd been told to respect, the impulse that takes over when the adult in the room is failing and you become the adult by default. The invisibility clenched. The stuttering light helped; every blink of the bulb erased an inch of her. She kept the rhythm: move on darkness, stillness on light.

She reached the table's corner. The pistol lay a foot from her fingers.

The hum thrummed like a wire about to sing itself apart. She knew that pitch now: the threshold tone, the one that had always preceded the pull sideways into nothing. She did not want that here, now. She could not. Carrying someone... she'd never even tried with weight heavier than a spoon, a thought, a breath.

Please, she told the current. *Not yet. Not until I touch her.*

The current eased. Not away, a hand loosening on a leash.

She crouched, her knees a creak she hoped the fluorescents swallowed. The girl had been watching the phone man, her focus pinned where the threat was loudest. Maya put her face level with the girl's and shook her head once: no sound, no sudden jerks. The bandana gag hid the child's mouth, but the eyes widened a fraction more, not with fear but with recognition. Children have a sense for what adults have forgotten how to see. The girl's gaze flicked to the empty aisle behind Maya, then back to where Maya was; she could see *something* there, the way heat shimmer lets you know the road exists.

Maya extended two fingers. The girl tipped her face down, pressing the gag against them, a trust so clean it made Maya dizzy. The plastic at the girl's wrists sawed against metal. Maya's invisible fingers found the knot at the back of the bandana. She pulled. The fabric didn't give. She needed a blade. She didn't have one. The table had a box cutter tucked under its lip with a strip of duct tape.

Phone man picked up his phone again, impatience back in his shoulders. "Yes. Yes, now," he hissed. "I said bring the van. No, the other one."

Maya slid her hand along the table's underside, found tape, metal, the cold delicious weight of an answer. She peeled the box cutter free, breath held until her chest burned. The hum under her ribs wanted to swell and burst; she kept it small and tight. *Consent, not command. Listen, don't force.*

She reached for the gag knot.

The hum changed again. Lower. Closer. Behind her.

She felt it before she heard it: a small mechanical readiness, oil and intent.

A handgun being racked.

Her skin flashed cold across the shoulders, a cat's hackles raised by a sound that needs no translation. She didn't turn because turning would be the same as offering her heart to a circle of metal. She looked at the girl instead, and the girl did what you do when a grown-up tells you *it's okay*, she held perfectly still even though nothing was okay.

Maya's mouth tasted like copper. Her heart did the arithmetic and went very quiet. The hum inside her met that quiet with a steadiness that felt like the edge of a precipice. The Weave wasn't shouting now. It was offering a hand.

Behind her, a voice she hadn't heard yet spoke American vowels smoothed thin by years of swallowing them. "Don't move," he said. Not a shout. Not a bark. A bored instruction issued by someone who didn't think it would be disobeyed.

The box cutter felt very small and very stupid in her hand.

The pistol on the table was an arm's length too far.

Maya breathed once, the way you breathe when you have already decided and your body is the last to hear it.

The command hung in the air—*Don't move*—and for a breath, she obeyed. Then she moved.

The sound of the hammer locking back was so small, so clinical, that it didn't register as a threat until her pulse found it. Then the room seemed to tilt around that sound, the world narrowing to geometry and breath.

The hum inside her ribs rose in sympathy, an electric tremor too deep for hearing. It vibrated in her bones, threading through her breath, whispering that stillness wasn't safety; stillness was consent.

Her invisibility faltered. It didn't flicker out all at once, it *peeled* away from her skin, retreating like frost melting off glass. The man behind her, square frame, gun steady, saw movement where there hadn't been any, and his curse hit the same instant her shape coalesced in his sight.

"Jesus," he spat, and the barrel snapped toward her face.

Maya's body decided before her mind did.

She lunged sideways, shoving off the crate, her shoulder slamming into the edge of the table. The gun on the rag clattered to the floor, spinning under the seated man's boots. Startled, the man behind her fired, once, reflexively.

The sound didn't come right away. The first thing she felt was *impact without pain,* the way thunder rolls through your stomach before the lightning hits your ears.

Then the sound arrived, compressed, warped, wrong.

A shriek ripped through the warehouse lights, the fluorescents screaming as every bulb surged at once. The hum inside her chest leapt into a new pitch, a note sharp enough to slice thought. The air fractured.

She saw it. She *felt* it.

"The world cracked like glass, and light spilled through the seams."

The bullet had left the gun, but it hung there, silver glint frozen in air halfway between his hand and her body. Everything else moved slower than it should have: dust curling through light, the girl's wide eyes reflecting a warped image of Maya mid-turn, even the smoke trailing from the muzzle hanging like an unspooling ribbon.

Her breath tore out of her throat, ragged and hot. The world stuttered, and she realized she could *see* the Weave.

It wasn't light exactly, more like threads of movement, thin filaments vibrating through space, invisible until now. They clung to everything: to her, to the bullet, to the men, to the girl's bound wrists.

Every line shimmered with rhythm, all converging toward the spot where Maya's heart was hammering itself raw.

The hum became a roar.

Move now.

She did. She threw herself forward, instinct trumping reason, diving for the child.

The man behind her yelled, fired again, but the sound hit too late, lost in the distortion already flooding the room.

Maya reached the girl. The Weave pulsed like a heartbeat, hers, the child's, something older in between. She grabbed the girl's wrist, skin to skin, and the sigil burned alive on her palm.

Light exploded from that contact, a blinding white that wasn't brightness but *absence*, a hole torn through the visible.

For an instant everything existed as one sound, one vibration, one impossible chord. The heat, the smell of oil, the gunmen's shouts, the gagged sob, all drawn together, folded, inverted.

Pressure dropped. The warehouse imploded inward and exhaled.

The hum peaked into silence so pure it rang.

Then the world let go.

Maya felt herself *stretch*. Not just her body, but her being. Her awareness elongated through a thousand directions at once, up, down, outward, sideways through things that weren't supposed to have sides. The Weave flashed around her in ribbons, threads converging and snapping as if in pain. She was moving without moving, a pulse through fabric rather than space.

She felt the child's small wrist burning against her hand, and that touch anchored her, one point of gravity in a flood of nothing.

They weren't falling. They weren't flying. They were *becoming elsewhere.*

A second heartbeat, too big, too ancient to be human, echoed through her veins. She didn't know if it came from the Weave or from inside herself. The sensation wasn't language, but she understood it.

Not yet fear. Not yet loss. Only motion.

Her mind tried to find an edge, something solid. She remembered breath. She remembered light. She remembered the word *home.*

That was enough.

The light around her folded like origami and sealed itself shut. The silence broke with the rush of air.

They hit the floor hard.

Maya landed first, shoulder cracking against polished tile. The girl's body tumbled onto her, small and trembling but alive.

For a heartbeat Maya thought she'd gone deaf, the silence still clung to her, but then a man's voice shouted, "What the hell?" and the world slammed back into volume.

Footsteps. Metal scraping. Radios barking.

They weren't in the warehouse anymore.

She blinked up into fluorescent light, different, cleaner, institutional. Walls the color of oatmeal. The smell of floor wax and burnt coffee. A red sign by the door read **Salem Police Department – Main Lobby.**

Officers froze mid-conversation, donuts half-raised, the day collapsing around them. The displacement had brought a puff of wind, scattering papers and knocking a coffee cup onto the tile, dark liquid blooming like ink.

The girl whimpered once and buried her face against Maya's chest. Maya could feel the child's heart hammering fast enough to hurt.

"She's, she's safe," Maya gasped. Her lungs stung as if she'd run for miles.

An officer unholstered his weapon but didn't point it, eyes wide, pupils dilated. "Ma'am, what, how?"

"Warehouse," she rasped, blood slicking her upper lip. "Docks. Blue door. He's there," She swallowed the rest, realized she was shaking.

Someone moved closer, hand on her shoulder. "Miss, you're bleeding."

She pressed her fingers under her nose, saw red, forced a shaky laugh. "Yeah. He, he hit me. When I got her loose."

The lie came so smoothly it scared her.

Another officer scooped up the child, cutting the ties, murmuring soft comfort. "We got you, sweetheart. You're safe now."

The girl pointed weakly at Maya, voice hoarse behind the torn gag. "She... came out of the light."

Every head turned.

Maya wanted to disappear again, not teleport, not Weave, just *vanish* into anonymity. But the Weave around her hummed differently now, stronger, steadier, a current she could almost surf on if she closed her eyes. The power no longer screamed; it *breathed*.

Her reflection in the polished floor lagged half a beat behind when she lifted her head.

The officers didn't notice. Cameras did.

Somewhere, in another room, a security monitor recorded the burst of white and the impossible appearance of two bodies in the station lobby. The time stamp blinked red. The system buffered, then saved.

Maya sat against the wall while paramedics checked the girl. The buzz of voices blurred around her. Someone asked if she needed a hospital. She shook her head, too tired to lie again.

The hum inside her settled into a low vibration, equal parts heartbeat and machine. It wasn't angry. It wasn't wild. It was... waiting.

She touched the mark on her palm. It was cool again. Faintly luminous under the skin, like moonlight through fog.

For the first time since it began, she didn't want to push the power away. She didn't fear it. She *understood* it, at least enough to know what it wanted: movement born of compassion, not control.

She looked across the lobby. The little girl met her eyes, smiled shakily, and whispered something Maya barely caught.

"Thank you."

Maya smiled back.

And in the Weave, just for a heartbeat, she thought she heard another voice answer, not in words but in tone: *You listened.*

The overhead lights flickered once, then steadied.

Outside, sirens began to wail, far away, moving toward the docks.

Maya exhaled and closed her eyes.

The world, for a moment, was still.

Then someone said, "Ma'am? We need your statement," and she realized there was no going back.

The police station lot buzzed like a hornet's nest. Red and blue lights pulsed against wet asphalt, sirens crying somewhere down the next street as more cruisers arrived. Maya sat on the open tailgate of an ambulance, a foil blanket crinkling around her shoulders. Every sound, the slam of car doors, the crackle of radios, felt too sharp, as if someone had turned the world's volume up a notch too high.

A paramedic crouched in front of her, checking vitals on a handheld monitor. His breath smoked faintly in the cold. "You sure you don't want to go in for a scan? Pulse is elevated. You took a hit, right?"

Maya blinked hard. Her head still rang from the jump. "Yeah. He, uh, hit me when I tried to grab the girl. Just adrenaline, I think. I'll be fine."

He looked unconvinced but didn't push it. "You're lucky," he said, peeling the bloodied tissue from her hand and replacing it with gauze. "You did something good in there. Kid's safe, that's what matters."

She nodded, voice too quiet to carry. The truth, that she hadn't run, hadn't fought, hadn't even *walked* out of that warehouse, sat behind her teeth like a secret burning for air.

The sergeant who'd taken her statement earlier approached. "Miss Rodriguez? I just wanted to thank you again. The girl's already talking to our people. Brave work following that bastard. You probably saved her life."

Maya forced a brittle smile. "Anyone would have done the same."

"Maybe," he said, "but you *did*." He tapped his pen against his notebook and added, "We might want you for a formal interview later today, but for now? Get some rest."

She nodded again, waiting until he walked off before exhaling. The word *brave* lodged somewhere near her ribs. It didn't feel like bravery. It felt like surviving a lightning strike.

She watched as the little girl, wrapped now in a too-large police jacket, was lifted into another ambulance. Their eyes met for an instant through the open door. The child managed a tired smile.

Maya smiled back.

Then the cameras started flashing.

Reporters had gathered at the edge of the cordon, already forming the circle predators make around fresh story meat. Phones lifted. Someone shouted, "Hey! Is that her? The woman from the lobby video?"

Another voice followed, male, triumphant: "That's the *appearing angel!*"

The phrase cut through the noise, absurd and chilling all at once.

Maya turned her face away, pulling the blanket tighter around her shoulders, and started walking. She didn't know where she was going, just *away*. Every time the flashbulbs went off, her pulse tripped, and the air shimmered faintly at her edges. The Weave, whatever it was, still lingered close enough to taste.

She muttered under her breath, "Not here. Not again."

The hum beneath her skin agreed. It wasn't a sound, more a vibration threading through her blood, faint but steady. Even without the Codex nearby, she could feel it, the same pulse that had dragged her across space now brushing lightly against her thoughts.

It wanted her to move. She refused.

A young officer jogged up from behind, calling out, "Ma'am, you need to stay for debrief," but the look on her face stopped him. Whatever he saw, fatigue, shock, something stranger, made him hesitate.

"Tomorrow," she said softly, and kept walking.

She ducked through a narrow gap between the vehicles and slipped down a side street. Her shoes splashed through shallow puddles; rain had started again, fine and whispering. She leaned against a brick wall, shivering.

The cold felt good. It was real. Solid.

She pressed her hands to her face and breathed through her fingers, trying to steady the tremor in her chest. The city's noise faded to the dull hum of tires and wind.

Somewhere in the distance, church bells struck the hour.

In the space between the chimes, she could feel it again, the faint presence of the Weave, humming across miles like a distant radio station she couldn't quite tune in. A residual echo of power, vibrating against her heartbeat.

It wasn't coming *from* her apartment. It wasn't *in* the Codex. It was in *her.*

A terrifying thought bloomed: what if the Codex had only awakened what was already there?

She closed her eyes, testing the thought the way you'd test the weight of a blade.

Her pulse synchronized with the hum, one-two-three, until she felt the edges of herself start to blur. The same disorienting pressure she'd felt before a jump tugged at her spine, light bending at the corners of her vision.

"No," she whispered. "Control it."

The tug subsided, reluctantly, like an animal obeying a command it didn't fully understand.

Maya exhaled, slow and measured, her breath steaming in the cold. She stayed like that until the tremor passed. Then she opened her eyes again and looked up at the sky, low, gray, and empty.

Somewhere up there, a camera drone buzzed, still circling the station. Her stomach turned. They'd be replaying the footage already, frame by frame, feeding it to news cycles that would spin her into a myth before the day was out.

The *appearing angel.*

She almost laughed at the irony.

She'd spent her whole life trying not to be noticed, and now the world had decided to worship the ghost of her.

When she finally pushed away from the wall, the hum within her had faded to a low, sleepy murmur. The city felt normal again, or at least close enough to pretend. She started walking home, every step a small prayer that the Codex would still be sitting where she left it, quietly waiting, as if nothing had changed.

But everything had.

And deep down, she knew it was only beginning.

The video feed looped again, the same ten seconds of impossible footage replaying on Senator Victor Hargreaves's monitor.

White flash. Static. Then, from the void, a woman and a child, falling onto the floor of a police station lobby.

The senator leaned back in his leather chair, swirling the ice in his glass. The clink of melting cubes filled the office, steady and deliberate.

"Freeze it," he said.

His aide, Raymond Cho, paused the frame. The lobby camera had caught the woman mid-motion, hair flaring, mouth open, her hand still gripping the girl's wrist. The surrounding pixels bent, like heat distortion in summer air.

Hargreaves frowned. "And you're telling me this isn't doctored?"

"No, sir." Cho stood a step back, holding his tablet against his chest. "We ran the raw file through three independent verifiers. No compression artifacts, no splices. It's... genuine."

"Define genuine," Hargreaves said flatly.

Cho hesitated. "As in, it happened."

Hargreaves's smile was small and humorless. "Christ." He unmuted the audio. The lobby commotion filled the office, officers shouting, a child crying, someone saying *She just appeared!*

He played the clip again, slower.

Light. Absence. Then materialization.

No transition. No blur. Just *there*.

He sipped his drink and leaned forward, elbows on the desk. "Find me her name."

"We already have it. Maya Rodriguez. Twenty-two. Bookstore employee. Local to Salem. No record, no history of mental illness or medical anomalies that match this kind of... whatever this is."

He tilted his head. "Any scientific theories?"

"Online chatter's a mix of quantum nonsense and divine intervention. A few tech analysts claim it's a teleportation glitch caused by sensor lag."

"But the witnesses saw it," Hargreaves said.

"Yes, sir."

"Then it wasn't lag."

He rose and walked toward the window. The Capitol dome gleamed white in the distance, washed in sunset. Below, traffic moved like veins of light, feeding the city's machinery.

"This is what happens when something new appears," he murmured. "The world doesn't know whether to worship it or dissect it."

Cho glanced up from his tablet. "Sir?"

Hargreaves turned, smile tightening. "And we're very good at doing both."

He walked back to his desk and paused the feed again on Maya's image. The expression on her face fascinated him, not defiance, not confidence, but confusion. The look of someone caught in their own miracle.

"She's scared," he said softly. "That's good. Fear makes people cooperative."

Cho cleared his throat. "What should we do, sir?"

"Keep it quiet for now. I want every file she's ever existed in, employment, tax, social. I want her phone metadata, her credit trail, her blood type. Have her followed. But no federal involvement. No official record of contact."

"Understood."

"Raymond," he added, turning toward him, "the difference between a witness and an asset is timing. Don't be late."

Cho nodded, uneasy.

As the aide moved toward the door, Hargreaves said, "And Raymond, if she *can* do what this video says she can, then she's about to have a lot of new friends. Some of them won't ask nicely. Make sure we get there first."

"Yes, sir."

The door clicked shut.

Hargreaves sat back down and opened his laptop. The cursor blinked in a new message window as he typed:

To: m.kellar@tacnetintel.org

Subject: Possible Vector, Salem

Incident reviewed. Civilian female exhibits unexplained displacement event.

Acquire quietly.

Prioritize containment over explanation.

Full details classified under Project HECATE.

He read it once, smiled faintly, and hit send.

The hum of the air conditioner filled the room. Outside, Washington's skyline flickered with light from office towers.

For a long moment he sat still, staring at the darkened window. His reflection stared back, orange lamplight framing his face. Then something in the reflection shifted.

Not him, *behind* him.

A ripple in the shadow along the wall, like smoke swirling through deeper darkness.

He turned. Nothing there. The lamp buzzed once, dimmed, then steadied.

Hargreaves chuckled under his breath. "Long day," he said to the empty room.

But as he reached to switch off the monitor, the reflection in the glass still showed movement, a faint, slow pulse of darkness that didn't match his own.

He didn't see it. Or maybe he chose not to.

The lights dimmed again, this time without flickering back.

The apartment felt smaller that night.

Quieter, too, though not the kind of quiet that meant peace.

Maya stood just inside the doorway, rain dripping from her jacket, staring at the overturned bowl of cereal still dried in a halo on the kitchen floor. The spoon glinted from beneath the table, dusted with flakes of milk crust gone gray.

She hadn't cleaned it before. She hadn't expected to need to.

Her eyes drifted to the bookshelf.

The Codex sat exactly where she'd left it that morning, upright between two paperbacks on mythology, its leather cover dull, its silver runes faintly etched but inert. The mundane air of the room almost convinced her it had all been some elaborate hallucination.

Almost.

She hung her jacket, stepped out of her shoes, and walked barefoot into the kitchen. Every movement felt detached, her body operating on leftover adrenaline.

On the counter, her phone buzzed with missed notifications, calls from the station, local reporters, even a voicemail from her boss, Gary, asking if she was "involved in some TikTok stunt." She didn't listen to any of them. She powered the phone off and slid it beneath a towel, as though even its glass screen might accuse her.

She poured herself a glass of water, but the moment she raised it to her lips, her hands started shaking. The water rippled, catching the reflection of the overhead light, pulsing once, twice, in time with her heartbeat.

The light above flickered in perfect synchrony.

Her breath caught.

For a moment, the air in the apartment carried a charge, faint as static before a storm. Her skin tingled, her pulse syncing with something just beyond her hearing. It wasn't danger; it was *recognition*.

She put the glass down. The trembling stopped.

Later, she sat cross-legged on her living room rug, the Codex open before her. The apartment was dark except for the dim orange glow from a streetlamp outside, bleeding through the blinds.

Her reflection looked ghostly in the window, tired eyes, a smear of dried blood beneath her nose, a woman who'd been somewhere the world didn't have a name for.

She inhaled slowly.

Held it.

Exhaled.

"Just breathe," she murmured. "You're home."

But the word didn't feel true. *Home* suggested safety, and she could feel the air vibrating, subtle, like the hum of a distant engine.

She placed her hands on her knees, palms up, and closed her eyes.

At first, there was only darkness. The natural kind that lives behind your eyelids. Then, slowly, it thickened, taking on texture, like silk catching light. She breathed deeper, and the darkness unfolded.

Threads of light rose around her inner vision. Dozens of them. Hundreds. Some faint, like cobwebs catching starlight; others alive with color and motion, weaving through the air as though suspended in invisible water.

They moved when she breathed.

When her heartbeat quickened, they brightened.

Each thread carried a *tone*, a hum, low and resonant. Together, they made a harmony that wasn't music so much as intention. The longer she listened, the more she understood: this wasn't sound, but structure. The quiet order beneath everything.

One thread in particular drew her focus.

Golden-white.

It pulsed more slowly than the rest, as if bound to a deeper rhythm.

When she reached toward it, without thought, without will, it responded, flaring gently.

A memory not hers passed through her mind: a figure of light, dissolving into the same radiance. A man's voice carried through the echo, distant but resolute. *Ethan.*

The pulse shivered outward, connecting the golden thread to countless others, and for an instant she saw their lattice, a vast network stretching into infinity, every light a life, every vibration a breath.

Then, softly, beneath it all, came the whisper.

"Threads remember."

It wasn't spoken in her ear but through her. The words vibrated in her chest cavity, in the small bones behind her eyes. They weren't a command. They were a truth, a greeting.

Her eyes snapped open.

The apartment had gone very still. The lightbulb above her swayed slightly, though the air was calm.

The Codex lay open on the rug, pages fluttering without breeze. The runes along its spine glowed with a faint silver luminescence, the same rhythm she'd just witnessed behind her eyes.

Her throat felt tight. "You... heard me," she whispered.

The runes flickered once, answering like a heartbeat.

She stared at them for a long time, unsure whether she was more frightened or awed.

Then, slowly, her expression softened.

"If threads remember," she murmured, "then I'll remember too."

The glow dimmed to a steady pulse, one... two... three... then faded altogether, leaving only the faint scent of ozone in the air.

Maya closed the book gently, her fingertips brushing the worn leather. The hum inside her body had settled now, not silent, just resting, like the ocean after a storm.

She rose, crossed to the window, and looked out over Salem. The rain had stopped. Puddles mirrored the city lights, and for a fleeting second, she swore she saw faint filaments of gold rippling through their reflections.

She blinked, and they were gone.

But the whisper still echoed in her mind.

Threads remember.

And this time, she didn't flinch from it.

She simply nodded to the quiet, as if answering an old friend.

5

Sparks of Connection

The television wouldn't stop showing her face, or what little of it the security footage had caught. Every channel looped the same grainy clip: the police-station lobby frozen in fluorescent light, a sudden white flare, and then two figures crumpling onto the tile. A child. A woman. The chyron scrolled beneath in anxious capitals: **"THE GHOST RESCUER OF SALEM."**

Maya muted the sound, but the captions kept chasing her across the screen: *'Appearing Angel,' some call her... unexplained phenomenon... experts baffled...*

She turned off the TV and the silence that followed was worse. The apartment hummed faintly, the same quiet tremor that had haunted her since the warehouse, but now it blended with the world's static. Her phone buzzed on the counter again, one alert after another: missed calls, voicemails, DMs from usernames she didn't know. The subjects blurred together, *You're a hero! Tell your story! Are you an angel? Can you teleport my sick daughter?*

She swiped through them mechanically, a reflexive scroll that left her pulse jumping. Then came one from Gary, her manager at the bookstore:

Saw the news. If this is a PR stunt, HR's gonna kill you.

She snorted, half-laughing, half-ready to throw the phone across the room. Of course Gary would think it was marketing. Of course the world would. She could still hear his voice from that last shift, condescending, nasal, alive with petty authority. The idea almost made her smile. *Maybe disappearing had been the right career move after all.*

Ping. Ping. Another message: *Local radio wants an interview.*
Then another: *Fox News calling you the "Appearing Angel."*
Then something darker: *We know what you are.* No sender listed.

Maya held the power button until the screen went black. The quiet afterward was clean, almost holy. She set the phone face-down and leaned both hands on the counter, breathing through her teeth.

The blinds were drawn, but pale daylight leaked through the slats, striping the kitchen with gray bars. She hadn't stepped outside since the night at the station. The hum inside her blood had subsided to a pulse you could mistake for anxiety, but when she moved too quickly, lights still flickered in sympathy. Electricity no longer trusted her.

She crossed to the window and tilted one blind.

Outside, two news vans idled half a block away, their satellite dishes turned skyward like listening ears. A cluster of reporters leaned on the hoods of their cars, plastic ponchos glistening in drizzle, camera lenses pointed toward her building. Across the street, a woman in a pink raincoat held a handmade sign that read: **"ANGEL SAVES CHILD, A SIGN FROM GOD."**

Maya let the blind fall shut.
"Perfect," she muttered. "I save one kid and now I'm the end times."

The laugh that followed cracked in the middle. It wasn't funny, not really. Just pressure venting through a fault line.

She moved around the apartment like a ghost in her own space, coffee table, couch, the worn paperback she'd left face-down days ago. Each object carried a memory of normalcy, but none of it felt hers anymore. The Codex sat closed on the shelf, still and heavy, runes dull in daylight. For the first time since the incident, she was grateful it stayed quiet.

Her stomach growled. That, at least, was ordinary.

Maya pulled on jeans, a hoodie, a baseball cap, and a disposable mask from the drawer. If anyone looked closely, she'd just be another Salem twenty-something avoiding eye contact before caffeine. She hesitated by the door, fingers on the latch. The hum inside her chest fluttered like a held-back breath.

"It's just coffee," she told herself. "People do it all the time."

The building's hallway smelled of wet carpet and detergent. Downstairs, a reporter's voice drifted faintly through the glass of the entryway. Maya paused behind the door, peering through the slit between blinds. The woman with the sign had company now, two cameramen and a young guy holding a microphone. They were talking to the landlord, poor man, who gestured helplessly toward the upper floors.

Maya exhaled and slipped out the side exit instead, ducking into the drizzle. The air felt good against her skin, cold enough to make her remember she was solid.

She walked fast, head down, across two blocks toward the coffee shop on Derby Street. Every puddle mirrored fragments of her: the flash of a hood, the white of her sneakers, the vague blur of motion that might or might not have been a person.

Halfway there she caught sight of her own reflection in a storefront window, slightly out of sync, like an old film reel missing a frame. She stopped. The reflection stopped a heartbeat later.

Her pulse jumped, and the hum under her ribs answered with a small sympathetic vibration. She forced herself to look away and kept walking. Not here, not now.

At the corner, someone held the door open for her, and she mumbled thanks without looking up. The smell of roasted beans hit her like a drug. Inside, the shop was warm, crowded with students and tourists sheltering from the rain. No one looked twice at her. The sound of milk steaming, spoons clinking, the low murmur of conversation, all of it felt impossibly precious.

She ordered a black coffee, voice steady despite her shaking hands. When the barista turned to pour, she glanced at the tip jar, half-full of coins and folded bills, and thought how easy it would be, with a single thought, to vanish from every camera, every eye. The idea both tempted and sickened her.

The barista handed over her cup with a polite, distracted smile. "Crazy weather, huh?"

"Yeah," she said. "Crazy everything."

She took a seat near the window, back to the wall, steam warming her face. Outside, the reporters' vans waited in the drizzle, unaware their miracle woman was three blocks away, hiding behind paper cups and condensation.

For a few minutes she let herself pretend none of it had happened. She sipped. She breathed. She watched rain stripe the glass.

But the reflection in the window still lagged by a fraction of a second, and when she looked closer, she could swear the lips of her mirrored self moved first.

Maya laughed quietly to herself, half-fear, half-defiance. "Guess you're the famous one," she said to the glass, then took another sip.

The reflection smiled back a heartbeat late.

Outside, thunder rumbled over the harbor.

Inside, the hum beneath her skin began to stir again.

Her coffee was already cooling, which felt like a waste, but the warmth of the cup steadied her hands. She kept her cap low and her mask tucked under her chin. On the wall behind the bar, a chalkboard listed specials in cheerful handwriting. Rosemary latte. Cardamom mocha. A doodle of a fox reading a book.

The barista was a young guy with black curls and a T-shirt that read RULES ARE JUST REALLY PERSISTENT SUGGESTIONS. He moved with the easy rhythm of someone who knew where every cup lived. Bright eyes. Quick smile. He worked the line, then slid a ceramic mug to an older woman with the same care a sommelier might give a vintage bottle. When the crowd thinned he hopped the counter half a step and opened a slim laptop at the far end. The wallpaper caught Maya's eye before she could stop herself.

Not a landscape. Not a game menu. An illustration of constellations drawn like a living map. Lines of light connected stars into a lattice. The paths looked like threads under tension. There were runes in the margins, not any language she knew, but the shapes felt familiar. The image tugged at her in a way that made her sit up straighter.

He looked up, caught her glance, and grinned as if she had spoken. "It is nerdy, I know," he said. "I promise the coffee still tastes normal."

"What is it," she asked, then winced at how curious she sounded. "The wallpaper."

"Homebrew map art." He turned the laptop so she could see. "I am building a tabletop campaign. Threads of Power. I wanted the sky to look like it remembers where everyone has been."

The hum in her chest shifted. Not louder. Closer. "You drew that."

"Yeah." He shrugged, pleased but trying not to show it. "Alex. I pull shots here three days a week and build games the other four."

"Maya," she said. The name felt like a coin on her tongue. She set her cup down so she would not crush it.

He leaned a hip against the counter. "So. You are either a cartographer in disguise or you saw something in this mess of dots that did not annoy you."

"The lines," she said. "The way they feel like they are under tension. Like if you plucked one it would sing."

He blinked at her. For a second his expression softened into something like recognition. "Most people say it looks busy. Or they ask me why I drew spiderwebs in space."

"Spiderwebs would be messier," she said. "This looks like it has rules."

He laughed quietly. "You have no idea how happy that sentence makes me. Coffee on the house for a sentence like that."

She shook her head. "You do not have to."

"I want to." He poured from a fresh pot into a clean mug and set it on the bar. "So. Rules. Pitch me your favorite."

She hesitated. The word favorite felt like a trap. The first rule that rose in her mind was not from any book. It came from blood and pain and the way the world had buckled in a warehouse. She took a breath anyway.

"Power should cost something," she said, and watched his face.

Alex did not laugh it off. He did not roll his eyes or make a joke about mana bars. He nodded, slow and thoughtful. "I agree. The price is how you know it is real."

"Then why do so many games make it free," she asked. "Cast and cast and cast until you solve the room."

"Because it feels good to be unstoppable in a pretend world," he said. "And because balancing tables is hard. If you want it to feel earned, you have to let the players break sometimes. Fall down. Lose things. Most people do not come to a Friday night session to watch their wizard have a migraine and go home."

Maya sipped the new coffee. It was better than the first one, or maybe she was just ready to taste it now. "What do you do in your game," she asked. "For the cost."

"Every spell is a thread you pluck in the world," he said. "Threads vibrate. That ripple goes somewhere. If you pull too hard, you pay. If you pull cleverly, you can shift the pattern without tearing it." He paused, then added, softer, "If you do not listen, the pattern ignores you."

Her throat tightened. She tried to smile so he would not see it. "You make them listen."

"I encourage it." He held up his hands. "I do not tyrant-GM. I just offer consequences that feel like they belong. A long cast leaves a nosebleed or a headache. A teleport makes you lose your sense of direction for a while. A big ritual steals hours out of your day."

Maya set the cup down a little too quickly. "Teleport."

He watched her carefully now. "Yeah. We have a threadwalking build. I like rules that make distance feel like a substance."

She looked at the wallpaper again. The lines were not straight. They bowed around blank spaces, then joined in gentle arcs. Alex followed her gaze and tapped the screen near a cluster of stars.

"See that gap," he said. "If you force your way across it, you punch a hole. You can get through once. Maybe twice. Then the map starts deleting you. I do not let players brute force a weave. They have to respect the empty places."

She laughed, but it sounded thin in her own ears. "How do they take it when you tell them the map can delete them."

"They laugh until the first time it happens."

He tilted his head. "You look like you know that feeling for real. Sorry. That came out weird."

"It is alright," she said. "I just like when fiction treats cause and effect like physics."

"Same," he said, relief relaxing one shoulder. "You would be surprised how many people argue with gravity."

She wanted to ask a dozen questions. She wanted to know why he had drawn five slightly longer lines that met in a circle in the lower right corner. She wanted to know if he had seen anything like the way her reflection lagged a heartbeat behind her. Instead she asked, "Do you run games here?"

"After close on Tuesdays," he said. "We drag the tables together and pretend it is a tavern. You should come. No pressure. I can park you in the back with a pregen and you can heckle the party with a slingshot."

"I have a job," she said, then thought of Gary's voicemail and their stockroom and the way the shelves had looked while she tried not to exist. "Most nights."

"Most nights can spare two hours for a tavern," he said. "Where else are you going to find a safe place to argue with fate."

A little silence settled between them, and for the first time all day it did not hurt. The jazz shifted into something older. Rain thickened on the glass. The café's door opened and closed in a pattern that felt almost like breathing.

"You draw like the sky remembers," she said. "That line was not just clever."

"I had a good teacher," he said, then amended, "Several teachers, all of them fictional. I write code sometimes too, so I think in systems. Even when I sleep."

"That sounds exhausting."

"It is," he said, cheerful about it. "So I drink a lot of espresso, and I make art that tells me the rules are worth it."

She studied him. He had the bright, slightly feral energy of someone who lives on ideas and too little sleep. It should have set her nerves on edge. It did the opposite. He looked like a person who believed in patterns, and who would not mock her for saying she could feel one.

"Tell me your thesis," she said. "About magic."

He warmed to it at once. "Magic is consent between a mind and a pattern. The pattern says here is what I allow. The mind says here is what I ask. The cost is the agreement. If you try to skip the consent, the pattern punishes you. Or worse, it pretends to help until you forget how to live without it."

Maya looked down at her hands. The skin over her palm felt normal again. No heat. No glow. A fine tremor sat in the tendons, more memory than symptom.

"Fair," she said. "That sounds fair."

"Fair is the only way it stays beautiful," he said. He watched her a beat longer. "I am talking too much. Sorry."

"You are not," she said. "I asked."

He smiled. "Then I will risk one more question. Are you okay?"

No one had asked her that yet without a microphone waiting. The answer formed and collapsed three times. She settled on the one that did not betray her or insult him.

"I am trying to be," she said.

"That counts," he said. "Trying counts a lot."

A couple at the far table waved for refills. Alex lifted a finger in apology and headed back behind the bar. He moved like he knew he would come back to this conversation, which surprised her with how glad it made her. She sipped her coffee and studied the map on his screen again. The longer she looked, the more she saw. Tiny notations. A series of small circles that marked crossings. Someone had loved this structure.

He returned with a rag and wiped the bar. "I will be done in ten," he said. "If you want to see the rest of the worldbuilding notebook. No pressure."

"Maybe," she said. Her voice wanted to sound braver than she felt.

He nodded. "Cool."

A student dropped a stack of coins in the tip jar and left. The room emptied a little. The rain eased. A patch of lighter sky opened over the harbor like a promise. Maya's nerves steadied, slow as a tide. She became aware of her breathing again. In. Hold. Out. The tiny hum in her chest settled to a steady undernote. Alex's map glowed on his screen, constellations connected by lines that looked almost like veins.

Guarded sarcasm had gotten her through the door. It did not feel like the right tool anymore. She looked up at Alex.

"I like your thesis," she said. "Consent between a mind and a pattern."

He smiled, quieter this time. "Thanks."

"Cost makes it honest," she said. "Maybe beautiful too."

He set the rag aside. "You talk like you have seen it."

"Only in books," she said, which was true for the first half of her life, and now also a way to survive the second.

"Books can be good teachers," he said.

Behind him the espresso machine hissed like a tame dragon. The fox on the chalkboard kept reading its drawn book. The café door opened for a new customer and a drift of cool air moved across the floor. It smelled like wet stone and the sea.

Maya glanced at the laptop once more, then back to him. "Maybe I will stop by on Tuesday."

"Great," he said, and the word landed like a small light in the room. "I will save you a chair."

The rain had thinned to mist by the time Maya turned onto Essex Street, her coffee cooling in her hand. The city smelled like wet leaves and exhaust, and the streetlamps drew halos in the fog. She pulled her hood up and kept walking, half lost in the rhythm of her steps, half watching the puddles for threads of light that never quite appeared.

A car door clicked somewhere behind her. Not loud, not hurried. She didn't turn.

"Maya Rodriguez?"

The voice was male, careful. Not a question meant to corner, but one meant to ask permission.

She stopped anyway. The man stood a few paces back on the sidewalk, under the awning of a closed bookstore. His coat was soaked at the shoulders, tie loose, face pale with sleeplessness. She recognized him before he said another word—the same jawline she'd glimpsed in the news photo, next to a woman holding Emily Jameson's school picture.

"I'm David Jameson," he said quietly. "Emily's father."

For a second she couldn't breathe. She almost told him he had the wrong person. But something in his expression, a mix of exhaustion and fierce gratitude made lying feel cruel.

"She's... she's okay?" she asked.

"She's home," he said. His smile cracked around the edges. "Won't let the police out of her sight, but yeah. Home."

Maya nodded, eyes lowering. "Good."

"I know you didn't want attention," he said. "They said you left before the cameras could get to you. I wouldn't have found you except..." He tapped his phone pocket. "I recognized you when you walked past the corner."

"I really don't want..."

"I know." He reached inside his coat, produced a slim envelope, and held it out. "The reward. Twenty thousand. We promised it, and you earned it."

"I don't want your money," she said, sharper than she meant. The words felt too small for the moment.

He didn't flinch. "I know that too. But take it anyway. You saved my daughter's life. Let me do one human thing that isn't just saying thank you."

Rain drummed softly between them. She looked at the envelope. It wasn't fat, wasn't flashy, just a folded check inside a plain white sleeve, edges already damp from the air. She hesitated long enough that he added, "It's not about buying anything. It's about closing a circle."

She reached out, finally, and took it. The paper was warm from his hand.

He nodded once, relief crossing his face. "She asked me if you were real," he said. "When I told her yes, she said she thought angels didn't like being thanked."

Maya managed a breath that almost became a laugh. "Tell her I'm definitely not an angel."

He smiled, weary and genuine. "I'll tell her you said that."

He stepped back toward the curb. "You don't owe us anything else. You did more than enough."

"I didn't do it for," She stopped herself. "Just... keep her safe."

"I will."

He started to turn away, then paused. "She keeps drawing you," he said softly. "In her notebook. There's always light around you."

Maya didn't answer. He gave a final nod and walked off into the mist, his figure dissolving into the wet glow of the streetlights.

She stood there for a long time, the envelope cold in her hand. Then she slipped it into her coat pocket and kept walking.

The rain began again, thin as thread.

And somewhere deep inside her, the hum stirred once softly, approving and went quiet again.

The Tuesday rain had thinned to a mist by the time Maya reached the game shop. Its windows glowed with soft yellow light that pushed back the dark like a campfire in a cave. Inside, laughter rose over the click of dice and the soft scrape of chair legs. A cardboard dragon the size of a housecat sat in the front display beside a stack of fantasy novels and a chalkboard sign that read: *Campaign Night – Threads of Power.*

She hesitated in the doorway. The part of her that still expected the world to tilt sideways at any moment told her to turn around and keep walking. But Alex looked up from behind a mountain of character sheets and caught her in the reflection of the window. His smile came easily, warm without being invasive.

"You made it," he said, standing. "Wasn't sure you'd brave the nerd den."

Maya pulled her hood back and shrugged. "It was raining. Seemed safer in here."

"Best endorsement we've ever had," one of the players said, earning a laugh from the group.

The shop was cozy in the way only old buildings could be; uneven floors, the faint smell of paper and varnish, every corner packed with color. Four players sat around a table under a hanging lamp: a teacher with a spiral notebook, a tattooed student wearing a hoodie with a pixelated sword, and two older guys whose enthusiasm could have powered the lights if the grid failed.

Alex's Dungeon Master screen, painted with a mountain and a storm, was propped up like a small stage. He motioned for Maya to sit near the counter. "Grab a drink, spectator's choice. We're mid-session. Just in time for the boss fight."

She found an old stool, unzipped her jacket, and wrapped her hands around a paper cup of coffee. It was the first place in days that didn't smell like panic.

At the table, Alex leaned forward, voice dropping to a storyteller's hush. "The cavern shakes as the ley-threads tremble. The mage has drawn too deep, and the Weave itself begins to hum."

The word hit her like a soft slap. She blinked, almost spilling coffee. He hadn't noticed.

The players leaned in. "What's the save DC?" one of them asked. Alex grinned. "Nineteen. Failure means your spell collapses, and the backlash tears a thread."

A die clattered, bounced twice, and rolled into the light. Cheers followed. Maya smiled despite herself.

She watched them play, how their laughter softened when the tension built, how they finished one another's ideas mid-sentence, how easily they trusted a shared imagination to hold them. The simplicity of it made her ache. They could make the world obey them by pretending; she did it by accident and paid in blood.

When Alex described the climactic blow, light shearing through shadow, a heartbeat of silence before victory, she flinched. The sound in his story was too close to what she'd felt in the warehouse.
And yet, the room was so alive that she couldn't look away.

Eventually, dice stopped clattering. The players leaned back, talking over one another, laughing about near-death rolls. The teacher mock-groaned, "I'm never trusting your portal traps again."
"That's the spirit," Alex said. "You survived. Barely. Heroic level achieved."

He glanced toward Maya as if to ask if she'd survived too.

When the group started packing up, he stayed seated, scribbling notes in a leather-bound journal. The title embossed on the cover caught the light: *Threads of Power.*

Maya drifted closer, drawn by equal parts curiosity and unease. "That's what you call your game?"

"Yeah." He smiled without looking up. "I started sketching the idea a few years back. Wanted to see if I could make a system where magic isn't free. Every spell costs something."

"What kind of cost?"

He looked up then. "Depends. The stronger the bond, the stronger the spell, but break a bond, and it bites you. Magic runs on connection. The trick is knowing when to pull and when to listen."

She stared at him. "Where'd that come from?"

He tapped the side of his head. "Dream, maybe. Or something I read and forgot I read. The idea of threads that bind people... I liked the poetry of it. Less *fireball*, more *fidelity*."

Her throat felt tight. She remembered the Codex's first page: *The Covenant Was Never Broken.* She remembered the lattice of light in her dreams, the pulse of threads humming like veins through the dark. "You'd be surprised how real that sounds," she said, her tone lighter than she felt.

Alex caught the edge in her voice and softened his. "Hey, don't let the lore scare you. I promise no one's going to summon anything worse than a pizza."

Maya smiled, but the gesture felt fragile. "I think I've had enough of magic for one lifetime."

He studied her a moment, then closed his journal gently. "You don't have to believe in it to understand it. Most of this," he gestured to the table, "it's about connection. People sitting together, sharing a story. Belief's just the thread we use to keep it from unraveling."

"That's almost wise," she said.

"Almost," he agreed. "But hey, proof isn't what makes a thing real. If it changes you, that's enough."

Their eyes met. For a second the shop's noise, the whir of the fridge, the scrape of boxes, the hum of the heater dropped away. The silence wasn't awkward. It was the kind that listens back.

Then one of the players called, "You closing up, man?"
"Yeah," Alex said, still looking at Maya. "Five minutes."

The others said goodnight and drifted out into the rain. The bell over the door chimed, leaving only the two of them and the faint smell of wet pavement leaking through the cracks of the old window frame.

Alex opened a drawer under the counter and pulled out a small velvet pouch. Dice spilled into his hand, tiny planets in amethyst, gold, and jade. He picked one up, a deep purple twenty-sided die, edges sharp and numbers inked in silver. "Here," he said. "Token of appreciation for surviving your first campaign audience."

She blinked. "I didn't even play."

"Then call it a welcome gift. Or a charm. Depends on how dramatic you want to be."

She hesitated before taking it. "Do I roll it?"

"Always," he said, sliding a tray toward her. "Rules of the universe."

The die felt heavier than it should have, solid and warm from his hand. She rolled it across the felt. It clicked once, twice, and spun in a lazy spiral. When it stopped, the twenty gleamed up at her like a small sun.

"Natural twenty," he said, mock solemn. "That means fate owes you one favor."

"Or it's just math," she said, smiling faintly.

"Yeah, but I like my version better."

Something under the table rattled, a soft metallic tremor that ran through every die in the tray, setting them spinning half an inch and stopping all at once. Alex laughed, glancing toward the ceiling vent. "Old ductwork," he said. "This place hums whenever it rains."

Maya didn't answer. The vibration in her chest had flared and then gone still, perfectly timed with the dice. She pressed her hand to her ribs, pretending to fix her coat. The hum there responded once, faint as a whisper acknowledging another.

Alex didn't notice. He leaned against the counter, arms folded. "You know, there's a superstition about dice. The ones that roll high the first time belong to the player they favor."

"They favor me?"

"Seems so. Might be a sign you should come back."

She laughed softly. "You're persistent."

"Occupational hazard," he said. "Half my job's convincing people that worlds can coexist on a table."

Maya slipped the die into her pocket, feeling its warmth settle against her palm. "Maybe next time I'll play."

"That's not a maybe," he said, smiling. "That's a promise waiting for courage."

The remark caught her off guard, simple, unflinching. She wasn't sure if it was the rain or his tone that made her throat tighten. "Goodnight, Alex."

"Night, Maya."

She stepped outside. The mist had thickened into a fine silver drizzle, coating her hair with cold droplets. Through the glass she could see him moving around the counter, wiping down the table, switching off the lamp. The shop's sign flicked to *Closed,* and the reflection of his motion shimmered across the wet pavement like a ghost of light.

She touched the pocket where the die rested. A faint pulse answered from beneath her skin, gentle this time, not the electric surge of power, but a heartbeat syncing with her own.

The rain whispered along the street. The Codex's hum remained silent, but she could feel its echo under the city, deep and slow, as though the Weave itself was listening in.

Maya smiled despite the unease curling in her gut. For the first time in weeks, she didn't feel like a glitch in someone else's reality. She felt anchored, even if she didn't know why.

She looked back one last time. Inside, Alex was stacking chairs, framed in the yellow warmth of the café's light. His shadow moved easily, unafraid of its shape.

Maya turned up her collar and started walking. The die clicked softly in her pocket with each step, a tiny rhythm that sounded almost like laughter, or maybe the beginning of a new thread pulling taut between two lives.

Alex locked the shop and flipped the sign. The bell gave one last tired chime. Rain softened the street to a sheet of silver, shallow streams running along the curb. Maya pulled up her hood and started toward Essex. Footsteps fell in behind her. She glanced back and saw Alex tucking his hands into his jacket pockets.

"Headed this way too," he said. "I park three blocks up."

They fell into an easy pace. The rain made talking feel private. Car tires hissed. A dog barked once from a balcony that was more iron than shelter. Their shoes clicked on wet brick. The city was tired and kind at this hour.

"You hungry?" he asked.

"Tea is better," she said. "I have some at home."

He nodded. "Tea is safer than espresso at this hour. Lead on."

She did not invite people to her apartment. She heard that fact in her own head and felt a small spin of alarm. The feeling passed. The die in her pocket made a soft clack with each step, a tiny metronome that kept her from drifting. They turned at the corner where the streetlamp always buzzed. Reporters were gone tonight. Only the rain watched.

Inside, her apartment smelled like paper and detergent. She flipped the lights to low. The Codex sat in its usual place on the shelf, dull in the warm room light. The sight of it made her throat tighten. She pushed the feeling aside and kicked off her shoes.

"Make yourself at home," she said. "Kitchen is there. Kettle is on the back burner. There is honey. There is also honey that tastes like it has seen better days. Choose wisely."

"Copy that," he said, amused. He set his jacket on a chair and took in the room as if it were a new map. "You read a lot of history."

"It was cheaper than therapy," she said, then softened the line with a small smile so it did not land like a bruise.

He moved toward the kitchen. Water filled the kettle with a cold rush. She opened a tin of Assam and one of chamomile. She chose chamomile. He chose Assam. It felt like a joke the world made for them. Something steady and small.

Steam drifted. Cups warmed their hands. Rain tapped the window. For a minute there was nothing to solve and no one to save.

He drifted toward the bookshelf while the tea cooled. "Family photos," he said, tilting his head toward a small frame. "That your grandmother?"

"Great aunt," she said. "More or less. The lines are a little crooked in my family."

He nodded. His gaze moved to the leather spine of the Codex. It looked unremarkable if you did not know it. The silver on its edges had dulled to the color of rain on stone.

He reached toward it and paused. "Old," he said. "Is that an heirloom?"

"Something like that," she said. Her voice came out tight. "Be careful."

He looked back at her with a crooked smile. "I am always careful."

His fingers touched the spine.

What happened did not slam the room. It entered like a chord held under a whisper. The runes along the Codex's margin woke and filled with blue-white. They did not flare like fire. They filled the way a candle fills a glass. The light slid into the silver lines and lived there. A tone moved through the air, clean and harmonic. It found the same pitch in the radiator and made it hum along. The cups on the counter shivered once and settled.

Maya felt it at the same moment. Two heartbeats inside her chest. Her own, quick and high. A second, steady and near, as if her ribs had made room for it without asking. It lasted a breath. It was enough to change the shape of the world. She staggered half a step and caught herself on the table.

Alex froze, hand still on the book. His eyes were wide, not with panic, but with the startled comprehension of a person hearing a note that belongs to them.

The two of them jerked their hands back at once. The light went down as if someone had turned a dial. The tone softened. It did not stop. It drifted lower. The pitch settled into the room like a cat curling into a corner. The Codex did not go dark. It kept a thin line of blue in the deepest grooves of its runes, a pulse that timed itself to a new rhythm.

For a second they only breathed. The kettle clicked as it cooled. Rain moved on the glass in slow lines.

Alex was the first to find words. "You felt that, right?"

Maya nodded. "I think it felt us."

His gaze stayed on the book. "Is it going to do that again?"

"Not if we do not touch it," she said. She tried to make the line light. It came out careful. The second heartbeat inside her had faded, but the memory of it clung to her ribs. She placed a hand over her sternum without thinking. The skin there tingled as if a night breeze had blown through bone.

He noticed the gesture. "Are you okay?"

"I will be," she said. "It was not pain. More like... company."

He let out a slow breath. "Company. That is one word for it."

They stood looking at the thing they had woken. The Codex did not pretend to be a book now. It felt like a listening animal. The hum in the room had changed since he touched it. Lower, warmer. Not a warning. A recognition.

Maya picked up her cup and drank to hide the shake in her hands. The chamomile had cooled. It tasted like quiet fields and heat. She stood straighter.

"Family heirloom," he said softly, repeating his earlier guess because plain language was a bridge when magic tried to make ladders out of light.

"Sort of," she said. "I found it in a place that belongs to my family. It did not belong to anyone else."

"And it reacts like that when anyone touches it?"

"No," she said. She looked at him. "It reacts like that when you touched it."

He swallowed. "Then maybe I should not touch it again."

"That is probably wise," she said. She set the cup down and stepped closer. "It did not feel angry."

"No," he said. "It felt like a tuning fork. Like the room agreed with itself."

The word agreed eased something in her. She nodded. "That is close."

He sat on the arm of the couch, cup in both hands now. His smile looked a little stunned and a little delighted, the way people look after a comet or a sentence they waited years to hear. "I do not believe in magic," he said, and then stopped himself. "Correction. I did not think I did."

"You do not have to label it," she said. "You only have to admit you felt it."

"I felt it," he said. "Two heartbeats. That was new."

"Mine too," she said. She let the confession sit. "It never did that with anyone else."

His eyes softened. "That sounds like a lonely sentence."

"It was," she said. The room did not flinch from that truth. It absorbed it like rain into wood. "Tonight is less lonely."

He smiled at that. Not big. Honest. He studied the Codex again and then looked around the apartment. "Is everything going to hum at me now?"

"Only if it likes you," she said.

"Then I hope the radiator is a fan."

They both laughed. It took the edge off the fear without dismissing it. Outside, a siren slid past, thin and far away, then dissolved back into rain. The lights in the apartment did not flicker. They held steady, as if whatever had moved through the room had chosen to leave the wiring in peace.

Alex sipped his tea and set the cup down. "If I ask questions I am going to fall into a hole that is too deep for a Tuesday. I do not want to be rude. I also do not want to pretend that was nothing."

"It was not nothing," she said. "It was the opposite."

"What is the opposite of nothing."

"Listening," she said. Her voice surprised her with its certainty.

He nodded. "Then I will listen."

They stood a little closer to each other without planning it. The Codex kept to its slow glow, a heartbeat confined to a spine and a set of runes that no longer looked like art. The pitch of its hum had settled into a lower register since he touched it. She could feel that change like a weight added to the bottom of a scale. Recognition. That word again.

He reached toward the bookshelf, stopped short of the leather, and withdrew his hand. "Not touching. Promise."

"Good," she said. "I do not think either of us should try that again until we have slept."

"Agreed."

He glanced at the clock over the stove. "I should go. I do not want to leave, but I should. Also, I am aware that is a sentence that contradicts itself."

"It is a true one," she said. "I get it."

He slid into his jacket. The normal action felt gentle after the room had decided to sing. He moved to the door and hesitated. "Maya?"

"Yes."

"Thank you for trusting me."

"You didn't run," she said. "That counts."

He smiled. "I will see you Tuesday. Or sooner if your kettle needs a union rep."

She walked him to the door. The hallway light was an honest yellow. No one waited outside. The building smelled like wet stone and dust. He stepped into the hall and turned back.

"Goodnight," he said.

"Goodnight," she said.

She closed the door and rested her forehead against it for a second. The apartment was still. The Codex kept its quiet pulse, lower now, as if the room had lowered its voice out of respect for sleep.

Maya crossed to the shelf and looked at the runes. The blue-white was faint but present. She placed her palm on the leather without pressure. The hum answered, not with force, but with recognition that had learned a second name.

"I felt it too," she whispered.

The tone shifted one note and settled again. She took her hand away and turned off the light in the kitchen. The city rain found its rhythm outside. Inside, the apartment finally matched it.

Curiosity had brought him in. Awe had sat them down. Fear had told them to stop. The room held all three like a chord that had learned how to be true without breaking apart.

Maya slipped the amethyst die from her pocket and placed it on the table. It caught the dim light and kept it, a small moon in a small sea.

She breathed in. She breathed out. The hum in her ribs met the hum in the room. For one quiet moment they were the same sound. Then both sounds rested.

After Alex left, the apartment took a long breath and held it. The kettle clicked once in the quiet. A drip from the dish rack marked time. The Codex rested on the shelf with its runes still faintly lit, not bright, just a slimmer version of the blue that had filled them when his hand touched the leather.

Maya stood a few feet away and watched the glow collect in the grooves. It did not feel like danger. It felt like awareness with its eyes half closed. She let her palm hover above the spine. The light answered with a small throb that matched the slower pitch the book had adopted once Alex was in the room. She pulled her hand back, not from fear, but from a sense that the thing was listening and did not need more volume.

The amethyst die sat on the table by the couch. It had caught a strip of light from the street and held it like a drop of evening. She turned it with one finger. The faces slid from twelve to seven to one. Her body remembered the soft vibration when every die in the shop moved as if the air had tapped them. She felt a mild echo of that in her ribs and then nothing more.

She made a small ritual of closing the blinds two thirds of the way. The rain had thinned to a few threads that the streetlamp caught and lifted into the air like silk. She washed both cups and set them upside down to dry. She placed the die on the spine of a paperback and watched it balance at the edge, steady as if the page had a lip.

The room was still, so the smallest sounds arrived with shape. The radiator breathed and went quiet. A neighbor down the hall walked to the stairwell and paused, perhaps listening, perhaps counting keys. Somewhere beyond the brick, a car door closed and a new song from the wind began. Not a gust. Not a whistle. A rhythm.

She stood by the window and tried to pretend she could not hear it. The wind did not care about pretending. It carried a steady vibration that rose and fell in a pattern she could not call music because music would have insisted on melody. This was pulse. The kind of repeating that belongs to tides and heartbeats and the noise that lives under a city you love.

She unlocked the window and raised it two inches. Cold air slid along the sill and brought with it the rhythm in a clearer voice. She did not hear words. The meaning arrived anyway. The message fit inside a single thought that felt older than language.

Others are waking.

She let the window stay open and did not answer out loud. She could feel the response forming in her chest without the shape of words. Something like relief turned very slowly toward light. She looked down at her hands. The faint warmth under the skin of her palm returned for a heartbeat, then passed like an animal crossing a path at dusk.

She turned and faced the room. The Codex shimmered. Not a flare. More like the way a fish turns in deep water and offers the surface its silver for a blink. She could not tell whether the glow came from what she had understood or from something distant that had understood her in return.

She crossed to the shelf and slid the Codex gently away from the other books. The leather felt cool. When she opened it, the first page unreadable to her eyes even now, the lines of silver along the margin answered the city's wind with a vibration she felt in the bones of her fingers.

"Others are waking," she said, finally giving the thought a shape in air.

The pitch lowered, as if agreeing. She closed the book and held it against her chest. The weight grounded her. The apartment stopped feeling like a room that had borrowed her life. It felt like a place she could stand without apologizing.

She set the Codex back in its place and turned off the overhead light in the kitchen. The room shrank to two pools of yellow. One from a lamp near the couch. One from the hallway fixture that always added a note of amber to the air. She went to the window again and pushed the blinds apart with two fingers.

Salem lay quiet under a thin veil of cloud. The harbor lights blinked with calm authority. Streetlamps lined Essex like a necklace. The occasional headlights painted the wet pavement with a slow brush. The breeze shifted to carry a softer version of the same rhythm, less chant now, more breath. She stood very still and tried to match it without forcing herself to keep time.

Her heart complied. Two beats quick, one slow, and the slow one felt like it belonged to the room more than to her. It did not alarm her. It arranged her. The city lights did a small trick then. She saw them blink in a cadence that fit her chest. She told herself it was coincidence. She did not believe herself. The pattern repeated once more and then returned to ordinary.

She stayed at the window until the chill asked her to close it. She left it open a fraction. The wind found a new voice when it met the glass. It sounded like a low vowel held under the hum of the street. The idea that human voices might be adding to it in other rooms did not feel foolish. She pictured someone on the far side of town sitting on the edge of a bed, unaware of anything mystical, yet touching the same thread of quiet and thinking of calling a friend for the first time in months. She pictured an old man rubbing his thumb over a rosary and pausing because the bead suddenly felt like it had been carved by a patient hand that was not his. She pictured a child too young for words humming out of sync with a lullaby and finding that the new rhythm made sleep easier. The pictures came and went like the lights on the harbor.

Maya closed the blinds and sat on the floor. The rug pressed soft patterns into her calves. She took the die from the paperback and set it in front of her. Her phone was still off. She did not reach for it. She did not want other people's names for what was happening. She wanted the one that made her fear move to the side and let something else sit.

She closed her eyes. Darkness settled behind her eyelids, not empty, more like velvet that had been warmed by a hand. She listened in the style Alex had named. Not belief. Consent. The hum under her breastbone rose a little and then evened. The threads appeared as they always did when she managed to be still for more than a breath. Thin lines of light that discovered themselves by vibrating. Tonight there were more of them. Not crowded. Present. The lattice stretched farther than before, as if someone had opened a curtain in a room she had lived in for years and showed her that the wall was a window.

She moved her attention slowly along the lines. Some pulsed in a familiar way. One shone with a steady gold that made her think of the man who had become a part of the pattern rather than a hand trying to pull it. Others glowed with colors she could not name. She felt three distant pulses that did not belong to the city. They were not close. They were distinct. A thought crossed her mind that she did not want to claim yet. She let it pass and noted the directions the pulses seemed to favor, then let that go too.

Her breath faltered when the lattice brightened across the skyline. She opened her eyes at once and saw a hint of the same thing in the room with her eyes. Not full lines. Suggestions. The way smudged glass hints at an image before you wipe it clean. Filaments lay across the city as if some giant hand had placed veins under the night for a single second. She saw them above the river where the bridges carried their metal. She saw them like pale ribs under the old streets that had taken too many years to decide where they wanted to lead. The filaments retreated and left the ordinary view in place. She realized she had been holding her breath. She let it go slowly, the way a swimmer surfaces once the shoreline feels close.

Her fear rose with a reflex honed by nights in the last week that ended in blood and a howling in her ears that had not belonged to weather. The fear did not sit in the chair it usually took without asking. It stood near the door instead and watched her from there. It did not leave. It yielded. Behind it another feeling stepped forward. Not triumph. Not even confidence. Something like acceptance with a small light placed in the center of it.

She spoke without lifting her voice. "I am not alone in this."

The room did not answer in words. The lamp shade shifted very slightly as if a hand had passed near it. The Codex held its thin blue. The radiator released a warm breath and went still.

She picked up the die and closed her fingers around it. The edges fit her palm. The weight reminded her that the body can be an anchor and not only a thing that hurts. She laid the die back on the floor and wrote in the margin of the small notebook she had been using to keep track of symptoms. She wrote fewer numbers tonight. The words arrived more easily than timers and durations.

Others are waking.

Listening lowers the cost.

The city breathes too.

She capped the pen and set the notebook on the low table. She lay on the rug for a minute and let her spine lengthen against the floor. The old wood gave a little and then held her.

When she stood, the hum in her chest had settled into something she could carry without effort. She turned out the lamp and left the hallway light. The apartment darkened to kindness. She went into the bedroom and sat on the edge of the bed. The window there faced a different street. It offered a different color of silence.

Maya pulled the blanket up and lay back. The Codex glowed faintly in the next room. The wind kept its rhythm. The whisper that had carried no words earlier repeated once in the place where breath turns into sleep. Others are waking. The thought did not crowd her. It diluted the loneliness that had stained every good thing for days.

She closed her eyes and did not try to vanish. She let the city's pulse count her breaths until the numbers fell away. The last thing she saw before sleep flattened the night was a tiny flare of blue-white on the edge of a page that no longer looked like paper. The last thing she felt was hope light enough to float but heavy enough to stay.

The night had gone still again. No traffic, no wind strong enough to stir the curtains. The air carried that late-hour hush particular to coastal towns, the pause between the city's pulse and the ocean's.

Maya sat at her window, the Codex open across her knees. The glow had faded to a quiet silver, not gone but resting, like coals beneath ash. The leather was cool beneath her fingers, its weight oddly comforting.

Her pen hovered above the page. The Codex had stopped resisting her ink days ago; now the nib met the paper without drag, as if the surface invited it. Her handwriting had begun to change under its influence, loops sharper, strokes more deliberate.

She looked out the window before she began. The street below was empty except for the lamplight pooled around the nearest post. Raindrops clung to the glass in perfect stillness. The hum in her chest had gentled into a rhythm so soft she could almost mistake it for calm.

She started to write.

When I listen, the world listens back.

The words formed in a darker ink than she'd loaded into the pen. They shimmered faintly, each letter releasing a pulse that faded into the fibers of the page.

She stopped, watching.

At first nothing followed. Then a low vibration crept up through the paper, less sound than sensation. The words themselves began to resonate, each letter ringing in the bones of her wrist. It wasn't threatening, just impossibly aware.

Maya's throat tightened. "Maybe it's listening now," she whispered.

The Codex responded. The hum deepened, a single, sustained note that filled the room without echo. The inked words glowed faintly, then dulled again. The page stilled.

Outside, the nearest streetlamp flickered once, a soft blink perfectly in time with the beat of her heart. She froze, half expecting the others on the block to follow. They didn't. Only that one answered. It was enough.

She leaned back in the chair and let out a long, uneven breath. The exhaustion she'd been carrying since the warehouse, since the first disappearance, finally settled into her bones. She felt the weight of discovery and the edge of something larger pressing at the world's seams.

The line between wonder and danger had never looked thinner.

She reached out and closed the Codex carefully. The runes along its spine dimmed to a color somewhere between moonlight and breath. The hum receded into silence.

In that silence she thought about the words she'd written: *When I listen, the world listens back.*

The truth of them frightened her more than anything she'd seen in the mirror, yet it also steadied her. If the world could hear her, then it was capable of understanding. If it could understand, it might forgive her for what she didn't yet know how to control.

Maya rested her forehead against the cold windowpane. The glass trembled once beneath her skin, faint as a heartbeat under ice.

Below, the lamplight pulsed again, one, two, three, and then held steady. She smiled in spite of herself, the kind of fragile smile that belonged to people too tired to be afraid.

"Goodnight," she murmured to no one. Or maybe to everything.

The Codex stayed quiet, but the warmth it left in the room lingered, a memory of light that refused to leave completely. The city outside exhaled in the same rhythm she did.

Maya turned from the window, the pen still between her fingers. She set it beside the Codex, switched off the lamp, and crossed to the bed. The dark felt thicker now but not unfriendly.

In the quiet just before sleep, she heard it, one faint note, neither outside nor within, a tone the size of a breath. It thrummed once through the floorboards, through her chest, through the cooling pages of the Codex.

A small sound of acknowledgment.

She smiled into the dark.

Discovery achieved. Safety gone.

The Weave was awake.

6

Experiments and Consequences

Wednesday morning the light over Salem came in gray, washed thin by drizzle that clung to the apartment windows like a film. Every sound was muted, even the city traffic, reduced to the slow sigh of tires through wet streets. Inside, Maya had transformed her living room into something between a science lab and a séance.

Chalk lines crossed the hardwood floor in measured geometry: three circles nested together, joined by faint arcs of salt. Sticky notes formed a constellation across the walls, handwritten hypotheses, half-legible formulas, reminders in blue ink that looked like prayers disguised as notes.

"Stay calm," one said.

"Listen first," said another.

Near the couch sat a set of kitchen scales, her phone on top recording sound; two timers; and a half-drained cup of coffee cooling beside a notebook labeled in neat print: **Control Trials**.

The Codex rested open on the table's edge like a silent observer. The runes on its spine shimmered faintly, more like breath than light. It had been quiet since the last night's hum, but she could feel it watching, not judging, only waiting.

Maya knelt at the center of her chalk circle, tucking loose hair behind one ear. She'd dressed for practicality, sweatpants, bare feet, an old MIT hoodie from a thrift store. If she was going to risk breaking physics, she might as well be comfortable.

"Okay," she murmured, pressing record on her phone. The red dot blinked. "Trial one, Wednesday, eight forty-two a.m. Objective: confirm short-range displacement of small metallic object."

She picked up a coin, an old quarter from her change jar, and set it on the mark inside the innermost ring. It looked ridiculously ordinary sitting there. She steadied herself and placed a hand over her sternum, counting the rhythm of her pulse. Four in, hold two, six out.

The hum answered on the third breath.

It started in her ribs, faint, the way you sometimes hear your own blood when the room is too quiet. Then it gathered into tone, clean and single-note, the same pitch she'd first noticed the night she saved Emily Jameson.

Her thumb hovered over the tuning app on her phone. The pitch read somewhere between A-sharp and B, wavering with her heartbeat. She smiled despite the nerves. "You have a frequency," she whispered, almost giddy. "Of course you do."

She adjusted her breathing again. Calm heartbeat, harmonic tone, clear intent, her new commandments.

The coin began to vibrate.

Not shake or rattle but vibrate like a string plucked beneath the skin of reality. The light around it thickened, edges softening, the shadow on the floor blurring to gray. Maya felt her own breath align with it, each inhale brightening the shimmer, each exhale dimming it.

"Focus," she told herself. "Just a few inches."

She pictured the spot across the circle, nothing more. Her hand tingled; the air thickened. There was a faint *snap*, the smell of ozone, and the coin was gone.

For one dizzy heartbeat she thought she'd failed, that it had burned out of existence or fallen through the floor. Then, a soft *plink* came from the other side of the circle.

It lay there, glinting harmlessly under the gray light, exactly six inches from its starting point.

Maya exhaled so hard she nearly laughed before the sound even formed. Then she did laugh, loud and bright, the kind of sound that hadn't belonged to her since before the Codex had found her. "You've got to be kidding me," she said, half laughing, half gasping.

The phone's recorder caught everything, the hum, the silence, the coin's faint arrival. She grabbed it, replayed the clip, and heard the impossible: the hum rising through her body matched perfectly to the distortion spike just before the sound of impact.

She wrote quickly in her notebook:

Trial One: Coin. Displacement 6.3 in. Duration: 3.4 sec. Recovery: minimal. Emotion: calm, curious. Hypothesis confirmed.

She underlined *confirmed* twice.

The thrill didn't fade. It built. She pressed her hand flat to the floor where the coin had been, feeling for that faint pull in the grain of the wood. The hum still existed, but soft now, satisfied.

Maya grinned, rolling the coin between her fingers like a magician about to perform a second trick. "Again."

She reset it on the chalk mark. "Trial two, variable intent speed."

This time she didn't close her eyes. She kept them open, tracking every flicker of light, every quiver in the air. The hum began sooner, as if it remembered her. The lines of chalk glowed faintly, so faintly she might have imagined it, until the coin lifted a fraction off the floor and vanished.

The sound of return came quicker, two seconds. The coin landed neatly on her open palm.

She froze, half-laughing again, disbelieving. "You came back."

Her heart pounded in rhythm with the hum. Her hair prickled with static. She was sweating now but couldn't stop smiling.

On her phone's spectrum analyzer, the frequency had shifted slightly lower, her calmer pulse changing the note. She wrote that down too, hand shaking.

"Trial three," she said to herself, voice hushed like a scientist with a secret. "Variable emotion."

The warehouse returned to her mind: the child's fear, the gun, the impossible pause of that bullet. The hum spiked at once, sharp enough to make her teeth ache. The coin skittered across the chalk as if shoved by invisible wind but didn't move the way it had before.

She backed off quickly, forcing herself to breathe until it calmed again. "Friction," she murmured, jotting the word down. "Emotion creates resistance."

The idea made a strange kind of sense. The Weave didn't respond to command, it responded to harmony. When she fought it, it fought back.

She reset, slower now, and ran the test again.

The coin winked out. A heartbeat later, it dropped from the air above the table, missing her coffee by an inch.

She whooped in triumph, nearly upsetting the mug. "Okay, okay," she said, laughing. "Now we're getting somewhere."

She lined up three more coins and started mapping the distances, alternating her breathing rhythm and emotional tone each time. Her notes filled quickly: harmonic rise under calm focus; discordant pulse under fear or anger; lowest resistance during curiosity.

By the time she reached her tenth trial, her hands were trembling from fatigue, and sweat dampened her hairline. But the results were consistent. Every repetition shaved a fraction off her recovery time. Every attempt proved that the hum wasn't random, it was responsive, alive in the way a melody is alive when someone plays it right.

She glanced at the Codex. The cover had darkened, the runes glowing faintly beneath the surface like something pulsing under ice. It felt approving, or perhaps merely attentive.

Maya sat cross-legged on the floor, coins scattered like breadcrumbs across the chalk lines. The air smelled faintly of copper and static. Her pulse had steadied to match the room's invisible vibration.

"Trial eleven," she whispered. "Variable distance."

This time she aimed farther, across the room to the kitchen counter. The hum deepened. The air felt thick, elastic. Her ears popped as pressure shifted. The coin trembled on the floor, then blinked out with a sound like a finger snapping underwater.

She turned just in time to see it clink softly against the glass of the coffee pot.

Maya threw both arms up, laughing helplessly. "Science, meet sorcery," she said.

Her laughter echoed briefly before the hum faded into the floorboards again. For the first time since the Codex had entered her life, she didn't feel like prey to a force she couldn't name. She felt like a participant.

She gathered the coins into her hand and pressed them together until the metal warmed in her palm. "Trial complete," she whispered.

On the table, the Codex shivered once. One of the runes along its spine brightened, a subtle acknowledgment, as if the book itself had taken note.

Maya looked up toward the window. The rain had stopped. Light spilled through the wet glass in thin bars, bright enough to break the gray. The reflection staring back at her was still her own, but steadier now, eyes bright with something new.

Control.

Magic no longer felt like an accident. It felt like a method.

By late afternoon the apartment looked like a cross between an evidence locker and a child's science fair project. Maya had expanded her chalk rings into a sprawling network that touched the base of every wall. Sticky notes now numbered in the hundreds, her handwriting slanting from neat observation into feverish shorthand. Empty coffee mugs had gathered on the windowsill like spectators at a strange recital.

She sat in the center, hair pulled up, sleeves rolled high and took inventory.

"Trial three," she said softly to herself. "Control object: pen."

She placed a blue ballpoint at the ring's inner edge, switched her phone recorder on, and exhaled until the hum returned. It came faster this time, more cooperative, like a muscle remembering movement. The pen wobbled, its shadow doubling as if two versions briefly overlapped. Then, with the faintest *tick* of pressure release, it blinked out of existence.

Maya didn't move. She listened.

There, behind her. The pen clattered gently against the leg of the coffee table, rolling once before stopping.

She smiled. "Displacement, twenty-three inches. Directional control, inconsistent."

The Codex vibrated faintly on the table. The hum in her chest echoed it, a small harmonic rise, pleased but patient.

She lifted the pen, studied it as if it might tell her what it had seen. "No burn marks. No distortion." She placed it back on the line and checked her stopwatch. Recovery: 1.7 seconds.

Her earlier tests with the coin had left her dizzy and sweating. Now the only sensation was a mild tingling under her skin, like standing too close to static electricity.

"Trial four," she recorded. "Increased mass, ceramic mug, half full."

The mug was her favorite, chipped at the rim, faded constellation print around the sides. She centered it carefully and backed away a few inches.

The hum came slower, reluctant. She realized her pulse had picked up; her muscles were tensed without her meaning to.

"Breathe, Maya."

She tried again. The mug trembled, a faint shimmer around its edges. The Weave didn't like tension. She could feel it, the friction building between her heartbeat and the hum's steady rhythm. It wasn't pain yet, just resistance, the same way two magnets repel when you try to force them together.

"Trial four-point-one," she amended. "Observation: friction disrupts field stability."

Her heart rate slowed. The hum smoothed out. The mug blurred, shimmered, and vanished.

She turned in time to see it drop gently onto the counter near the sink, sloshing coffee onto the tile.

"Trial four-point-two," she murmured, laughing under her breath. "Success."

She wiped her hands on her hoodie and paced, energy buzzing under her skin. The Codex glowed faintly in the corner of her eye, pages rustling as if caught in a draft that didn't exist.

The pattern was forming. She could feel it: harmony mattered more than force. When she tried to *push* the power, it snarled. When she *listened* and breathed with it, the current moved with her.

She jotted in her notebook:

Principle: The Weave = resonance field. Emotional static increases resistance. Harmony decreases loss.

The handwriting trembled with excitement. She underlined *harmony* three times.

Next, she set out a pair of keys, her apartment tag glinting under the lamplight. "Trial five," she announced. "Predictive control."

The hum greeted her like an old friend. She imagined the keyring landing on the small end table beside her couch. Her pulse synced to the rhythm. The edges of the room softened.

The keys vanished with a sigh and reappeared exactly where she pictured.

Maya broke into a wide grin. "Nailed it."

The success pulled laughter out of her again, wild and breathless. She leaned against the couch and let herself laugh until tears pricked her eyes.

When the sound faded, the apartment seemed to breathe with her. The lightbulb overhead brightened in rhythm with her heartbeat, then dimmed.

She sat on the floor cross-legged and took a sip of water. "Trial five results: predictive aim possible. Mental clarity essential. No nosebleed. Minimal fatigue. Duration of hum: thirty-eight seconds."

The Weave purred faintly at the edge of perception, content.

Maya rubbed her temples. The rhythm inside her had changed. It was no longer a foreign presence; it was her, extended into a layer of the world she'd never known existed.

Her gaze drifted toward the Codex again. Its runes were faintly illuminated in shades of silver and blue, as if reflecting an unseen sky. She reached for the book but hesitated.

"You're not running this experiment," she said to it, almost teasing. "I am."

The glow softened, and for a moment, she imagined it approved.

She leaned back and looked around. The room was chaos, but it was *her* chaos, order in fragments. Every object that had flickered or moved held a kind of reverence now, proof that her life wasn't just reacting anymore. She was creating.

She pressed record again. "Trial six: multiple objects, simultaneous displacement. Aim: measure focus degradation over two targets."

A coin and a pen this time. She centered both, drew a breath, and felt for the hum. It rose smoothly, easy as muscle memory. Her fingers tingled.

The air thickened, not unpleasantly but full, dense with quiet electricity. The pen and coin blurred, shimmering in tandem.

Then, the friction hit. A crackle at the base of her skull. Static jumped across her fingertips like a mild shock.

Pain bloomed behind her eyes, white and fast.

"Too much," she hissed, dropping focus. Both objects reappeared midair, tumbling to the floor.

She pressed the heel of her hand to her temple, waiting for the pain to ebb. When it did, she found herself smiling again despite the throbbing. "Trial six," she said weakly, "result: simultaneous displacement triggers feedback. Field limit reached."

She wrote it down before she forgot. The key detail came to her halfway through the note: when she'd forced both objects, the tone had fractured. The single hum had split into two dissonant notes that fought each other until both collapsed.

Her breath caught. "Friction versus harmony," she whispered again, as if the Codex might be listening. "Every push creates a pull."

The phrase felt important. She wrote it in the notebook margin and circled it three times.

The apartment had gone still again. Rain drummed faintly on the window, slow and steady. She stood, stretching, every muscle humming with a strange contented fatigue.

She took one last look at her work: the chalk circles, the notes, the coins and keys scattered like a map of small victories.

"Trial seven," she said with a tired grin. "Observation: wonder outweighs exhaustion."

She clicked off the recorder and leaned back against the wall. The Codex fluttered open on its own, pages riffling until they stilled. The faintest hum answered from within it, low and warm, as if echoing her conclusion.

Maya closed her eyes and whispered, "We're getting there."

And for the first time, she could swear the Weave agreed.

The rain had given up by midafternoon. Sunlight slipped through the blinds in pale bars and laid themselves across the chalk rings like quiet ribbons. The room smelled faintly of wet concrete from the street below and the mineral dust of chalk. A drip in the sink kept time with the soft tick of the wall clock. Somewhere outside, gulls argued over nothing.

Maya stood in the doorway for a breath and let the quiet settle. Heat still flushed her face from the morning work, but the jitter had gone. She had drunk water, stretched, and given herself ten minutes without touching the Codex. The result was a steadier pulse and a confidence that felt earned rather than borrowed.

She moved through her checklist. Window unlatched a crack for air. A folded towel spread on the far side of the room. A bottle of water within reach. Phone on the tripod, camera centered on the chalk rings, audio recorder running beside it. She tested the levels and clapped once. The room clapped back, thin and accurate.

She sat, then checked her pulse against the watch. Sixty eight. Seventy two on the next count when a gull shrieked. Back to seventy. She wrote it down, added a line about the faint tingling in her fingertips left over from the last series, and circled the note. The Codex sat closed on the table. The runes on its spine were dull silver, not asleep, only waiting.

"Test A," she said, enough voice to mark the moment without breaking the stillness. She picked a thick hardcover from the stack. Four hundred pages. Good weight. She placed it on the inner mark and settled onto her heels.

Three breaths. She hummed the stable pitch under her breath, soft and human, until the deeper tone that was not her joined it. Air seemed to gain weight. The edges of the book lost their sharpness and turned to haze. A handspan above the cover, the light bent as if the room were made of water.

A soft snap. Not loud. The sound of a suction cup letting go.

The book was no longer on the floor. It sat on the couch arm within her sightline, slanted at a polite angle as if someone had placed it there while thinking about the next step.

Maya held still, feeling for backlash. None came. Her breath stayed regular. Her heart ticked along with the recorder's little red dot.

"Result," she murmured. "Displacement one point eight meters. Field time two point three seconds. Recovery six to eight seconds." She waited another six for good measure, then stood and crossed to the couch. The book was warm where her fingers had touched it earlier and no warmer. No smell of ozone. No singe on the cloth cover. She lifted it, smiled, and set it on the table.

"Mass is not the enemy," she said to the quiet. "Forcing is."

She looked around the room and thought about water, slosh, momentum inside a container. She did not want to learn that lesson by accident. She filled a metal kettle halfway at the sink and dried the outside with a dish towel. The handle was set forward and to the left so it would not catch if it arrived at an odd angle. She placed the kettle on the mark and spread the towel at the target spot with care, as if setting a landing strip for a small craft.

She rolled her shoulders back. "Test B. Kettle at half capacity. Abort if the pitch splinters or if the headache spikes."

She sat. Three breaths again. On the third, the pitch lowered. The tone was strong, then wavered when her mind jumped to the image of water slamming into metal. Anticipation itself was a kind of shove. Prickles of static rose along her forearms. A thin chill slid across the room.

She tried to push through. The tone rasped at once. The kettle did not move. Pain bloomed behind her eyes, clean and fast.

"Abort," she said, and backed out, shaking her hands like someone warding off a cramp. The rasp faded. She drank water. She waited until the clock ticked through thirty seconds and the pain settled into a steady dullness.

"Course correction," she breathed. "Listen."

She lowered her gaze to the towel at the far side and pictured the kettle sitting there, handle still forward, water intact. No metal tearing sound. No splash. She gave the image weight. She thought about calm dock pilings and the way water wraps things it respects.

The pitch cleared. Not higher, cleaner. It compressed in her chest like a drawn bowstring that did not resent being drawn.

The kettle blurred. Light dimmed, not by much, enough to make her eyes water. It vanished.

Silence collapsed inward as if the room had been holding a breath longer than she had. The edges of her vision tunneled. Gray crept in from the sides. She reached out without meaning to and felt air that did not agree on where it belonged. The lights refused to flicker. They refused to move at all.

Something heavy hit towel and floor on the far side. Water hissed across fabric. The sound arrived as if it had to fight through a thin door.

The gray finished its work. The floor came up. Cold wood met her cheek. Taste of copper.

The clock ticked. A footstep passed somewhere in the hallway outside. Traffic laid a soft ribbon in the distance. The room returned in pieces. First the feel of chalk dust in the cracks between the boards. Then the throb of pain behind her eyes, less white now, more human. Then the sense of her own hands under her chest.

She rolled to one side and sat, head forward, both palms to the floor until it stopped breathing like a ship's deck. She checked the tripod screen. The time stamp did not lie. Two minutes, forty seconds.

Nosebleed. Minor. She leaned forward and pinched the soft part of the nose, grabbed a tissue from the table without looking and ruined it at once. Her hands shook a little. She let them. After a few breaths the tremor eased. She kept pressure for another count of sixty and then let go. The drip had stopped. The smell of blood hung thinly around the coffee smell that never really left the room.

She scanned the floor. The kettle sat near the towel, dented in one side as if an impatient thumb had pressed into it. Water sprayed away from it in a comet shape across the towel and onto the boards. She checked her legs and arms for heat and sting. No scald. She wiped up the worst of the spill, then set the kettle upright, angry at it for a heartbeat and then grateful that it had not chosen her foot for a landing.

She turned to the devices. The camera had captured a brief bloom of white the instant everything went wrong. The audio showed a line of silence that ate a second whole. She scrubbed back and listened to the hum run from four hundred forty five hertz toward four hundred thirty eight right before the drop. Then a low thump that did not come from any object she could see. She would name it later. It felt like a heartbeat gone wrong.

The Codex was closed. Its spine runes pulsed with a steady glow that matched nothing in the room but felt correct for what had just happened. A faint warmth came through the leather when she laid her palm on it. Not heat. Attention.

She measured what she could control. Displacement two point four meters. Impact dent depth one centimeter at the deepest part by the ruler. No deformation at the spout. Handle slightly twisted. She took photos. She breathed through another small wave of headache and logged it. Vision steady at the three minute mark. Pain at a four out of ten and holding steady.

She wrote.

Internal fluid plus mass magnifies field stress. Anticipatory fear introduces friction that multiplies cost. Abort at rasp. Never push through static.

She paused. The words felt like something she would need later, not as information but as law. She turned to a fresh page and wrote the thesis clean, centered, and large.

Harmony before motion.
Force equals fracture.

She added two supporting lines.

Visual anchor reduces slosh instability.
No escalation to living cargo until blackout risk is under thirty seconds.

The Codex answered in the small way it had learned to use with her. One rune brightened and then faded. The tabletop hummed once, too low for the recorder to care about, exactly the right size for a human to hear.

She set the pen down and leaned back against the couch. The tissue in her hand had a diluted smear of red near the edge. The sight of it pulled the air out of her chest for a second, then put it back. She was not afraid of the power. She did not enjoy the reminder that the body pays all bills.

Sunlight crept across the floor and climbed the kettle. The dent caught it and made a small crescent of brightness inside the larger gleam. The towel had already gone from wet to damp. The room smelled like clean metal and spilled water and the chalk dust that always found a way into the air.

"No more at this weight today," she said. "Map the tones. Lower risk. Gather insight."

She closed her eyes. The hum came as a friend rather than a test. She pictured the city grid and the places where the air had throbbed for her before. She let the tones divide into lanes and then recombine into something like a map. It would be enough work to keep her from doing anything foolish.

She opened her eyes again and looked at the kettle, the chalk, the phone's little graph still lingering on the last seconds of sound. The method worked. The body kept the score. Respect both.

She picked up the notebook and underlined the thesis once more, slow and dark so the pen would remember. Then she turned off the recorder and let the apartment be quiet. The gulls had moved on. The clock ticked without opinion. The Codex warmed her palm for a heartbeat and then cooled, as if signing off the entry in its own way.

Maya rinsed the towel in the tub and wrung it until the water ran clear. The dented kettle sat beside the sink like a patient that had survived a minor surgery. Her head still throbbed in a low, manageable way. The worst had passed. The chalk rings looked softer in the late light, their edges blunted by the sun as it leaned toward evening.

She laid a fresh sheet of paper on the floor next to her notebook and pulled a thin black pen from the cup. The Codex was closed, close enough to touch. She did not open it. She wanted to hear without the book answering first.

She sat cross legged, palms up on her knees, and let her breath find its own pace. Four in. Hold two. Six out. The room obliged, growing quiet around the rhythm. The tick of the clock settled into the background like a metronome that had decided to cooperate.

The hum rose from the base of her lungs and moved outward. It was small at first, the way a pond remembers a stone, a single ripple that does not yet know what to do with itself. She did not reach for it. She let the sound notice her before she noticed it back.

On the fifth breath the tone broadened. Her body felt longer by a fraction. The hum was not in her ribs anymore. It had found the floorboards. It spread there and came back through her hands. Each fingertip tingled as if she had pressed them against a quiet fence charged by a small, patient current.

She half closed her eyes and saw nothing. Then she saw texture in the darkness. A thin grain, like silk stretched across water. The grain shifted when she breathed, and the shift made lines. She leaned into the sensation without pushing at it. The lines strengthened.

They traveled under the room first, not across air, but along what felt like the bones of the building. They followed joists and old nails and whatever else holds wood accountable over decades. Then they moved out beyond her building and into Salem.

Her breath caught. The lines were not just under her. They were everywhere. The city rested on a lattice she had never been taught to see. Each line hummed at a slightly different pitch and the difference mattered. Some thrummed low and slow like a barge engine half a mile away. Some flickered like insects near water, quick and bright. She did not try to count them. She would lose the sense if she tried to own it too fast.

She opened her eyes to a slit and set the pen down on the paper. Her hand moved as if it belonged to the hum more than to her. A long stroke for Essex. Another for Derby. A curve for Lafayette bending toward the water. She marked the square where the bookshop lived because the air there often pressed on her ears. She drew a thin line from it to the Common where she had once felt the ground ring when a marching band was not there to claim responsibility.

The map formed in small decisions. She did not measure. She listened. When a line thrummed in her left ear she shifted the pen left and down. When the pitch cooled, she lifted the line and lightened the stroke. The page began to look like a spiderweb someone had tried to translate into music.

She whispered to the room without meaning to. "Every place has its own pitch."

The words did not change the hum. They arranged her attention. She could feel the harbor from here. It pulled at the lines like a tide pulls at kelp. Several threads leaned toward that effort and met one another near the piers. The intersection was not a node as much as it was a knot. It did not feel hostile. It felt old. She drew a small circle there and shaded it lightly.

Other crossings showed themselves after that. One near a church that had always smelled to her like cedar and wet wool even when the air was dry. Another near Gallows Hill where she had walked once on a dare and wished she had not. She did not shade that one. She left it open, a ring with room inside for trouble.

Her headache loosened a notch, not because the work was easy, but because the work was right. She sensed lines threading under her own apartment building and curving out toward the water in two shallow arcs. One of those arcs passed under the bookshop. The other ran east and rose under a block where the town kept nothing now but locked maintenance doors and a mural from the eighties that deserved a better wall.

She traced both and set small dots at their crossings. The dots gathered in a pattern she would not have predicted from street names and one way signs. The crossings favored older ground. They respected stone that had been placed by hands centuries ago and had not been moved since.

She closed her eyes again and tested the thought. The tones grew more pronounced under those places. The hum liked what had lasted. It treated new steel with politeness. It loved granite.

Her breath slowed. She shifted back into the room and then out again. With each pass the lines became easier to follow. She added a short note in the margin.

Old stone deepens pitch.
Intersect near water carries more weight.

She marked another place that had begun to buzz at the edge of her attention. A sliver of park that most people used to cut between streets on foot. Even as she drew it she remembered a time she had paused there for no good reason last winter when the air had tasted sharp and clean. The map claimed it as if it had been waiting for her to notice she already knew.

The pen moved faster the longer she listened. She did not think of obstacles. She thought of flow. She sketched a narrow band down the center of Derby Street where tourists liked to gather in the warmer months, then lifted that band slightly where a covered passage bridged a gap. She drew a crescent over the old burying ground and felt the hum swell in her bones like a choir warmer than the air.

She set a triangle over three crossings that seemed to converse with one another. The shape steadied the page. She breathed out and tracked a thin filament that threaded behind a row of old brick and met another running in from the direction of the museum. The two did not collide. They braided and separated, respectful of each other's work.

Her focus narrowed. Wonder shifted to something hungrier. She wanted to name every thread. She wanted to walk each street with her palm held an inch above the ground and confirm the notches in the pitch with the soles of her feet. She wanted to know why the line near the docks dipped and rose again as if skipping a beat under the oldest pier. She caught herself gripping the pen too hard and put it down to stretch her fingers.

The kettle flashed in the corner of her vision. The dent caught the light. She looked at it and then turned back to the map. This was safer, she told herself. This was insight without blood. The thrill that rose in her throat felt cleaner.

She made a second sheet and began again, this time focusing only on crossings. Dots became a constellation. She connected a few with a faint line and then stopped herself. She did not want to invent relationships that were not there. She listened, then connected a different pair because the hum made them family.

Minutes passed. Maybe more. The light shifted on the floor. The clock ticked. The room smelled like paper and chalk and a small amount of steam leftover from the kettle's mistake. The Codex stayed closed, its spine warm where the sun reached it.

The harbor knot deepened in her awareness. It pulled her attention the way a well pulls water. She set her palm on the page and pictured the place. Old planks. Salt. A ring in the wood so polished by hands and rope that it shone like bone. The hum quickened. She marked the knot again, darker, then drew a small arrow from it toward the Common. She did not know why she drew the arrow. Her hand knew. Her body accepted its decision.

She wrote in the margin.

Carry begins at intersections.
Rest occurs where lines widen.
Noise rises where lines are shallow.

She flipped the page and drew a simpler map, a child's version for speed. She marked the bookshop, her apartment, the Common, the harbor, Gallows Hill, the old church. She drew paths between them that felt truer than routes any app would suggest. She looked at the paths and understood that if she followed them, the jumps would cost her less. The city had lanes. She had stumbled through them before. Now she could use them on purpose.

Obsession took the chair that wonder had been using. She felt its weight and let it sit. She wanted to go now. She wanted to test the map while the lines were still singing to her skin. She wanted to feel the pitch change underfoot and know she had read the score correctly.

Her head reminded her what a blackout felt like. The kettle dent added a small, bright argument. She swallowed, set the pen down, and closed her eyes.

The map hummed lightly through the paper under her hand. The room waited. The city listened without asking anything yet.

She opened her eyes and placed the map beside the notebook. She wrote one last line at the top of a clean page, then underlined it.

Route planning lowers cost.
Listening precedes motion.

She looked at the harbor again in her mind. The knot pulsed once, as if to wave, then went still.

Maya breathed out and finally stood. The room steadied around her. The kettle did not look offended anymore. The Codex warmed her palm when she touched it and then cooled. She did not open it. She did not need to.

She turned off the recorder and took a photo of the maps with her phone for a second copy. The light in the room softened to gold. She rolled up the maps carefully and slid them under the table so she would not trip on her own lines later.

The hum remained in her chest, small and companionable. It would be easy to confuse that comfort with permission. She would not. Not tonight.

She touched the circled harbor on the top map once with her fingertip. The skin there tingled in answer. She smiled, not wide, not careless, and said to the room, almost quiet enough that the words did not need to exist at all.

"Tomorrow."

The map lay rolled on the table, still warm from her hands. Maya was rinsing the last traces of chalk dust from her fingers when the news cut into the background music on her phone. She glanced over. A reporter stood beside a trailhead sign just outside Salem, the picture grainy with dusk and drizzle. Words scrolled beneath: Search underway for missing hiker in Pine Hollow Reserve. Last seen at four fifteen.

The audio crackled. Not ordinary static, but a thin ribbon of sound that matched the low note sitting in her chest. She reached for the volume and did not touch it. The hum rose on its own. The field microphone on the reporter's jacket hissed again, exactly in rhythm with her heartbeat.

Her breath slowed. The map in her head unrolled without help.

"Pine Hollow," she whispered. Her fingertip pressed a dot she had circled that afternoon, two streets from the reserve. The line had drifted out of the city there and slid into the trees like a current seeking deeper water. She heard it now, not loud, just certain.

She pulled on her jacket and stuffed her phone and a small flashlight into the pocket. No Codex. She left it on the table and turned the latch on the window for luck. She told herself she would walk. She told herself she would listen first and move second.

The reserve lay a fifteen minute ride away and then a short walk from the bus stop. It smelled of wet leaves and hemlock and the sweet damp rot that feeds forests in spring. Park rangers had set a folding table near the trailhead, paper maps held down by rocks, a thermos with steam rising from its mouth. Two volunteers in reflective vests took names and handed out strips of orange flagging tape. The last of the day's light had pulled back into the trees and left the paths bruise colored and soft.

Maya kept to the edge. She did not sign in. She did not want her name written on any clipboard tonight. She put the hood up and let the hum guide her past the table and the people who looked tired already.

The first turn came quickly. A spur trail hung a right around a granite outcrop. The hum favored it. She followed, breath steady, steps light. The map in her head matched the real ground so well that she felt a small thrill of relief. She had not imagined the lines. They ran under her now, strong and cool, braided with the root systems that stitched this patch of woods into itself.

She tried her first blink at a mossy boulder. Two steps back for a run-up would have been ridiculous, so she did what she had trained herself to do. Four in. Hold two. Six out. She pictured the boulder's far side where the ground flattened and the hum thickened like the low chord of a piano.

Air pressed. The tone in her ribs slid lower, then clicked. Space folded a fraction. She was there.

No sting. No heat. A brief dizzy tilt, then balance. She grinned into the hood and moved again.

The trail narrowed. Stones showed at odd angles like knuckles under thin skin. Ferns tugged at her calves. The hum gathered and stretched ahead in easy hills. She blinked from tree to tree, never more than a body length or two, always with the picture of the next landing clear and small. Each time she arrived, the recovery time shortened. Each time, the world felt less offended.

She stopped at a fork where the official sign pointed one way, and a faint footpath cut into the leaves pointed another. The hum preferred the footpath. She checked the ground. The mud there held a wide print, the edge softened by rain. A running shoe. Fresh enough to hold its shape. The print angled downslope, not toward the lookouts and their easy views, but toward the part of the map she had shaded that afternoon, a simple dot that had begun to feel heavier than ink.

"Do not be careless," she told herself, quiet enough that the trees would not feel included. She followed the footpath. The forest closed in a little. The light thinned.

She blinked again to a fallen trunk and crouched. The bark was slick under her palm, cold with rain. Her breath fogged. The hum thickened. It led her to a shallow gully where water would run hard in a storm. Tonight it moved only in thin threads, whispering against stone. The print was here too, smeared now, and another beside it where someone had slid a foot and caught themselves. She looked up.

"Hello?" she called, not loud, the way you would ask a house if anyone was home. The forest answered in water and bird calls and the small rustle of something that did not care about her at all. Under it, the hum carried a new disturbance. A low rasp that made her think of metal scraping rock.

She followed that sound the way a person follows a smell. Twenty paces. Then another blink. Then another, short as a breath. The rasp returned, closer. She stepped up onto a flat rock and saw a shape below in the shadows tucked against a blowdown.

A man's leg stuck out at an odd angle from beneath a mat of branches. His jacket sleeve moved, a slow drag up and down that could not be wind. She slid down the bank on her heels and landed in a crouch, both hands up and open so he would see a person coming and not a threat.

"Sir," she said. "Can you hear me?"

The jacket stilled, then twitched. A face turned toward her, pale against wet leaves. He was in his thirties maybe, beard beginning, eyes wide with pain. A section of small dead limbs held his left thigh pinned. A larger trunk lay across them, not heavy enough to crush, heavy enough to keep him where the forest had decided to place him.

"Help," he said, a dry croak, as if the word had been waiting behind his teeth for an hour and had just gotten the order to move.

"I am here," she said. "You are not alone. I am going to check you for anything urgent." She kept her voice calm and even as if that tone could knit things.

She checked his head for bleeding. No scalp wound. Pupils even. Breath shallow but regular. No chest deformity. The leg was the problem. The trapped thigh was swelling against the denim. When she touched near his knee he flinched with a sharp inhale.

"Name?" she asked.

"Jason," he said, as if giving her the answer to a riddle at school.

"Okay, Jason." She slid her jacket off and folded it under his head. "I am Maya. I am going to get help. But I want to see if I can make you a little more comfortable first."

She peeled smaller branches away and tossed them into a pile. The larger trunk would not budge. She left it alone. The hum pressed at her back like a hand trying to get her attention. She ignored it just long enough to untie his shoe. Swelling would fight the laces later. He hissed again but did not argue. She found his phone in his jacket pocket, battery dead, and placed it beside her own.

"Cold?" she asked.

He nodded once.

She took the scarf from her neck and tucked it under his jacket at the collar. "I need to leave you for a few minutes," she said. "I will bring people. I promise."

His hand clutched at her sleeve. "Please do not leave."

She put her palm over his knuckles and let the hum move through that contact. It came up through her arm and settled. It was the same note she had felt around Emily's wrist in the warehouse, not loud, not dramatic. Present. She held the touch for three breaths and did not look away.

"I am coming back," she said.

He released her.

She stood and checked the ground. The route back to the path cut up the bank and through a tangle of roots. She tested a blink to the top and felt the field catch at the edges of her vision, a warning nudge. She set that aside. No long jumps now. She needed her head clear when people asked questions.

She took out her phone and switched the flashlight on and off three times for herself, then started back at a steady pace. The ground was soft and kept her marks. She did not try to hide them. She widened her steps where she could, scuffed the heel in places, and bent a sapling branch to hang the orange flag she had quietly lifted from the table on her way in. She tied another to a root a little farther up. Footprints and flags. Enough for any trained eye.

When the main trail widened and the glow of a lantern showed between trunks, she broke into a jog. A group of volunteers stood with a ranger, map open, fingers tracing lines that had nothing to do with the ones she had drawn at home.

"I found him," she said, a little breathless. "He is conscious, leg pinned. He needs a litter and a saw."

The ranger's head came up so fast the brim of his cap clicked against his collar. "Where?"

She turned and pointed the way she had come. "Take the spur to the granite outcrop, then the footpath beginning to the right of the sign that says stay on trail. Follow the flags. My footprints will take you off the footpath to a gully. He is just beyond a blowdown on the left bank."

The ranger held her gaze a beat, measuring for panic or invention, and found neither. He nodded once, clipped, and spoke into his radio. "Possible subject located, conscious with leg entrapment, Pine Hollow east gully. Litter, saw, medic. Team Bravo with me." He looked back at her. "You can show us?"

"I will walk ahead," she said. She did not add that she would not lead them more than necessary. She did not want anyone to feel they had been pulled by a force they could not name.

They moved. Boots on wet leaves. Packs shifting. The ranger's light cut a path, and her flags did the rest. She kept her pace steady and her steps heavy enough to leave clear prints. The hum ran alongside her like a dog that understood the job.

At the blowdown she stopped and stepped aside. The ranger slid past, kneeled, and spoke the kind of calm words she had used. Jason's reply came out rough and grateful. The medic fell to work. The saw buzzed to life and drowned the forest's small sounds. The group moved with quick gentle competence, the kind of dance people perform when they have practiced together for a long time.

Maya drifted back to the treeline, not far, only far enough that she could watch without being watched. The forest felt different with other heartbeats in it. The hum in her veins answered theirs and then settled.

When the first red rescue light flared between trunks, something inside her answered. A faint pulse moved through her blood like a hand closing once around hers. It did not belong to fear. It belonged to relief. It belonged to a quiet yes.

She exhaled and let the trees take back their shape around her. The ranger lifted a hand in her direction without looking to see whether she was still there. It meant thanks. It meant you did the right thing. She lifted her own hand in answer even though he could not see it with his attention on the saw and the boy and the work.

They shifted the trunk. The medic spoke. The litter came forward and lowered. The saw went silent. Voices replaced it, some tired and some lighter, as if a weight had moved off all their backs at once.

Maya stayed until the team had Jason up and ready to travel. When they passed the spot where she stood, one of the volunteers glanced toward the shadow and blinked as if unsure whether anyone had been there at all. She let the forest hold her a little deeper and smiled.

She took a last slow look at the path, her flags bright against the dim, the footprints clear where the mud held them, and then turned toward the main trail. She did not blink again. She walked, calm and careful, and let the hum settle into its smallest size.

At the trailhead the folding table had acquired another thermos. An old woman in a purple raincoat ladled hot chocolate into paper cups and pressed one into Maya's hands without a question. The drink tasted like childhood and tired victory. She sipped, nodded thanks, and stepped aside as the team came out to the lot with the litter. A cheer rose that the woods swallowed in a heartbeat.

She set the empty cup on the edge of the table and moved back into the dark, far enough to watch without being counted. The rescue vehicle's lights spun once, then steadied. A soft wind moved the tops of the pines. The hum in her chest gave one more pulse and rested.

Fear had carried her into the woods. Purpose had taken her down the gully. Exhilaration hovered at the edge of her vision and did not push. It would wait until she was home and the map was on the table again to make itself known.

She pulled her hood tighter and walked for the bus stop, the night suddenly so normal that it felt like a joke. Only her hands knew the truth. They shook once as if clapping, then were still.

The next morning came pale and uncertain, the kind of dawn that looked unsure whether to stay. Rain had returned sometime in the night, thin and silver against the windows. Maya woke to the sound of her phone buzzing on the nightstand, one persistent notification after another, piling faster than she could blink sleep away.

She sat up, hair tangled, the room still smelling faintly of chalk and metal. The Codex sat closed on the table, innocent, its runes dark. She ignored it and reached for her phone. The lock screen was a wall of alerts; news feeds, messages, and one headline repeated across several outlets, each more breathless than the last.

GHOST RESCUER OF SALEM STRIKES AGAIN

She read it twice before her brain caught up. The story below played like an echo of the first time: a child saved in impossible circumstances, now a man found against all odds. The article quoted the ranger, describing "a mystery volunteer who led them straight to the missing hiker." It mentioned "a woman in a hood," then blurred into speculation.

The local blog had gone further. **"Same description as the police station event last week."**

She set the phone down, stared at it, then picked it up again. The reporter's language was everywhere now; ghost rescuer, miracle worker, divine intervention. Some threads turned the phrase into a joke; others turned it into scripture. One even offered a blurry image someone had snapped near the trailhead: a silhouette, indistinct, mid-turn.

It looked vaguely like her.

She pressed her palms to her eyes. The memory of the night before, the hum, the rain, the quiet pulse that had guided her to Jason was still too fresh to feel real. The internet had already decided to make it legend.

Her stomach twisted. She hadn't done it for attention, hadn't even meant to be seen. She'd left footprints, flags, all deliberate, to make it easy for them to find him. But she'd also left traces of something else.

She pulled her laptop closer and opened a private browser. Burner account, anonymous handle, no photo. She typed **"Ghost Rescuer of Salem"** and hit search.

Hundreds of posts.
Dozens of theories.

Some called her a vigilante. Others said she was an angel, sent to "cleanse the city's sins." One thread spun a government-experiment theory complete with grainy screenshots from the police station's security footage. Someone had circled her reflection in a frame and claimed it glowed. Another post, buried deeper, described her teleportation as a "quantum displacement anomaly," with diagrams that looked stolen from a high school physics class.

A new comment blinked into existence as she scrolled.

u/Watcher1776: "If this woman's real, she's being tracked already. No one just disappears twice and walks away."

Her fingers hovered above the keyboard. She should close the window, delete the search history, step away. Instead, she clicked the username. The account was blank, created this morning. No posts. No history.

Her breath slowed. The hum in her chest stirred faintly, the same low note she'd felt before something shifted. She shut the laptop, pushed it aside, and got up.

The mirror over the sink showed a face she barely recognized: circles under the eyes, hair in loose waves from sleep. She splashed cold water on her cheeks and laughed under her breath, the sound brittle. "Ghost rescuer," she said to the empty air. "Great."

Outside, Salem was still waking. She needed normalcy, coffee, conversation, anything that didn't vibrate with cosmic resonance. She grabbed her hoodie and crossed the street to the café.

The bell over the door chimed. Steam and warmth folded around her. The smell of espresso and sugar made the morning almost ordinary. Alex wasn't behind the counter; a different barista smiled at her with polite recognition. Maya ordered her usual and found a seat by the window.

She scrolled her phone while she waited, telling herself it was just curiosity. Another news station was running the story now, their banner looping the same phrase: **GHOST RESCUER RETURNS**.

The clip showed aerial footage of Pine Hollow, search teams moving through the woods. Her heart clenched when she saw the gully, lit by floodlights. Then the frame froze on a single blurry figure, the hooded outline of her leaving the scene.

"Authorities are still searching for the unidentified woman who led rescuers to the injured hiker," the reporter said. "Witnesses describe her as calm, almost serene, before she vanished into the trees."

Vanished. She hadn't vanished. She'd just walked away.

A laugh escaped her, half disbelief, half surrender. "I can't win," she murmured.

The barista set her coffee down with a smile that was a little too bright. "Crazy story, huh? They're saying she's local."

Maya forced a smile. "Yeah. Wild."

The barista lowered her voice conspiratorially. "My roommate says it's gotta be a setup. Some viral marketing thing. No way a person just... blinks around like that."

She nodded, eyes fixed on the foam. "No way."

She went back to the counter, humming off-key.

Maya turned her focus to the window, letting the glass blur the street. Cars passed in slow motion through the mist. The world looked soft, manageable again. She sipped the coffee, closed her eyes, and exhaled.

When she opened them, she noticed the sedan.

Black, polished even under the drizzle, parked across the street with its engine idling. The driver's window was cracked an inch. A man sat inside, his profile mostly shadow. The coat, dark, expensive, military-cut, hung too neatly on him to belong to an ordinary commuter. He wasn't on his phone. He wasn't reading.

He was watching the bookshop.

Her bookshop.

Maya's pulse quickened. The hum inside her ribs answered, faint and warning. She lowered her gaze and pretended to stir her coffee. In the reflection on the window, she caught his movement, a slight tilt of the head, just enough to confirm he was still looking.

Across the room, someone's laughter broke the tension for a moment, grounding her. She forced her breathing to slow, counting again. Four in. Hold two. Six out. The hum calmed with her, but the instinct didn't fade.

She reached for her phone, opened the camera, and pretended to check a message while angling the lens toward the window. The photo snapped with a faint sound. The man didn't react.

She looked at the picture. The sedan's license plate was half visible, the driver's face blurred by rain. The image meant nothing by itself, but it meant someone was paying attention.

Not the Weave. Not fate. Not coincidence.

People.

She gathered her things, finished the coffee in a few quick sips, and left a crumpled bill on the table. As she pushed open the café door, the bell chimed again. The sound felt sharp in the morning quiet.

Across the street, the sedan's brake lights flared, then dimmed. It didn't pull away.

Maya walked toward the corner instead of home, keeping her pace steady. Her reflection moved beside her in the glass storefronts, the hood pulled low. She cut down a side street lined with parked cars and wet brick. The hum tracked with her heartbeat, steadier now but alert.

At the next intersection she glanced back. The sedan had turned the corner behind her. Same car, same driver. The distance stayed the same, careful, practiced.

By the time she reached the next block, she ducked into an alley that opened toward the rear of the bookshop. A delivery van blocked the far end. Perfect cover. She pressed herself against the wall, heartbeat fast, the hum vibrating just beneath skin.

A few seconds later the sedan passed the mouth of the alley, slow enough to see the driver's eyes flick in her direction before he looked away and kept going.

She waited until the sound of the engine faded. Only then did she exhale.

Back inside her apartment, she locked the door and leaned against it. The Codex sat where she had left it. The runes were awake again, silver-gray in the dim light. They pulsed once, faintly, like a heartbeat.

"I saw him," she said softly.

The book didn't answer, but the hum did, a low, sympathetic tone that reminded her she wasn't imagining the overlap between worlds. The Weave watched. Now, so did someone else.

She sank into the chair, phone still in her hand, and scrolled through the headlines one last time. Every article, every thread, every wild theory, all of it pointed back to her.

A hero to strangers.

A miracle to some.

A target to whoever sat in that sedan.

Maya closed the laptop and whispered to the quiet, "You wanted control. Now you've got attention."

Outside, the rain slowed to a drizzle. The café's neon sign across the street blinked once, twice, then steadied.

Validation lingered for a heartbeat, warm as light through fog. Then unease replaced it, a cold thread winding through her pulse.

The Ghost Rescuer of Salem had returned.

And this time, the world was watching.

Night wrapped around Salem like a held breath. The rain had stopped an hour ago, leaving the streets slick and reflective, every puddle a trembling mirror. Maya sat cross-legged on the floor, lights dimmed, the city glow leaking through the blinds in soft gold stripes.

The Codex lay open on the coffee table. She hadn't meant to open it. She'd come home from the café, shaken, poured herself tea, and told herself she'd leave the book closed for once. But it had other ideas. When she'd passed it on the way to the kitchen, the faintest vibration had brushed her fingertips, as if something behind the leather had drawn a breath.

Now it waited, silent but awake.

She exhaled, slow, deliberate. "You've been quiet all day," she said, half to herself, half to it. "That usually means trouble's next."

The Codex didn't move. But the hum did.

It began low in her ribs, then widened outward, not louder, just larger. The sound wasn't inside her this time. It came from the room itself, woven through the air like threads tightening in invisible hands.

She froze, tea halfway to her lips. The mug rattled against the saucer.

The light in the ceiling flickered once. The shadows on the wall shifted in rhythm, as if breathing with her.

Her first instinct was fear, quick, cold, rational fear. She'd spent the week teaching herself control, mapping invisible lines, proving that magic could obey reason. But this was different. This wasn't her. This was something listening back.

The hum layered. Beneath her own steady tone another began to rise, a harmony, distant but distinct. It moved just out of sync with her pulse, an echo that refused to mirror perfectly. The two notes rubbed against each other, dissonant for a heartbeat, then blended.

She set the cup down and reached toward the Codex. "Okay," she whispered. "If you have something to say, I'm listening."

Her fingers brushed the page.

The runes ignited in soft blue light. Not blinding, not searing, just illumination, alive and deliberate. They flowed like liquid silver beneath the surface, rearranging in subtle ripples. The hum shifted again, deepening until she could feel it in her teeth.

Maya didn't recoil. She let the vibration move through her hand, her wrist, her arm. It wasn't pain. It was presence. The same way she had felt the ley lines beneath the city, alive, aware, patient.

The Codex pages turned on their own. Once. Twice. Then stopped near the center, on a blank sheet that hadn't been there before.

Her pulse jumped. The hum steadied. A faint blue filament rose from the surface of the paper, thin as smoke, wavering like a candle flame in a wind that didn't exist. It hovered for a moment, then split into two, weaving around each other before sinking back into the page.

She heard it then, beneath the tone, a whisper. Not words. Not yet. Just shape and cadence, like the world forming the outline of speech but not filling it.

The air thickened with the scent of ozone. The light flickered again, steadier this time, as if synchronizing to the rhythm.

Her heart raced, but she didn't pull away. Instead she reached for her pen and turned to the margin.

The world watches when I act. It listens when I stop.

The ink glowed faintly when she lifted the pen. The hum answered, a low, approving sound that wasn't quite external anymore.

Maya leaned back, hand trembling. "So that's what you wanted to tell me," she murmured.

The Codex didn't move again. But she could feel its agreement, not as sound but as gravity.

She looked toward the window. The blinds were half-open, show-ing slivers of the Salem skyline. The old rooftops gleamed damp under the streetlights, and beyond them, faint mist hung above the harbor.

Something shimmered there, faint, nearly invisible.

At first she thought it was residual light, the trick of wet air catch-ing reflections. But the shimmer moved with intent, not wind. Thin blue filaments stretched across the city, flickering along streets and rooftops, tracing the same invisible map she had drawn that after-noon.

They pulsed once, in perfect rhythm with her heartbeat.

Maya stood, stepping closer to the window. Her breath fogged the glass. The filaments brightened for a moment, then dimmed again, as if embarrassed to have been seen.

"They're real," she whispered. "I mapped them, and they're real."

Her reflection stared back from the glass, eyes wide, face pale, the faint blue light painting her skin in ghostly relief. For one terrifying, beautiful second, the world felt awake. Not the hum, not the Weave, not even the Codex, but the world itself, every stone, every drop of water, every wire running under the streets.

Alive. Listening.

The thought thrilled her and terrified her at the same time.

She backed away from the window, pulse hammering. "If it listens," she said softly, "then it learns."

The hum quieted but didn't disappear. It lingered like the aftertaste of lightning.

She closed the Codex gently, palms flat against its cover. The warmth beneath her fingers faded to stillness.

The room seemed too small now, too bright, even in half-light. She turned off the lamp. The darkness felt cleaner, more honest. Outside, the city's heartbeat slowed again. The filaments dissolved into mist, leaving nothing behind but rain-slick streets and the faint reflection of her own uncertain face.

Maya stood for a long time in that quiet. She wanted to believe the glow had been a hallucination, the product of exhaustion and adrenaline. But deep inside, she knew the truth. The Weave had shown her its body. Salem was not just streets and buildings anymore, it was part of the pattern.

And the pattern had eyes.

She sat again, the Codex before her, the pen still warm from her hand. Her last note caught her attention.

The world watches when I act. It listens when I stop.

She added one more line beneath it:

Listening is never harmless.

The hum acknowledged that, faint but present. Then silence reclaimed the room.

Maya rubbed her thumb over the dented kettle on the counter, the lingering reminder of cost. She looked back to the window. The skyline had gone ordinary again, but she could still feel the rhythm beneath it, the city breathing, the lines pulsing in secret measure.

"Discovery achieved," she said softly. "Safety lost."

The Codex gave one final flicker, a pulse of light through the runes like a closing eye.

Maya stood, turned off the last lamp, and let the darkness settle around her.

Outside, Salem exhaled, a single pulse through the unseen filaments, and was still.

7

The Book of Shadows

The apartment looked like it had been holding its breath all evening.

Maya stood in the kitchen with her hand on the light switch and decided, firmly, not to flip it. The overhead fixture felt like too much. Screens felt like too much. Fluorescents, LEDs, anything that hummed on its own. She was full of other hums already.

Instead, she reached into the drawer under the stove and pulled out a half-used sleeve of tea lights. She set three in a crooked triangle on the coffee table and one on the windowsill. The lighter clicked, once, twice, then each wick caught, little disks of fire cupping themselves in metal.

The city outside stretched along the glass in soft smears of yellow and red. No sirens. No shouting. Just the occasional hiss of a passing car on wet asphalt and the distant horn of something on the harbor. Salem was quiet tonight. Or pretending to be.

On the counter, the dented kettle sat where she had left it, a dull metal bruise in the candlelight. The warped spot caught a weak glow and held it, small crescent of brightness trapped inside the curve. A reminder that even experiments that went right had teeth.

Maya ignored the electric lamp beside the couch. Its pull was familiar, but it belonged to the part of her life that could be turned off with a switch. The thing she was about to open did not.

She padded barefoot to the coffee table, the wood cool under her soles, and sat cross-legged on the rug. The Codex lay waiting, its leather dark and matte, spine creased with angles that refused to match any modern binding. The runes along its back were a soft ghost-silver in the flicker, not shining exactly, just refusing to be fully dark.

Her phone lay face down to one side, screen dark. She had already silenced every alert, backed away from headlines and forums and theories about ghosts in police lobbies and angels in the woods. None of those people could help her understand the thing that had taken up residence on her table.

She placed both hands lightly on the cover. It was warm. It had no right to be warm.

"Okay," she said quietly. "Just reading. No tricks. No bleeding. Just... reading."

The book did not respond. Not yet.

She opened it to where she had left off two nights before, somewhere past the family names and incantation fragments, in the section that had refused to choose a language. Half the page was composed of looping characters that had never belonged to any alphabet she knew. The other half looked like English seen through broken glass. Words she almost recognized, tense and warped, sliding away when she tried to pin them.

Tonight, the page felt different.

She leaned closer. The candle beside her breathed smoke and small light across the parchment. The top line wavered. At first she thought it was only the flame. The ink seemed to shimmer in rhythm with the flicker, letters sinking and rising as if written on water instead of skin.

Her chest tightened. She held her own breath to watch better.

One of the curved runes near the margin loosened at the edge, its tail pulling free from the stroke beside it. The motion was slow and deliberate, like melted wax deciding which way to drip. The line slid sideways and folded into another loop, forming a shape that looked a little less alien, a little closer to something she could sound out.

"Are you serious," she whispered, more to the room than the book.

The hum answered before the Codex did. It stirred in the low back of her lungs then climbed, a note she had learned to recognize as the Weave's version of attention. The candle flames nearest the book reacted, thinning, then flaring, their sway synchronizing to the rise and fall of the tone in her ribs. Light and sound worked in lockstep.

Ink responded next.

The runes across the top line began to move, one after another, as if some decision had been made and the page was only now catching up with it. The change was not dramatic, no jerking, no cracking, just a patient rearranging. Lines slid into other lines. Curves untwisted. Tiny barbs at the ends of strokes straightened out.

Shapes she had never seen before started to resemble letters she had. Old ones. Text from woodcuts and facsimiles of medieval manuscripts she had shelved a hundred times at the shop.

She blinked and sat back an inch. The text froze mid-change, as if her distance had cooled it.

"Okay," she said, more wary now. "If I am hallucinating, this is very well organized."

She leaned in again. The hum rose, interested. The ink resumed its slow migration.

The half-legible section that had once looked like it had been written on top of itself began to separate. One layer sank back, ghostly, retaining its runic curl and clearly belonging to something older and harsher. Another layer floated forward, the same strokes drawn anew but with different angles, different weights. It became English letters rendered in a hand that belonged to no one alive.

Her mouth went dry.

She reached out, fingers hovering just above the page, not touching. Heat floated up from the parchment, more than wax and flame could account for. Her palm tingled, the sigil there warming in sympathetic recognition.

The letters finished their shift and settled.

She tested herself. She looked away, counted three heartbeats, then snapped her gaze back.

They stayed.

Her throat made a weak sound, half under her breath, almost a laugh, almost a prayer. She could read this.

She skimmed the first line and her eyes snagged halfway through. The letters were English, but the words slotted into each other in a pattern that carried an accent from another century.

"*Concerning that which remaineth when all threads are drawn,*" she murmured aloud.

The sound of her own voice in the small apartment sounded too loud, spilling into corners that did not belong to a human tone anymore.

The hum deepened in her chest. The candle nearest the page leaned toward her, its flame stretching thin and bright for three seconds, then easing back. The wax edge drooped in a ring.

She closed her eyes, took a breath, opened them again, just to be sure this was not another case of reality slipping sideways.

It was all still there. Legible. Waiting.

She checked herself one more time. "You are doing this on purpose," she told the Codex, as if it could hear sarcasm and decide whether to be offended.

The binding creaked gently as the spine flexed, like old leather taking a deeper breath.

Between the two central candles, the ink near the top margin pulled itself into a line more careful than the rest. This time the change was simple and direct. Strokes thickened and thinned where someone had once lifted a quill and re-set it. The script resolved into words that looked intentional in a way the rest of the page did not.

Her eyes traced them, one by one.

Fragment XXVII: On the Nature of the Unmaking
Written by Myrddin Emrys, Keeper of the Second Song.

She swallowed, throat suddenly tight. The word Unmaking felt heavier than the letters that composed it. It sat on the page like something that would not move if pushed.

The hum did not spike like it did before a jump. It sunk lower, into her spine, a resonance she recognized from the ley intersections she had sketched that afternoon. The candle flame in front of the title steadied, no longer flickering, as if something had cupped a hand around it.

Maya sat very still. Curiosity pressed at her ribs from the inside. Thrill pressed back from the page. Behind both, a thin thread of wariness tugged, reminding her what usually followed when the Codex decided to be helpful.

She considered closing the book, right then, while the letters were still fresh and her mind had not yet wrapped itself around that new word. She glanced at the dented kettle in the kitchen, at the rolled maps of ley lines under the table, at the sticky note on the wall that read in her own handwriting, Listen before you move.

"Listening counts as moving too, huh," she muttered.

The page waited. The heading did not fade. The old ghost script that still lingered beneath the English version looked almost like a shadow, just out of focus. She could feel the age of it, not as a number of years but as weight. Someone far older than her had written this. Someone who thought in terms like thread and residue and silence between songs.

Her pulse sped up. The hum answered, sympathetic.

"This might be too much," she said to the empty room.

The emptiness did not agree or disagree. The candles danced in time with her heartbeat. The word Unmaking seemed to lean toward her, the curve of the capital U catching the light.

She pulled her notebook closer, clicked a pen open, and settled her eyes on the first line beneath the fragment title.

If the book had gone to all this trouble to speak plainly, walking away felt worse than foolish. It felt like leaving a door unlocked in a bad neighborhood and pretending the street did not exist.

"Fine," she whispered. "Tell me, then."

She lowered her gaze to the text, the candlelight catching the curve of every letter, and began to read.

Maya traced the title with her eyes, not her fingers.

Fragment XXVII: On the Nature of the Unmaking

Written by Myrddin Emrys, Keeper of the Second Song.

The word sat at the top of the page like a stone in a pond. Everything around it seemed to ripple a little. The candle flame closest to the book leaned in, then shrank back as if reconsidering.

The heading settled, ink still glistening faintly in the candlelight. Beneath it, a signature curled in older script: *Myrddin Emrys.* Maya frowned, mouthing the name. She had read it before, in a set of brittle translations from the rare-book section downtown. *Myrddin Emrys,* the name used by Merlin in the oldest surviving texts. Merlin of King Arthur's court, the myth that refused to die. Her pulse quickened. The Codex was not quoting legend; it was *written* by it. She swallowed and began to read.

The script was English, but old English, its spelling slipperier, its phrasing bending at odd angles. The first line unfurled slowly in her head.

When the first threads were drawn from thought into matter, all things were carried in one concord.

She mouthed the words without sound. The hum in the room answered, low and approving.

The paragraph continued, ink neat and deliberate. Merlin had not been in a hurry when he wrote this.

From that concord came motion and rest, light and its absence, heat and the mercy of cooling, each their own proper voice in the Song. Yet no song, however perfect, may be held forever without strain.

She copied that into her notebook, pen scratching softly.

No song, however perfect, may be held forever without strain.

Her own handwriting looked strange beside the elegant script in the Codex. Rounder. Faster. Human in the present tense.

She kept reading.

Merlin described the Weave first, and not as some abstract diagram. He called it a song, a breath, an ordering that lived underneath things. Threads, he wrote, were not lines but relations. They bound intention to form, idea to flesh, memory to stone. All magic, all miracles, all prayers that ever truly landed had moved along those threads.

She felt the hum under her palm as she rested it lightly on the margin. It agreed.

Then the tone of the fragment shifted. The letters seemed to lean a degree sharper. The ink grew minutely darker, as if more pressure had been used here, more care.

Yet even in concord, there is waste.

She paused, pen halfway to the page. Waste. Her first instinct was to think of pollution or refuse. Merlin meant something larger.

When a thread is drawn, there is fraying. When a light is kindled, there is smoke. From the first making there remained that which could not be drawn back into the Song, for it matched no note within it. This remainder I have named the Residuum of Will.

She wrote that down slowly.

Residuum of Will.

The letters looked heavy in her notebook, like they wanted to sink through the paper.

As she wrote the name a strange thing happened. For half a second, her script thinned and curved in a way she did not intend, the pen forming elegant tails and hooked flourishes that were not hers. The hum in the spine of the Codex swelled at the same moment, warm, intimate.

It was like someone older had put a hand over hers and guided the stroke.

She pulled her pen back, heart ticking a little faster. The style shifted back to her usual cramped print as soon as she broke contact.

"Not yours," she said under her breath, glancing at the book. "You do not get my handwriting too."

The candle nearest her sputtered, then steadied.

She drew a line in the margin and wrote, in her normal letters:

All creation leaves a remainder.

The idea made her skin tighten. There was something brutally honest about it. Even the gods, Merlin implied, could not create without byproduct. The Weave was harmony, yes, but in the gaps between its notes, something extra collected.

Merlin called that extra a residue. He described it not as a monster, not as a demon, but as a byproduct of perfection held too long, of power used without a place for all its shadows.

She read on.

Beagron, who walked where matter had not yet quite decided to be, first named it in my hearing. He spoke of it as the ash that will not return to the flame, though all else burns clean. It is what remains when Will has wrought more than form can justly bear.

She underlined Beagron hard enough to tear the surface of the page a little.

Beagron.

She had seen that name once already, briefly, in another fragment bleeding through the dream of a black stone. Now it came with context. Someone else had seen what Merlin saw. Someone who had been there earlier. Someone who had left warnings in talismans and runes.

"Okay," she murmured. "So this is not just your theory."

Her pen moved again, this time less shaky.

Margin note: Beagron = primary source. Oldest witness.

She could almost feel the book approve of that summary.

The fragment went deeper.

Merlin spoke of the Unmaking, though he did not always use that word. Sometimes he called it the Shadow Current. Sometimes the

Leftover Silence. The Residuum of Will. The thing that gathers in corners when threads strain and cannot break, only fray.

He described its nature with a kind of reluctant respect.

It is not alive as men reckon life. It seeks no throne. It plots no kingdom. It does not say I.

Her eyes lingered there. She copied the line with care, then added beneath it:

Not alive. No "I". Just reaction.

The candle flames bent toward the page as if drawn.

Yet it is not absent of mind. It knows imbalance as a wound knows pressure. Where the Song grows too loud, it moves to hush it. Where form runs longer than its measure, it moves to shorten. It is not hatred, but correction gone blind.

Her pen moved faster now, notebook filling with paraphrase.

Energy unclaimed seeks a vessel, she wrote. Not evil. Just correction without perspective.

The act of writing calmed the fear a little. Analysis was a familiar shelter. She was good at reading things no one else wanted to read, at folding horror into language and shelving it safely between covers. If she could name this, perhaps it would not feel so much like the cold draft that had brushed her neck in the catacombs.

Still, the word Unmaking kept catching her.

Every time her eyes tripped across it on the page, the nearest candle flame dipped. Not extinguished, just a quick bow, like a head lowered in the presence of a superior.

She tested it, half disbelieving.

She looked away, focused on the wall, and just thought the word Unmaking a single time, fully and clearly.

The flame sagged immediately, shrinking low to the wick, then sprang back up.

"Okay," she said softly. "I hate that."

The hum in her chest held steady, neither growing nor retreating. The book did not move. The only visible sign that anything had reacted to the thought was that tiny candle bow.

She licked her lips and went back to reading, slower now.

The fragment shifted again, more personal.

Merlin wrote of his own attempts to touch the Unmaking. He had not done it casually. The tone in the script tightened, as if even remembering unnerved him.

I have stood in the presence of its flood, upon the rim of a nexus when the threads strained near breaking. It is no beast, to be banished with name and circle. It is the noise between all names, the breath taken after all circles break.

Maya's skin prickled. She tried to imagine him, mythic Merlin, not as robed stage magician, but as a tired man standing at the edge of something large and uncaring.

He admitted fear in the next line, not bluntly but in the way he circled his own limits.

I, who have spoken with stones and heard their answer, will not hold the Residuum in my bare thought for long. It gives back nothing. It offers only the rest that is not mercy.

She underlined that twice.

Rest that is not mercy.

Her gaze blurred for a second. The words made a quiet sense she wished they did not. She thought of the numbness that had crept into the edges of her mind when she had blacked out after the kettle. The way it had felt good, for half a heartbeat, to stop existing as a conscious shape and just be pressure and quiet.

Dread traced a small circle in her stomach.

She flipped a page, careful not to smudge the ink.

The next section read more like warning than observation.

Those who despair are nearest to its reach, for they loosen their hold upon their own thread. It finds ready harbor where purpose has been abandoned.

She scrawled in the margin:

Human despair = open door.

Her handwriting had begun to tilt, letters leaning toward each other. Little hooks appeared at the ends of her Ts and Ys, small flourishes she did not intend. The Codex hummed faintly with each of them, as if approving an essay.

"Stop that," she said, more sharply this time. She shook out her hand and deliberately wrote her next note slow, all block letters.

IT DOES NOT HATE. IT CORRECTS.

Seeing the sentence in her own blunt print made it worse, not better. Correction sounded reasonable. This was not reasonable. This was the universe's version of rot, growing wherever something was left unattended too long.

She inhaled and read the next paragraph.

Some would name it Evil, for it unwinds what they would keep. Yet evil is a matter of aim and choosing. This thing chooses nothing. It is the sum of all excess, and excess must go somewhere.

She thought of landfills. Of runoff. Of the way river foam gathers behind rocks. Cosmic trash. Only this trash remembered what had been thrown away.

"All creation leaves a remainder," she repeated softly, touching the first note she had written.

The candle at the edge of the table wavered, just once.

Merlin named Beagron again later, crediting him with the first glimpse of the problem.

From Beagron's stone I wrung the truth that no act, even of gods, is without shadow. The making of worlds is not clean. There is always that which does not fit back into order.

Stone. Talisman. The memory from her dream floated up again, the sense of something black and heavy humming under water.

She wrote in the margin: Talisman of Beagron = recorder of waste.

Her hand wanted to curl its letters into the same long loops the fragment used. She forced herself to stop, to draw a line under the note and sit back a bit.

As she leaned away, the hum eased. The pressure in her ears quieted. The candle flames grew less rigid, allowed to sway with drafts again instead of an invisible metronome.

The physical pull of the page had been subtle but real. She realized she had been inching closer without meaning to, shoulders creeping over the book as if trying to climb inside it.

She sat up straight, rolled her neck to loosen it, and took a breath away from the Codex.

The distance helped. Awe stepped back a pace. Fear had room to stretch its legs properly.

It unsettled her more than anything else that Merlin, who could feel this power in ways she was only beginning to, sounded cautious. Not reckless. Not hungry. Wary. He did not write as a conqueror of forces. He wrote like someone who had lived long enough to know what not to touch.

Maya glanced at the dented kettle again, its warped metal catching a line of candlelight.

"Even you were afraid of this," she murmured, eyes on the fragment. "And you could probably move mountains with a sentence."

The room breathed with her. The hum in her chest stayed low, but she felt a new thread in it, something cooler, more distant, like a harmony waiting its turn. The word Unmaking floated at the back of her tongue even when she did not speak it.

She tested it one more time, just thinking it.

The center candle dipped, wick bowing in a quick, precise nod.

She closed her notebook a little too quickly, the pen clicking as she capped it. The sound made the room feel normal again for half a second.

Awe hummed in her blood. Analysis kept laying down lines of ink as if that would keep anything at bay. Underneath both, dread unfurled, slow and thin, knowing that now that she had read these words, something in the world had turned its head.

She placed her hand flat over her last margin note.

Energy unclaimed seeks a vessel.

Her palm warmed in answer. Not hot, not burning, but aware.

She pulled her hand back and blew out one of the candles. The small plume of smoke rose between her and the fragment title. For a moment it twisted itself into a shape almost like a spiral, then dispersed.

The two remaining flames flickered in the slight draft, then steadied.

"Enough for tonight," she told the Codex, voice only a little hoarse.

The book did not protest. The hum sank another fraction, as if something had taken its measure of her and retreated a step. Not gone. Never gone. Just waiting behind the next breath, the next page.

She closed the cover gently and sat in the dim, the word Unmaking echoing in the measure between her heartbeats, making each pause feel a shade too long.

The Codex stayed open even after she closed her notebook.

It sat on the table like a patient animal, pages relaxed, Fragment XXVII waiting in the middle of the candlelight. The heading seemed darker now that she had read it, Unmaking carrying more weight than ink should.

Outside, Salem went on pretending it was ordinary.

Somewhere down on the street, a car rolled past slow, tires hissing through shallow puddles. Voices floated up from the sidewalk, sharp and tinny through the old glass. A woman laughed. A man answered, tone edged. The sound thinned as they turned the corner and vanished into the brick.

Maya kept her eyes on the fragment.

Her finger traced the space beneath the last line she had read, careful not to touch the ink. The cut of the letters carried a tired precision, as if Merlin had been carving his warning into stone, not paper.

She let her gaze fall to the next paragraph.

It has no appetite for joy, nor for the heat of striving. It feeds most swiftly where grief is left untended, where despair is nursed in solitude, where will is wasted upon remembering what cannot be made again.

Her chest tightened.

For a second she thought it was the content, the bruise of the idea that something in the universe took special notice of people who had lost too much. That should have hurt. It did. But the pain did not match her thoughts. It rose too fast, too sharp, like someone else's sob catching high in her ribs.

She sat back a little, hand pressed to her sternum. The hum that had lived there as a single tone began to shift.

It moved outward first, sliding along her bones into the air. The candle flames twitched in response, all three leaning toward the book, then away, then toward her. The sound was not louder. It was wider. It seemed to touch the walls and the window before coming back through her skin.

Her eyes went to the door.

In the hallway outside, someone thumped against the plaster. A voice rose, muffled by wood and paint. A man's, low and slurred at the edges.

"You never listen," he snapped, words smeared by cheap whiskey and something older. "You never listen."

Another voice answered, higher, a woman's, the words indistinct under the tone. Tired. Defensive. The rhythm of people circling the same argument they had worn into the floorboards years ago.

The tightening in Maya's chest flipped.

Sadness drained away, replaced by a hot, sudden spike of anger that did not belong to her. It flashed up through her stomach to her throat, a fierce, irrational urge to shout back through the wall. To slam a door. To throw the Codex across the room just to hear something break.

She gripped the edge of the table instead, knuckles whitening. Her own thoughts riffled like a deck of cards. The anger did not match any of them. It surged and broke on a schedule her mind was not keeping.

Then the hallway voices cut off.

The anger vanished with them, snuffed so abruptly that she almost swayed. The hum in the room fell a half step, as if someone had turned down a dimmer switch.

She sat perfectly still, listening.

The quiet between her apartment and the next felt crowded all at once. She could almost picture the air as water, disturbed by stones thrown into it from either side of the wall.

"Okay," she whispered. "That was not mine."

She looked back at the fragment. Her throat had gone dry.

It feeds where grief is left untended.

Her hand moved before she meant it to. She flipped her notebook open and wrote in a slanted rush:

While reading about despair, felt sadness that did not match thought. Shifted to anger when neighbors argued. Vanished when they stopped.

She underlined not mine three times.

The hum in her chest gave a small, questioning pulse. It did not feel like it had earlier, one distinct note. There were layers now and each one had a temperature.

She closed her eyes, exhaled, and let her attention sink into the sound.

At first all she heard was the familiar tone, the one she had learned to use as a lever for moving coins and kettles. It sat in the center of her body, steady as a held note on a violin string. That was hers. She knew its shape.

Under it, another frequency fluttered, quick and jittery. It flicked up and down the scale like a hand tapping nervously on a tabletop. It made her fingers want to move, to drum, to pace. Somewhere above her, a floorboard creaked in a repeated pattern. She pictured the grad student in 3B who always wore headphones and walked figure eights in his living room when he was studying.

She focused on that smaller tone. It sharpened in her awareness, bright and thin. Her heart tried to match it and she snapped her attention away before it could.

Another layer sat lower and slower. It felt like a heavy drum hit every few seconds. The sensation tugged at her shoulders, trying to fold them toward the floor. A weight behind her sternum that wanted company. The woman across the hall, maybe. The one who left the TV on all night at low volume and sometimes cried along with the commercials.

Her eyes opened. Candlelight made halos on the ceiling.

"Emotions have pitches," she said, barely more than breath. Saying it out loud did not make it less strange. It made it more real.

The realization carried its own horror. She could sense them without meaning to. If she let herself, she could follow those tones like threads, down through the building, across the street, into other lives that had never invited her in.

Her stomach rolled.

She flipped to a clean page and wrote, more carefully this time:

Ambient hum shifts = people near?

She tapped the pen on the paper, listening again. The jittery tone from upstairs faded as footsteps moved toward the back of the building. The heavy drum from across the hall softened, as if whoever carried it had sat down and changed the channel.

Only her note remained clear, the one that felt like a middle C stretched across her bones.

She wrote beneath the first line:

Can pick out layers that are not mine.

No training. Unwanted.

The thought of walking down a busy street with this turned on made her want to crawl under the bed. Every fear, every irritation, every unresolved grief from every stranger pressing through her skin. No. She would go mad by noon.

The pen hovered.

She took a breath and did the only thing she knew how to do with something that threatened to own her: she experimented.

"Try filtering," she told herself quietly.

She set the pen down, closed her eyes again, and called up an emotion on purpose. Not the jagged ones. Not fear or anger. Curiosity. Plain and steady, the feeling she got when she stood in a library aisle and ran her fingers along the spines of books she had not yet read.

She thought of the warehouse, not the gun or the bullet, but the moment after when she and Emily had landed and the girl had looked at her with something like wonder. The sense that she had been a bridge, not a weapon.

Curiosity rose in her chest. What else can this do? Who built this song? How long has it been humming under everything?

The central tone responded at once. It steadied, smoothing out into a single clear note. The jittery and heavy layers dimmed, not gone but quieter, like someone had closed a door between rooms.

She breathed with that, in on the note, out on the note, letting it fill her lungs without spilling into panic.

The relief was immediate and sharp. She had control here. Not complete control, but a way to decide what came through and what stayed out.

"Okay," she said to the empty room. "You are not just a floodgate. You are a filter too."

Her hand found the pen without her looking.

She wrote:

Can tune by choosing my own state. Calm curiosity steadies field. External noise reduces.

The words settled something inside her even as they unsettled something else.

This power was not only moving things through space. It was changing the way space felt. The Weave did not just carry objects. It carried people, their feelings, the echoes of their choices. She was starting to hear it the way some people heard harmonies in a chord. Beautiful if you wanted it. Overwhelming if you did not.

The thought slid sideways to the fragment again.

It feeds where grief is left untended.

If she could sense despair like this, so could the Residuum. It would not think of it as invasion. It would think of it as gravity.

A chill walked up her spine that had nothing to do with any draft.

She glanced at the nearest candle. Its flame stood straight and ordinary. When she thought the word Unmaking, it dipped, then rose.

She set her notebook aside and pressed her palms flat on her thighs to stop them from shaking.

This was incredible. It was also invasive. To feel people without their consent, to accidentally carry their moods like pollen. She could see how that would be a gift in a crisis. She could also see a hundred ways it could break her if she let it.

She turned her focus inward again deliberately, pulling the tone of the building back out of her body and leaving only her own.

"I am not your vessel," she whispered into the quiet.

The hum slid back into its familiar place, centered, hers.

Outside, a car honked. Somewhere a dog barked once and went quiet.

The city's emotional noise settled behind the walls, changed but contained.

She picked up the pen one last time and wrote at the bottom of the page:

Hearing others = power and risk.

Use carefully.

The letters stayed in her own hand this time. No extra flourishes. No borrowed loops. The Codex hummed once, low and almost approving, as if acknowledging that she had passed some test it had not told her she was taking.

Wonder sat beside unease in her chest, both of them awake now, both refusing to sleep.

She closed the notebook and let her fingers rest lightly on the cover of Fragment XXVII again, not to read, not to ask, just to feel the quiet that had taken up residence between her and the world.

The quiet felt thin. As if anything could press through it now, if it wanted to.

The candles had burned low enough that their flames sat in little cups of wax, thin and trembling. The apartment smelled like smoke and old paper, heat from the earlier kettle trial long since gone from the air. The Codex lay open on the table, Fragment XXVII staring back at her like an eye that had finally chosen to blink.

Maya closed the notebook over her last line.

Hearing others = power and risk. Use carefully.

Her handwriting slanted more than usual. The words themselves felt heavier than the page could really hold.

The hum in her chest had calmed, mostly. The layers of other people's feelings had receded behind the walls. The building sounded like itself again. A pipe knocked somewhere. Someone flushed a toilet. A muted laugh rose from a television two floors down.

Inside her skin, though, everything still felt too full. She had spent the night sitting still while her mind ran laps. That was the problem. The Codex had filled her with theory, warning, names. Unmaking. Residuum. Will turned to ash. Now the knowledge sat in her like static with nowhere to go.

She stood abruptly. The chair creaked as it shifted weight.

Movement. She needed movement.

Coins and kettles were one thing. Lines on paper another. But all of that meant nothing if she could not trust her body to move through the world without punishing her every time she tried.

She looked at the dented kettle on the counter. Light from the nearest candle caught the curve of the metal, silver on the bent edge. Harmony before motion, she had written. Force equals fracture. She was not about to repeat that mistake tonight.

Keep it small, she told herself. Keep it close.

The apartment stretched around her in familiar shapes. Couch. Rug. Coffee table with the Codex. Narrow slice of kitchen beyond, tiles cool and ordinary in the dim light. The doorway to the hall, left of the bookshelf, a vertical shadow at the edge of her awareness.

A very simple thought formed.

From here to there.

She stepped onto the rug and planted her feet shoulder width apart. Just being on that spot made her chest loosen. This was where she had done most of her experiments, where she had plotted trajectories with sticky notes and coins. The hum knew this place. So did she.

She closed her eyes for a moment and listened.

The central tone came easily now. It rose in her ribs like a familiar song waiting for lyrics. Under it, she felt the faint pull of the lines she had mapped that afternoon, the ones that ran under the building and out into Salem. They were not loud. They were simply present, like a static grid over the world.

A vertical line dropped through the stairwell on the other side of her wall. A horizontal thread ran shoulder height along the hallway, a path she had not known she followed every day when she came home from work. The intersection under her feet hummed a little louder when she noticed it.

"Trial," she said out loud, the word quiet in the candlelight. "Short Blink. Living room to kitchen threshold."

She opened her eyes and fixed them on the border where wood become tile. It was no more than ten feet away. Less, probably. Before the Codex, she would have walked it without thinking. After the warehouse, she had moved across distances she did not understand and paid for it with blood. Tonight, this would be something between breathing and walking.

Four in. Hold two. Six out.

She let the hum meet her breath. There was no rush of power like before, no sudden spike of adrenaline. The tone simply deepened, aligning with her, not barreling through her like a train.

She set a gentle intent on the threshold. Not a command. A request.

Here.

Air thickened around her shoulders. The candle flames leaned inward for a heartbeat and then steadied. The wooden floor under her feet felt less like material and more like a suggestion.

The world folded, then unfolded.

There was no flash. No noise. The transition felt like the hiccup in a video when a frame drops. One moment she stood on the rug, the next her toes met cool kitchen tile. Her stomach did a small flip, the same feeling she got when stepping off a curb she had misjudged in the dark.

She braced for pain.

Nothing.

No needle of white fire behind her eyes. No sudden hot trickle from her nose. Her vision did not dim. The only sensation was a soft rush at the back of her head, like standing up too quickly from a couch.

She put a hand on the counter to steady herself. The surface was pleasantly solid. The hum in her chest had already begun to settle, tapering off instead of cutting cleanly in that frightening way it had before.

She laughed once, sharply. "Okay. That happened."

She counted under her breath. One. Two. Three. By five, her balance felt completely normal. Her heart rate had barely budged.

She walked back into the living room on ordinary feet, partly just to prove to herself that she could. The chalk circles from earlier had smudged into soft rings. The notebooks lay open like witnesses. She grabbed the nearest one and scrawled without sitting down.

Short Blink: rug to kitchen doorway. Approx. 10 feet.

Recovery: under 5 seconds.

Symptoms: mild head rush, no pain. No bleed.

She put the pen down slowly. This was new. This was important.

The mark on her palm warmed quietly, not the sharp coin heat of the Amber Alert morning, but the gentle pressure of a hand placed over her own.

She pressed the heel of that same hand to her sternum, feeling for any sign of backlash. The tone there purred low and satisfied.

The room still held more energy than she liked. Her muscles wanted to move. Her mind buzzed.

One more, she thought. Slightly bigger. Through something solid this time.

Her eyes went to the apartment door.

The hallway outside was no more than twelve feet of distance away, plus the thin wall. She had done longer without intending to. The idea of passing through the barrier made her skin prickle, but she had mapped the line that ran down the stairwell. It was a vertical lane, a kind of Weave conduit that seemed to favor circulation. She would use that.

"If this goes wrong," she said to no one, "you get to tell me you told me so."

She stood in front of the door, barefoot on the worn patch of wood where she always turned the deadbolt. She closed her eyes again, letting the hum drop into place.

This time she did not just feel the tone inside herself. She listened outward.

The stairwell line hummed faintly behind the wall, a vertical string connecting basement to roof. Someone on the floor below shuffled across their kitchen. Their television murmured at a low volume, all bright chatter and canned laughter. A small burst of anxiety pricked at the edge of her awareness, not hers. She let it slide past and chose her own state instead, the way she had earlier.

Curiosity. Calm. Intent without fear.

Her tone steadied. The emotional noise of the building faded to background. Her body felt very clear to her, an outline in the Weave.

She pictured the landing outside her door. The gray carpet. The railing on the right with one loose spindle that creaked when anyone leaned too hard. The faint smell of dust and old paint. She had seen it a thousand times. She gave the image weight.

Here.

Breath in. Hold. Breath out.

The world shifted sideways.

There was a momentary feeling of coolness on her skin, like walking through the tail end of someone else's shadow. Then she was standing on the landing, socks sinking slightly into thin carpet.

The hallway light flickered once overhead, then steadied. A hum of television laughter floated up from below, unchanged.

She turned in a slow circle. The stairwell yawned down and up, familiar. The door to her apartment stood at her back, paint chipped in the bottom corner where someone had once moved a couch without enough care.

Her body waited for the punishment.

She leaned forward, resting both hands on the railing, and held still.

Her head did feel light, but not in the splitting migraine way. It was the gentler emptiness of exhaling too long. A little vertigo. Nothing more.

She counted again. One. Two. Three. Four. Five.

The tone in her chest withdrew to a low murmur. Her palm tingled pleasantly. No stabbing pain. No ringing in her ears. No blood.

A laugh caught in her throat and came out in a shaky exhale.

"That was it?" she whispered. "That is the cost now?"

She stayed like that a little longer, fingers curled around the railing, letting the reality catch up with her. The body that had once crumpled under the strain of moving a kettle across a room had just passed through a wall and twelve feet of space and was complaining less than it did after a long shift on her feet at the shop.

She straightened, put a hand flat on the door, and pushed it open.

Inside, the apartment looked almost exactly as she had left it. Candles near stubs. Codex open. The dented kettle quietly reflecting a small oval of flame.

She moved to the notebook and sat down at the table, knees suddenly watery in a way that had nothing to do with magic.

She wrote:

Blink 2: apartment interior to stairwell landing. Approx. 12–15 feet through solid barrier.

Recovery: under 10 seconds.

Symptoms: light drain, no pain. Emotional input from neighbors present but filterable.

She tapped the end of the pen against her chin and added, beneath that:

Teleport under 1 mile: minor dizziness only. Cost decreasing with practice.

Listening = lower friction. Forcing = pain and blackout.

She underlined listening and forcing in different colors, blue for one, black for the other, a small private code.

Her palm brushed the page as she moved the pen away. The sigil there warmed again, a mild, steady heat. It felt like a nod.

She sat back in her chair, the fatigue of the day finally sliding into her bones in a way she recognized. This was not the hollowing-out she had felt after the warehouse, after the kettle. This was the ordinary drain of having learned too much in a single day.

Concern, sharp and tight, eased a little. In its place came a different kind of awareness. The Weave did not want to break her every time she moved through it. It demanded respect and practice. When she met it halfway, it treated her less like an intruder and more like a student.

She let her eyes close for a moment. The hum was there, smaller now, like a cat settling into a coil at the base of her ribs. Her hand lay open on her thigh, sigil facing up, palm warm but not burning.

"Okay," she whispered. "We can work with this."

Outside, a car door slammed. Someone laughed on the sidewalk. These sounds did not rush in to claim her. They stayed where they were supposed to, safe on the other side of the walls.

Inside, the air smelled of candle smoke and metal and paper. Her notes lay in front of her, clear evidence that the cost curve was changing.

She opened her eyes again and stared at the dented kettle on the counter. It still stood as a warning. Now, the small jump she had just done sat opposite it on the scale.

Cost. Skill. Consequence. Control.

Her world was still dangerous. The knowledge in Fragment XXVII had made that clear. But tonight had proved something else.

With each step she took into the Weave, the Weave took one step closer to meeting her without crushing her.

She picked up the pen one last time and wrote, small but sure, in the bottom corner of the page:

Practice changes the price.

The sigil in her palm glowed softly in agreement.

Maya drifted back toward the table on bare feet, notebook still open in her hand. The adrenaline from the short jumps had thinned into something quieter now, a low glow in her veins instead of a spike. Every part of her felt used, but not in the way that left her wanting to lie on the floor and not move for an hour. This felt earned.

Practice changes the price, she had written.

The Codex still lay exactly where she had left it, heavy and patient. Fragment XXVII stared up at her, ink dark against the parchment. Merlin's neat, spare hand began halfway down the page, the line she kept coming back to underlined twice in her own pen.

All creation leaves a remainder.

She sank into the chair. The candles had burned even lower, stubs in their glass jars, wax cooled into little white lakes. The apartment was quiet enough that she could hear the tiny crackle of wick as one of the flames guttered and then steadied.

She flipped back through her notebook, past maps of ley lines and scrawled metrics from the kettle trial, until she reached the page where she had copied fragments of Merlin's words.

Energy unclaimed seeks a vessel.

She read it again, slow, tracing the letters with her eyes. There was something in the phrasing that would not leave her alone. It was not just poetry. It was warning disguised as definition.

She moved her pen over the line, not touching the paper, just following the curve of each letter.

The air in the apartment changed.

It was subtle at first, like the feeling on the back of your neck when a cloud moves in front of the sun. The kind of shift you could blame on imagination if you wanted to. The hum in her chest stayed quiet, but the space around it braced.

She lifted her head. The hair on her arms rose in a tight wave.

The room temperature dropped in a way that did not feel like night chill. A minute ago the air had been warm with candle heat and the residual warmth from her own movement. Now her breath came out in a pale fog, visible for a second in front of her mouth before it vanished.

She heard no draft. No rattle at the windows. No hiss from the old radiator. Just that new, dry cold, slipping over her skin as if the room had been hollowed out.

Her gaze went to the nearest candle without her choosing it.

The flame had grown taller, stretching thin and white, as if reaching for something it could not name. Then, in the space of a breath, it narrowed. The core darkened, not to red or orange, but to a small absence, a vertical thread of black inside the light. The edges of the flame still burned gold. The center looked like nothing at all.

Maya's stomach tightened. She leaned forward, watching as that dark line pulsed once, then shrank back into orange.

The candle did not go out. That somehow made it worse.

She set the notebook down very carefully. A chill pressed between her shoulder blades. She searched the room without moving her head too much, as if big motions might encourage whatever was listening.

There, across the room, the cheap mirror above her dresser caught her eye. She had bought it at a thrift store, narrow and full length, the kind of thing you hang by the door to check for spinach in your teeth before work. Tonight its surface looked ordinary. The taut line of her own reflection stared back: hoodie, messy hair, the faint shadow of tired under her eyes.

Then the outermost edge of the glass changed.

Not the whole surface. Just a narrow frame, maybe an inch wide all the way around, went wrong. The reflection there rippled, not like water, more like the air above a highway in August. Heat distortion. Except the room was cold.

The center of the mirror remained steady. Her reflected face held still. Her eyes did not blink.

The ring of distortion around that calm center moved like a slow, delayed echo, a frame around her made out of time that refused to match her.

She swallowed. Her throat clicked loud in the quiet.

Her pulse said look away. Curiosity chose otherwise.

She raised her right hand in front of her, fingers spread, and watched the mirror.

Her real hand moved smoothly.

The one in that thin outer frame moved a fraction of a beat behind.

So small, she thought at first she might be imagining it. But the delay did not go away. Every time she shifted her fingers, the reflected version followed just a little late, like someone repeating a word they had not quite heard the first time.

Her stomach knotted. The sensation reminded her of hearing her own voice on a recording half a second late, the way it makes your brain flinch. This felt like that, except it was the world that was lagging.

She stood slowly, chair legs scraping very softly on the floor. The motion put her a step closer to the mirror. The delayed frame tracked her, always a little behind.

Her breath fogged the glass. The center reflection fogged with it, normal. The outer ring did not. The distortion there did not care about breath. It did not care about anything that belonged to bodies.

Merlin's words surfaced without her permission.

The silence between the heartbeats of the world.

She thought of the way he had written about the Residuum, the Unmaking, as static between notes. Not sound, but the absence that wanted to be the only thing left.

Her heart beat faster in her chest.

Between those beats, just for a moment, the hum inside her stuttered.

A tiny draft touched the back of her neck, cold and dry, as if someone had opened a freezer door a foot behind her and then closed it again before she could turn. The fine hairs there stood up. Her skin shrank tight over her spine.

She did not need to reach for the window to know it was closed. She had latched it earlier after rinsing chalk dust off her hands. The air in the room had nowhere to come from and nowhere to go.

She looked back at the mirror.

Her reflected eyes stared back as normal in the center. The delayed frame around them still did its half beat lag, and now, as she watched, the distortion swam in a little closer, as if curious. The inch of oddness widened to two. The border between normal and wrong got inside the corners of the glass.

Her stomach churned. She lifted her left hand this time, palm open toward her own face.

"Enough," she said quietly. Not to the Codex. Not to the Weave. To whatever it was that thought it could practice timing on her body.

The hum in her chest answered, but not in the usual way. A new tone had braided itself under the original. The familiar Weave note ran steady and low. Beneath it, or perhaps between it and silence, there was something else.

Not sound.

Not exactly.

It sat at the edge of her hearing the way very deep bass does, more felt than listened to. Except this did not vibrate. It un-vibrated. It felt like a pull from the other side of nothing, a suggestion that if she leaned even a fraction in the wrong direction, the note would take, and the rest of the music would follow.

Absence, Merlin had called it. The residue that wanted to finish what creation began.

Her fingers trembled. The mirror caught that too, the delay making it look worse than it was.

The candle nearest the Codex flared again, tall and thin. The dark thread in its center expanded just enough for her to see that there was no depth to it. No glow. No line. Just a straight cut through light, so black it might not exist at all.

The runes on the Codex's spine dimmed as the flame did that, silver gray fading to flat gray, as if something was feeding on their glow. The book itself felt different now. Its quiet attention had always been weight. Tonight, for a breath, it felt like a weight that had been picked up and stretched thin.

Maya stepped away from the mirror.

One step back, then another, until her calves hit the couch. She sat hard, the notebook still in her hand, Fragment XXVII open across the table like the world's worst bedtime story.

The cold focused on her for one more long, uncomfortable heartbeat. The void note in the hum pressed at the edges of her mind. It did not push. It did not rush. It simply reminded her that it knew she knew its name now.

She thought of the line she had copied, the one she had underlined too many times for comfort.

It does not hate. It corrects.

"This is not your house," she said through her teeth. Her voice came out smaller than she wanted, but it was steady. "I am not your vessel."

For a second the silence argued with that.

Then something in the air let go.

The temperature ticked up a degree at a time, the way it does when a heater kicks on, except nothing mechanical moved. Her breath stopped fogging. The candle flame shrank back into a normal teardrop of light. The black core dissolved into harmless orange.

The distortion along the edge of the mirror smoothed. The outer frame fell back in line with the center. Her reflection blinked once, the real and the glass matched again.

The new sub note in the hum receded, not gone, but farther away, like a sound heard from another room when a door closes.

On the table, the runes along the Codex's spine brightened slowly, threads of silver light seeping back into the grooves of each symbol. The book warmed under her palm when she reached across and touched it, a faint, exhausted heat.

She realized she had been holding her breath. She let it out slowly and then, because her body needed evidence that it still worked, she did it again.

In, hold, out.

The familiar tone rose and fell with her, no interference this time.

The notebook lay open in front of her, Merlin's lines and her own cramped script side by side. For a moment her eyes refused to focus. When they did, they landed on the phrase she had written earlier that night without yet understanding how true it was.

Silence between heartbeats = Residuum?

She picked up the pen with fingers that only shook a little and added, beneath it, in smaller letters:

It heard me read. It does not think, but it notices.

Her own handwriting, usually plain, came out with a slight curl to it, the same subtle stylizing that happened when the Codex hummed under her hand. She glanced down at her palm. The sigil there was faint, skin tone and memory, not glowing, not hot. It felt like the one part of her the cold had not been able to touch.

She sat very still for a long minute, listening to the apartment. The clock ticked above the stove. A car drove by three floors below. A neighbor coughed once in the hallway and shuffled past. None of those sounds carried anything extra with them. No echo. No lag. No void hitching a ride.

Only when she was sure the room belonged to her again did she close the notebook and slide it a few inches away from the open page of Fragment XXVII, as if giving the text a little more space would help.

The heading at the top of the page stared back at her.

Fragment XXVII: On the Nature of the Unmaking

Written by Myrddin Emrys, Keeper of the Second Song.

She reached out and laid two fingers gently over Merlin's name.

"You were afraid of it too," she whispered. "And you still listened."

The candle nearest the Codex flickered once, normally this time.

The urge to blow them all out and sit in the dark tugged at her. So did the urge to turn every light in the apartment on and sleep with the television running all night. She did neither.

Instead, she pinched one wick between damp fingers, then another, until only the smallest stub burned by the sink, a little anchor of ordinary flame.

She left Fragment XXVII open, but she pushed her chair back from the table and went to sit on the edge of her bed instead. From there she could still see the feel of the page, the shadow of letters, but not the words themselves.

Pride at what she had just done with the Weave still warmed her, but now it had something cold layered under it.

She knew more. She could move farther with less pain. Her control was real.

Something else knew that too.

Maya pulled the blanket over her legs and curled her fingers in the fabric, grounding herself in cotton and weight. The hum slipped down toward silence, leaving behind a faint vibration, not unlike the feeling of a train passing far below ground.

She closed her eyes.

Between one heartbeat and the next, she thought she heard a whisper that was not a whisper at all.

Not yet.

The bed did not move. The air did not change. Her breath stayed her own.

Still, when she finally slept, it took longer than it should have, and when dreams came, they were full of mirrors that did not quite keep up.

8

The Offer

Closing took longer than it should have.

Two nights had passed since the mirror had rippled and Merlin's warnings had crawled under her skin. In the time since, Maya had tried very hard to be boring. Work, sleep, coffee, shelving paperbacks about normal murders and normal heartbreak. No Codex tonight. No experiments. The Weave had stayed politely at a distance, a low vibration under everything, like a refrigerator you forget is running until it stops.

The shop smelled of dust, rain-damp paper, and the faint bitterness of old espresso grounds from the café next door. Now, near closing, it was mostly empty air and spine glue. The overhead lights hummed in their tired fluorescent way. The jazz playlist had already looped to silence; the only rhythm left was drizzle against the window.

Maya stood behind the counter, tapping the edge of the register with one fingernail and working through the closing checklist. Card machine off. Drawer counted. Receipts zipped into a folder. Rituals that made the world small and human, numbers behaving, pens staying where she left them.

The Weave hummed under all that, steady and low.

She powered down the terminal, watched the screen fade to black, and let the dimness settle. The shop always felt different once the

165

lights dropped, less public, as if the books could finally exhale. She flipped the sign from **OPEN** to **CLOSED**, slid the deadbolt, and watched streetlight spill in soft stripes across the floor. Rain blurred the glass, turning the city beyond into watercolor.

Her phone buzzed.

A message from Alex: a meme about sleep schedules and cursed libraries. She smiled despite herself, typed *ha*, then locked the screen. Normal. She could do normal.

She did one last walk through the aisles, fingertips grazing dust jackets, a small comfort in repetition. A stray paperback on astronomy went back to **Science**. A fantasy hardcover straightened on its stand, *Merlin and the End of Magic* flashing faintly under the light. The irony made her snort, then pause. That flash of gold lettering stirred something. *Arcana of the Weave.* The little green leather volume waited halfway down the Occult shelf, right where she'd left it weeks ago. She hadn't meant to touch it again, but the sight of it tugged at her, quiet and certain, like a name half-remembered in a dream. Before she could second-guess herself, she pulled it free, thumb tracing the worn spine. The hum in her chest answered, faint but familiar. She hesitated only a moment before tucking it under her arm, slipping it into her locker, and scribbling a note on the clipboard: *Pay for this tomorrow.*

At the back door she pulled on her hoodie. The building creaked the way old buildings do, pipes knocking once, roof timbers sighing. She raised her hood, more against habit than weather.

At the front, she paused and listened. Her inner hum matched the shop's quiet heartbeat. No dissonance.

She turned off the final lights. Streetlamps painted the room in amber and shadow. For a moment, everything was peaceful.

Then the Weave shifted.

It wasn't violent, just *wrong*. A thin buzz threaded through the harmony, metallic and insect-bright. Machinery riding on top of song. She felt it first in her teeth, a vibration behind enamel.

Her hand froze on the door handle.

Outside, the street looked ordinary: rain-slick pavement, sodium light pooled in puddles, a neon sign from the diner down the block bleeding red into water. A bus hissed and moved on. Two strangers passed under umbrellas, laughter muffled by drizzle.

The mechanical undertone stayed.

Maya's pulse sped up. She focused, the way she had learned to in the quiet after the kettle, layer by layer, identifying tones. Her own note sat centered, steady. Above it fluttered the light, nervous frequency of the café barista locking up next door. Below, the slow, weary drumbeat of the man at the bus stop.

And beneath all of it: something new.

Not emotion, too cold. A precision hum, faintly digital, the vibration of servos through bone.

She stepped away from the glass, into the narrow shadow behind the display. Between stacks of bestsellers she peered toward the street.

A black sedan idled in the loading zone opposite the shop. Headlights off. Rain collecting on the hood. A shape in the driver's seat, unmoving. Every time she looked straight at it, the static in the Weave spiked.

Her mouth went dry.

Not tonight.

She backed toward the stockroom, planning the route, through the alley, cut left toward her apartment. If needed, one short blink to clear the corner. She still had that control.

The door rattled behind her.

Three quick knocks. Polite. Wrong.

She stopped. The Weave's static deepened, a filament under her skin.

Another knock. "Sorry, are you still open?" A man's voice, casual, warm. The mechanical note under it crawled along her jaw.

"We're closed," she called, keeping her tone even.

A pause.

Then, "Understood." His politeness held the shape of a smile. "Could we have a word anyway?"

We.

Her stomach knotted. She edged sideways to the window slit. Two figures stood under umbrellas now, coats dark, clothes neutral. The sedan's silhouette waited behind them.

Average faces. Forgettable. Forgettable on purpose.

The hum in her chest recognized neither warmth nor life, only training and static precision.

"We won't take much of your time," he said. "Federal task force. Private matter."

A badge flickered, gone before she could focus.

"No, thanks," she said. "Come back during daylight."

Rain filled the silence that followed.

"Maya Rodriguez," the man said finally, tone changing. "It's important."

Her lungs forgot how to work. They knew her name. Of course they did.

She took one step backward. "Then send a letter," she said. "Good night."

She turned and walked quickly toward the rear hall. Shelves threw long shadows as she passed. The static followed, crawling across the Weave.

The back door loomed ahead. Freedom. She reached for the latch.

A different lock clicked open somewhere to her left.

Not the front. Not the back.

The side, an internal security door connecting the shop to the office stairwell. It was supposed to stay dead-bolted.

Supposed to.

The latch gave. Hinges whispered.

Two people stepped through, umbrellas folded, coats dripping. Up close, they looked even less like individuals, their features settling into an algorithm's idea of normal.

The man smiled. "Thank you for your time."

Her hand went for the Weave on reflex.

Power rose, fierce and bright, until something foreign crawled up the same lines she was reaching through. The hum fractured, replaced by white-noise static that made her ears ring.

"Please don't," the woman said softly. "It's safer for everyone if you stay calm."

"Who are you?" Maya demanded.

"People who want to keep you alive," he said. "For that, we need you to come with us."

"Hard pass."

She edged backward, fingers searching for the latch behind her.

He sighed, almost regretful. "This would be simpler if you cooperated."

A flick of his hand.

A glint of metal.

Pain stabbed her arm, a quick, burning puncture. She jerked back but too late. A syringe slid away between his fingers, clear barrel, viscous contents already inside her.

"What did you," she began.

The Weave shrieked.

Her balance went. Sound warped, stretching and slurring. Fluorescents buzzed in slow motion. Somewhere a book fell, the thud reaching her two seconds late.

Her knees buckled. The man caught her under one arm, efficient, almost gentle. "Easy," he murmured. "Breathe."

She tried. Air turned syrup-thick. Her muscles slackened; her tongue went heavy.

The Weave thrashed, looking for purchase in a mind going dark. Threads bled across her vision, lines of light bending like wet ink. The city's glow outside smeared into silver and gray.

She saw herself reflected in the glass of a framed poster, two images out of sync, one already falling. For a heartbeat, the lag looked just like the mirror from two nights ago.

Then everything folded inward.

Neon bled into rain.

The static roared.

The Weave's music shredded into silence.

Her last coherent thought was pure anger.

The floor tilted. The agents became silhouettes. The world narrowed to a tunnel of dim yellow and red.

Sound collapsed. Color followed.

Maya fell through the gap between them and the light went out.

The first thing she noticed was the color.

White, not clean, but overexposed.

The second was the sound.

A constant hiss, too even to be silence. Not fluorescent buzz, not ventilation, something deliberate, mechanical.

Maya's eyes opened to that noise.

Ceiling, lights recessed into matte panels. Walls seamless, curving slightly into the floor like poured resin. A camera in one upper corner blinked its little red pulse.

She lay on a padded bench that could have been a hospital gurney if hospitals came without windows. One wrist was strapped lightly, more as a reminder than a restraint. A thin patch covered the injection mark on her arm.

Memory reassembled itself in flashes: the shop, the door latch, the syringe, the static that had split the Weave like a struck bell. Then nothing.

Now, this.

She sat up slowly, the strap giving with a soft click. Someone hadn't bothered to lock it properly. Her head ached faintly, not from the sedative but from the noise. The room wasn't quiet enough to rest in; it was the wrong kind of quiet.

She swung her legs off the bench and planted bare feet on smooth flooring. No seams. No thresholds. No sense of orientation.

The hum pressed against her skin, the sort of sound that made dogs hide and humans grind their teeth. She felt it vibrate through her bones, a dull shimmer that crawled under the skin.

Someone had filled the room with static.

She could almost hear the justification for it: "electronic containment," "acoustic field," "spatial stabilization." Words that sounded smart in a memo.

They thought it would stop her.

Maya closed her eyes, letting the Weave's tone rise inside her chest the way it always did when she breathed past fear. The hiss interfered at first, fluttering through her rhythm like sand in gears. Then the deeper note asserted itself, steady and alive.

The static wavered.

Not silence, irritation. The Weave didn't like being drowned. It ignored the noise with contempt, pushing its resonance through the cracks between frequencies.

They hadn't caged her. They'd just built a room that gave her a headache.

Footsteps. A click of a lock.

A section of wall slid open with surgical precision.

Two uniformed technicians entered first, checking readings on tablets. They didn't speak. Their movements were slow, rehearsed, like people afraid of waking something.

A voice followed, male, calm, amplified through the room's hidden speakers.

"Good morning, Ms. Rodriguez."

She turned toward the sound. No figure, just the voice. It carried the smooth authority of someone who never needed to raise it.

"Where am I?" she asked.

The far wall brightened. A large panel of glass clouded, then cleared to reveal a screen. On it, a man's face resolved: late fifties, silver hair, precise features that never quite smiled. Senator Victor Hargreaves. She knew him from the news, foreign relations, defense appropriations, the kind of politician who made himself sound like a compromise everyone could live with.

"I apologize for the manner of your arrival," he said. "Your situation required discretion."

"My situation?"

He folded his hands on the desk in front of him, the gesture practiced. "You're a national-security anomaly, Ms. Rodriguez. What you did at the police station, at the rescue site, it's caught more than public imagination. My office oversees certain emerging-threat protocols."

"I'm not a threat," she said flatly.

"Neither is electricity, until someone mishandles it."

The static hissed a little louder. She resisted the urge to press her palms over her ears.

"I didn't ask to be here."

"No," he said mildly. "But I imagine you prefer this to being dissected by people with fewer scruples. We're offering structure."

"Structure?" she repeated.

"Containment with civility," he said. "Cooperation keeps you free."

She laughed once, short. "That's a contradiction."

"Freedom without oversight isn't freedom, Ms. Rodriguez. It's chaos. People panic over what they can't control. Right now, you are that panic."

He leaned closer to the camera. "We're trying to get ahead of it. For everyone's sake, yours included."

She watched his mouth move and felt nothing human in it. Just calculation, smooth and polished as glass.

"You want to study me," she said.

"I want to make sure you survive the next six months."

"That a threat?"

"A forecast." He smiled, just enough to show teeth. "Power attracts attention. Not all of it friendly. The last thing I want is for you to fall into the wrong hands."

Her pulse quickened. "And yours are the right ones?"

The Senator's expression didn't change. "You misunderstand me. I'm not your enemy. I'm the one person in this government who understands that whatever you can do must have limits. If we define those limits now, we avoid tragedy later."

The Weave stirred again, low and annoyed. It hated lies, especially polished ones. Maya's skin tingled with the urge to prove she wasn't caged.

She could leave. The hum was there, muted but reachable, sliding under the white noise like a bass line under static. But she didn't. Not yet.

She needed information.

"What happens if I don't cooperate?" she asked.

"Then the people who replace me won't ask."

His tone didn't rise, didn't sharpen. That was what made it worse. He didn't need to threaten. The bureaucracy did it for him.

He nodded to someone offscreen. "Demonstrate."

The two technicians turned toward her console. The hiss deepened into a low thrumming pulse. A faint shimmer appeared between her and the door, like heat haze.

Maya watched it and felt the Weave's tone stumble. Not stopped, just irritated, like a singer forced to harmonize with a detuned instrument.

The Senator's image flickered. "An electromagnetic field tuned to counter resonance anomalies," he said. "You'll forgive the jargon, my people assure me it prevents accidents."

"Does it?" she asked softly.

He didn't notice the edge in her voice.

"I prefer not to test it," he said. "I'd rather we talk."

Maya looked at the wavering air and smiled. The smile wasn't for him. It was for herself.

"It doesn't work," she said under her breath.

"What was that?"

"Nothing."

The hum inside her chest steadied, cutting through the static. The shimmer in the air flexed once, as if acknowledging defeat, and went still. She could feel the threads beyond it, faint but present, waiting.

He continued speaking, filling the room with reason and bureaucracy. She barely heard him.

On their readouts, the world was flat and stable. In her skin, it was humming with doorways.

Hargreaves leaned forward again. "We can make this easier, Ms. Rodriguez. Cooperate, and you can walk out of this facility tonight. No one else has to know you were ever here."

The hum in her chest answered, an almost musical chord of anger and restraint.

"I'm sure you believe that," she said.

He studied her for a long moment. "You're remarkably calm."

"I've had practice."

The static in the walls fluttered like tired breath. The lights overhead flickered once. not from power fluctuation but because the Weave twitched when she smiled.

Hargreaves' image glitched for a heartbeat, then righted itself. He didn't seem to notice.

"Rest," he said. "We'll speak again when you're clearer."

The screen went black. The technicians left without a word. The door sealed.

The hiss resumed its steady, oppressive rhythm.

Maya sat on the bench, the white glare washing every shadow flat, and let the hum in her body answer it.

It was still there. The Weave had never left her.

The noise wasn't a prison. It was just bad music.

She leaned her head back against the wall and smiled, small and tired but real.

"Nice try," she murmured.

The door hissed instead of opened, as if it had to think about it first.

Maya looked up. She had been watching the hairline crack between wall and ceiling, following it with her eyes like a lazy constellation, pretending it was something as simple as age and not cameras and microphones she could not see.

The young man who stepped in did not wear a suit. That was the first surprise. Gray hoodie, navy chinos, sneakers that had seen a city sidewalk recently. He carried a plastic pitcher and two paper cups on a metal tray, like this was a college counseling office instead of whatever it really was.

He nudged the door with his shoulder and it sealed behind him with a soft hydraulic click.

"Hydration," he said, offering a quick, almost apologetic smile. "Basic human kindness. We still do that."

The restraints around her wrists tugged when she shifted. Not metal shackles, but wide fabric cuffs anchored to the underside of the chair. If she leaned too far forward, they bit just enough to remind her she did not own her own distance.

"You could just untie me," she said.

"Not my call." He set the tray on the small table in front of her and took one of the cups for himself. "I'm Evan."

She stared at him. The fluorescent light washed the color out of his face. Up close he looked younger than she had first thought, maybe early thirties, maybe less, with the kind of tired under his eyes you got from too much screen time and not enough sleep.

"Do I get a last name, Evan?" she asked.

He hesitated. "Not one that means anything to you."

"Okay, Agent Not-My-Call," she said. "What do you want?"

He poured water, the sound small and domestic in the sterile room. The air conditioner kept humming its same low note, a mechanical drone that scratched at the edge of the Weave. The static field they had set up for her still buzzed against her skin, an irritant, like cheap wool on bare arms. It did not stop the deeper tone beneath it. It just made everything feel like listening to music through bad speakers.

Evan slid the cup toward her, stopping just short of her fingers. "It has a mild sedative in it," he said.

She raised a brow.

"For anxiety," he added quickly. "Nothing heavy. Nothing that touches motor control. We need you awake."

"Wow," she said. "You really know how to reassure a girl."

His mouth twitched. "You do not have to drink it. But it is there."

She left the cup alone.

He took the chair opposite her, dragging it a few inches so they were not directly across the table like interrogator and subject. More like two people at the end of a bad group project.

For a moment he did not speak. He just sat there, hands around his own cup, letting the silence weight itself.

Maya closed her eyes for half a second and let the hum widen. She had been avoiding that since she woke up, afraid of what other people's fear and anger would feel like in a box like this. Now she let it in, cautiously.

Her own tone sat center, a clear wire of sound running through her ribs. Under it, wrapping the room, was the RF buzz of whatever they thought would contain her. Beneath that, like notes played too softly on an out of tune piano, sat the emotional noise.

Evan's field was close. Jittery at the edges, a quick tremor of guilt and something like genuine concern. Beneath that, a pocket of fear that did not point at her. It pointed somewhere up and out, toward the people who gave him orders.

He believed in something. Stability maybe. Lives not falling apart. But the belief had seams.

She opened her eyes again.

"All right," she said. "Do your speech."

He looked almost offended. "I am not here to do a speech."

"Then why are you here, Evan?"

He took a breath. "To give you a choice."

She laughed once, flat. The restraints tugged against her wrists as her shoulders shook. "Sure. Because everything about this says choice."

He looked at the cuffs, then back at her. "You're right. It is coercive." The admission came quickly, before he could decide not to say it. "But it is not without options."

"That sentence does not mean anything."

"It means," he said carefully, "that there is a path through this where you walk out of here. Not tonight, not unsupervised, but free. Eventually. With some control over how people talk about you."

"Alive, you mean," she said. "You are offering not being disappeared."

A muscle in his jaw ticked. "We are offering partnership. You know who spoke to you already."

"The senator," she said. She did not bother to say his name. It tasted like metal.

"Hargreaves," Evan said. "He does not talk to many people like that directly."

"Is this the part where I am supposed to feel honored?"

"No," Evan said quietly. "It is the part where you should understand the level of attention on you."

The camera in the upper corner clicked softly, a tiny change in angle. Someone was watching this live. Maya kept her eyes on Evan.

"Order versus chaos," she said. "I heard the pitch. He thinks he can put me in a box."

"You know what happens when the public finds out there is someone who can do what you do?" Evan asked. He did not sound like he was quoting anyone. "Markets crash. Conspiracy groups explode. Every nation on earth starts wondering who gets to use you first. Or stop you first."

"And your boss wants to be the one holding the leash." She tilted her head. "Somehow this is not comforting."

"It is better than a thousand other hands reaching for it," Evan said. "I work with people who keep really bad things from spilling into the public. Weapons. Data. People. You are not the first anomaly I have seen. You are just the most... versatile."

"That is a terrible compliment."

He almost smiled.

She shifted in her chair, the cuffs biting enough to pull her attention back to the present moment. "So what is the demand," she asked, "under all that concern?"

He watched her for a second, then put his cup down.

"We need an extraction," he said. "One time. You help us, we file you under cooperative asset. That buys you latitude. We can protect you from other programs, other governments. Decline, and this stays adversarial. You end up in a hole somewhere, or worse, you end up on the wrong radar with no one to buffer the blow."

She let that settle, the way you let a dropped glass settle on the floor before you decide whether to pick up the pieces or just back away.

"Extraction of who?" she said.

He hesitated just long enough to confirm it mattered.

"A detainee," he said. "High information value. Currently held at a site overseas. Officially, he does not exist. Unofficially, he has information that, if released uncontrolled, could destabilize a region and cost a lot of lives."

"Region," she repeated. "Lives. That is some excellent vagueness."

"We monitor leak channels," Evan said. "This one has been a problem for a long time. Your abilities could let us take him out of a situation where everyone loses and put him somewhere he can be managed. Legally, eventually. Quietly at first."

"Managed." The word tasted bitter. "So that is what you want from me. Ghost taxi service for black sites."

"It is not like that."

"How is it not like that?"

He shifted in his chair, shoulders tight. The guilt note in his field spiked.

"He is not a spy," Evan said. "He is press."

The room seemed to pull into itself.

"Press," she said.

"A journalist," he clarified. "An investigative reporter who made enemies in the wrong places. He dug into campaign finance streams, foreign shell companies, defense contracts. Some of what he found ties back to donors who have leverage over Senator Hargreaves. Some of it ties to people with less patience."

"Why is he in a black site," she asked, voice thin.

"Because he kept publishing," Evan said. "Because nobody could shut him up with a lawsuit. Because the people he was going after decided to skip straight to removal. We did not put him there." He glanced toward the camera, then back. "We cannot publicly pull him out without exposing operations that make this country very nervous. But we also cannot guarantee no one puts a bullet in him before the election cycle ends."

"And that would be such a shame for your polling," she said.

His mouth thinned. "I am not here to talk about polling."

"No? Because everything about what you just said sounds like this is about votes and donors and optics."

"It is about stability," Evan said. "If his evidence drops in the wild tomorrow, unvetted, you get mass protests, targeted violence, maybe a few governments collapsing in places that really cannot afford it. Then you get opportunists stepping into the chaos. Real people die. Kids. Not just men in suits."

"And if you sit on it forever," she said, "what do you get?"

He did not answer.

"The offer is this," he said instead, voice smaller. "We give you coordinates. You get in, you get him, you get out. No one else is harmed. We can leak what he found slowly, in ways that let systems adapt instead of shatter. We can move him into protected custody under a new name. You go back to your life with us as a firewall between you and everyone who wants to cut you open to see how you work."

Silence settled between them. It felt thick, layered with his anxiety and something like honest hope that she would say yes.

Maya stared at the table. At the pattern the overhead light made in the grain. At her own pale knuckles where the restraints cut in. She thought of Fragment XXVII, of Merlin warning that excess power without perspective only corrected, never healed. She thought of Hargreaves on the screen, talking about order as if it were the same thing as safety.

"You could prevent chaos," Evan said softly. "You could keep this from turning into something worse. For a lot of people."

The Weave stirred in her chest, a low, dissonant note. She felt it flare under her skin, catching on the static field and peeling it aside, the way fingers separate cheap plastic wrap.

Her restraints trembled against their anchors.

Evan noticed. His eyes flicked to her wrists, then up to her face. "Maya," he said carefully. "No one here wants to hurt you."

"Too late," she said.

He flinched, just a little.

She let the hum rise another half step. Enough that the cup on the table buzzed faintly against the metal tray. Enough that the thin hair on his arms stood up.

"You think you are offering me a deal," she said, voice quiet, steady. "What you are really saying is: do our dirty work and maybe we will not throw you in a deeper cell."

"That is not fair."

"Do you think that man in your black site thinks anything about this is fair?"

Evan's mouth pressed flat again. The guilt note in his field climbed, high and thin.

"Order is not peace," she said. She met his eyes and did not look away. "It is fear wearing a uniform."

He swallowed. The cameras whirred again, a tiny adjustment in the corner.

"If you walk out of here without our help," he said, "you will not stay free long. We are not the only ones who have seen what you can do."

"I know," she said. "That does not make you better. It makes you first."

The restraints shivered harder. The hum built, finding the seams in the static field and pushing through in clean harmonic lines. To his ears it was probably just a rising pressure, a sense of storm before thunder. To her it was possibility, fanning itself out under the floor.

He leaned forward, hands empty, palms up. "I am trying to give you a way to survive this," he said. "Not as a prisoner. As someone who has some say in how she is used."

She almost laughed. "You hear yourself, right?"

"Tell me you do not care about the people who will get crushed if this blows up wrong," he said. "Look me in the eye and say you do not care."

She opened her mouth to say she cared about a man in a cell in the middle of nowhere more than she cared about donors and senators and their delicate reputations. The words stopped in her throat.

She did care. That was the problem.

"I will not be your weapon," she said instead.

"We are not asking you to kill anyone."

"You are asking me to make it easier for people who do," she said. "You do not get to outsource your moral math to me and call it structure."

He sat back, expression pinched.

For a long moment they just breathed, the hum filling the space between them, the static washing over it in useless waves. Somewhere, behind the glass, someone was radiating impatience. She could feel it as a hot flicker at the edge of her awareness.

Evan's shoulders sagged.

"They will not like that answer," he said.

"I am not talking to them," she said. "I am talking to you."

He looked at her. Really looked, like he was trying to decide whether the person in the chair matched the file on his tablet.

"Then what do you want to happen?" he asked. The question sounded honest.

She did not have an easy answer. Not yet. But the line in her head had gone sharp and clear.

"I want him out," she said. "On his own terms, not yours. I want people to know what was done to him. I want you and your boss to stop deciding who gets to be human and who gets to be 'asset.'"

"That is not how this world works," he said, almost gentle.

"Maybe that is the problem," she said.

The hum in her bones felt like a growing tide. She did not pull it any higher. Not yet. There would be a moment when pushing would mean fracture. Right now, listening was enough.

They sat there in the bright white room, two people in the middle of a diagram someone else had drawn, and for the first time since she woke up, Maya felt something like clarity.

They had taken her freedom. They had tried to wrap her in static and procedure and language about national security. But the Weave did not recognize their jurisdictions.

They could call her anomaly, threat, asset, whatever made their memos feel cleaner.

She knew which side of the line she stood on now.

The Weave woke her first.

Not with sound, but with tension, the subtle warning hum she had come to recognize as *someone coming*.

Maya sat still, head bowed as if defeated, but her pulse had already synced with that inner frequency. The static field scratched faintly at her nerves, but now it was background noise, irrelevant. The hum beneath it had changed pitch. Not threat. Not command. Something familiar.

Fear.

And not hers.

A voice blared over the intercom. "Containment breach in Sector Twelve. Repeat, breach in—"

The speaker cut out mid-sentence, replaced by the wail of a siren and the thudding rhythm of boots on tile.

Maya looked up. The far door, the one the technicians had used, burst open. Two armed guards rushed past the glass partition beyond, rifles up, eyes wild with confusion. Someone shouted about an intrusion on the perimeter. Her Weave sense expanded reflexively, mapping emotional signatures: urgency, fear, adrenaline... and one sharp thread of terrified focus that didn't belong here.

Alex.

She stood before she thought about it. The restraints at her wrists had been left loosely fastened after Evan's visit, a sign of condescension, or faith in their static field. They parted with one clean tug, the sound masked by the klaxon.

"Maya, sit down!" a voice barked from behind the mirrored glass.

She didn't.

The Weave thrummed louder. Her breath steadied to meet it.

Somewhere, maybe a hundred yards away, Alex was running blind through a place built for secrets. She could feel his panic in bursts, like a shortwave signal breaking through static. Each pulse of it brushed her awareness, rough and bright. He wasn't hiding; he was looking for her.

She stepped into the center of the room and closed her eyes.

Beyond the white walls, the facility stretched like a maze: corridors, offices, loading bays, all drenched in sterile light. But over that, threaded through concrete and steel, the Weave shimmered faintly, indifferent to walls or wires. It didn't care about architecture.

She reached toward it.

The static fought her at first, a hundred mechanical frequencies grinding at the base of her skull. She pushed past them, found her note, and let it resonate outward.

There. A spark. A heartbeat not her own.

Alex's fear flared like a flare against the dark.

He was cornered. She could feel it, the press of multiple intentions moving toward him, all sharp-edged. He'd made it into the warehouse, bypassed one of the external locks, probably on the signal trace from her phone. Clever. Stupid. Brave.

Her phone.

The connection was weak, the signal distant but unshielded. He'd used it to triangulate, to find her through the layers of interference. That's what she felt now, the faint echo of the Weave aligning along a technological trail.
He didn't even know he'd done it.

"Maya Rodriguez!" one of the guards shouted, appearing in the doorway. "Down on the floor!"

She looked at him and said nothing.

The air around her thickened, shimmered faintly as her heartbeat steadied into rhythm with the hum. Her skin tingled; her palms itched.

He took one step forward.

The lights flickered once, not failing, just flicking out of sync with the siren. The guard froze. The muzzle of his rifle trembled.

Maya closed her eyes and reached.

The world dissolved into tones and light.

Through that unseen geometry, she found him, Alex, heart hammering in the dark, somewhere near the loading bay. Every emotion he had was raw: fear, guilt, determination, and something else under it all, small and bright, trust. He believed he could save her, even though he had no proof she was still alive.

She followed that thread through the static.

The Weave folded, layers overlapping like translucent film. For a moment she was between notes, between heartbeats, in the silence that wasn't empty but *waiting*.

When she opened her eyes again, she stood in a hallway she'd never seen.

Dim emergency lights pulsed red. Alarm klaxons bled through the air like a migraine. Alex was twenty feet ahead, crouched behind a crate, phone clutched in one hand, his eyes wide with disbelief.

"Maya?" he said, voice cracking.

"Yeah," she said, breathless. "You picked a bad night for fieldwork."

He laughed once, strangled. "You're supposed to be, I mean,"

"Later," she said. The Weave flared again, warning her of motion. "They're coming."

Heavy boots clanged against metal grating down the corridor. Three signatures, closing fast.

Alex stood, fumbling with his phone. "I can jam the,"

"No time."

She reached for him.

"What are you doing?"

"Getting us out."

He didn't move, too stunned to object. The lights strobed around them, red on gray, gray on red. The static field here was weaker, thin enough that the Weave pushed through like sunlight through fog.

Maya felt the threads converge, hundreds of tiny harmonics intersecting. At the center: her heartbeat. She closed her fingers around his wrist.

"Hold on," she said.

"To what?" he managed.

Her smile was quick, almost a challenge. "To reality."

The first guard rounded the corner. Another shouted orders.

The hum in her bones went sharp, high, clean, resonant.

She didn't push this time. She listened.

The air thickened. Pressure dropped.

The smell of ozone burned the back of her throat.

A flare of blue-white light erupted around them, silent and total.

For a fraction of a second, Maya felt two heartbeats in one body, hers and his, overlapping, colliding, then synchronizing. Space folded around them like paper drawn through a flame. Her vision stretched, color separating from sound, everything drawn thin and luminous.

Then the world inverted.

A single note rang through her head, pure as struck glass.

The white corridor vanished.

They stumbled into darkness and rain.

Maya caught herself against a brick wall, one arm still locked around Alex's. Her knees nearly buckled. The smell of ozone hung in the air; her ears rang with silence.

A narrow alley, slick with water. Dim streetlight flickering overhead. The city, her city, back around them.

Alex blinked hard, his breath coming fast. "Where, what," He looked around like the buildings might fall apart if he touched them. "Did we, you,"

"Yeah," she said, voice hoarse. "We're out."

He doubled over, hands on his knees, trying to catch his breath. "You, you grabbed me and the *room folded*. Do you know what that looked like?"

"Do you want the short answer?"

He stared at her. "Yes."

"Impossible."

That broke him, he laughed, half-hysterical, rain dripping off his chin. "God, Maya, you, they're going to,"

She pressed a hand against the wet brick, forcing the dizziness down. The world still spun slightly; her vision ghosted at the edges.

The Weave inside her buzzed, stronger than ever but threaded with exhaustion. Carrying someone else had doubled the strain.

Alex straightened. "You're bleeding."

She touched her nose. A thin line of red. "Occupational hazard."

"Where are we?" he asked.

She looked up. The skyline of Salem loomed faintly through the fog, neon blurring in the drizzle. "East side, near the waterfront."

He gave her a dazed grin. "You, you just *teleported* us!"

"I blinked," she said automatically, the term she'd used in her notes. "Short-range. Two miles, maybe."

He stared at her like she was speaking a different language. "You can do that with *people*?"

"Apparently," she said, voice soft.

She sank to a crouch, back against the wall, trying to slow her breathing. Her hands still trembled. Each pulse in her veins hummed like an echo of the Weave's tone. "You shouldn't have come."

"Yeah," he said, still laughing under his breath. "You're welcome."

For a long minute they just sat there, rain pattering on asphalt, both of them shaking with adrenaline and disbelief. Somewhere distant, sirens wailed, not the facility's this time, but police. The ordinary kind.

Alex finally sank down beside her, drenched, exhausted, eyes bright. "That was,"

"Insane," she finished.

"Beautiful," he said.

She gave him a sideways look. "You're crazy."

"You did it," he said. "You got us out. You, you just broke a government black site."

She let her head rest against the brick, closing her eyes. "And now we run."

He exhaled, shaky. "Yeah."

For a long time neither of them spoke. Just the rain, the breathing, the hum beneath her skin. It wasn't quiet, it was *alive*. She could feel the city around her like a current, pulsing in soft sync with her heart. The Weave had accepted the Passenger. It had expanded.

It had also taken something from her, energy, stability, maybe even a fraction of her certainty.

Alex glanced at her, then at the sky. "You okay?"

She opened her eyes. The rain caught in her lashes, turned the streetlight into a halo.

"I will be," she said. "As soon as we figure out who's still chasing us."

He nodded slowly. "Then I guess we better move."

Maya stood, still a little unsteady, and looked down the alley, the wet street beyond glowing with reflected neon. The hum followed her pulse like a second heartbeat, stronger now, sharper. She could feel the shadow of what she'd done, the echo still hanging somewhere between here and there, like the Weave hadn't finished folding.

She took one last breath of the cold night air.

"Let's go," she said.

They slipped into the rain, their reflections following a half-beat behind.

The apartment was darker than she remembered. No hum of street traffic yet, no neighbor's TV. Just the soft tick of the clock over the stove and the whisper of rain against the window.

Maya stood in the doorway, soaked through, her hand still pressed against the frame as if the wood might reject her. The air smelled faintly of candle wax and smoke, the echo of what she'd left behind two nights ago. The dented kettle caught the first light creeping under the blinds, a dull silver scar on the counter.

Alex shut the door behind them and leaned against it, breathing hard. His hair clung to his forehead; his jacket dripped onto the floorboards. For a moment neither of them moved. The only proof that they'd actually escaped was the smell of ozone still hanging in their clothes.

Maya peeled off her hoodie and dropped it over a chair. "Sit," she said quietly. "Before you fall."

He obeyed. The chair creaked under his weight. "You sure this place is safe?"

"No." She crossed to the kitchen, turned on the faucet, and filled the kettle without thinking. The hiss of water felt almost normal. "But it's mine."

When the flame lit under the burner, she flinched. Memory, the flash of her first experiment, the hum gone wild, the metal collapsing inward on itself. She watched the blue cone of fire steady, breathing with it until her pulse matched its rhythm.

Alex's voice came from behind her, rough and low. "They'll come again."

"I know." She turned, bracing on the counter. "They'll find nothing but ash."

He frowned. "That's not funny."

"It's not a joke."

The kettle rattled faintly as the water began to warm. Maya's eyes flicked to it, then back to him. The Weave still hummed under her skin, restless. It wanted to move, to defend, to finish what it had started. Every instinct said *stay still*, but stillness was getting harder to pretend at.

Alex ran a hand over his face. "You just," He broke off, shaking his head. "You disappeared with me. We were there, and then," He snapped his fingers. "Nothing. You shouldn't even be *possible*, Maya."

"Tell me something new," she said, but the edge in her voice didn't last.

He looked up at her then, really looked. In the faint dawn light she seemed half-transparent, every shadow around her soft-edged. The air shimmered faintly near her shoulders, a distortion that didn't belong to heat or light. For the first time he saw what she'd meant about the hum. It was visible in the way dust motes swirled toward her and then away again, orbiting without touching.

"You're still glowing," he said before he could stop himself.

Maya blinked. "That's not possible."

"Look in the mirror."

She didn't. She didn't want to see what he saw.

The kettle began to whine, low and steady, a sound too close to a human cry. She shut off the burner before it could scream. Steam drifted upward, curling through the faint shimmer around her hands.

Alex exhaled. "You scared the hell out of me."

"I scared the hell out of myself."

"No, I mean," He pushed up from the chair. "You were gone. I thought they killed you. Then you showed up like a lightning strike and dragged me out of there." He paused. "You moved us through a wall, Maya. Through *space*."

"I didn't have time to explain the physics," she said softly.

He laughed once, dry and nervous. "Physics doesn't cover whatever that was."

She poured the hot water into two chipped mugs, one with a hairline crack down the side. "It wasn't supposed to work with another person," she said. "The Codex called it a passenger blink. I thought it would kill us both."

"Good thing you were wrong," he said. Then, quieter: "Or right enough."

Steam rose between them. He took the mug she offered, fingers brushing hers. His skin was still cold.

"You could have left me," he said. "You should have."

She met his eyes. "I wasn't leaving anyone else behind in that place."

The silence after that stretched. Outside, the rain lightened to a fine mist. The first birds were starting to test the morning. For a moment, it almost felt ordinary, two people standing in a kitchen before dawn, waiting for the day to decide what it was going to be.

Then Alex spoke again, quieter now. "I'm not afraid of you."

She looked up sharply. "You should be."

"I'm afraid *for* you." He said it simply, like fact. "They're going to hunt you. And the more they fail, the bigger the story gets. You're not a secret anymore."

Maya wrapped both hands around her mug, letting the heat anchor her. "Then I learn faster than they do."

"That's not what I meant."

"I know." Her gaze drifted to the kettle. The dented metal reflected the faint shimmer of her own light, warped and small. "But it's what I have."

Alex took a step closer. "You can't keep burning yourself down just to prove you're in control."

Her laugh was a small exhale. "You saw what control looks like, remember? It's a cage with polite lighting."

"That's not all there is."

"It is to them." Her voice softened. "And I won't go back."

He opened his mouth, closed it again. The words he wanted, the protective ones, the pleading ones, died somewhere behind his teeth. He'd seen the inside of that warehouse. He knew what kind of men called that order peace.

Maya turned off the light above the stove. The room fell into half-shadow. The shimmer around her dulled, but it didn't vanish.

"They'll come again," Alex said, repeating it because he had nothing else.

"Then they'll find nothing but ash," she said again, quieter this time, almost a vow.

He studied her face, the calm that wasn't calm, the exhaustion that hadn't found a way to rest yet. There was steel in her now, and something luminous under it. He understood then that she wasn't just carrying power. She *was* power, will given shape, consequence made visible.

It terrified him in ways he couldn't name.

Maya seemed to feel that thought pass through him. Her expression softened. "You don't have to stay," she said.

"I know."

"Then why are you still here?"

He looked down at the dented kettle, the faint reflection of her light bending across its surface. "Because someone has to remind you where the line is," he said. "Before all that light burns everything else away."

She almost smiled. "And if I already crossed it?"

"Then I'll cross after you," he said.

The silence that followed was fragile and human. For a few seconds, it held.

The hum in her chest eased, no longer war-song, just heartbeat. The air between them steadied. The kettle cooled, its metal sighing as it released the last of its heat.

Dawn spilled a pale line across the floorboards. Neither of them moved to close the blinds. The world was coming back whether they were ready or not.

Maya lifted her mug. "To whatever comes next," she said.

Alex clinked his against hers. "To surviving it."

Steam ghosted between them, curling upward and fading into the morning light.

The bathroom mirror looked like it had been waiting for her.

Gray light seeped in through the tiny frosted window, smearing the edges of everything it touched. Maya braced her hands on the sink and stared at her reflection. Same face as always: dark hair shoved into a loose knot, smudge of exhaustion under each eye, the faint impression of a sigil on her palm when she lifted it to push stray strands back.

For a few seconds, she looked ordinary.

Then the echo slid into view.

At the outer edge of the glass, just where the silver backing had begun to freckle with age, a second version of her appeared, faint as breath on cold glass. It was not a full duplicate, just a rim of double image, like someone had traced her outline, hesitated, and left it a fraction of an inch behind.

She frowned and lifted her chin.

The main reflection moved in time. The echo followed half a heartbeat later.

Her stomach tightened. She raised one hand slowly, fingers spread. The mirror hand rose with hers. The echo lagged again, then caught up, like a bad video call where the audio and picture could not agree.

"That is not me," she whispered.

Her voice fogged the mirror. The center of the glass blurred with condensation, her mouth and nose briefly erased. The halo at the edge did not fog. It rippled instead, as if made of air itself, sucking the mist inward before letting it go.

The hum under her sternum reacted, not rising, not dropping, just tightening, like a muscle remembering an old wound. Beneath it, lower and colder, there was the faint suggestion of that other note she had felt before, not quite sound, not quite silence. The space between.

She set her jaw, grabbed the hand towel from the hook, and wiped the mirror through the center. Her main reflection cleared. The echo at the edge stayed stubbornly a half beat behind.

"Not yours," she told it. Then, louder, "And not today."

She flipped off the bathroom light and stepped into the bedroom.

Alex lay half on, half off the couch, one arm flung over his eyes. The backpack she had dragged out for him rested open on the floor, half filled with clothes and whatever he had grabbed in the first frantic pass. His shoes were still on. Sometime in the last hour he had surrendered to exhaustion without meaning to.

"Alex," she said softly.

He twitched, then shoved his arm away from his face. "What time is it?"

"Too early," she said. "And too late. We need to move."

He pushed himself upright, wincing as muscles protested. "Right. Right. Plan."

"Such as it is," she said.

They worked without talking at first. Silence felt safer, less likely to wake something in the walls.

Maya moved through the apartment with the efficiency of someone cataloging a life she could not take with her. A change of clothes, socks, first-aid kit, flashlight. The notebooks went in next, stuffed into the backpack like contraband. Her printed maps of Salem stayed; the hand-drawn ley sketches slid carefully into a plastic sleeve and then into the pack.

On the table, the Codex waited. Its runes were a steady, low glow, no theatrics this time, just presence.

She touched the cover. The hum in her chest deepened in answer, a quiet mutual recognition.

"You sure you can carry that around without it eating the world?" Alex asked.

"It eats less when it is with me," she said. "That is the best I can do."

He accepted that with a grim nod. "Food, water, batteries. You got a death wish if you think we can live on metaphysics alone."

He rummaged in the kitchen, stuffing protein bars, instant coffee packets, and a half-stale bag of pretzels into his side of the pack. The dented kettle watched from the counter, warped metal catching the watery light. It looked smaller now, but more important, an exclamation point in steel.

Maya paused with a sweater in her hands, eyes on the kettle. "We will not be back soon."

"Good," Alex said. "I was starting to hate your landlord's wiring anyway."

It should have been funny. It was not. The apartment felt less like a home and more like a shed skin.

She turned back toward the bookshelf, meaning to do one last sweep, and froze.

An absence tugged at her. Not in the room. From somewhere else.

Green leather, worn smooth at the corners under her fingers. Gold title faded to a whisper: Arcana of the Weave.

The memory came back in a rush. Two nights ago. The shop. The pull she had felt standing in front of that little volume, the way it had seemed to lean toward her in her peripheral vision. The choice to tuck it into her locker instead of bringing it home, because she had planned to pay for it properly the next day.

Then the door opening, the umbrellas, the syringe.

Her chest constricted. Of course her most useful reference manual would be sitting in a metal box in a building that might already be under surveillance.

Alex noticed the way she had gone still. "What."

"Arcana," she said. "At the shop. I left it in my locker."

"You want to go back there," he said, dead flat.

"I need that book." She forced the words out steady. "The Codex is... not neutral. Arcana is like a field guide. Human hands. Human panic. I trust both."

"That place is burned," he said. "Hargreaves's people know you worked there. They will have cameras, cops, alphabet soup. You walk in, you are not walking out again."

"I will not walk in," she said. "Not exactly."

He stared at her. "You just got drugged and kidnapped for doing exactly that."

"This is different," she said. "I know more now. I can keep it short."

He scrubbed both hands over his face. "I hate that I know what you mean by short."

"It is early," she went on. "Too early for customers. The owner never opens before ten on Saturdays. Hargreaves is a bureaucrat. His people prefer paperwork to dawn raids. I can get in, get the book, and be gone before anybody realizes the lights flickered."

Alex paced once, twice, from couch to door and back. "And if you are wrong."

"Then at least they will not catch both of us in the same net," she said. "You take the packs and go ahead to the mausoleum. You remember the route."

He did. The old cemetery on the hill, the family crypt she had once described as a pocket of quiet inside the city's noise. Stone, deep and old. The kind of place the Weave loved. The kind of place cameras hated.

"I am not leaving you," he said.

"You are not," she answered. "You are making sure one of us is still out here if I miscalculate."

He hesitated, then nodded once. "Fifteen minutes. If you are not at the gate by then, I am coming back."

"Do not," she said. "If they have me, you will not get near me."

He looked ready to argue, then thought of the warehouse, the white walls, the polite smile on Hargreaves's face. "Fine," he said. "Twenty, then. I am bad at following instructions."

She almost smiled. "Understood."

She slung the Codex across her shoulder, the strap cutting a familiar line across her chest. The backpack followed. Her phone went into her pocket, then came back out again when she caught Alex's look.

"They tracked you with that once," he said. "You really want to give them a sequel."

She popped the back off the casing, pried out the SIM with a butter knife, and dropped the little rectangle into the dented kettle. It made the faintest click against metal.

"Consider it an offering," she said.

He snorted, half a laugh, half nerves.

They stepped into the narrow front hall. The apartment seemed to gather itself around them, light pooling in thin bars on the floorboards, chalk dust still hiding in the cracks, the faint ghost of her maps on the table. For a moment she felt the building as part of her, threads running down through its spine into the street.

"Ready," Alex said.

She took his arm, just long enough to steady herself. "See you at the tomb."

The hum rose, clean and practiced now. She pulled her awareness in, then out along the line that ran under Derby Street toward the shop. The image of the alley beside the building was clear in her mind: dumpster, brick wall, faded graffiti of a ship with no sails.

Here, she thought.

The world stuttered. Tile became damp asphalt. The smell of coffee and paper dissolved into wet trash and sea salt. She leaned against the wall, breathing through the brief swimmy feeling.

The alley was empty.

She circled to the front, hood up, head down. The shop's front windows were dark. An Out of Office sign hung crooked on the door, yesterday's announcement. No police tape. No official seal. Yet.

Keys, she thought, then remembered she did not need them.

She mapped the interior of the staff room in her mind, the lockless corridor behind the fiction section, the row of gray lockers. Hers, third from the left, with the small chipped corner from an overenthusiastic delivery box.

The hum obliged.

Blink.

She was inside, air stale and cool, the humming refrigerator the loudest sound in the little room. Her knees wobbled. She caught herself on the locker row and listened. No footsteps overhead. No voices.

She spun the combination with fingers that remembered the sequence on their own. The door opened with a familiar squeak.

Arcana of the Weave lay where she had left it, small and green, gold title catching the weak fluorescent light. Beside it, her folded note: Put cash in till tomorrow, M.

"Sorry," she whispered. "Running a tab."

She slid the little book into her pack, closed the locker, and drew breath for the return jump.

Something pricked at the back of her neck. She turned her head, scanning the staff room.

The cheap metal sink. The bulletin board with its faded notices. The tiny square mirror above the hand sanitizer, used mostly to check for stray crumbs or ink on chins.

Her reflection stared back from the mirror.

At the edge of the glass, the echo waited. A fraction behind. Exactly like the bathroom.

Her pulse thudded. "Not now," she said under her breath.

The echo did not speak. It just blinked slower, like someone learning the timing of her body and getting closer with every try.

She shut her eyes, reached for the hum, and let the line to the mausoleum tug at her.

Stone. Oak door. The cool stillness of old crypt air.

Here.

The shop dissolved.

She arrived at the cemetery gate with gravel crunching under her shoes, breath fogging in the morning chill. The world steadied around her, gray stone and iron fencing coming back into focus one heartbeat at a time. No sound but the rustle of bare branches and the distant hum of waking traffic.

For a few minutes, she stood alone, hand gripping the cold iron rail, eyes fixed on the narrow road that wound up from town. Her pulse still hadn't found its ordinary rhythm. The Weave hummed low and steady in her chest, quiet, but alert.

Headlights crested the hill.

Alex's borrowed sedan rolled to a stop on the shoulder, engine ticking as it cooled. He climbed out fast, scanning the tree line until he saw her. The relief in his face hit harder than she expected.

"You made it," he said, voice raw.

"I told you I would," she answered.

He crossed the road, slinging both packs over one shoulder. "You got it?"

She tapped the side of her own bag; the faint shape of the green leather volume pressed against the fabric. "I got it."

Some of the tension left his shoulders, though his eyes still flicked toward the road as if expecting headlights behind them.

"Let's move," he said. "Before anyone gets curious."

Together they slipped through the old gate, the hinges giving a tired sigh as the iron swung inward.

They threaded through leaning headstones and old trees. At the far side of the grounds, half hidden by ivy, the mausoleum waited, a low stone building with a heavy door and iron ring. The hinges complained when Alex pulled it open. The air inside smelled of dust, old stone, and that peculiar stillness that only accumulates under centuries.

They set up their little camp in one corner. Bedrolls, backpack, flashlight on the floor like a small altar. Maya set the Codex and Arcana side by side on the marble ledge of an empty niche, modern leather and older leather sharing space.

The hum from the Codex deepened at once, as if it approved of the stone, of the age.

She felt it resonate through her bones, a low chord that matched the way the mausoleum sat in the Weave, heavy and rooted.

"For now," Alex said, slumping onto his bedroll, "this is home."

"For now," she echoed.

Outside, the first rays of real sun touched the cemetery. Inside, the crypt kept its own time.

Far across town, in the apartment they had just left, the air thinned.

If anyone had been there to see it, they would have noticed the way the light shifted, the way the dust motes stopped swirling and hung for a single, perfectly still second. Blue filaments, thin as hair, slid through the cracks around the windows and under the door, spreading through the rooms in a slow ripple.

They brushed over the chalk ghosts on the floor, and the marks faded as if they had never been there. They passed through the impression of her hand on the table, the notches in the mattress where she had slept, the warmth lingering in the cushions of the couch. Each sign of her presence dimmed, then disappeared, not physically erased, simply rewritten to match what the layout should have been if no one like her had ever lived there at all.

The dented kettle remained on the counter, mute witness. The light that struck its warped side shifted, just a little, as if whichever law governed reflections had been asked to forget a particular shape and was trying, clumsily, to comply.

For a heartbeat, in the dark glass of the television screen, a faint double image of her appeared, standing in the center of the room. The echo wore no expression. It lagged nothing. It simply stood, perfectly still.

Then the image smeared, blurred, and vanished, leaving only an empty room and the hollow hum of a place that had been edited.

In the mausoleum, the Codex vibrated once, hard enough that Maya's hand jumped where it rested on the cover. The hum in her chest answered, thinner at the edges, as if something had been trimmed from it without permission.

She shivered.

Alex glanced over. "You okay?"

She nodded, but her eyes were fixed on the dark leather. "Something just let go," she said softly. "Like the city pulled a page out of itself."

"Is that good?" he asked.

Her fingers tightened. "I do not know if good is the right word."

The Codex's resonance sat lower now, a bass note that made the stone itself seem to listen.

Her reflection, wherever it was, had one fewer place to live. The part of the world that remembered her apartment had been thinned, corrected, scrubbed.

Temporary calm settled over the crypt. Underneath it, quiet dread unfolded, patient and sure. The humans were hunting her body. The Unmaking, whatever it chose to call itself, had started hunting the outline she left behind.

9

Threads of Others

The moon was full over Salem, bright enough to turn rooftops silver. Clouds drifted high and thin, their edges glowing where they crossed the light. The wind carried salt from the harbor and the faint metallic tang of cold stone.

Two days since Maya and Alex had taken refuge in the mausoleum, two days of restless sleep, whispered arguments, and the constant sense that someone, somewhere, was still looking for them. The tension between them hummed like low current.

Maya walked alone, her boots crunching frost at the edges of the path. Gallows Hill lay quiet this late, just a few streetlamps on the road below and the distant buzz of traffic, softened by the cold. The informational plaques about the trials gleamed faintly, their bronze surfaces gathering the moonlight. She passed them without reading. She didn't need words to feel the history in the air. The hum told her everything.

Alex thought she was taking a short walk to clear her head. He didn't ask questions when she'd slipped out of the mausoleum, and she hadn't offered answers. She needed silence. The kind that wasn't an absence of sound but a space where sound could be understood. The Codex and *Arcana of the Weave* rested in her pack, the leather pressing lightly against her spine like a heartbeat that wasn't hers.

She climbed to the top, where an old foundation ringed the crest of the hill. Weathered stones jutted through the grass, arranged in a circle that might have once supported a wall. The air felt heavier here, charged. The map she had drawn weeks ago, the one showing the ley intersections through Salem, came to life in her memory. One of the strongest lines crossed right beneath this hill.

Maya settled on a flat slab of granite, setting the Codex beside her, the smaller green *Arcana* tucked under her jacket for warmth. She drew a slow breath, hand over her chest, feeling her pulse thrum against her palm. The dented kettle flashed through her mind, the day she'd pushed too far, the ache behind her eyes, the thin thread of blood she hadn't meant to shed. Power always came with cost.

Tonight, she didn't want power. She wanted understanding.

She pressed her bare hand against the stone. It was cold, smoother than it looked. Beneath the surface, she felt the hum waiting. It rose gently, like a voice hesitant to speak until it knew it was being heard.

"Okay," she whispered. "I'm listening."

The vibration deepened, subtle as a cat's purr at first. Then it thickened, gathering rhythm. Not random, not chaotic, measured. She could feel patterns in it. Each breath she took adjusted the pitch. Her heartbeat entered the rhythm like a drum joining an orchestra already playing.

She closed her eyes. The Weave under Gallows Hill didn't sound like the soft humming she felt in the apartment or the muted tones near the harbor. It was lower, fuller. There was sorrow buried here, centuries of fear and injustice condensed into a single long note that quivered under her skin.

As her breathing steadied, the tone around her expanded into harmony.

She felt directions take on voices. To the east, the harbor sang high and thin, a keening whisper through iron and salt. The Common pulsed at midrange, steady and human, full of footsteps and lives still unfolding. Beneath her, Gallows Hill's tone was the bass line, old and solemn. Together, they aligned like parts of a chord.

It wasn't music she could hum or write down, but she recognized intervals. Fifths, octaves, harmonics rising from the spaces between. She smiled slightly. *A choir,* she thought. *A city singing to itself.*

The sensation soothed something raw inside her. Since the abduction, her nerves had felt strung too tight, like she was always half a breath from snapping. Here, the tension unwound. For the first time in days, her mind wasn't chasing threats or shadows. It was simply *present.*

Her fingers brushed the edge of the Codex. The leather was warm from her body heat, faintly pulsing in rhythm with the tones beneath the ground. It didn't feel alive exactly, more like it was resonating, as though the book itself were remembering.

She leaned back, eyes closed again. The sound spread outward, layers folding and unfolding, a spectrum that wasn't limited by her ears. Every living thing in the city had its tone, its pulse in the Weave. She could sense hundreds, thousands, all faint and distant. It should have been overwhelming, but instead it felt right. Connected.

This is what it's supposed to be, she thought. *Not fear. Not control. Harmony.*

A memory stirred, Merlin's words from the Codex, *The Weave is harmony, and the Unmaking is its silence.* She had written that line in her notes, underlined twice. Tonight, the truth of it resonated through her bones.

She stayed that way for a long while, just breathing, feeling the city's song expand. She didn't realize when the edges began to blur, when the individual notes started to stretch beyond Salem itself.

At first it felt like wind shifting across her skin. Then it was a pull, gentle but insistent, like threads being drawn outward from her center.

The tones changed timbre. The Salem chord thinned, and beneath it came faint echoes from elsewhere, notes not bound to this city at all.

Her breath hitched. She wasn't just hearing local resonance now. The Weave was opening further, the way it had when she'd first touched the ley lines on the map.

Somewhere far away, other voices began to sing.

She opened her eyes. The city lights looked distant, unfocused, as if viewed through water. The moon hung directly overhead, haloed in a thin frost of mist. For a heartbeat, she felt the ground tilt, not with vertigo, but with expansion.

She gripped the stone edge beneath her to steady herself. The hum rolled outward, the world stretching with it.

And for the first time since she had discovered the Weave, she felt something beyond it, threads, taut and trembling, pulling at the edges of perception. They were not Salem's. They belonged somewhere else, to someone else.

Her pulse quickened. Her breath fogged the cold air.

"Not local," she murmured, half in awe. "You're not local at all."

The tones surrounding her shifted in response, a chord modulating, opening into distance.

Maya sat perfectly still, heart hammering. The night had gone perfectly quiet. Even the wind seemed to pause.

Then, beneath that silence, a faint tug, fingers brushing invisible strings, reached from somewhere far beyond the horizon.

Something, or someone, was singing back.

The tug grew stronger the longer she sat still.

It was not a hand or a voice. It was the feeling you get when you stand at the edge of a lake at night and know, without knowing how, that something is moving beneath the surface toward where you are.

Maya let her eyes half close.

She could still feel her body. Stone under her, cold and unyielding through the denim. The chill on her cheeks. The faint ache in her lower back from sitting too long. The pack against her spine, weight of Codex and Arcana both. Her fingers resting on the granite, palm open, sigil warm against something older than any book.

All of that remained.

It just stopped being the most important thing.

The hum in her chest, that familiar center note, did not vanish. It spread. It became one voice in a choir that had waited a long time for her to shut up and listen properly.

She exhaled and let her attention move outward along the lines she had mapped weeks ago on paper. On those maps, the ley routes had been ink and guesswork. Tonight they felt like braille pressed into the world.

The line under Gallows Hill ran north and east, a deep tone that tasted of old stone and older fear. She followed it without force, the way you follow a current in shallow water, not swimming yet, just letting your feet lift.

Salem slipped a little out of focus.

The harbor note thinned. The chatter of human lives in the Common drifted to background. Her sense of the hill, of the damp grass, of the informational plaques and their careful, wrong words, became something she knew but did not need to hold with her hands.

The Weave did the carrying.

Her awareness stretched, not like a body being pulled, more like a lens being widened. The chord of Salem stayed underneath her, a home key. Over it, higher and lower, other tones started to come in, faint at first, then stronger.

Her pulse hitched. She almost pulled back.

Instead she remembered how the kettle had crushed her when she pushed, how much better everything worked when she listened. She let the current decide what to show her.

The first new presence arrived like a note held very cleanly on a distant instrument.

Bright, steady, unwavering.

It sat somewhere inland, far beyond the reach of her mental map. If Salem was a cluster of lights along a shoreline, this presence was a lighthouse miles away on another coast, beam sweeping back and forth at perfect intervals. Its tone was high but solid, clear in a way that made her own note feel rough by comparison.

It was not a place. It was a person.

She felt that as certainly as she felt the stone under her. The Weave did not hum like this for cities or hills or lines of granite. This was a human mind that had learned to rest its weight inside the field, the way she had, only more. Longer. Better.

Her breath caught.

Before she could lean toward that beacon, another presence flared.

This one did not hold steady. It flickered, changed pitch so quickly it made her throat tighten. The tone juddered up and down the scale, jagged like a heart monitor in a medical drama that is not going well.

Heat clung to it. Concrete. Metal. A smear of noise that felt like a city that never slept. Somewhere dense and breathless, full of glass and steel and too many people sitting under fluorescent lights at two in the morning.

Panic threaded that tone. Fear. A will that touched the Weave not in curiosity, but in crisis.

Her chest clenched in response. The empathic layer of her power tried to join in, to taste the feeling directly. She held it back. Even from here, at this distance, the chaotic thread made her bones want to pace.

Her own tone wobbled in sympathy. She steadied it deliberately, matching the hill instead, letting Gallows Hill feed her the bass line again.

As she did, a third presence stirred.

This one hit her like a memory she had not known she had.

The note was not bright like the beacon. Not jagged like the one in crisis. It carried a strange mix of both, high harmonics braided with a low, dark resonance that felt almost, but not quite, like a shadow.

The familiarity made her jaw tighten. She could not place it. She knew she had brushed this tone before, lightly, in the way you brush a stranger's coat on a crowded sidewalk. It had registered and then vanished into the noise.

Tonight, the Weave would not let it vanish.

The third presence sharpened, as if some part of the field had decided that if she was looking, she might as well see.

Light formed, but not the kind you see with eyes. It was the impression of a shape made out of recall and consequence. The Weave did not bother with hair color or eye shape or height. It cared about how someone fit into the pattern, not what their face looked like in a mirror.

She felt hands first.

Hands that had learned what it meant to move energy, not just objects. Fingers that had traced sigils, maybe in air, maybe in blood. Palms that had known the weight of talismans and stones and something like the Codex, but not exactly.

Around those hands, a body resolved in outline, made of light braided with shade. The shadow in it was not absence. It was memory, the afterimage of something that had burned away and left a shape behind.

Her breath came faster. She knew, without knowing how she knew, that the owner of this outline had died once. Or come close enough that the Weave had begun to lay claim to him. He had walked into the field willingly. He had not entirely walked back out.

The Codex hummed at her hip, muffled by the pack, a sudden sympathetic vibration. The Arcana of the Weave, tucked under her jacket, warmed. Both answered this presence as if greeting an acquaintance.

Not a stranger.

A predecessor.

No words spoke, not the way Merlin's ink spoke. Yet something like a phrase slid into her mind without sound.

He walked the pattern before you.

Images followed, quick and disjointed, like flashes cut from a film.

Rain on asphalt. A stone that drank light. A young man standing between two currents, one bright, one black, hands outstretched as if refusing to choose between them and choosing anyway.

She did not see his face. She felt his decision. The sense of someone who had understood that the Weave was not a tool or a toy, but a responsibility. A bridge and a battlefield at the same time.

Emotion punched through the connection, sharp and clean and not hers.

Love, fierce and stubborn.

Grief, heavy and long.

Resolve, the kind that makes people step into impossible places because there is no one else left who will.

She made a small, involuntary sound, the back of her throat catching. The outline wavered. For a heartbeat she felt a thread from his presence touch hers.

Not pulling. Not binding.

Tagging.

As if the pattern itself were marking her as the next point in a sequence that had started long before she was born.

The Codex hummed louder. Her pack vibrated faintly against her spine. The name Myrddin Emrys floated up from her memory of last night's reading, but he did not feel like Merlin. This one was more recent. Less legend, more wound.

She did not know his name yet. She only knew that he belonged to the same story, and that realization landed with a weight she had not expected.

She was not unique.

The idea shivered through her, knocking pride loose and replacing it with something heavier.

Responsibility.

If there were others, then the universe had not bent all its hopes around one woman in Salem who liked books and wrote color coded notes. She was one thread among many. A relief, at first. The burden in her chest lightened.

Then came the second thought.

If there were others, they were all doing this alone too.

The outline of the man in light and shadow pulsed once, as if in agreement. Then his thread faded back into the larger chord. Not gone, only less foregrounded. A melody line retreating so the rest of the orchestra could resume.

Maya swallowed hard.

The bright beacon inland thrummed again. Closer now, or perhaps she was simply paying more attention.

It felt old. Anchored.

Snow lay around it in her mind, whether that was literal or just her brain trying to make sense of tone. She tasted stone, thick and cold, the sort used to build monasteries or fortresses or universities that never closed. The presence at its center felt calm, not because nothing bad had ever happened to it, but because it had lived with this hum for so long that it had learned how to breathe around it.

She tried to lean toward that one, to ask a question without words.

The Weave acknowledged the intent with a slight change in pitch. The beacon answered with a tiny rise in volume, a greeting of sorts. But when she tried to peer closer, to focus on it the way she had on the outline of the man who might once have been Ethan Moore, something resisted.

Not a hand pushing back. More like a polite hand redirecting.

Not yet, the sensation implied.

She let that one sit, a steady star on the horizon.

The chaotic thread, the one that felt like a person in crisis somewhere in a city that did not sleep, flared again.

Its tone shot high, then plunged low, then skittered in jagged intervals that made her jaw clench. Heat rolled off it, thick and humid, the opposite of Salem's salt chill. Her shirt dampened at the back of her neck with phantom sweat.

Whatever that person was doing, they were not sitting on a hill under a full moon meditating on responsibility. Their contact with the Weave felt accidental. Panicked. Like someone had fallen into a river and was grabbing at anything they could find to keep from going under.

She reached it on instinct.

Her own note stretched toward that chaos, offering a harmonic, a kind of support. She did not know how to help from here, only that doing nothing felt unbearable.

For a heartbeat they brushed.

Her gut lurched. Fear hit her like a physical blow, sharp and sour. Voices shouted in a language she did not know, words lost but tone clear. Sirens. Footsteps pounding up stairs. The taste of smoke. The pressure of eyes watching from cameras.

She tore back before her own mind could drown in it.

The Weave answered that retreat with a shudder.

Not angry. Alarmed.

Her own tone wobbled wildly for a second, threatened to match the chaos. Gallows Hill steadied her again, its low note sliding under her like a hand at her back.

She gasped, breath steaming in the cold air. Her fingers dug into the stone. For a moment the world shrank back to boots on frost and moon above and the smell of damp grass.

She let that anchor hold until the shaking in her hands eased.

Then, more carefully, she extended her awareness again, this time not to touch, only to listen.

The three presences remained.

Beacon in stone and snow, calm and distant.

Thread of light and shadow, another walker in the pattern, partly gone and yet still woven through it.

Chaos in heat and concrete, flaring and fading, dangerously bright.

They felt like she did to the Weave.

Humans whose will had found purchase in the field. Each with their own tone, their own way of leaning into the Song. She recognized the shape of that leaning the way a musician recognizes another musician by the way they carry themselves in a crowd.

Wonder swelled, surprising her. It lifted her chest until she almost laughed. For months she had carried the quiet fear that she was an accident. A glitch. The Weave had never said she was the only one, but the silence had allowed that illusion to grow.

Now the field itself had corrected her.

She was part of a pattern that spanned more than one city, more than one life, probably more than one era. It did not reduce her. It located her.

Awe followed, slower, deeper. Her own story shrank down to the size it actually was, a few inches of thread in a tapestry too large to see. The abduction, Hargreaves and his talk of order, the Ghost Rescuer headlines and the dented kettle and the quiet mausoleum where Alex slept tonight, all of that mattered. It just was not everything.

If others were out there, they might be facing their own Hargreaves. Their own Unmaking. Their own dented kettles.

That thought hurt.

Questions pushed at the inside of her teeth.

Could she reach them, ever? Should she? Would contact help them, or paint targets on all their backs? If she could barely keep herself safe from a task force with a neat acronym and a sedative, what right did she have to try to pull anyone else into her mess?

She did not get to answer any of those.

Because as she turned more of her attention toward the steady beacon, just to drink in its calm for a second longer, the harmony under everything wobbled.

It was small at first, the way a record warps by a fraction and makes one note come out wrong for a beat.

The tone of Gallows Hill dipped, then rose too fast.

The harbor note scratched, as if dragged across something rough.

The lighthouse presence inland flickered, not much, just enough to make her shoulders tense.

An entirely different vibration rose under all of it.

Deep enough to make her teeth ache.

It did not sound like the threads. It did not sound like stone or water or human will. It was the absence of all of those pressed into a shape that the Weave could not quite absorb.

The Codex in her pack went cold against her spine.

Her skin crawled.

Somewhere in the back of her mind, Merlin's neat script uncurled from memory.

It feeds where sight lingers too long.

Her tongue tasted metal. The hairs on her arms stood up.

The new vibration did not reach for her. It did not have to. It simply existed, and in doing so, it made the spaces between all the other notes feel thinner and more fragile.

The Weave had noticed her noticing.

And something in the Residuum had noticed too.

The change announced itself the way winter does in October, first as a feeling you can't name, then as breath you can see.

Under the city's chord, beneath the layered voices of harbor and Common and hill, another presence rose. It wasn't sound. It was what happens to sound when someone cups a hand over it. A pressure at the edges of hearing, a subtraction that made everything else too bright.

The lines she'd been following quivered.

Not like plucked strings, like wires under snow when something heavy crosses them in the dark.

Maya's breath shortened without her permission. The cold around her was not the honest cold of night; it was the clean, dry chill of absence. The stone under her palm felt suddenly slick, as if frost were forming under her skin instead of on the rock. Her chest hitched. Between one heartbeat and the next, there was a pause that lasted just long enough for her body to panic.

Merlin had a line for that. The silence between the heartbeats of the world.

Her pulse restarted, too fast, like a bird freed from a hand.

The not-sound did not strike. It did not even reach. It thickened, and in thickening it found the places where she had been looking. Attention had weight. It left dents. The thing beneath the Song curled itself along the edges of those dents like cold fog pooling in footprints.

The bright beacon inland flickered once. Not much. Just enough for the certainty of it to become a question. Something passed between her and that calm star, not touching it, only blocking her view the way a shadow moves over a sundial.

The chaotic thread in heat and concrete pulsed harder, signal fighting through a sudden squall of static. For a heartbeat its frequency doubled, panicked, then dropped so low her teeth ached. She flinched and nearly reached again before the memory of the gully and the ranger and the discipline she'd bled for stopped her hand.

The third presence, the one that felt like light braided with shadow, brightened in outline as if answering a call that wasn't a call. For an instant it seemed nearer, the way a face resolves when a projector focuses. Then the cold edged around even that, tasting the place her mind had been, pressing its cheek to the glass where she had leaned.

The Codex warmed against her spine.

Not hot. Not warning. Recognition. A hum under leather, a resonance that answered words she had copied in her own hand two nights ago.

The residue stirs where sight lingers.

It didn't hate. It corrected. It moved toward imbalance the way water moves toward the low place. Her attention made low places. Not because she meant harm, but because she was not a passive observer. Sight bent the field. Naming put weight on things. She had followed the chord outward like a searchlight, and the shadow had followed the beam.

Guilt bucked in her chest, quick and stupid.

She could feel the temptation to argue with physics like a child arguing with rain. I didn't invite you. I only looked. But looking, here, was participation. The Weave had taught her that the first day it let a coin slide across her floor. Every breath she took adjusted the pitch. This was only the other side of that truth. Attention was gravity. Gravity had consequences.

Her heart stuttered again. The pause stretched. Half a second too long. A fraction longer than fear could pretend was normal.

She pulled back.

Not with panic. Not with a wrench that would tear what she was trying to save. She had learned better than that. She gathered herself the way she had gathered the kettle's image, carefully, with respect and drew her awareness up and in.

The inland beacon sheathed itself in stone again, steady beyond her need to examine it. She let it go, even as relief and loneliness argued under her ribs.

The chaotic thread writhed once more. She did not reach. She released the picture of its city. She released the heat. She released the imagined stairwell with the shouting and the sirens. The signal dimmed to a distant pulse, still there, no longer under her hand.

The outline of light and shadow blurred, as if a veil slipped back into place. The Codex hummed once, then quieted, appeased by her restraint.

She narrowed and narrowed until only Salem remained, harbor whispering high, Common walking at midrange, Gallows Hill a low note that fit her spine like a brace. The subtraction tone stayed under everything, a cold river flowing beneath bedrock, but the current's pressure stepped down a fraction once she stopped pointing.

The air eased. Not much. Enough that her breath stopped fogging and returned to simple white in, gray out. The stone no longer felt like ice under skin. Her fingers uncurled from their hook on the granite.

Beauty soured in her mouth, like a song gone flat at the last bar. A minute ago she had been part of a choir. Now the choir had teeth.

Discovery braided itself to dread, tight enough to be one rope. She had wanted to know whether there were others. Wanting, here, was a lever. She had leaned on the lever and moved more than she meant to. The cost of looking too far was not hers alone.

Her eyes opened on reflex. Moonlight stung.

Salem reassembled, the wrong bronze of the plaques, the brush of dry grass at her boots, the thin frost on the shadow side of the stone. Far below, a car turned at a light, tires whispering on damp pavement. No siren. No drama. Ordinary night.

The Weave didn't let go of her entirely. The hum stayed in her bones, smaller now, the size of a held breath. Her pack vibrated once against her back, a small, precise buzz, like a phone receiving a message from another century.

She slid the pack off her shoulders and set it in her lap. The Codex's leather felt warmer than the air, a heart under skin. The Arcana's smaller spine had a steadier heat, the kind of warmth that comes from cloth hid under a coat.

She didn't open either.

Not yet.

Her palm lay flat on the Codex cover. The sigil in her skin answered with a mild glow, more reassurance than flourish. The hill's tone sat behind it, patient as granite.

"Noted," she whispered to the dark. "I see the rule."

Sight made gravity. Gravity drew residue. Curiosity and care had to learn to share a skull.

She blew a long, deliberate breath out through her nose and counted her way back into her body. Four. Hold. Six. Again.

The cold under the song did not vanish. It receded, the way the taste of metal recedes after you bite your lip. Awareness of it remained like a bruise you stop pressing.

She waited until her heartbeat stopped trying to double the tempo and slipped back into its ordinary time. The pause between beats shortened to what it had been before. Not mercy. Just normal.

Somewhere behind her, down the slope, a fox moved through old leaves with the sound of careful paper. The night accepted the fox without comment. She tried to accept the night the same way.

The pack's zipper rasped too loud in the quiet. Maya winced, glanced downslope for any late dog-walker or patrolling cruiser and then tugged the flap back the rest of the way. Cold bit her fingertips. The Codex lay where she had tucked it, wrapped in a scarf to keep the leather from scuffing, as if scratches could matter to something that old. Beneath it, the green Arcana of the Weave pressed a steadier warmth into the canvas, a smaller, tidier pulse, like a space heater compared to a furnace.

She slid both books into her lap. The Arcana hummed, reassuring as a manual with tabs and diagrams. The Codex did not hum. It waited. Its gravity sat in her hands, a pressure that was not weight exactly, more like the feeling of standing at the mouth of a tunnel and knowing the air moves differently inside.

Her breath came out as fog over the leather. She wiped it away with the back of her wrist and set the Codex on her thighs. For a moment she only held it, palms flat, listening for the hill's chord and her own pulse and the absence underneath both. The cold lived in her knuckles. The fear from the deeper listening had receded, but its echo stayed.

"Fine," she said softly. "Say it."

She lifted the cover. The spine flexed with a patient creak. Pages fanned and then settled, not on Fragment XXVII where she had left an old coffee ticket as a marker, but three leaves forward, near enough that she could feel the residue of the Unmaking in the air but not so close that the word itself looked back. The leaf the book chose was blank. The parchment smelled faintly of ozone, the way air does after a lightning strike far away. It made the tiny hairs on her wrist rise.

Ink formed before her eyes.

Not the slow, melting reshaping of runes she had watched by candlelight. This was direct, as if an invisible nib had lowered to the page and begun to write. Strokes drew themselves in a hand as familiar now as her own notes from the last two nights. The same measured angles. The same careful pressure changes. The same habit of widening the tail on a capital that did not need widening.

The words came one line at a time, no flourish, no preface.

The residue stirs where sight lingers.

She did not breathe. The second line followed, the nib that did not exist lifting and setting down again with exact pauses between.

It follows the gaze that names it.

Her fingers had already found her notebook without permission. She balanced it against the Codex, thumbed to a clean page, and began to copy even as the script on the parchment finished drawing itself. For a half breath her pen matched the cadence on the page beneath. Her letters fell in the same rhythm, the same spacing. Then her hand slipped back into her own speed, slightly faster, slightly sloppier. Human again. The Codex's line ended with a neat dot. Hers ended with a dot that bled a little too much.

As she lifted her pen, more ink appeared. A small caret, an insertion mark as tidy as any proofreader's, grew between the two lines. A three-word clarification wrote itself into the space.

Where attention is weight.

Maya almost laughed. The sound that came out of her was too thin. She wrote that too, then looked at what she had made: her notes and a book's voice, stacked, the edges barely offset. It felt like taking dictation from a teacher she could not see.

She let the pen hover and then made herself translate, not to obey, but to own it.

Margin note: *Looking is not neutral.*

Another line, tight and blocky.

Awareness is invitation.

Her script wavered. She underlined invitation and did not like the feeling that underlining it made the word heavier, as if the page might tip if she wrote too many lines on one side. She shook her hand out and wrote a slower sentence beneath.

The more I map, the more it has paths.

The Codex did not protest the tone. It did not correct her. It did not add a third line at once to argue with her phrasing. It did something worse. It agreed by continuing.

More script unfurled, the same hand that had labeled Fragment XXVII and signed Myrddin Emrys at the top of an older page.

A name gives shape. Shape gives purchase. Let sight be a light that moves, lest it burn a hole.

She copied that too, pen scratching. Her breath fogged once more and blurred the margin. She brushed the dampness away with her sleeve and saw, then, what had not been there a heartbeat earlier.

A tiny side note had appeared near the bottom gutter, crammed into a space no respectful scribe would have chosen, as if someone in a hurry had squeezed a thought into the only available room. The letters were smaller than the main text, narrower, with a tired grace that was less Merlin's tidy patience and more an older hand that had learned to write with a blade before it learned a quill. The ink looked a shade browner, as if age had pressed some of it back into the page.

Beware the one who sees only the pattern, not the people in it.

Maya's throat tightened. She did not write at once. She only stared at the words. The admonition carried a voice she could not place. Not Merlin. The line felt older, or wider. Beagron. Ethan. Someone else tied into this chain who had spent too much time looking at the world from above.

She wrote it out carefully anyway, then boxed it with a thin rectangle so she would not smear it with the side of her hand later. Underneath, in her own uneven letters:

Don't become a cartographer of harm.

The wind lifted and fell across the top of the hill. She felt the Codex hum under her palms again. The sensation traveled up the bones of her forearms. Her script changed for a heartbeat, her Ys taking longer tails, her Ts curling back on themselves in a way she would never have chosen if she had not been trying to keep up. It was not possession. It was contagion. Style infected by resonance.

"Enough," she said aloud, but quietly. "You can speak. I will not let you steer my hand."

The hum settled into simple warmth.

She sat back a little and looked at the page as a whole. Two lines in Merlin's hand, a small interlineal phrase, and that cramped warning in the gutter. Her own notes crowding the right margin, modern ink cut by older strokes. It was not a record anymore. It was a conversation. Worse than a conversation. It was a ledger. Every insight she had given herself the luxury of feeling privately could have an entry. The thought tasted like surveillance.

Her mind tried to push the idea away and could not. Even if no human eyes but hers ever saw these pages, she was being folded into something that had a long memory. The Codex was not only where others had written. It was a device that wrote back, that added, that braided her into the same rope. She had wanted a teacher. She had not accounted for being drafted as a link.

The Arcana pressed steady heat through her thigh, grounding as a textbook. She leaned over, pulled it from under her jacket, and cracked it open one-handed to a plate she remembered from a late-night skim weeks ago: a diagram of sympathetic correspondences, radiating circles labeled with human states and tonal intervals. It was clean and theoretically wrong in places the Codex did not bother to argue about. She set it on the stone beside her, the way a diver sets a rope beside a dark opening in case the water decides it prefers you below.

Her eyes went back to the Codex. The pen in her hand felt heavy now that she had the sense she might not be its only driver. She made herself finish the translation work anyway.

Looking is not neutral. Awareness is invitation. Paths can be built by the act of noticing.

She drew a small triangle next to the three ideas and labeled the points with quick initials: L, A, P. Then she traced a loop around them to remind herself that they fed one another. If she could make the book's lines hers, if she could make the vocabulary belong to her mouth, then maybe she could keep herself from becoming a conduit someone else could use.

The page brightened a fraction, as if the ink had been glossy all along and she had only now tilted it to the light. She closed the Codex halfway to break eye contact. The parchment sighed as the cover lowered, the smell of ozone lifting as if a storm had stepped a mile farther off.

She looked out over the city. The rooftops had gone more silver. Frost held on in the grass where her boots had bent it. Salem hummed under everything, its chord patient, its intervals familiar enough now to find even when the cold under-song tried to pull her under.

"Beware the one who sees only the pattern," she said into the air, testing the warning against her own tongue. "I hear you."

She glanced at the Arcana plate again and then slipped the green book back under her jacket. The Codex went into the pack, not closed all the way, just to the point where the page she had been reading would not catch and tear. The leather warmed the side of her ribs. The weight at her spine steadied her.

Intellect buzzed in her head like a swarm. She could sit here and take dictation until her fingers cramped. She could build a glossary. She could go home and pin maps to the walls until the room looked like a conspiracy, lines converging on places tourists thought they understood. She could do what frightened people do with knowledge: hoard it until it rotted.

Or she could test the world the way the world had tested her.

The hill's bass note nudged that choice.

She wrapped the scarf back around the Codex, zipped the pack two-thirds shut, and stood. The stone under her hand felt less like a monument now and more like part of a circuit. Trails down the slope shone as slightly darker ribbons where frost had not set. Far east, the harbor's high thread called like a wire under tension. North, a line she barely knew yet tugged at the thinner bones of her sense, hinting at routes she had not taken out of fear or prudence or simple lack of time.

She checked herself for that pause between heartbeats. It was there, but no longer reaching for her. The residue had tasted the weight of her sight and moved on when she stopped pointing. She could not pretend ignorance would keep anything safe, but she could decide how long she stared and where.

She pulled her gloves on and set her palm against her sternum for one steady breath. The sigil warmed, consent and caution in the same small glow.

"Intellectual insight is useless without practice," she said to the hill, to the Codex in the pack, to the air that had learned the shape of her voice. "Let's see what these tracks can carry and what they ask in return."

She started down, every step a measure, every measure an answer. The city waited, humming. The currents under the streets felt less like a map and more like rails. She would ride them toward the water and then beyond, measuring cost against distance, listening to the price change as she chose care over hunger.

Behind her, the stone kept its chord. In her pack, the Codex warmed once as if in agreement, then cooled, the ink on the blank leaf drying to the same quiet black as the rest of the book's long memory.

The mausoleum was cold in a way stone always remembered. The kind of cold that had more to do with history than temperature. Maya crouched on the floor, her pack spilled open beside her and spread her maps across the uneven slab. Candle stubs flickered in alcoves, throwing long shadows across the chalk lines she had drawn hours earlier.

Alex sat on the steps, arms around his knees, exhaustion written in the tight set of his shoulders. Every few minutes he glanced toward the entrance, as if expecting black sedans and heavy boots to appear through the iron gate.

"They're not coming tonight," she murmured, not looking up.

"You don't know that."

"I don't have to know. I can feel it. The city's quiet."
She tapped one of the sketched ley intersections. "Here. Here. And here. These are pulling harder than the others."

Alex rubbed both hands over his face. "Maya, you just found out you're not the only person in the world who can," He gestured vaguely at the maps, at her, at the nameless thing living in her chest. "—do this. And your first instinct is to take it on a field test?"

"It's not a test," she said, tracing a fingertip up the coast. "It's survival. If Hargreaves can find me once, he can find me again. And the Shadow Current," She hesitated, not wanting to say its name inside a building meant for the dead.
"it's tracking my attention. The only way to stay ahead of either is to understand how the lines *want* to move."

Alex leaned forward. "I'm not saying don't practice. I'm saying don't do it alone."

She finally met his eyes. He was scared. Not for himself, he had already proved that, but for her. That mattered. It always did.
But fear wasn't going to keep the world from shifting under her feet.

"I'll be back in minutes," she said softly. "You'll barely have time to panic."

"That's not comforting."

"It's the best I've got."
She slid the Codex into the pack, tucked Arcana of the Weave beside it, and stood, brushing dust off her jeans. The air in the mausoleum thrummed around her, the Weave acknowledging her decision with a faint, anticipatory note.

Outside, the sky was paling at the edges. Pre-dawn fog clung to the grass. The harbor wind cut sharp across her face as she walked toward the water.

Alex followed her to the threshold.

"Just... come back," he said.

She nodded once, then stepped into the fog.

The harbor looked different at this hour, no tourists, no lights on the docks, just dark water breathing against the stone. The place where she had first mapped the coastal line sat between two old granite blocks. The intersection hummed under her boots like a tuning fork pressed to bone.

She set her feet exactly on the seam.

The usual hum rose inside her chest, steadying into its note. But tonight she didn't try to *generate* anything. She reached outward instead, listening.

The coastal line answered.

It felt like a river made of tone; slow, deep, patient. A highway humming with centuries of repetition. She followed its sound north, letting her awareness stretch between the fishing boats, the marsh grasses, the rocky beaches curving away from Salem.

The line wasn't going straight. It arced and dipped, following an old geological spine. Ipswich sat directly on that path.

She exhaled.

"Okay," she whispered. "Take me with you."

The world didn't snap. It leaned.

The air thickened around her calves. A soft, pulling sensation, not suction, not force, but invitation, tugged her forward. For once, she didn't brace. She let her weight shift into the motion.

Her vision flickered: docks → reeds → dark road → salt marsh lit by moon → a brief flash of gravel drive → old gray shingles → then—

She stood on different stone.

The smell told her first: seaweed, colder and cleaner than Salem's harbor. The fog here was lighter, drifting in thin sheets across a quiet shoreline. The pitch under her feet rang a degree higher, as if the land itself breathed differently.

Ipswich.

She let out a shaky laugh. "Holy hell."

Her legs wobbled, but only from adrenaline. No sharp pain behind the eyes. No bleeding. No collapsing. The dizziness felt like she had sprinted up three flights of stairs too fast, not like the blackout after the kettle trial.

Her body was adapting.

Or the lines were.

She walked a few steps, taking in the unfamiliar houses, colonial roofs sloping toward the water, narrow lanes of cobblestone and old brick. The Weave sang differently here. Not as burdened by history. Not etched with the scream-lines of trials and death.

This place felt elderly, not haunted.

Her skin prickled with a strange peace.

"Okay," she murmured. "Ipswich hums in D. Good to know."

The Shadow Current was still there, somewhere beneath the world, but quieter. Like background static instead of a presence waiting to step into her breath.

She wondered if the bright steady thread she'd sensed earlier lived somewhere out here, anchored in stone and snow and old memory.

She wondered what they'd felt when her attention brushed them.

Her chest tightened with guilt.

Looking is an invitation, the Codex had warned.

She inhaled deeply to steady herself. She could not fix that now. But she could control what she did next.

The return route vibrated differently. Where the coastal line had felt like a river going north, the southward version felt like a returning tide, slower, heavier, but smoother.

She stood where two narrow paths crossed, feeling the earth's tone in her shinbones.

"Take me home," she whispered.

The slide began again, this time easier, as if the Weave recognized her pattern. The flickers resolved faster: marsh → dunes → coastal road → harbor glow.

A puddle reflected moonlight right before she landed.

For a split second, her reflection looked back at her.

But it was delayed.

A half-beat behind.

The Echo.

It snapped into alignment as her foot touched the wet ground.

She stumbled back. "No, no, no,"

But the puddle was still again, reflecting only her real face, lit by the faint gray of the approaching dawn.

The Echo was following the vectors now.

Her heart raced as she leaned on the harbor railing, replaying the moment. That delayed reflection, first seen in the mirror after reading the Codex, faint in the warehouse blink, then ghosting in a puddle,

It was growing clearer.

Her body remembered Alex's weight in her arms, the way the Weave had doubled the strain when she carried him through the blink.

Two minds on a line deepened resonance.

Two minds deepened Echo.

She closed her eyes, reaching inward.

The hum inside her answered with a wary tremor, the kind that meant *not yet.*

"I wasn't planning to take him with me," she whispered, shaking her head. "Not until I know the cost."

A gust of wind lifted strands of her hair. The Weave around her rose in a quiet, approving note. Practice had brought her here. Practice would keep her alive.

But practice also left footprints.

She opened her eyes.

It was time to return.

She was halfway back up the hill toward the cemetery when she saw it, still water pooling in a ditch beside the road, the sky reflected in its dark, frost-lined surface.

She slowed.

The puddle reflected the trees.

The gravel.

The pale dawn light.

And her.

Or, her twice.

One Maya stood straight, breathing steam into the cold morning. The other stood a fraction behind, posture skewed, outline flickering like a paused video frame catching up.

The delayed version blinked late.

Raised its hand late.

Exhaled late.

Exactly half a heartbeat behind.

Her lungs locked.

The Echo smiled.

She hadn't.

A tight, involuntary sound escaped her throat.

"Stop," she whispered. "You're not me."

The reflection stuttered, then collapsed back into ordinary stillness, just a puddle, showing only one woman standing alone in the cold.

Maya staggered backward onto the gravel shoulder, heart thundering.

The Echo was evolving.

And it had learned to step out of shadows and water now.

She ran the last stretch, boots crunching frost, breath ragged, fog curling behind her like a ghost of its own.

The mausoleum gate squealed when she pushed it open.

Alex looked up instantly from where he waited on the steps, tension in every line of him.

"Jesus, Maya, what happened?"

She dropped her pack beside him, chest heaving.

"I can ride the lines," she said breathlessly. "Long distances. Almost no cost."

He stared. "Okay, that... that's good. Right?"

"Yes."

She swallowed hard.

"No."

His brow furrowed. "What do you mean no?"

Her voice cracked, the memory of the delayed reflection still scraping at her nerves.

"Because something came with me."

So she told him. Not everything at once but in fragments, like pieces of a dream retold before it fades. The choir of the hill. The lines that weren't Salem's. Three threads flaring like distant stars, one steady, one erratic, one familiar. The cold pulse that crawled up the song. The new lines that had written themselves into the Codex. And the trip to Ipswich, the ride along the natural corridor, the ease of it. The way her reflection lagged behind her landing.

Alex listened without interrupting. His eyes were bright with fatigue, but sharper with something like grief.

"So there are others like you," he said at last, voice low. "Like this."

"Not like." She pulled her knees up, folding her arms around them. "Parallel. We're touching the same thing, but from different angles. Some are stronger. Some are... gone."

His gaze flicked to the Codex, then back to her. "And something under all of it is watching you watching it."

"Yes." Her voice didn't waver. She'd already gone through the fear outside. "And it will watch you too, if you get too close."

He swallowed. The candle beside him guttered, throwing a brief tremor of shadow across his face. "I believe you."

She nodded, waiting.

"That's what scares me," he added. "Not the magic. Not the... teleporting. Not even the thing in the water or whatever's under the ground." He exhaled sharply. "It's listening to you. And you're describing it like it's a storm pattern, not something that wants to eat everything you are."

"It doesn't want," she said softly. "It reacts. It corrects."

"That doesn't make me feel better."

Silence stretched between them. The mausoleum was never fully quiet; small echoes lived in the corners, soft breaths of stone settling, outside wind pushing past the door. But across the short distance between them, the quiet felt heavy.

"I'm not afraid of you," Alex said suddenly, eyes locked on hers.

Her throat tightened.

"I'm afraid for you. Because none of this feels survivable. Not in the long term. Not if this thing keeps following you back from everywhere you look."

"I'm getting better," she said, too quickly.

"You're getting deeper," he corrected.

She tried to joke. "Well, depth is important in any,"

"Maya." The word stopped her. He wasn't smiling. "You jumped with me once. If you hadn't... I'd be gone. I know that. And I'm grateful. But that jump almost killed you." His jaw tightened. "And now there are echoes of you appearing in puddles."

She closed her mouth. Humor felt like a thin sheet of paper over a crack in the floor.

They arranged the blankets without speaking. Shifts, they decided. Half practical, someone had to stay awake in case HECATE got close. Half emotional, they both felt the need for distance and hated that they needed it.

Maya lay on the left side of the mausoleum, head near the stone entry arch. Alex lay on the right, near the wilted flowers and idle candles. Between them sat the Codex and Arcana, stacked like a pair of silent sentinels.

The gap between their bedrolls seemed wider than a few feet. It felt like the mouth of something she couldn't name.

She watched the doorway. A sliver of moonlight cut across the floor like a blade. Her pack sat just inside that line, steel thermos hanging from the strap.

As clouds drifted over the moon, the thermos' metal sheen flickered. For an instant, she saw her reflection in it, tiny, warped by curve and shadow. A second face appeared beside hers, one beat late.

Her pulse stuttered. The image vanished as the moon disappeared behind cloud.

Maya exhaled shakily and closed her eyes.

Under the cemetery, she felt the Weave's lines steady and ready, a calm hum rising through the earth. But beneath that, quieter and colder, a pulse waited like a question.

Her last thought before sleep was not one she would admit aloud:

She was no longer moving through a pattern.

The pattern, and the thing under it, was beginning to move around her.

10

Fractured Reflections

The mausoleum woke slowly, the way old stone does. Pale light seeped through the ironwork gate and the narrow slit windows near the ceiling, soft and colorless. Candles burned low on a ledge, small pools of wax hardened around their bases. Alex slept on the far side of the room, wrapped in his jacket, one arm over his head, breathing deep and steady.

Maya pushed herself upright, stiff from sleeping on stone. For a moment she allowed herself to pretend it was an ordinary morning, a cramped Airbnb, maybe, or a friend's spare room, anywhere but this crypt of borrowed silence. But then the smell of cold granite and wilted flowers drifted in, and reality settled back around her ribs.

She stood, walking quietly across the mausoleum. The air was chill enough that her breath barely fogged, but not cold enough to sting. A small metal wall plaque hung near the door, commemorating a family line long gone. They had been using its polished surface, dulled by decades but still reflective enough, as a makeshift mirror.

She leaned in, running a hand through her hair before checking the bruise forming along her wrist. The restraint marks were fading. Her eyes were tired, ringed with shadows. Otherwise, she looked normal.

Until she blinked.

Her reflection blinked a fraction of a beat after she did.

Maya froze.

She blinked again. Slow. Deliberate.

The image in the plaque followed, just late enough to be wrong, early enough to mimic truth.

She lifted her right hand. The reflection hesitated, then lifted its own. A half-beat behind. Exactly like the ditch water outside Ipswich, like the puddle under the streetlamp, like the flicker she'd caught in the kettle before she left her apartment for good.

Her stomach tightened.

She tilted her head to the left.

Lag.

She stuck out her tongue.

Lag.

She narrowed her eyes.

Lag, soft but unavoidable.

No cold wind this time. No ripple of temperature. No humming distortion. That almost made it worse. This wasn't an attack. It wasn't an event. It was simply there.

Settled, routine.

Like a bruise becoming part of the skin.

She touched her sternum, feeling for the hum. It was faint, resting, the way it always was in the quiet moments after waking. But the reflection's rhythm, that wasn't the hum. That was something else. Something clinging to her outline.

Resonance burn, she told herself. After effects. You pushed too hard. You mapped too far. All side effects.

But the Codex had been clear, in its own quiet way:

Residue rides patterns, not choices.

She drew a slow breath, stepped back from the plaque, and watched the image shrink. For a moment she thought it had stabilized, then, as she turned away, the reflected profile in the metal turned a fraction later.

A delayed echo, baked into the surface of her shadow.

"Just the echo," she whispered under her breath, though the words tasted hollow.

Behind her, the plaque stayed silent.

Still reflective.

Still wrong.

She didn't wake Alex, she didn't look again.

Instead, she wrapped her arms around herself and went back to the center of the mausoleum, pretending the chill in her bones was only the morning air.

Something else would find her soon enough And when it did, she wouldn't be looking at a reflection.

When Alex woke up, he stepped outside to check the perimeter, or maybe just to breathe air that didn't smell like stone and old dust. Maya listened to the iron gate creak shut behind him. Silence settled back over the mausoleum, heavy as a lid.

She pulled the Codex from her pack, flipping past Fragment XXVII to look for anything that matched what she'd just seen in the plaque's reflection. The Arcana of the Weave lay open beside it, a green leather echo of the larger book. Between them, she found only scraps: a penciled note in an old hand about *tainted scrying surfaces,* another referencing *Residuum clinging to images.*

Nothing that said, "Your reflection will lag behind like an echo trying to remember you."

Maya exhaled sharply. "Great. Very helpful."

She carried the Codex back to the polished wall plaque, their makeshift mirror. The bronze surface caught the early morning light in uneven glints, warping her features slightly. At first glance, the reflection behaved the same as before: a half-beat late, her motions echoed just out of sync.

"Okay," she murmured, touching the plaque lightly. "Whatever you are, you're just residue. Environmental static. Nothing more."

But the reflection didn't agree.

As she watched, the delay stretched, not longer, but deeper, as if the echo were trying to remember something else entirely. Her reflected eyes seemed to look past her shoulder, focusing on a point that didn't exist in the mausoleum.

Maya's pulse jumped. "No. No, don't..."

The reflection shifted.

The face staring back at her was still hers, at first. But behind her reflected shoulder, a second figure bled slowly into view. A girl. A teenager. Long hair matted, edges charred as though smoke were still rising from it.

Isabel.

She looked exactly as she had the night she died, only without the terror. Her eyes were clear, solemn. Alive in a way they hadn't been in years.

Maya froze, breath locked in her throat.

"Isabel," she whispered.

Isabel's reflection smiled faintly, a soft, sad curve of the mouth that never reached her eyes. The background behind her wasn't the mausoleum. It was stone, yes, but lit by a wavering, impossible orange glow. As though embers were drifting somewhere just out of frame.

When Isabel spoke, her voice did not come from behind Maya or from the room.

It came from the plaque.

"The flames still burn beneath stone."

Maya's knees weakened. "Is this real?" Her voice broke. "Or is it just my guilt getting creative?"

Isabel tilted her head as if listening to a sound Maya couldn't hear. "Guilt does not hum like this." She glanced around the edges of the reflection, as if she could hear the Weave itself resonating. "You are standing on old fires, Maya. Not just mine."

Something cold tightened in Maya's chest. "Why are you here?"

Isabel didn't answer immediately. Instead, she looked at Maya's reflected outline, specifically at the slight lag behind her movements, the same delay Maya had seen all morning.

Finally, Isabel whispered, "You are not the only one reflected."

Maya swallowed, throat dry. "What does that mean?"

"Something else has learned your outline," Isabel said gently. "It tries to walk where you walk. To echo where you echo."

The warmth in her voice fought with the terror in her words.

Maya reached out a trembling finger toward the plaque. "Can it use you? Is that why you look—"

But Isabel flinched. The reflection wavered, as if another image pressed up behind her, a shadow mimicking her shape, a second Isabel slightly out of phase.

For a heartbeat, Isabel's mouth moved with no sound, like something was choking the words off before they could reach Maya.

Then everything snapped.

Isabel's form dissolved.

The plaque reflected only Maya again, tired eyes, messy hair, and the echo lagging half a beat behind her.

A faint rustle behind her broke the silence. The Codex had opened itself to a new page, an incantation near the spine marked with a single line of ink:

For glass that remembers what it should not.

Maya's breath hitched.

"This keeps getting worse," she whispered.

But she couldn't look away from the plaque.

Because this time, even after Isabel vanished, the echo seemed to smile.

Late.

Too late.

As if someone else were trying on her face.

Midmorning light slanted through the mausoleum's narrow windows in thin, washed-out bars. The air felt colder than it had at dawn, though Maya knew that was probably just nerves, or the echo of Isabel's face still imprinted behind her eyes.

Alex stood near the gate, jacket pulled tight, scanning the cemetery as though expecting black sedans to rise from behind the headstones. He had accepted Maya's weak explanation that she wanted to "try a small fix," but his posture told her he wasn't convinced this was wise.

"Five minutes," he said. "Then I'm dragging you outside, ritual or no ritual."

"Deal," she lied gently.

She knelt beside the stone shelf where she'd propped the bronze memorial plaque. Its polished surface held her faint reflection, and, thankfully, only hers. The delayed blink was still there, faint but insistent, like a second heartbeat trying to sync with hers.

The Codex lay open beside the plaque, pages trembling lightly in the draftless air. It had opened on its own again when she carried it inside, this time to a page she'd barely skimmed before, a thin column of text beside an ink drawing of a palm over glass. Radiating lines sketched outward like cracks in ice.

A note in the margin read:
Burn out shadow-latched images. Restore concord to the face of seeing.

Arcana of the Weave lay open as well, offering a more practical annotation in a tidy librarian's hand:
For scrying mirrors or reflective mediums presenting delayed resonance. Risk of incomplete banishment. Do not attempt on living water.

Maya exhaled slowly, grounding herself. The sigil-marked palm tingled with anticipation or warning, she couldn't tell.

She uncapped her water bottle and poured a thin stream across the bronze. It beaded and ran in narrow silver paths. She sprinkled a pinch of salt from a packet she'd taken from Alex's pack, she would apologize later if he discovered it missing.

Then, as the Codex instructed, she traced a small circle over the wet surface with her sigil hand. The bruise on her wrist, almost healed, ached faintly as she moved. When the circle was complete, she drew a single straight line down its center.

Nothing happened at first. Then the bronze rippled under her fingers.

Maya swallowed and began the incantation. The language was old, older than Latin, older than English. But the Codex had been shifting its script for her for days, and now the words came into her mind with a strange, instinctive ease.

"En draelien… sorath ven… cala dimme…"

It felt like humming backwards.

The plaque darkened as though ink were bleeding from beneath the metal's skin. Hairline fractures spidered outward from the corners, not audible cracks, just thin white lines that caught the light like frost.

"Maya?" Alex called softly from the door. "Everything okay?"

"Fine," she said, but the word came out thin. "Just… finishing."

The plaque pulsed once, just enough to jolt her fingertip. Then something impossible happened.

Shadow began to fall.

Not rise. Not smoke or vapor or anything she could brush away. It *fell* inward, toward the center of the plaque, defying the direction of gravity. A fine dust of darkness poured from the spiderweb cracks and gathered in a small, shifting pool, like soot collecting in a bowl that wasn't there.

Maya's heart slammed against her ribs.

This wasn't cleansing.
This was concentration.

She suddenly understood: the ritual wasn't meant to *banish* shadow residue. It was designed to pull it out of its spread, invisible layer and force it into a single point so it could be dealt with.

She had just pulled it in.

"Not good," she whispered.

The shadow pool thickened, tightening into a knot of darkness no larger than a coin. The edges quivered like something alive, or something remembering it once had shape.

"Maya?" Alex's voice sharpened.

She shook her head once, she didn't dare look away from the plaque. "Stay back."

The knot pulsed.

A breath of cold slid over her knuckles. The bronze chilled under her palm.

And under her feet, the Weave's hum hiccuped, stumbled, like a record skipping.

Her pulse froze.

The plaque vibrated once.

The shadow knot sank straight downward through solid metal, as if the bronze were only a surface of water and she had dropped a pebble through it.

It vanished without so much as a ripple.

The hum under the mausoleum floor stuttered again, harder.

Maya jerked back, heart hammering as the plaque returned to normal, no cracks, no stain, no sign it had ever held anything other than her own faint reflection.

Except the reflection wasn't alone.

Behind her in the metal, just for an instant, a second silhouette watched her.

Not Isabel.

Not Alex.

Not human.

Then it blinked out, a beat late.

The floor's vibration rose like a held breath about to break.

And Maya realized, far too late, that she had not cleansed anything.

She had just called it home.

The temperature in the mausoleum dropped so suddenly Maya's lungs seized. One breath ago the air had been cool and stale; now it hit her chest like winter water. Her exhale ghosted white in front of her.

Alex turned sharply from the gate. "What ?" He stopped. Whatever he saw froze him mid-step.

Every candle flame in the room thinned. Their warm gold narrowed to needles of light with black threads running through the center, thin, vertical seams of pure midnight. She had seen that thread once before, in her apartment's mirror. Now there were six of them, wobbling inside the flames like dark veins.

Then the hum vanished.

Not everywhere. She still felt the Weave beyond the stone walls, alive and thrumming like distant traffic. But inside the mausoleum, inside a perfect circular radius around her, there was nothing. No tone. No pulse. No warmth.

A silence so complete it felt physical.

Maya's hand hovered over the ritual plaque as if it could anchor her. Her skin prickled, tiny pins-and-needles racing across her fingertips. Inside her chest, her heartbeat stuttered.

One beat.
Another.
Between them, a pause that stretched too long, as if the world was deciding whether to continue.

Something darkened the air above the plaque.

It was not a shape, not in the way shapes belonged to objects. It was a patch of space that refused to hold light. The edges shimmered like heat haze, but instead of brightening, they blurred into deeper gray.

It flickered in her peripheral vision like a shadow moving without a source. When she tried to stare directly at it, it became nothing but a bruise in the world, colorless and shifting. Through it, the far wall appeared half a second late, as if seen through a glitching screen.

"Don't look at it straight on," she whispered.

Alex didn't answer at first. His gaze kept skidding away from the distortion like his eyes were physically unable to focus. Finally he rasped, "Maya. What did you just do?"

She couldn't speak. Her throat was locked.

The thing, *the absence*, did not move toward them like a creature. It simply began to erode what it touched.

Lines on the stone floor blurred, edges melting and reforming like wet paint. Her bedroll's outline softened, sinking and reappearing in a smear. A single dried flower in the corner collapsed into a spill of shadow for the length of a blink before popping back into brittle shape.

The Unmaking did not devour. It un-wrote.

And it curled itself most strongly around three points:

The ritual plaque.

The Codex.

And the air just above her sternum, where her tone in the Weave usually sang the loudest.

Maya felt her empathic sense wither, not shut off, but mute. Emotion from Alex, usually a steady, anxious hum in the air around her, thinned to nothing. The silence wasn't just auditory. It was psychic.

"Alex," she managed, her voice barely a breath. "Back up. Slowly."

He didn't move. His knuckles whitened around the strap of his pack. "That is not normal shadow."

"No," Maya whispered. "It isn't."

Merlin's words surged back:

The Unmaking is not a creature. It is the silence between heartbeats, the correction that consumes the unaligned.

And she had just *summoned* it. Concentrated it. Given it a point to push against.

The thing pulsed.

The flames bent inward, thin knives of light tugged toward the distortion. Another heartbeat stretched long, too long, before slamming back into her ribs with painful force.

"Maya," Alex said again, fear cracking his voice this time. "Do something."

She reached instinctually for the Weave, for the familiar hum, her anchor,

Nothing.

Inside this bubble, the hum was gone, stripped clean. Her power felt like reaching for a door that wasn't there.

Her pulse hammered.

The distortion jittered, growing slightly, edges fraying deeper into the gray. The world behind it lagged again, worse this time. Her peripheral vision shook.

"I have to get us out," she whispered.

Alex swallowed. "You can't jump in here, you said the lines,"

"I don't have a choice."

She reached deeper. Past fear. Past the silence. Past the deadened space around her.

And there, far outside the mausoleum's walls, she felt it. A faint thread. Weak, distant, almost extinguished, but present. The Weave waited beyond this bubble. If she could just reach that far,

The distortion twitched, as if it sensed her intention. The stone floor beneath it rippled. A crack on the far wall slid along the mortar, unmaking and remaking itself in a stuttering shiver.

Her breathing sped. "Alex. Come here. Now."

He stumbled toward her, eyes locked on the thing. "Tell me what to do."

"Hold on to me."

He grabbed her arm. His hand shook.

The distortion flared once, soundlessly, and Maya felt something brush the edge of her awareness. Not a mind. Not a presence. A pressure. A cold fingertip tracing the outline of her shape, memorizing it.

She gasped.

Her heart skipped, and didn't immediately start again.

That broke her.

She reached for the Weave like reaching for breath, for life, for escape.

And the world cracked open.

The distortion pulsed once, soundless, colorless, but deep enough that her knees nearly buckled. Maya didn't wait for a second warning.

"Alex. Now."

He was already moving, his face pale, jaw clenched. When she grabbed his arm, he gripped back without hesitation. No question. No protest. Just trust, raw and terrified.

She pulled him close, hand splayed over his wrist, fingers shaking. "We're getting out," she whispered, more to convince herself than him.

Her mind leapt to the cemetery gate, stone pillars, iron bars, frost-glittered gravel. It wasn't the calm, focused image she was used to summoning. It came ragged, sloppy, smeared at the edges by fear.

The Weave answered with a flicker of tone. But inside the mausoleum's deadened bubble, it was thin, like a rope half frayed.

She inhaled, reaching for stability.

And heard two notes.

One was hers: bright, rising, the familiar pulse that lived beneath her ribs.

The other slid between her heartbeats like oil, the absence-tone she'd felt blooming above the mirror. A pitch made of silence.

She didn't have time to untangle them.

She pushed anyway.

The world snapped,
and then stalled.

Not the clean fold of space she knew. Not the rush of air displacement or the soft realignment of gravity.

This was a stutter.

Maya gasped. The mausoleum flickered around them like a bad projection. The cemetery gate flickered too, half-formed, half-present. Between them was a thick gray, not fog, not shadow, but something without depth or light or meaning.

Alex's hand crushed hers. "Maya,"

"I know," she choked.

Then the backlash hit.

A needle of ice drove straight down her spine. Her vision fuzzed white-hot. Her nose burst warm with blood, dripping instantly onto her shirt. The freezing air turned the smell copper-sharp.

Alex folded slightly, gasping. She felt the spike of his fear through her half-dead empathic sense, not fear of the distortion, but fear for *her.*

The distortion followed.

Not physically. Not like a creature.

It wrapped around the outline of her body mid-jump, tracing her shape like fingers skimming cloth. It was learning her. Learning the arc of her will. Learning the *route* she carved when she moved through the lines.

They hung suspended between spaces for three agonizing beats.

Two worlds.

Zero footing.

The gray swallowing both.

And in the flicker, one of the stone plaques along the wall flashed past her vision, reflecting the half-formed scene.

She saw herself.

And she saw the after-image behind her.

A delayed version, a half-second out of sync, repeating her motion like a ghost stuck in an echo. Only its face wasn't a face, just a soft hollow, a smear of absence shaped roughly like her head.

"No, no, no," she whispered, panic tearing through the pain.

The Weave finally screamed back, its frequency climbing in a desperate surge, as if refusing to let her go.

The jump buckled.

The world snapped inward, and spat them back into the mausoleum with brutal force.

Maya hit the stone floor on her side, air punched from her lungs. Alex crashed down beside her, catching himself on one knee with a ragged cry.

Her vision tunneled hard, shrinking to a narrow pinhole of gray light. Her hearing dimmed. The Weave's hum cut out completely.

And in that terrible gap, a peace washed through her. Perfect quiet, perfect stillness.

Not mercy.

The "rest that is not rest," the kind Merlin had warned about, the kind that exists only when a flame gutters out.

Her mind sank toward it.

Then the Weave slammed back into her with a force that felt like defibrillation. Her spine arched. Sound flooded in, sharp and painful. The cold receded in a rush.

"Maya!" Alex's voice came from far away, shredded by her fading consciousness. "Stay with me, Maya!"

But she couldn't hold on.

Her body collapsed sideways, skull hitting cold stone. Her blood smeared the floor beneath her cheek.

Darkness rose.

And just before it took her, her perspective drifted, not from her own body, but from behind it. From the Echo's vantage. Watching her fall.

For a moment, there is no Maya.

There is only *a shape* collapsing through space, viewed from a half-second behind the present, as if the world itself is buffering.

The mausoleum tilts, slow and liquid. Candlelight smears into pale gold arcs. Alex's shout lands in the air with the weight of a delayed thunderclap, audible only after the mouth that formed it has already closed.

Her body hits the stone floor.

And the one who sees it is not in that body.

A point of view hovers a few feet above the scene, a place with no breath and no heartbeat, just the cold clarity of watching. Maya's collapsed form lies curled, one arm flung out toward Alex, her other hand pressed weakly to her sternum as if she'd been trying to hold a thread inside her chest. Blood beads and drips from her nose, dark against the gray stone. Her lashes flutter once, then still.

The perspective drifts, no footsteps, no sound of movement, only a shift, as if gravity has forgotten to apply.

Alex lands beside her on one knee, chest rising and falling with ragged effort. His hand reaches for her shoulder. The fingers blur for a fraction of a second, resolving only after they've already touched her. Sound follows even slower, "Maya, Maya, stay with me," hollow, distant, as if spoken from underwater.

But the viewpoint does not answer him. It does not share his panic.

It merely observes.

The edges of the mausoleum buckle slightly, the stone lines rippling like heat over asphalt. The candle flames in their stubs droop, then stretch tall in the wrong direction, upward, then sideways, then trembling between shapes. Time behaves like a frayed film reel: a frame sticks, jumps, then resumes.

The Codex sits open on the stone shelf, runes dimming and brightening on a slow pulse. Something unseen studies that dimming, leaning closer without ever stepping forward. The pages shiver though no draft touches them.

Maya's body stirs. Barely. Her ribs quiver in a micro-movement, a breath trapped between beats.

And the watcher tilts its attention.

In the warped reflection on a metal plaque half buried in candles and dust, another Maya looks back. Not the one on the ground. A faint, pale echo, her head turned at a slight delay, her blinking out of sync, her eyes two dark, depthless hollows where color should be. This version moves only after the real body stops moving, like a puppet whose strings are pulled by someone watching the original.

The reflective Maya lifts her chin a fraction too late.

Her lips form a shape, not quite a word, more like the start of one.

Then she flickers.

Once.

Twice.

Gone.

The hovering perspective dips lower, closer to the unconscious girl on the floor, as if memorizing the exact angle of her fall, the line her arm traces, the fading glow at her sternum where the Weave has pulled back to protect itself. It lingers on her outline, mapping it, learning its edges, filing her pattern away.

The hum of the Weave is still absent inside the bubble of silence, like someone has turned off a world-sized machine. But beyond the walls, faint and distant, the lines of Salem vibrate, confused, calling for the thread they momentarily lost.

The watcher... listens.

Maya's eyes finally roll closed all the way. Her body goes still.

The viewpoint withdraws, not up, not back, but *sideways*, slipping into a direction that does not exist on any map.

Before it goes, it leaves one final impression in the quiet, less a thought than an imprint:

The pattern remembered how she fell. The silence remembered where she would land.

Darkness folds over everything.

11

The Voice Beneath Salem

Maya woke with her cheek pressed to stone.

Cold, wet stone, grain rough enough to bite her skin, nothing like the mausoleum floor she remembered a heartbeat before the world folded and the echo swallowed her sight. She drew a sharp breath. The air tasted metallic, sharp as a coin held too long between her teeth. A hint of salt clung to it too, like the Atlantic trapped underground.

She lifted her head.

Darkness stretched in every direction, but not an ordinary dark. Here, the walls breathed with light.

Pale-blue veins, thin as hair in some places, thick as rope in others, glowed inside the stone. Not on it. **Inside** it. They pulsed slowly, in a slow heartbeat that did not belong to her. Each pulse brightened, then receded, leaving ghost-sparks wandering through her peripheral vision.

She pushed up onto her elbows.

The floor shifted under her like she'd risen on a rocking boat. Gravity didn't feel wrong, just undecided. She pressed a palm to the slab beneath her, grounding herself in the only stable thing she could reach.

The stone was warm where the light veins passed under it. Warm, then cold, then warm again, in a rhythm she could almost hear.

Drip.

A single drop of water fell somewhere far down the tunnel.

Drip.

The echo arrived a moment late, as if sound itself was struggling to travel through this place.

Her balance wavered. She blinked hard, taking in what little she could see.

She was in a corridor, but not one carved by human hands. The tunnel arched overhead like the inside of a ribcage, joints of stone curving naturally, almost organically. She could not tell where the stone ended and the Weave began, because here, the Weave wasn't a layer above reality. It was *in* the walls, in the floor, in the air.

"This isn't the cemetery," she whispered.

Her voice didn't echo correctly. It sounded close, too close, as if the space swallowed the edges of her words before they could bounce away.

She moved a hand to her forehead, no cut, but her nose still had the tacky dryness of a bleed. She remembered Alex shouting her name, the jump collapsing, the sudden peace like falling into warm water.

Then nothing.

Now this.

She sat fully up. Her breath fogged faintly in the air, then thinned, then returned, temperature fluctuating with the Weave's pulse.

"How deep..." She trailed off. Talking to herself made the silence feel crowded.

She looked at the glowing veins again, tracing one as it snaked along the wall. The light was soft, not like electricity or flame, but like moonlight caught under ice. She reached toward it without thinking. Her fingertips hovered a hair's breadth from the stone, and the vein's pulse responded, brightening, matching her breathing for a moment.

A tremor ran down her arm.

The Weave was louder here. Denser. Thick like woven rope instead of thin thread.

And old. Older than the trials, older than Puritan settlements, older than Gallows Hill. Older even than whatever ruins this tunnel might once have been. This place hummed with a version of the Weave she had never felt before, one that felt less like a tool and more like a presence.

She closed her eyes, just to listen.

Her chest hum synced with the walls for a single, perfect breath. Then fell out of sync, like she'd stepped into a song halfway through. The Weave didn't hurt her, but it didn't welcome her either. It simply was, immense, foundational, real in a way that made the surface-world Weave feel like a faded copy.

A shiver ran through her, not from cold, but from recognition.

She wasn't just beneath Salem.

She was beneath *history*, beneath the strata where human time meant nothing.

Her pulse stuttered. "Where are you?" she whispered, not to anyone living, but to herself, trying to map memory onto darkness.

The Weave responded with a long, slow vibration that traveled through the floor and up her spine. A whisper of insight slid through her mind:

The city was built on top of something far older.

Not ruins.

Not caves.

A *foundation of the original Weave*, a junction from the age when the Guardians still shaped the mortal side of the Seal.

Her mouth had gone dry.

Water dripped again. Only once.

She forced herself to her knees, then to her feet. The ceiling felt too low until she blinked and realized it was her sense of space bending, not the stone. Each breath made her feel taller or shorter, like the world changed scale around her.

A tiny laugh escaped her throat, thin and humorless. "Great. Perfect place to have a breakdown."

But she didn't break. She steadied.

"Alex?" she called, louder this time.

Silence answered. But not an empty silence. This one felt watchful.

She took a tentative step forward. The veins in the wall brightened with each footfall, as though the tunnel were aware of her movement, aware of her presence in its long-forgotten arteries.

The Weave thrummed again, lower, deeper, resonant enough to make her bones ache.

Something moved in the distance.

A soft scuff.

Not the drip.

Not the pulse.

A footstep.

Maya froze.

The sound was deliberate, heel, then toe, light enough to belong to someone familiar. Someone who knew how to move quietly.

A figure emerged from the darkness ahead.

For a moment, only the faint lines of blue lit her silhouette.

Then the figure stepped into a brighter vein-glow.

Maya's breath caught.

"...Isabel?"

The cavern breathed in with her, the veins brightening, as something warm and impossible stepped closer from the deep.

The figure's approach warmed the air.

Not a temperature shift, something deeper. A soft glow rose from behind the silhouette, blooming gold through the blue-lit veins. The cold stone at Maya's back eased. Her pulse steadied, warmed. The metallic smell thinned into something sweeter. Sunlit.

Then Isabel stepped fully into view.

Unburned, Whole, Alive.

Her dark hair fell the way Maya remembered, loose curls brushing her shoulders. Her eyes were clear and bright, not clouded with pain or smoke. Not screaming. Not fading. Her skin held the warm flush of someone lit from within, as though every breath she took pulled more light into being.

"Hi, M," she said softly, the nickname brushing against Maya's memory like a warm hand on the cheek. "You don't have to hurt anymore."

Maya's knees nearly buckled.

It wasn't the words themselves. It was the tone, gentle, familiar, the kind Isabel used when waking her from nightmares after long study nights or when coaxing her out of self-blame. It was the voice Maya had buried under grief and what-ifs.

"The flames can be undone," Isabel continued, stepping closer. Her bare feet didn't disturb dust or echoes. The Weave's glow bent around her like sunlight through morning branches.

Maya swallowed hard, voice catching. "You, this isn't,"

Isabel's hand lifted. Not touching, just hovering near Maya's shoulder. The heat of it reached her anyway, convincing, heartbreakingly real.

The blue veins in the walls flickered once and shifted. The darkness around them softened, reshaping as though the cavern were exhaling.

The stone melted into linoleum.

Suddenly Maya stood in her childhood kitchen. The one with the dent in the fridge door and the mismatched floor tiles. Warm lamplight glowed. A pot simmered on a stove that had never worked right. The air smelled like cumin and oranges, her mother's comfort-soup.

Isabel stood beside her, unchanged, folding seamlessly into the memory like she belonged there.

Maya's breath hitched. "No. This isn't real."

Isabel smiled, warm, easy, exactly how she'd smiled after kissing Maya the first time under the stacks at Peabody. "Real isn't the same as true."

Before Maya could respond, the kitchen blinked, blurred, like a slideshow cycling too fast.

The world snapped into the library aisle where she and Isabel had first met. Dust motes hung suspended in the orange glow of late afternoon. Isabel reached out, running a finger along the spine of a book Maya had forgotten she loved.

"You've carried so much," Isabel murmured, turning back toward her. "Loss, guilt... power no one prepared you for."

Maya felt the sting of tears gathering. "Stop. Please."

"You don't have to be strong here," Isabel whispered. She stepped closer, her warmth radiating like a memory made flesh. "You don't have to fight anymore."

The scene shifted again.

Now her mother stood at the doorframe, young, laughing, wearing the green sweater she'd only ever worn in the good years. Her smile was full, bright, unbroken. Maya's eyes burned. Her chest tightened.

"Mom?" she breathed.

Her mother's laughter echoed through the aisle. "Mi estrella."

The golden light wrapped around them like a blanket. Maya felt it seep into her bones, loosening every knot of fear, tension, exhaustion. The Weave here hummed harmoniously, brightening to match the gold of the illusion. A cradle-song cadence. A lullaby turned right-side-out.

She wanted, God, she wanted, to lean into it.

She took a half step forward without meaning to.

The cavern's cold, the black stone, Hargreaves, the Echo, all of it blurred like dreams dissolving at sunrise. The warmth was so real. As real as Isabel had been, before the fire. As real as her mother had been, before everything broke.

But something inside her, a thin thread of instinct, or experience, or stubbornness, twitched.

"Isabel," she whispered hoarsely. "You died."

Isabel's expression didn't falter, but the golden light brightened, too bright, washing out the edges of the library aisle.

"You don't have to hurt anymore," Isabel repeated. The words were almost a song. "You can be whole. You can have all of it back."

The air trembled. Gold haloed Isabel's hand as she reached out to her.

Maya closed her eyes.

Hope swelled in her chest, thick and sweet and dangerous.

She felt her boundaries thinning. Her logic dissolving.

The Weave itself leaned toward the warmth.

And Maya, exhausted, grieving, yearning, leaned back.

Just a little.

Just enough.

Just enough for the Unmaking to push its lure a fraction deeper.

The glow brightened to gold. She reached for Isabel's outstretched hand and the world held its breath.

Isabel's fingers brushed hers.

Warm.

Alive.

And the cavern dissolved.

The golden glow surged outward from the point of contact, flooding Maya's nerves with gentle heat. It wasn't the burn of power or the cold surge of the Weave. It was something far more intimate, something that felt designed for her. Tailored to the shape of every old ache.

The world around her unfurled like a book opening.

She stood on a quiet street outside a modest townhouse, morning sun soft and pink. The door opened. Isabel leaned against the frame, hair mussed, smiling with the sweetness of someone who had just woken up beside you.

"Coffee's almost ready," she said, voice lazy, warm. "You overslept."

Maya blinked, breath catching. Isabel stepped forward, took her hand like she had done it every day for years, and tugged her inside. The house smelled like toast, citrus, fresh laundry. Life lived in peace.

Maya's chest tightened, but the ache diminished as soon as it rose, absorbed into the golden warmth spreading beneath her ribs.

Then the scene shifted.

Maya sat in her parents' old kitchen, her father reading a paper, her mother humming as she chopped peppers. No shouting, no tension, no bitterness. Just quiet domestic ease. Her mother's hair was streaked with silver, more than she ever lived to have, but her smile was whole.

"We're proud of you," her mother said, touching her cheek. "You've always been enough."

Maya's breath shuddered. She hadn't heard those words in a decade, not with this softness.

The warmth in her chest grew, curling around her heart like a hand lifting her gently from inside. Her shoulders loosened. The exhaustion of the last week, the abduction, the echoes, the cold pulses of the Unmaking, fell away like discarded clothing.

The golden world folded again.

She watched herself walk across a university campus, backpack slung over one shoulder, coffee in hand, earbuds in. Ordinary. Blissfully, beautifully ordinary. No hum in her chest. No glow beneath the skin. No danger shadowing her steps.

No magic.

She laughed with classmates. She studied for finals. She texted Isabel about dinner plans.

Her future branched out ahead of her like a sunlit road with no monsters waiting at the end. A life without fire. Without fear. Without graves she couldn't stop seeing when she closed her eyes.

Maya's throat constricted. Tears stung her eyes.

"Is this real?" she whispered.

Isabel answered from beside her, not the living Isabel of this vision, but the glowing one, unchanged, steady, eternal. "It could be. It can be. You don't have to carry any of it anymore."

The warmth pressed deeper, wrapping around her chest with exquisite precision. It moved exactly where her hum lived, where the

Weave resonated, where power thrummed like a second heartbeat. But this wasn't the Weave. It was smoother. Softer. Flawless.

Too flawless.

Maya's fingers twitched inside Isabel's grip, but the glow soothed that flicker of doubt instantly, like a blanket tucking itself tighter.

Her breath slowed. Her pulse gentled.

The Unmaking didn't have to force her. It only had to give her everything she'd ever wanted.

She stood on the brink, half inside the dream, half outside. The golden world shimmered at the edges, ready to solidify the moment she let go.

"Stay," Isabel whispered. "You can rest here. You can heal."

The promise wrapped around her like a vow.

Maya closed her eyes.

For a moment, one fragile, dangerous moment, she let herself believe. Let herself lean forward. Let the warmth swell until it drowned out every sharp memory. She felt her real body loosening, her awareness sliding into the illusion like slipping beneath warm water.

Maybe she had fought enough.

Maybe she deserved one good thing.

Maybe,

A sound cracked through the golden haze.

Muffled. Distant.

But real.

"Maya!"

A voice strained with panic, fear, love.

Alex.

Her eyes flew open.

The golden kitchen flickered. Isabel's hand pulsed with light, too bright, the edges glitching like dropped frames in a video. Her smile froze unnaturally mid-expression.

Alex's voice came again, clearer this time, echoing through the stone. "Maya, please, wake up!"

The golden world quivered like a shattered reflection trying to hold shape.

Maya staggered back, clutching her chest. The perfect resonance inside her twisted sharply, the too-precise warmth slipping for a heartbeat. A seam opened in the illusion.

The campus walkway split down the middle, golden paving stones falling away into blue-lit cavern stone. The townhouse door flickered into a jagged hole in the undercity wall. Her parents dissolved into dust motes.

Isabel glowed brighter, too bright, face lagging half a beat behind her voice.

"Don't go," she said.

The echo-delay dragged the last word, stretching it unnaturally.

Maya saw it then, the pattern beneath the illusion. The same delay as the Echo. The same mimicking rhythm the Unmaking had learned from her reflection.

"Isabel," she whispered, voice breaking. "You're not her."

The warmth in her chest cracked.

And the golden world shattered.

The golden world trembled, just slightly at first, like a candle flame disturbed by a breath.

Then the breath formed words.

"Maya, Maya, please, wake up."

Alex's voice, strained and shaking, filtered through the stone-heavy air like a rope thrown down a well. The sound didn't belong to this warm illusion, and that mismatch cracked something in her.

A thin fracture tore straight through the false sunlight.

The kitchen tiles beneath her feet split. The warmth clinging to her skin dimmed. Isabel, perfect, unburned Isabel, froze mid-reach. Her smile glitched, stretching a fraction too wide before snapping back.

And there, in her eyes, Maya saw it.

The lag.

The exact half-beat delay she had seen in every Echo, every distorted reflection.

Isabel blinked.

Then her reflection blinked.

Two separate motions.

Maya's breath stuttered.

Alex's voice rose again, closer this time, desperate:

"Maya, please, where are you? Wake up!"

The golden walls shuddered. A hairline crack shot up the length of Isabel's arm like a bolt of lightning trapped under skin. Light leaked from it, not warm gold, but sharp electric blue, the same shade as the ley veins in the real cavern.

Maya's heart lurched.

This isn't real.

This isn't her.

The truth arrived like cold water thrown over her mind:

The Unmaking wasn't offering comfort.

It was wearing comfort like a mask.

Isabel's face flickered, a whole half-second behind her voice now. When she spoke, the lag doubled, her mouth forming words out of sync with the sound.

"Stay," she whispered.

But her reflected form mouthed stay late and slow, a puppet learning the wrong rhythm.

Maya staggered back, one hand pressed to her chest as the warmth trying to lull her split inward, revealing its seams. The glow faltered, replaced by phantom static rippling beneath her sternum.

Alex called again, shouting this time, voice raw:

"Maya! Come back, please!"

The illusion buckled.

The tiny library aisle where she and Isabel first met collapsed into dust. The street outside the townhouse folded like paper and vanished. The campus walkway dissolved mid-step, her foot slipping on nothing.

Only the cavern remained, blue veins pulsing along the stone like the heartbeat of something ancient and awake.

"Isabel" flickered harder now, her edges buzzing, failing. Her familiar face warped, first too smooth, then too sharp, like a bad memory trying to correct itself. The warmth around her twisted cold.

Maya felt that cold reach for her, careful, coaxing, almost tender. A lure, not an attack.

But Alex's voice, breaking with fear, split the moment:

"Maya! I'm right here!"

Her knees wobbled. Her breath shuddered free of her lungs.

He was real, this wasn't.

She stepped back.

The golden world shattered like glass dropped onto stone.

Illusion-rubble rained down in silent, weightless fragments that dissolved before hitting the floor. Isabel's figure splintered into echo-delayed smears of light, the lag growing so wide it pulled her form apart.

For the briefest moment, the false Isabel looked almost panicked, as if the thing wearing her face did not understand why Maya was stepping away.

Then the entire projection collapsed into a curtain of drifting ash that fell inward, sucked toward the cavern floor by a gravity that didn't match the air.

Maya gasped, knees hitting stone.

She pressed a fist to her sternum, grounding herself in her own pulse, a real pulse, flawed and human and hers.

Alex's voice reached her again.

"Maya?"

Softer now. Terrified.

She blinked hard, clearing the last golden afterimages from her vision.

"I'm here," she whispered, though he couldn't hear her yet. "I'm here."

The hum of the Weave returned, faint and strained but real, real enough to cut through the lies.

And when she looked ahead, the cavern's passage glowed with cold blue light, a path opening deeper into the truth.

The world steadied around her as the golden illusion collapsed. The false Isabel hung frozen in the dim air, hand still outstretched, smile caught between frames. For a heartbeat Maya almost reached for her again out of memory and habit. Then the image began to crumble.

A thin crack ran down the length of the figure's arm. Another split her cheek. The illusion broke apart along those fractures like pottery under pressure. What had looked like skin dissolved into pale drifting ash that lifted, swirled once, and then fell inward to the cavern floor without a sound.

The last fragment of Isabel's face was a single eye. It watched her for an instant that felt too aware. Then it faded into nothing.

Maya exhaled. The sound was rough and uneven. When she opened her eyes fully, the cavern had returned to its real shape. The walls rose in uneven stone arcs, their surfaces pulsing with faint blue veins of light. This glow was colder than the false warmth of a moment ago, but it was honest. It hummed in a way that matched the Weave, not the echo-pattern of the presence that had tried to seduce her.

She braced a hand on the damp rock and pulled herself upright. Her legs trembled. Her breath still carried traces of the illusion's sweetness. She wiped her mouth as if clearing it away. The Weave's hum filled her ears again. Not the harmonious choir she had felt on Gallows Hill, but a low ancient tone that felt carved into the bones of the earth.

Her fingers brushed the fabric over her sternum. The warmth there was fading, replaced by her own heartbeat. Real, imperfect, alive.

Fragment XXVII whispered through her mind.

The residue stirs where sight lingers.

It follows the gaze that names it.

She understood now. The false Isabel had not been brought to her. She had been drawn out of Maya herself, shaped from memory and longing and the echo-pattern the Unmaking had already learned. The thing beneath Salem had used her deepest wound as a doorway.

Maya lifted her chin and faced the dark.

"If you want me, come as you are," she said. Her voice filled the cavern, steady despite the tremor in her chest. "I will not walk into your dream."

The words echoed once, then dissolved into the stone.

The silence that followed felt alive. Not empty. Waiting.

A faint vibration traveled through the floor. The blue veins along the walls brightened, running liquid light toward a tunnel ahead. It glowed with a thin cold luminescence, as if the earth itself were drawing a path for her. Whether it was an invitation or a challenge, she could not tell.

Her pulse quickened. Fear still pressed at the edges of her thoughts, but there was something larger under it. Resolve had weight. She felt it settle into her shoulders and spine as she drew a slow breath and tightened her grip on the strap of her pack.

Her world had narrowed to a single choice. She could climb toward safety, toward Alex, toward light. Or she could go forward into what had tried to wear her memories like a mask. Running would only lead to more illusions. Standing here meant waiting for the next one. Moving forward meant facing it without disguise.

She stepped toward the glowing tunnel.

The light brightened in response, flowing deeper into the stone passage, illuminating carved shapes she did not yet understand. The air grew colder with every footstep. The hum grew more focused and intense, a pressure in her ribs and skull.

Maya did not look back.

She followed the ancient rhythm downward, into the heart of the city, where the true presence waited.

The tunnel narrowed for several yards before opening into a space that felt older than anything Maya had ever stood inside. The ceiling arched high overhead, carved by time rather than by human hands. The floor sloped down in a gentle bowl shape, as if some ancient force had pressed the earth inward to make a vessel.

A pool rested at the center.

Its surface was absolutely still, so smooth it reflected the ceiling like polished obsidian. The water gave no scent and no movement. Not even the faint drip of condensation disturbed it. It was a perfect mirror sitting in the heart of the cavern.

Maya descended the slope slowly. Each footstep sent tiny shivers of sound into the stone, but none reached the water. The pool did not ripple. It was waiting.

The faint blue Weave-light that threaded the walls dimmed as she approached, as if yielding attention to the object beneath the water. A low vibration pressed against her inner ear. She felt it before she heard it, a tone like the lowest note of a distant choir.

She recognized it at once.
The ash-note.

Fragment XXVII had described it as the resonance of the Residuum of Will. A colorless hum, neither life nor death. She had heard it during the mirror ritual, and again when the shadow distortion folded into the mausoleum. Now it thrummed under her feet, stronger and more focused.

She stepped to the edge of the pool.

The water was dark enough to swallow all light, yet transparent enough for her to see the stone resting at the bottom. It was the size of a large heart, smooth on the outer curves and sharply carved across the flat surfaces. Runes wound around it in looping, spiraling lines, glowing faintly as if lit from inside.

She had seen some of these symbols in the Codex. Others were older. The stone did not simply hold Weave power. It radiated it in slow pulses, one every few seconds, like a deep heartbeat echoing through the cavern.

The next pulse rose up and brushed against her chest. The air vibrated. The water quivered, but the pool did not ripple. The motion seemed to move inside the liquid rather than across it.

Maya crouched, bracing a hand on the damp stone. The cold seeped through her palm. The glow from the runes painted her face with thin lines of blue and silver as she leaned closer.

The reflection that looked back at her was clear.

Too clear.

Her own face stared up from the water, but when she blinked, the water-image blinked almost a whole second later. Her breath caught. She blinked again. The delay repeated. A fraction too slow. A fraction too familiar.

The echo effect.

She pulled back slightly, but her image remained, floating beneath the surface with its wrong-timed motion. It should have frightened her more than it did. Instead, she felt a strange steadiness, as if the cavern had narrowed her emotional range into something focused and sharp.

She leaned forward again.

Her water-reflection lifted a hand just after she did. A second late. Tethered by something she still did not understand.

But then, beneath that reflection, deeper still, the stone pulsed again. This time the pulse reached her bones. The water reflection wavered, but the stone did not. The Talisman's glow did not change. Its pulse was constant and confident, untouched by whatever was mimicking her movements.

She whispered, "You are not mine, and I am not yours."

The words sank into the stillness.

The cavern did not answer, but the pulse beneath the water deepened. It felt like a reply all the same. Her ribs vibrated with it. The air seemed thicker, heavy with expectation.

She reached toward the pool, fingers hovering just inches above the surface. The cold radiating from the water felt unnatural, like standing too close to a vacuum. Something below was drawing heat out of the air without touching it.

The moment her fingertips came near the surface, the water trembled.

Not outward. Inward.

As if the entire pool inhaled.

Her reflection collapsed into a ripple of shadows. The wrong-timed echo flickered and vanished altogether, swallowed in a single shiver of distortion. The pool stilled again instantly, perfectly flat, but the disappearance sent a chill up her spine.

She had not banished the echo. The Talisman had.

She pulled her hand back and rose slowly. The stone below glowed brighter now, runes shifting slightly as her shadow crossed the water. They did not rearrange like the Codex's runes did. They breathed. That was the only word for it. The entire pattern along the Talisman seemed to expand and contract.

She breathed with it without meaning to. The pulse resonated through her sternum. Along her arms. Down her spine. She felt as if the cavern itself were trying to imprint something onto her.

A knowing.

A memory.

An invitation.

She whispered its name. "Beagron."

The air changed. The blue veins in the walls brightened with a sudden flare. The pool shimmered as if struck by an unseen gust of wind.

A single deep pulse rose from the Talisman. It climbed up through the water. Through the air. Into her chest.

And something far beneath the pool pulsed back.

The sound was deeper. Older.

Not the Talisman.

Not her.

Something below.

The pool went perfectly still once more. The cavern fell silent, the way a person might hold their breath after saying something they regret.

Maya stepped back, heart pounding, unable to shake the sense that she had just announced herself to something that had been sleeping.

And now it was awake.

12

The Weave Revealed

The mausoleum had grown quiet again. Evening settled across the graveyard in a slow blue hush, and pale light filtered through the high slits in the stone walls. The candles Maya had left burning earlier were nothing but nubs now, their flames small but steady. The air had that stillness that came after fear had run its course, the kind of quiet where even dust seemed reluctant to move.

Maya knelt on the cold floor beside her pack. Water clung to the canvas in beads that slid down the stitching. She wrung out the bottom edge with both hands until the dripping stopped. Her fingers shook slightly from cold and leftover adrenaline, but she ignored the tremor.

Alex hovered near the entrance, leaning one hand on the stone arch. He looked exhausted, hair flattened on one side from where he had fallen asleep earlier while waiting for her. The relief in his eyes was unmistakable, even beneath the fear that had not yet faded.

He did not ask where she had been. She did not offer it yet. They both understood that some answers needed to be shaped before spoken.

Maya eased the Codex onto a flat stone slab that served as a makeshift table. The cover was cold against her palms. She opened it carefully, page by page, giving the damp parchment time to breathe. Thin curls of steam rose in the candlelight where moisture evaporated.

At first the pages lay still. Then the runes began to move.

The ink shifted sluggishly, as if waking from sleep. Lines stretched, curled, and flowed into new shapes. A few faded entirely as if sinking deeper into the page. Others rose, darkened, and settled in different patterns. Maya did not touch them. She only watched.

The movement was slow, deliberate. Not frantic. Not chaotic. It felt like someone organizing thoughts after a long silence.

Alex stepped closer. "Is that supposed to happen?"

"I don't think the word supposed applies to this book," she said softly.

The runes paused, shimmered, and then began to align themselves into lines of text. The letters straightened, sharpened, and grew more defined until the heading took shape in front of her eyes:

Fragment XXVIII

Concerning the Talisman of Beagron

Maya felt her breath leave in a tight exhale. The Talisman. The stone beneath the black water. The thing that had pulsed back when she approached it. The thing that had felt older than memory itself.

The parchment dried completely with a soft whisper of sound. The ink settled into place, dark and sure. She brushed her fingertips along the margin, not touching the words, only feeling the faint warmth emanating from the page.

Alex circled behind her and crouched, peering over her shoulder. He stayed quiet, but she felt the tension in him. He had seen enough by now to recognize when the Codex was preparing to teach her something new. And every lesson so far had come with a price.

Maya closed her eyes for a moment. She let the quiet of the mausoleum settle into her bones. The scent of old stone and burnt candlewick grounded her. Her pulse steadied to the faint hum she always carried now.

When she opened her eyes again, the heading on the page looked almost brighter. As if it were waiting for her to begin.

"Something is coming," she whispered.

Alex swallowed. "Then at least you have a guide."

Maya nodded once. She was not calm, not really, but she felt centered. The panic of the Deep had receded like a tide, leaving a space inside her that was ready to be filled with understanding. The Codex had chosen this moment to reveal its next fragment.

The stillness around them felt heavy, almost purposeful. Not oppressive. Not threatening. Only aware.

The book was preparing her.

And she felt herself preparing in return.

She turned the page.

Maya ran her fingertips lightly along the edge of the new heading, more to prove it was solid than anything else.

Fragment XXVIII: Concerning the Talisman of Beagron.

Her mouth felt dry.

"Read it," Alex said quietly behind her. "Please."

She nodded, swallowed, and let her eyes fall to the first lines beneath the title.

The script on this fragment looked different from the others. The ink had a faint metallic sheen that caught the candlelight in tiny glints. Symbols along the margin shimmered in a way she had not seen before, like they were catching light from inside the page rather than from the room.

"The parchment is... weird," she murmured.

"Weird how," Alex asked.

"Like someone built a spell into the margins. Water or blood keyed, maybe." She did not like how certain that guess felt.

She began to read.

The first paragraph spoke of Beagron. Not as myth, not as a god, but as a craftsman who had tried to measure perfection and accidentally recorded its failure. The Talisman was described as a stone cut from the root of the Weave, forged at the first moment sound had learned to become form.

Her gaze snagged.

"The Talisman of Beagron is no jewel and no star metal wrought for vanity," she read aloud, voice low in the mausoleum. "It is a stone that carries two harmonies at once. The Song that builds and the Silence that waits."

She lowered her voice on the last words without meaning to.

The hum inside her chest flickered in answer. It did not spike. It acknowledged.

She reached for her notebook in reflex. The pen felt clumsy in her cold fingers. She copied the line down, printing carefully.

The Talisman carries two harmonies at once. Song that builds. Silence that waits.

She underlined both phrases twice.

Alex stayed quiet, but she could feel his attention on her, almost as present as the hum. It made the mausoleum feel less like a tomb and more like a watchful room.

Maya kept reading.

The fragment shifted into first person. Myrddin's voice emerged in the script, plain and steady, the way it had in Fragment XXVII.

I have held the stone, he wrote. In its shadow I saw every working I had ever woven, unmade and returned to dust. I heard a voice that was not mine whisper that all creation leaves a remainder.

She whispered those last seven words under her breath and felt the old echo of Fragment XXVII answer in her bones. All creation leaves a remainder. Merlin had heard it at the first Unmaking. She had heard it on her apartment floor with a kettle and a nosebleed.

She wrote that line again anyway, as if writing it might pin it down and keep it from moving.

All creation leaves a remainder.

The ink in her notebook looked dull next to the Codex's metallic shimmer.

Her eye caught on the next lines.

When I asked what that remainder seeks, the stone grew cold. The stars outside the window forgot how to move.

Maya frowned. "Does that mean literal stars or metaphors for something else."

"Which answer is less terrifying," Alex said.

"Good point."

She copied the phrase stars forgot how to move, then circled it. That felt like more than poetic flair. The Talisman did not just observe power. It listened to it, measured it, slowed it.

Her gaze slid further down the page.

It is not meant to be wielded. It is meant to be endured.

The sentence stood alone in the center of the parchment, slightly larger than the rest. A second hand had underlined it at a later time, the ink a different shade, darker and more scratched. Merlin had gone back to emphasize his own warning.

Maya's throat tightened. She wrote that line in her notebook, hand careful and slow.

It is not meant to be wielded. It is meant to be endured.

On the page, the Codex ink looked calm. In her notebook, her script slanted a little too much to the right.

Her mind slid back to the cavern, to the black water and the heart sized stone beneath it. To the way the hum in that place had threaded straight into her skeleton as if her bones were instruments waiting to be tuned.

She could feel a hint of it even now, an echo in the back of her spine, like the ghost of a cold hand pressing between her shoulders.

"The Talisman is a stabilizer," she said aloud, more to organize her own thoughts than for Alex's benefit. "It gives shape to things that would just unravel. It counters the Silence by forcing it to take form."

"How is that a bad thing?" he asked.

She tapped her pen against the underlined sentence. "Because you cannot pick up a magnet without picking up what it attracts."

He watched her, brow furrowed. "In English."

She chewed the inside of her cheek, looking for words. "If the stone listens to the Silence, using it means the Silence listens back."

Alex let out a slow breath. "Of course it does."

Her eyes dropped to the next section.

The fragment shifted out of personal confession and back into something more like thesis. Beagron's name appeared several times, credited as the first to bind the ash-note into matter. The text described the Talisman as a recorder, a stone that remembered every stress in the Weave, every place where power had been held too long or used too hard.

Those who carry its note, the passage warned, carry the attention of what gathers in the gaps.

Maya copied that almost word for word.

Those who carry the ash-note carry its attention.

The phrase ash-note made her skin crawl. She remembered the void-pitch in the mausoleum, the feeling of nerves forgetting how to fire, the way peace had almost convinced her to stay in the gap between beats.

She underlined carry three times, pressing harder each time. The pen left a slight groove in the paper.

"That is the second time you have written attention like it is a curse word," Alex observed quietly.

"Attention is not neutral," she said. "Not here. Not with this thing."

Her heart beat a little faster. The hum inside her adjusted, shifting into a slightly higher key. The Codex warmed under her hand as if in response to her understanding.

She went back to the top of the fragment and let her gaze travel slowly down, this time not copying exact sentences, but pulling out the spine of the knowledge.

She wrote in the margin of her notebook:

Talisman = stone cut from Weave root

Holds both Song and Silence

Stabilizes by forcing remainder to take shape
Not tool. Warning.
Contact draws Residuum's attention to the holder.

The act of summarizing steadied her. She had always done this, even before magic. Academic writing, dense theory, obscure poetry, all of it had become survivable when she could break it into bullet points that made sense.

Only now the subject was not some philosopher safely dead for centuries. It was the thing under Salem that had tried to wear Isabel's face.

She glanced back at the Codex.

Near the bottom of the page, a single line had been written in a much smaller hand, squeezed between two paragraphs in the narrow strip of margin. The script was finer, almost spidery compared to Merlin's strong strokes.

Beware the one who hears only the pattern and forgets the people who live inside it.

A chill walked down her arms that had nothing to do with the mausoleum air.

"That is not Merlin," she whispered.

"Who then," Alex asked.

"I do not know," she said. "Feels older. Or just more tired."

She copied that line too, setting it alone on a blank part of the page.

Beware the one who hears only the pattern and forgets the people who live inside it.

Her pen hesitated halfway through the word people. It felt uncomfortably specific.

The hum inside her chest shifted once more. For a brief second, the Weave did not feel like something she was using. It felt like something that had invited her into a conversation that had been going on for a very long time.

She lifted her hand from the Codex and rested it on her sternum. The steady tone was there, the same note that had carried her from apartment to stairwell, from harbor to Ipswich and back again. Now it sat in her like a thread tied to two anchors at once.

The song that builds. The silence that waits.

Her teleportation, the way she bent space, had always felt like pulling on threads in a tapestry. Now, reading Beagron and Merlin, she saw something else.

Every jump was also a tear.

Small, quick, partially mended each time the Weave snapped back into place, but a tear all the same. A strain that left residue in its wake. The Talisman under the water existed because people like her, and beings far older, had been doing that since the first note had become form.

She drew one more line in her notebook, slower this time.

My jumps stress the pattern. That damage can either invite the Silence or be used to mend it.

The words looked too large for the narrow paper.

Intellectual curiosity cooled into something sharper, deeper. This was no longer about tricks in alleys or escapes from warehouses. The fragment had shifted the ground under her feet.

Responsibility. The word rose in her mind and did not go away.

Maya let the notebook fall half closed in her lap. The Codex page still glowed faintly where the ink caught the light. Fragment XXVIII sat with its warnings and its quiet sorrow, talking about a stone that listened and a remainder that never slept.

She exhaled.

"Okay," she said, voice rough. "So we have a stone that can hear the damage and the thing that is drawn to it. And a city sitting on top like kindling."

Alex rubbed a hand over his face. "And what do we have on our side."

She looked down at her palm, at the faint sigil there, and then at the fragment.

"Apparently," she said, "we have a song that can learn."

The words tasted like a prayer and a threat at the same time.

Maya read in silence until her eyes caught on a line near the middle of the fragment.

Beneath all thought there is a lattice.
Beneath all will there is a thread.
The stone hears where these strain.

The phrase lattice beneath thought tugged at her in a way the rest had not. It felt less like metaphor and more like coordinates.

She heard herself say it before she decided to.

"Beneath all thought there is a lattice."

The words rolled out into the mausoleum. The air answered.

The candle flames did not flicker. They straightened. The shadows on the walls did not dance. They froze, as if the room were holding its breath.

The hum in her chest rose, not in volume but in focus. It narrowed to a single, piercing clarity that vibrated behind her eyes.

"Maya," Alex said quietly. "Your pupils just did something very creepy."

His voice came from far away.

The stone under her and the cold air on her skin were still there, but they were suddenly less important than the tone that had just locked into place inside her ribs. It felt like slipping a key into a lock that had always been in her, only no one had turned it before.

Her fingers tightened on the edges of the Codex.

The ink on the page brightened, metallic flecks catching light that did not belong to any candle. The letters that formed the word lattice seemed to breathe.

The room faded.

Not all at once. First the lines of mortar between the mausoleum stones blurred, as if someone had taken an eraser to their edges. Then the texture of the slab beneath her knees softened into suggestion. The smell of melted wax and damp granite thinned.

The hum did not come from her chest anymore. It came from everywhere.

She inhaled.

When she opened her eyes, the mausoleum was gone.

She stood in the center of a sphere that had no floor and no ceiling, only distance in every direction. It was not empty. It was filled with light.

Threads stretched away from her in all directions, like lines on a star chart. Some were as thin as spider silk, some as thick as ship ropes, but all of them shone. They crossed and knotted and diverged, forming an endless lattice that curved back on itself so far away she could not see where it began or ended.

Each thread hummed in its own pitch.

Some sang a high, clear tone. Others thrummed low and slow. There were chords where many lines crossed, places where sound and light tangled and became something larger than either.

The entire web made one vast harmony. No melody she could pick out, but a sense of rightness that vibrated through her bones.

She turned slowly, or thought she did. It was hard to tell if her body was moving or if her viewpoint simply rotated through the threads.

The lattice beneath thought, she realized. Exactly as the fragment had said. This was what the Guardians had felt when they talked about the Weave. Not vague currents in the air or pulses under ground. This immense, interconnected choir.

On one line far above her, she sensed a bright steadiness she recognized. The presence she had brushed from Gallows Hill. Ethan, or whatever remained of him. Another thread glowed in frantic flashes, the chaotic presence she had felt. Others shone less brightly, but they were there, scattered through the structure. Human minds whose will had learned to lean on the lattice instead of just being carried by it.

Her own thread ran through her. She could feel it as surely as she could feel her heartbeat. It was not vertical or horizontal. It cut diagonally through the web, touching node after node, connecting places that had no business being close.

She watched it pulse.

Each time she drew breath, the line brightened a fraction. Each time her heart contracted, the vibration along that thread intensified. Her jumps had burned a pattern into it, a series of stressed points where she had bent space and insisted it obey.

Smallness welled up in her throat. She was one glowing filament in a structure that might as well have been infinite. Her problems, her fear, her guilt over one burned girl and one haunted city felt tiny against this scale.

The feeling lasted only a moment.

Then she saw what lived between the threads.

At first she thought it was just ordinary space. The gaps were dark compared to the light, so her mind labeled them empty and tried to move on.

Then one of the crossings dimmed, just slightly. The threads there did not go out. They fuzzed.

She peered at the gap between them.

It was not black. It was not void.

It was static.

A faint shimmer crawled through the spaces where no light should have moved. Not like dust motes in a sunbeam, but like television snow seen out of the corner of an eye. Pixels of almost nothing, flickering in and out too fast to track, gathering strongest where threads had obvious strain.

Where the lattice was perfect, the gaps between threads were quiet. Where a line had been pulled too hard, the static thickened.

Residuum of Will, she realized. The remainder. The Silence that waits.

She watched it pool.

Near one crossing point, several threads bent a little too close to-gether, angles tightened past comfort. The light trembled. In the space between them, the static brightened, like mold in the corner of a room that had been damp too long.

Her stomach turned.

She let her awareness follow her own thread again.

There, a jump from Salem harbor to Ipswich. The bright streak of action still clung to the line. At the point where she had forced the bend, the thread had a tiny notch, a kink that had not fully smoothed.

In the microscopic gap that kink created, a fine mist of static seethed. Nothing like the thick pools she saw at older scars in the lat-tice, but present.

Another kink, farther along. The warehouse escape. The passenger jump with Alex. That bend was deeper and more abrupt. The static there was brighter.

She saw the echo of her jumps as visible distortions in the lattice, a signature pattern of strain that belonged uniquely to her way of mov-ing through the Weave.

Every teleport she had ever made was marked.

Every one of those marks left a place for the residue to gather.

She thought of the mausoleum, of the way the Unmaking had rid-den the lane she tried to escape through, learning the shape of her route. Here, in this view, that event was unmistakable. Where the cor-ridor had opened and stalled, the static in the surrounding gaps had surged, filling in like water rushing into a trench.

Her throat tightened.

The Unmaking was not separate from this vision. It was part of it. The static lived in the same space as the threads, not intruding from outside, but growing wherever the lattice had been pulled, torn or held wrong for too long.

She looked around again, more carefully this time.

The entire structure glowed, beautiful and terrifying. In some re-gions the static was almost absent. Clean chords, steady light. In others, shadows of noise crawled in every gap, a mist of potential un-making.

Every act of creation left residue. Every spell, every miracle, every time someone like her insisted on rearranging the lattice for their own survival. The Talisman under the water was one place where all of that had been recorded on purpose.

She lifted a hand, or the idea of a hand, and set it against her own glowing thread.

The lattice vibrated. The static along her line hissed in answer, a faint, high noise she felt more than heard.

"If I keep doing this the same way," she said, the words somehow both thought and sound, "I am just making more places for you to gather."

The lattice did not answer.

The static did.

It brightened, infinitesimally, in every gap where her thread had bent.

Clarity cut through her like cold water.

Her jumps were not just a way of cheating distance. They were stress points in the pattern. The Unmaking was not chasing her because it hated her or even because it preferred her. It was chasing her because her route had become a series of perfectly aligned, perfectly repeated weak spots.

She could keep running that way. Tear after tear, kink after kink, until the static found enough purchase to turn one of those gaps into something like the void she had seen in the mausoleum.

Or she could learn to move differently.

Not as a knife through fabric, ripping and letting the fibers snap back as best they could.

As a needle. Something that threaded through existing paths, strengthening them, closing gaps instead of widening them.

She felt, suddenly, what Beagron must have meant by stabilizing. What Merlin had warned about enduring rather than wielding.

If she could bend in such a way that the threads learned to carry the tension evenly, the static would have less darkness to pool in. The Talisman had done that once. It had listened. It had drawn the ash-note into itself so the rest of the lattice could breathe.

The idea that she might have to do something similar lodged in her chest like a stone.

You cannot unmake the residue, she thought. But you can decide how much space you give it.

The sense of scale pressed on her, the weight of a network that touched every life on the planet. She was one glowing filament. One human. That should have crushed her.

Instead, the thought settled into a strange, steady place.

Smallness shifted to something else. Not importance, exactly. Relevance.

The lattice did not need her. The Song that built the world had been playing before she was born and would keep playing after she was gone. But her thread was part of it. Her choices mattered along its length.

She took her metaphorical hand off the line.

The threads shone. The static hissed. Somewhere far off, a bright knot pulsed in a slow, powerful rhythm that felt like an old friend she had never met. Ethan. The others.

She felt herself breathe.

The sphere of light dimmed a fraction. The sense of infinite distance folded in on itself, threads drawing back until they were once more a hum under her skin rather than a universe around her.

Stone returned under her knees.

Wax smoke curled into her nose.

The Codex lay open in front of her. Alex knelt just beyond it, eyes wide, one hand half lifted as if he had been afraid to touch her.

"Maya," he said softly. "You were gone. Sitting right here and totally gone."

She let out a breath she did not remember holding.

"The lattice," she said, voice hoarse. "I saw it. All of it. And the static between."

He swallowed. "And."

Her hand went to her notebook without thinking. She wrote, the pen scratching louder than it should have in the quiet.

Every teleport bends the lattice.
Each bend leaves a tear.
The Unmaking is following those tears.

She met his eyes.

"I cannot stop the residue from existing," she said. "But I can stop giving it such a neat trail to follow."

The hum in her chest settled, clear and low.

For the first time since the warehouse, her fear of the Unmaking did not feel like running from a monster.

It felt like listening to a flaw in a song and beginning to learn how to sing around it.

The Codex lay open where she had set it, pages still faintly damp, runes vibrating as if pleased that she had finally seen what they had been trying to tell her. The afterimage of the lattice still ghosted behind her eyelids, fading in slow waves. She rubbed her forehead and felt the echo of each thread like thin strings humming under her skin.

Alex sat across from her, waiting. He did not push. He rarely did when the magic was this close to the surface.

Maya looked down at the notebook again. Her own handwriting stared back.

Every teleport bends the lattice.
Each bend leaves a tear.
The Unmaking follows those tears.

She tapped the last line with the end of the pen. At first it felt like a confession of guilt, the written proof that she had been making everything worse. Yet when she closed her eyes, the memory of the lattice returned in sharper detail. She replayed the way the threads had strained and the way the static had crept in. She replayed, too, the way each stressed point had responded when she placed her hand against her own glowing line.

Not with collapse.

With tension redistributing.

With readiness to be guided.

She let out a slow breath.

"What is it?" Alex asked softly.

She shook her head, but not in dismissal. She was sorting through new logic, new instinct. "The tears only exist because the lattice tries to correct itself. The tension gets uneven. That is where the static gathers."

Alex frowned. "That sounds bad."

"It is bad," she said, then hesitated. "But it also means something. The lattice wants to return to balance. It wants to heal." She looked up at him. "It is not static by nature. The residue only appears where the Weave is already weakened."

He watched her carefully. "And what does that mean for you?"

"It means I have been pulling the threads wrong." Her voice steadied. "All this time, I have been jumping like someone tearing cloth. Fast. Desperate. With no regard for the grain."

She touched the Codex. The parchment warmed beneath her fingertips as if agreeing.

"But the lattice showed me something else," she continued. "If I jump along the existing lines instead of across them, if I match the pitch of the threads instead of forcing them to bend, then the strain redistributes. The tears begin to close."

Alex blinked. "Close. As in heal."

"Yes," she whispered. The word carried relief she had not allowed herself to feel in days. "Teleportation is not just damage. It is pressure. And pressure can be control if you know where to apply it."

The insight solidified inside her like a knot tightening in silk. Her so-called flaws, the strain she left in her wake, the Echo that stalked her reflection, all of it formed a map of the weak points. Places she could reach. Places she could fix.

She had never seen herself as anything but the source of the cracks.

For the first time, she saw herself as someone who could mend them.

Alex let out a slow breath. "That sounds like a lot for one person."

"It is," Maya said. "But the lattice is already moving with me. I felt it. It knows my thread. It has room to adjust." She touched her sternum. The hum responded, steady and clear. "And I can use that. The same flaw the residue is chasing can become the tool that stops it."

Alex leaned his head back against the stone wall, eyes closing. "You sound confident."

Maya considered that. Not bravado. Not detachment. Something more grounded.

"I sound like someone who finally understands the shape of the problem," she said. "And the shape of me."

Her guilt softened. Not gone but transformed into a weight she could lift instead of one that crushed her. The realization settled into her bones with surprising gentleness.

She was no longer the girl who tore holes in the pattern.

She was someone who could stitch it back together.

She closed the Codex and held it in both hands. The runes dimmed as if resting.

"The residue follows damage," she said quietly. "So I will make less of it. And where it already exists, I will learn how to close the tears."

Alex opened his eyes and looked at her. "So what does that make you?"

Maya glanced toward the darkening doorway of the mausoleum, as if she could still see the lattice glowing behind her.

"Necessary," she said.

And for the first time, she believed it.

They began at twilight, when the city softened and the hum of the Weave rose just enough to be heard beneath the surface noise of

Salem. Alex stood by the mausoleum gate with his notebook and a borrowed pen, the same posture he used when tracking her experiments in the apartment, though now his shoulders carried a different weight. This was no longer curiosity. It was a quiet, persistent fear wrapped inside steady devotion.

Maya looked over the hand-drawn map she had unfolded across a grave marker. Five nodes circled in ink. Five points where the ley lines braided tightly enough to make the air feel thick.

"Gallows Hill first," she said.

Alex nodded. "I will stay here and keep a log. Call if something feels off."

She gave a single breath of acknowledgment, then closed her eyes. The lines under her feet brightened in her mind, the way they had in the lattice vision. No tearing. No forcing. Just threads waiting to be followed.

She stepped forward and let the line take her.

The world shifted gently, not with the snap of brute teleportation but with a slow folding, as if she were moving along a silk ribbon already stretched between two points. The pressure in her ears was mild. Her breath remained even. When she opened her eyes, the top of Gallows Hill stretched before her, the grass frost-bitten, the air rich with the same low harmony she had felt during her meditation days earlier.

She stood very still, listening.

The hum rose beneath her ribs, matching the pitch she remembered. She did not need to reach for it. It stepped into her instead, filling her chest the way a violin resonates when touched by the right note. Her smile came without permission, small but real. It surprised her with how easy it felt.

She marked a stone with her boot to ground herself, then let the next thread pull her toward the Harbor Knot.

The second jump came smoother than the first. The line under the hill funneled her toward the sea as if guiding a bead along a wire. When she landed on the wooden edge of the harbor boardwalk, the fog curled between her feet like recognition. The hum changed too, brighter and sharper, carrying the taste of salt and iron. She inhaled and felt it brighten her entire body.

Her recovery took only a few seconds. No dizziness. No ache. No tearing sensation in the world around her.

Alex's voice crackled faintly through the static of her phone. "Second node?"

"Harbor Knot," she answered. "Stronger than before."

"Logging it."

She slipped the phone into her pocket and touched the railing. It warmed under her hand. The thread to the Old Burying Point waited at the edge of her senses, buzzing like a plucked cello string.

She followed.

This jump was more complex. The lines here were older, more tangled, shaped by centuries of grief and ceremony. When she appeared beside the Puritan tombs, the scent of earth and cold stone filled her lungs. The wind brushed through her hair with the gentleness of a passing whisper.

Her knees bent slightly as she steadied herself. Not from weakness, but from reverence. The pitch under the Burying Point was deep and resonant, almost like a human voice sustained across time. She whispered a thank-you to no one and everyone.

Back at the mausoleum, Alex scribbled notes as she spoke through the phone. His voice trembled between awe and worry.

"You sound different," he said.

"Different how?"

"Peaceful."

She let the word settle in her chest. Peaceful. She could not remember the last time that had been true.

"Next node," she said.

"Be careful."

She followed the thread north, letting the lattice pull her toward the Naumkeag Stone Ridge. The moment she stepped onto the rocky plateau, the world rang like struck crystal. The hum rose so clearly she could almost sing it. Old stone. Older memory. Untouched by the trials. Untouched by the modern city. A place where the Weave felt awake.

She stood there for a long moment, letting it wrap around her. Alex's voice reached faintly through the phone.

"Maya. Report."

She exhaled slowly. "I did not want to interrupt the music." She immediately blushed at how that sounded. "Sorry. It is good here."

A pause. "I believe you."

The final thread carried her away from the ridge and into darkness. The abandoned rail tunnel near Castle Hill waited like a sleeping lung. As she arrived inside it, the hum shifted again. Hollow. Metallic. But steady. The lines gathered here like breath drawn in and held.

Her flashlight cast a thin beam over rusted rails. She walked a few steps, feeling the tension of the thread settle into her calves. This node was raw. Fragile. A place where the lattice needed help.

"I can fix this," she whispered.

"You already are," Alex said softly through the phone.

He could not see her, but she nodded anyway. The idea of stitching the lattice here felt not only possible but right. She placed one hand against the tunnel wall and let her tone rise to meet the Weave. It responded. It strengthened.

She teleported back to the mausoleum with slow care, following the same ribbon-line she had taken out. The arrival was gentle, like lowering herself into her own skin. Alex looked up from the notebook, eyes wide.

"No nosebleed," he said.

"No pain," she added.

They stood facing each other, both breathing lightly, both aware that something had changed. Not in the Weave alone. In her.

Threadwalking had given her something she had never had before.

Mastery without violence.

Movement without damage.

Power without fear.

She rolled her shoulders, feeling warmth settle through her limbs. "I want to run the route again," she said. "Faster. Smoother. Until the lattice feels like second nature."

Alex hesitated, but only for a moment. He closed the notebook and stepped closer.

"Then I will keep watch," he said.

Her smile came again. Larger this time.

"Let's begin."

Maya felt it on the sixth circuit.

Up to that point, the night had been kind. The Weave carried her from node to node with the smoothness of a practiced melody. Gallows Hill to the Harbor Knot. Harbor Knot to the Old Burying Point. Burying Point to Naumkeag Ridge. Ridge to the old rail tunnel. Back to the mausoleum. Each jump sat clean in her body. Fatigue gathered in her muscles, but it was the honest kind, like walking a long trail, not the hollowed out collapse she remembered from the warehouse and the kettle.

She stood once more on Gallows Hill, breath puffing in the cold. The sky had thinned to a field of stars. The city lay below like a necklace of lights wrapped around dark water. Her bones rang with the hill's low note, steady and solemn.

"Sixth run," Alex said in her ear through the phone. "Everything seems normal. You still with me?"

"Still with you," she answered.

She closed her eyes and reached for the line that ran from Gallows Hill down toward the Harbor Knot. The thread lit up in her mind, a silver band that had become familiar. She let her weight tilt toward it, the way she had learned. No forcing. No tearing. Just stepping onto a current that already knew where to go.

Then something breathed under the ground.

It was not the soft inhalation of the hill's own hum. It was deeper, slower, like bedrock pulling air through stone lungs. The sound did not pass through her ears. It moved through her bones.

She froze mid step. The line to the harbor remained bright. The hill's note continued to vibrate under her feet. Under both, far below, a second pulse rose and fell once, very slow.

"Maya?" Alex's voice sharpened. "What is it?"

She opened her eyes. The grass looked the same. The informational plaque nearby caught moonlight on its bronze face. Salem slept in its ring of lights below. Nothing had changed. Only her.

"I felt something," she said. Her voice sounded thin to her own ears. "Under everything. It felt like a breath."

"From what?"

She listened again, reaching downward without jumping. The Weave answered in the familiar way, threads singing along the paths she knew. The deeper pulse did not repeat. It sat quiet, like a giant that had turned over once in its sleep.

"Not the city," she said slowly. "Not the Talisman either. Bigger than both. It came from the same direction as the cavern, just deeper."

Alex was silent for a moment. "Do you want to stop for tonight?"

She considered it. The sensible answer waited on the tip of her tongue.

"No," she said instead. "If it is waking up because I am moving, I need to know how much."

She heard the breath he took, the quiet acceptance wrapped in worry.

"All right," he said. "Logging that. Sixth run, anomaly noted. Proceed with caution."

She almost laughed. Proceed with caution sounded ridiculous in the face of whatever lay beneath Salem, but it steadied her. It meant they still had rules.

She stepped onto the line and let it carry her to the harbor.

The transition felt normal at first. Space folded with familiar softness. Her stomach did the small flip she had learned to expect. The smell of salt and diesel rolled in. She appeared on the damp boards of the Harbor Knot, exactly where she intended.

Then the light changed.

The streetlamp above her flickered, once, twice. That happened sometimes in old fixtures, but this flicker was wrong. The air around the pole glowed for a second with a thin, sickly blue, the same color as the undercity veins she had seen in the Deep. The color clung like bruise light, then vanished.

Maya's breath caught.

Her hum did not falter, but it felt as if some of its sound was being eaten. The harbor's bright, briny note came through thinner, like a trumpet muted with cloth.

"Maya." Alex again. "Status."

"Harbor Knot looks normal," she said. "Except the light just bled blue. The Weave here feels pinched."

"Pinched how?"

"Like something is pressing on it from below."

She knelt and touched the board with her fingers. The thread under the harbor still flowed, but it wavered. A faint tremor ran through it, not enough to break, just enough to make her teeth buzz.

The image of the lattice vision rose in her mind. Glowing threads. Static pooling in the gaps. The deep breath she had felt on Gallows Hill suddenly had a shape.

The nexus is moving, she thought. It is stirring in its sleep.

She stood, forcing her shoulders to relax, and reached for the line to the Old Burying Point. The corridor of the Weave flickered in front of her inner eye, then steadied. She let it pull her again.

The graveyard met her with its usual solemn quiet. Old stone. Cold air. The hum beneath the Burying Point came up strong and human, a chorus of remembered lives. It soothed her immediately.

She almost believed she had imagined the disturbance, until the note itself bent.

For one heartbeat, the tone of the node dropped half a step, like a choir voice that cracked. The air around her trembled. The hum recovered a second later, but she had felt it slip.

She pressed a hand to her sternum and to the nearest headstone at the same time. Her own tone answered, steady. The stone's song followed, also steady. The field between them, however, held a echo of that wrong pitch.

She swallowed.

"Node three," she said into the phone. "The Burying Point. Its tune just went out for a breath. Then came back."

"How bad?" Alex asked.

"Not bad. Just wrong. It felt like a missed step."

Silence crackled on the line. She heard him flipping pages in the notebook, the soft rasp of paper.

"That is two anomalies in one circuit," he said. "Maybe we should actually stop now."

"After the ridge," she said. The words came out before she could stop them. "I need to know if it is happening everywhere."

He cursed softly under his breath. She pretended not to hear.

She jumped to Naumkeag Ridge and landed among the rocks. Here the Weave still sang clean, high and cool. The node accepted her without stutter. No flicker. No blue. No bending. For a moment, relief washed through her.

"Ridge is steady," she told Alex.

"So it is not all of them."

"Not yet."

She walked to the edge of the slope and looked down toward Salem. The city glowed, unaware. Somewhere beneath its streets, the cavern and the Talisman lay buried in their bowl of rock and dark water. Beneath even that waited the deeper pulse she had felt.

Her skin prickled.

On her way back to the mausoleum, she took the long way on foot for the final stretch, letting her legs carry some of the burden. The jump from the rail tunnel to the graveyard settled in her bones like a sigh. The air above the cemetery was sharp and cold.

She cut through a path where last night's rain had left a shallow puddle pressed into the dirt. The water caught the moon and her face in one small circle of reflection.

She almost walked past. Habit made her glance down instead.

Her reflection looked back at her. Tired eyes. Wind tangled hair. A faint smear of dirt on her cheek.

Then it lagged.

Her eyes blinked. The reflection's eyes blinked a fraction of a beat later. Her mouth tightened. The reflection's mouth followed, just behind. The delay was small, but it was there. The Echo had followed her into this harmless scrap of water like a loyal shadow.

Maya stood very still, boots sinking a little into the soft ground.

The reflection did not do anything else. No second face. No Isabel behind her. No black thread of absence. Just that tiny, wrong gap between action and image.

She lifted her hand slowly. The water version lifted its hand with that same breath of delay.

"Maya." Alex again, his voice closer now. He must have seen her from the gate. "You are scaring me. Talk to me."

She tore her gaze from the puddle.

"I think I know what is happening," she said.

He jogged the last few steps, notebook under one arm, coat half zipped. "Tell me."

She looked back at the small circle of water and then toward the center of the cemetery, where the ground sat highest above the hidden catacombs.

"The nodes are breathing," she said quietly. "Something under Salem is waking up. When I walk the threads, it notices. When I move, it stirs."

"You mean the Talisman?"

She shook her head.

"No. The Talisman listens. This feels like something that answers. The nexus Merlin wrote about. The place where every line knots together. It is waking because I am pulling on its web."

The words settled in the cold air between them. Alex's jaw clenched.

"Then maybe," he said, "we have done enough calling for one night."

For once, she did not argue.

She stepped away from the puddle. Her reflection broke into ripples and vanished. The hum under the cemetery remained steady but deeper now, as if a giant heart had shifted a fraction in its sleep.

As they walked back toward the mausoleum, Maya felt the lattice beneath Salem breathe one more time. Slow. Heavy. A patient inhale.

It already knew her pattern.

Now it knew her path.

13

HECATE's Net Tightens

The cemetery was no longer quiet.

Long before sunrise, Maya felt the disturbance in the air. The hum that usually coiled through the gravestones had a stutter in it, like someone dragging a fork across a violin string. When she stepped outside the mausoleum, cold morning fog clung to the ground in thin sheets. At first she thought it was natural mist.

Then she heard the mechanical whir.

A drone drifted between headstones, its red sensors sweeping back and forth across the cemetery in a slow grid. Another drifted above the willow tree near the fence line, following a lazy circular pattern, as if smelling for something. Maya pulled back into the shadows and held her breath.

Alex joined her silently at her side. He pointed to the north fence where two men in dark tactical gear moved along the perimeter. Their jackets carried a symbol she now recognized: the broken circle of HECATE.

Alex whispered, "They are not here for random patrols. They are methodical."

The Weave confirmed it. The hum had a sharp, metallic edge she associated with modern interference tech. HECATE had brought devices that rattled the local lines but could not break them outright. She felt their pulses like small, irritating shocks against her ribs.

A second drone dipped lower. Its light washed over a row of granite markers. The beam flickered as it passed near where she stood, the flicker running through the ground like a crack of static. Maya pulled back and put a hand over her own mouth to quiet her breathing.

"They know the cemetery was a safe zone," Alex murmured. "They must have tracked the signature from the warehouse."

Maya whispered, "They cannot track Weave movement. They should not be able to."

Alex gave her that quiet, uneasy look he had started showing more often. "They are learning."

A distant shout carried across the grounds. "Open the secondary grid. Pattern Interdiction Team One, move to the northern quadrant."

Pattern Interdiction. Maya felt the term like a bruise under the skin. She had seen plans for that program once, buried in the same files that labeled her a possible energy weapon rather than a person.

A sudden pulse went through the earth like a ripple. She nearly staggered at the sensation. One of the interdiction devices had activated. It projected a cone of high-frequency disruption that made her connection to the Weave feel scratchy and distorted, like trying to listen to music through a wall of static.

"They are closing circles," Alex said. He pulled her down behind an overturned stone slab where roots had lifted it years ago. "If we stay here, they will box us in."

She peeked over the stone. The second unit had fanned out, cutting off the back path to the residential streets. The only direction open was deeper into the cemetery where the old crypts stood like silent sentinels.

A drone swept close again. Maya pressed her shoulder to Alex's. "How many teams did Hargreaves send?"

"Three at minimum. Maybe four. Enough to surround the entire block."

She felt the hum stumble again. Another interdiction pulse rolled across the ground. It made her bones vibrate. She clenched her jaw as her teeth chattered involuntarily.

Alex touched her wrist. "You are shaking."

"I do not like when the Weave gets torn like that," she whispered. "It feels like someone scraping the inside of my skull."

Across the cemetery, a third drone dropped into a lower altitude, its light bright and unwavering. It passed over a statue of an angel, then the statue crackled with a faint spark. The machine was reading energy that should not exist. Maya knew what would happen next.

She grabbed Alex's sleeve. "It is too close. We have to move."

They sprinted between headstones, keeping low, weaving through narrow rows. Twice a drone passed overhead. Maya felt each sweep like a flare in her senses, a slicing arc of technology brushing against the threads she lived inside.

Behind them, a voice shouted, "Team Two, I have a reading. Something jumped frequencies. Move to grid C."

Maya felt her pulse climb. Her throat tightened. "They are tracking resonance shifts. Not jumps. Just the way the Weave rings when we move too fast."

Alex kept his voice low. "You need to slow your breathing. You are vibrating the air."

"I cannot help it. Everything feels wrong."

They ducked behind a stone mausoleum as another interdiction pulse rolled toward them. Maya braced for the sting.

This pulse was stronger.

She gasped as the hum collapsed entirely for a second. The Weave reconnected a moment later, but the disconnection left her dizzy.

Alex steadied her with both hands. "Hey. Stay with me. It is alright. I have you."

She felt her pulse stutter back into rhythm. Alex's emotional field pressed around her like a warm blanket, steady and grounding. It was instinctual, not something he fully understood yet. It calmed her enough to keep moving.

Another shout: "We have footprints. Someone is here. Spread out."

Maya looked at Alex, eyes wide. "They are too close. If we jump, they will see the distortion."

"Then we need to get out of view first."

They moved again, slipping into the narrow path between two crumbling crypts. The air grew colder there. The hum steadied. They were momentarily outside the interdiction range.

But not for long.

Maya felt the drones turning. She sensed them adjusting their search pattern. They were tightening the loop.

"They are closing in," she whispered.

Alex nodded. "Then we need to close out."

He took her hand. She felt the resonance lock click between them, warm and subtle.

The searchlights swept the gravel ahead of them. Boots crunched on fallen leaves behind them.

Time ran short.

Maya drew in a breath.

This was no longer about escape.

This was about survival.

They huddled inside the shallow alcove beside the old crypt. The stone pressed cold against Maya's back. She listened for drones and footsteps, her senses stretched thin. For a moment the search pattern drifted wider, giving them a sliver of breathing room.

Alex reached into his coat and pulled out something wrapped in a torn piece of thermal blanket. He hesitated, then held it out to her.

"I took this while they passed the south gate," he whispered. "I was not sure when to show you."

Maya unwrapped the blanket. A government-issue HECATE tablet lay inside. Its screen flickered with a faint blue glow, half drained from whatever encrypted software it was running.

Her pulse stuttered. "Alex. This is tracked tech."

"It is in airplane mode. I killed the beacon before it pinged anything. Just look. You need to see what they are working with."

Maya tapped the screen. At first it displayed nothing except the HECATE logo and a loading bar. Then the home menu appeared. A folder sat centered on the screen as if daring her to open it.

WW CLASSIFICATION: LEVEL 1 TO LEVEL 3

The sight of it made her skin crawl.

"Walker-World?" she whispered, trying to guess the acronym.

Alex shook his head. "Walker. As in Weave Walker."

Her stomach dropped. "They already named us."

"Keep going," Alex said softly.

Maya opened the folder. Three profiles appeared in a clean vertical list, each marked with color-coded alerts. Beneath them, her own file sat highlighted in red.

Subject 01: Minneapolis Resonance Signature

Level 2: Cautious Containment

Notes: Subject displays high-stability fluctuation. Energy field self-regulates. Threat potential uncertain.

A blurry satellite image pulsed beside the text. The silhouette caught her breath. She did not know his name yet, but she recognized the hum from Gallows Hill: the calm presence like a lighthouse. Ethan.

She scrolled.

Subject 02: Miami Spire Incident

Level 1: Unstable. High-risk.

Notes: Erratic spikes. Possible burnout cycle pending. Track via thermal anomalies and eyewitness reports of "air shiver events."

A map of Miami flashed red with overlapping triangles, like a heartbeat out of rhythm. The chaotic presence she had sensed. Someone scared. Someone alone.

She scrolled again.

Subject 03: Colorado High Ridge

Level 2: Low activity. Subharmonic signature suggests deep grounding.

Unknown age.

Notes: Might be dormant. May predate modern Weave events.

This one contained no image, only a topographic map of mountains. The steady, ancient hum she had felt from afar. Someone older than her by decades. Maybe longer.

Maya felt the Weave in her chest tighten like a fist. "They mapped them. They mapped all three."

Alex nodded. "And they tried to map you."

She scrolled to the final file. Her name filled the header in bold letters:

Subject 04: Maya Rodriguez

Classification: Level 3

Designation: Walker-Class Threat

Her photograph stared back at her. A DMV picture. A clipped, sterile summary followed:

"Display of telekinetic resonance, short-range displacement, and potential long-range traversal. Interacts with field fluctuations in measurable patterns. Must be contained. Do not engage alone. High-liability asset. Potential weaponization pending."

Maya felt heat rise in her throat. Her hands shook. The Weave inside her vibrated in a dangerous pitch.

"Walker-Class Threat," she said, almost choking on the words. "They do not even know what we can do. They just want to cage us before they find out."

Alex watched her with alarm as the stone floor under her boots trembled lightly. "Maya. Slow down. You are ringing the lines."

"I am tired of running. I am tired of hiding." Her voice cracked. "They think they can take people like us and list us like inventory."

She swiped through the rest of her file. Surveillance stills. Heat signatures. A grainy image of the warehouse wall she broke when escaping Hargreaves' lab. A chart estimating her "energy expenditure ranges." A note from the senator himself:

"**Confirmed. Subject is active. Expect escalation. Prepare containment protocols.**"

Maya exhaled a shaking breath. "I am not a protocol. I am not a specimen."

The Weave answered her pulse as if ready to surge.

Alex placed a hand on hers. His touch grounded her. His presence softened the vibration inside her like dampening foam around a shaking wire. The lines steadied.

"I need you clearheaded," he whispered. "Not furious."

"They have files on the others," she said. "People who probably have no idea what they are. They are hunting us like animals."

Alex nodded slowly. "Then we need to reach them before Hargreaves does."

She stared at him. "Reach them how? I have no idea where they are beyond vague coordinates."

"The Weave knows. You sensed all three without even trying."

She swallowed hard. "What if finding them puts them in danger?"

"What if not finding them leaves them alone when HECATE arrives?"

The drones buzzed again, closer this time. Flashlights swept the gravel between headstones. A dog barked on the far side of the fence.

Maya closed the tablet. She wrapped it again in the thermal blanket and tucked it into her coat.

Her fury no longer burned outward. It crystallized, cold and sharp, into purpose.

"We are going to shut Hargreaves out of the Weave," she said. "And we are going to find the others. No more running."

Alex's eyes flickered with something new. Not fear, not awe. Something like acceptance. As if he already knew his place in this plan.

As the next drone passed overhead, Maya reached for Alex's hand again.

Their combined resonance hummed once, steady and clear. Stronger than the static tearing through the cemetery.

A sudden vibration runs through the tablet. A hidden subfolder unlocks itself:

"SUBJECT 05: Alex Caldwell — Pending Classification."

His resonance has been detected.

And Hargreaves is already watching.

The gravel outside the mausoleum shifted under heavy boots. Maya felt the pressure ripple through the Weave like a warning pulse. The search teams were close. Too close. Even the faintest breath risked giving them away.

Alex crouched beside her, pupils wide in the dim light. Sweat clung to his brow. His breath trembled, but he stayed near her shoulder, ready to move.

Through the cracked stone doorway, Maya saw HECATE agents sweep thermal scanners across the cemetery rows. A drone dipped low, its spotlight slicing through tombstones like a blade.

"We have to go," she whispered.

Alex nodded, jaw tight.

Maya grabbed his wrist. She reached for the Weave, searching for the hum beneath the ground, but the pressure outside, the fear inside, and the static left behind from the Deep all tangled with her pulse. The field felt slippery. Sluggish. Harder to grab.

Another beam of light cut across the entrance.

Maya inhaled sharply. "Hold on."

She tried again. She closed her eyes and summoned the Salem node beneath the hill. Usually the energy rose to meet her like a tide, but tonight it stuttered. The hum flickered in and out, as if someone had put a hand on the line to dim the current.

She pushed harder.

The air tightened. Her chest burned.

Alex squeezed her hand. "Maya, stop. You are hurting yourself."

"We do not have another way out."

One of the agents spoke into a radio outside. "Movement on the thermal. Fifteen meters. Prepare breach."

Maya tried to center her breath. Her hands shook. The hum wavered again. A jolt of fear shot through her like cold lightning.

And then Alex moved closer.

He touched her other hand, the one braced against the stone floor. His palm rested lightly over hers, not pushing, not pulling. Just anchoring.

"Maya," he said softly. "Look at me."

She lifted her eyes.

For a moment the fear in Alex's face sharpened into something else: focus. Clear, steady, resolute. As if he were listening to something she could not hear.

He closed his eyes and inhaled.

And the Weave shifted.

She felt it. A vibration. A tone tightening in the air between their hands. At first she thought she had finally locked onto the node beneath the cemetery. But the pitch was wrong. It did not rise from the ground.

It rose from Alex.

Her breath caught. The vibration settled into a perfect counterpoint to her own resonance. When she pushed forward, his pulse steadied. When her tone faltered, his filled the gap. When she reached for the Weave, he grounded the touch.

It was as if he were holding the field open for her.

A stabilizing harmonic.

A Listener's gift.

Her vision sharpened. The cemetery nodes came into focus. The hum aligned. The current rose like a breath drawn through both of them. The static that had been disrupting her earlier vanished under the steady pressure of his presence.

The jump flickered into readiness.

"Maya," Alex whispered, voice shaking. "I think I just heard something. Or felt something. I cannot explain it."

She stared at him, stunned. Her pulse hammered in her ears. "Alex. You heard the field. You heard me."

Outside, a boot scuffed against gravel. A hand touched the mausoleum gate.

Alex's eyes widened. "Whatever this is, do it now."

Maya focused on the node beneath the harbor. Alex kept his hand over hers. His resonance tightened again, the stabilizing tone rising and meeting her own. Their combined pitch formed a corridor in the Weave that she had never been able to open so cleanly before.

No effort. No strain. The field flowed toward them in a smooth arc.

A Listener-Class Walker.

His resonance fit hers like a lock meeting its key.

Light flickered at the edges of the room. The candles bent sideways as the corridor formed.

She whispered, "Alex. You are attuned."

His breath left him in a broken exhale. "I felt you reaching. I just tried to keep you from slipping."

"You did more than that." She tightened her grip. "You matched me."

The door handle rattled. Maya pulled the corridor fully open. The air snapped like a sheet caught in wind. Alex looked terrified, but not of the jump.

Terrified of what he had just become.

She held his gaze. "We do this together."

He nodded once.

The corridor brightened.

And when the door burst inward, they vanished in one clean, unified pulse of light.

The world snapped back into place with a hard jolt, and the two of them tumbled out of the broken arc of the jump into a patch of woods north of Salem. Moonlight spilled through bare branches, silvering the frost that clung to the fallen leaves. Maya hit the ground on her knees, palms sinking into cold dirt and damp foliage. Her breath tore in and out in ragged bursts. Every nerve in her body felt electrified, a thin sting running up her spine and into the base of her skull.

The Weave around them still vibrated with leftover distortion. The Static had not followed them fully, but it lingered like the fading echo of a scream.

Alex dropped beside her. He landed harder than he meant to, boots digging into the mulch. He looked shaken but unhurt, breathing fast, eyes wide with confusion and something like instinctive terror.

"Maya. Talk to me. Are you here?" His hands hovered over her shoulders, afraid to touch, afraid not to.

She tried to answer, but the words would not come. Her nerves were still buzzing, a loose electrical hum running through her chest where her sigil burned faintly under her shirt. The jump had torn open too much, the way it always did when the Static was close. It had slipped one cold finger into the arc as she folded space. She could still feel the residue trying to cling to her pattern.

Her fingers curled harder into the leaves, as if gripping the earth would help pull her back together.

"Stop," Alex said suddenly. "Here. Give me your hands."

She did not think. She simply obeyed. Her hands rose, trembling, and he caught them gently. His palms were warm, too warm, as if he had been standing near a fire.

The moment their skin touched, something shifted.

A pulse moved from him into her. It was not magic in the bright, sharp way she felt her own resonance. It was warmer, steadier, a low vibration that rolled through her like the slow exhale of a deep breath. Her chest loosened. The sting in her nerves softened. The static tremor along the edges of the Weave faded, like dust settling in sunlight.

Her breathing steadied. Her vision cleared. The cold grip of the Unmaking slipped back into the dark.

"Alex." Her voice came out hoarse. "What did you just do."

"I don't know." He swallowed, still holding her hands. "I saw you shaking. I saw that look in your eyes. I thought you were slipping again, so I just... focused."

"Focused on what?"

"You." He looked startled by his own answer. "I don't know how else to say it."

Maya closed her eyes and listened to the Weave. The hum around her, which had been jagged and unstable, was now smooth. She could feel Alex's presence in the resonance. It was not like hers. Hers cut through the field like a bright line. His covered it like a warm blanket. There was no sharpness, only grounding.

She whispered, "Alex. Your pitch is calming the field."

"That is not a thing," he said, shaking his head. "I'm not doing anything."

"You're doing everything," she said softly.

To test it, she lifted her left hand and shaped the smallest blink she could manage. Just a thread. Just enough to pull a fingertip into a fold in space. As soon as she opened the arc, the Static pricked at its edges, searching for an entrance the way cold water seeks a crack.

But Alex, still gripping her right hand, focused on her with fierce concentration. His brow furrowed. His breath steadied. The warmth in his resonance pulsed outward again. It spread like a soft ripple through the soil, the air, the Weave itself. The static intrusion faltered. The cold prickle vanished. The mini arc stabilized.

Maya gasped. "You are shielding me."

Alex blinked, stunned. "I didn't do anything."

"You did," she said. "Alex... you are blocking interference. You're grounding my signature."

He looked overwhelmed. "I am not a Walker. I am not anything like you."

"Yes, you are." She squeezed his hands. "You heard the field before I did. You steadied the jump back at the facility without knowing how. And now this."

Alex stared down at their joined hands, as if trying to see the current between them. For a moment he looked afraid of himself. Then he shook his head, voice barely a whisper. "I just didn't want you to break."

She felt something in her chest loosen. Not in the Weave. In her. She drew in a slow breath, letting the forest air fill her lungs, letting the tremor in her bones settle.

"Alex," she said, "you're not just attuned. You're a Shield."

The word hung between them, strange and true.

A leaf drifted down from the branch above, twisting in the moonlight. The silence of the woods wrapped around them. Far off, an owl answered something unseen. The Weave hummed at the edges of her senses again, steadier now, calmer. Not because she had healed herself, but because Alex had.

Fear slowly ebbed. Safety took its place, fragile but real.

They stayed there a long moment, hand in hand, both of them breathing as the wind moved through the trees and the world settled back into itself.

Finally Alex asked, voice quiet, "Is this bad for me? Whatever this is?"

Maya looked at him, her heartbeat steady for the first time in hours. "I don't know," she admitted. "But I know one thing."

"What."

"You are the reason I am still myself."

He swallowed and nodded once, accepting that truth even as it frightened him.

The clearing felt brighter. The Weave felt calmer. And Maya realized with a shiver that she was no longer facing the coming storm alone.

Alex was a Shield Walker. And he was her anchor.

They walked until the woods thinned into a narrow service road, little more than a strip of cracked pavement lined with frost-burned grass. Maya could still feel the vibration of HECATE's sweep teams across Salem. It wasn't sound. It was pressure. The field trembled in low, irritated pulses every time one of their Pattern Interdiction rigs fired up. Even out here, she felt the harmonic interference on her skin like the sting of cold static.

Alex paused at the edge of the road and looked toward the faint orange glow on the horizon. Search lights. Drone clusters. A ripple of distant engines. "They're locking down the whole city," he said quietly. "All the roads leading in. All the old districts too."

Maya closed her eyes and let her awareness sink into the ground. Alex's hand steady on her arm made it easier. His pulse was a warm anchor in the resonance, a slow harmonic that helped her push past her own exhaustion and into the current.

The ley-lines snapped into clarity. Not as bright as before. Distorted. Warped. Someone had thrown a net over Salem's natural harmonics, and the lines were straining under the weight.

"Something's wrong," she murmured. "The grid's shaking. HECATE's tech is interfering with the whole field. They're trying to isolate me."

"You? Or Walkers in general?"

She swallowed. "Both."

Alex's grip tightened just slightly. "Then we need to get ahead of them. Can you map a route?"

Maya opened her senses wider. Light bloomed in her mind, little flares where nodes used to glow strong. Now some sputtered. Others flickered out completely. The Harbor Knot was unstable. Gallows Hill was worse, humming like a drum pulled too tight. The Naumkeag ridge still held, but barely.

She shook her head, overwhelmed. "They're choking the lines, Alex. If I jump wrong, I could fall into the Static's path. Or drag you into it."

He stepped in front of her, forcing her to look at him. "Maya. Breathe."

Her lungs obeyed only because his voice reached her before the panic could spiral. His resonance followed a moment later. A warm, steady pressure that settled the Weave around her ribs and let her draw a full breath.

"Better," he said.

She nodded, though guilt rose like a tide. "I shouldn't run. The city's humming wrong because of me. The Talisman. The Current. All of it's moving because I'm moving. If I leave—"

"If you stay, they'll catch you," Alex said. "And then everything gets worse."

She dropped her gaze. "I hate that you might be right."

He lifted her chin gently. "I'm not saying give up. I'm saying regroup. You're not thinking clearly, not with the grid under that much strain. And they're expecting you to stay inside it."

He let go, only to gesture toward the distant line of hills. "What if we jump outside their net. Just far enough to breathe. Naumkeag ridge. You said that node's still stable."

"It's weak," she said.

"But it's accessible?"

She hesitated and then checked again, resting her fingertips on the cold pavement. Alex's presence steadied the field around her. The node's glow wavered in her mind but didn't vanish.

"Yes. I think so."

"Then that's our move," he said. "We go there. We get out of their grid. And we plan our next step when you're not about to collapse."

Maya let out a shaky breath. "It feels like running."

"It's not running," Alex said softly. "It's surviving. It's thinking. And you told me once that jumping is like choosing a line on a map. So choose one that keeps us alive."

She almost laughed, because he sounded more confident than she felt. "Since when are you the strategist?"

"Since you started shaking apart at the edges," he said. "Someone's gotta help you hold the pieces together."

She looked at him for a long moment. His face was pale from the cold, hair standing on end from static, eyes tired but clear. He had no training, no heritage, no magical legacy. And yet he grounded her better than anyone else ever had.

"Alex," she said, "your resonance... it changes mine. I don't know how, but it makes everything quieter. Not weaker. Just clearer."

He shrugged like he didn't know what to do with that. "Then use me. If it helps you see the next move, do it."

She nodded slowly. "Alright. Naumkeag ridge."

"Good," he said. "Tell me what to do."

"Just stay close," she said. "And keep your mind steady. If you panic, the field wobbles."

"Right. No panicking. Very easy for me." He gave her a nervous half-smile. "Do I... need to hold your hand again?"

She hesitated and then held it out. "It helps."

He took it, fingers tightening just enough to remind her he was real. Warm. Solid. Hers to rely on.

Maya lifted her free hand and shaped the arc. The Static pricked at the edges, hungry and familiar, but Alex focused on her instantly. His pulse steadied. His resonance warmed. The field smoothed out like ripples settling on a pond.

The blink circle opened clean.

"Ready?" Maya whispered.

"No," he said honestly, "but go anyway."

She pulled him through.

The woods vanished in a ribbon of pale green light, and the clearing fell silent as the arc snapped shut behind them.

For the first time in hours, the direction was clear. Not safe. Not perfect.

But theirs.

The tunnel swallowed sound.

The old rail line had been carved into the hillside and then abandoned, left to rot under creeping moss and rust. Rails long since torn up, ties half buried in dirt, the place felt like a throat that had forgotten how to speak. Only their lantern said otherwise, a small glass heart hanging from a broken bracket near the entrance, throwing a shaky circle of light against damp stone.

Maya sat on an overturned concrete block a few yards in, knees drawn up, pack at her feet. The cold from the ground seeped through her boots. A faint breeze moved down the tunnel from some unseen opening deeper in, carrying the smell of wet rock and old metal. Aboveground, HECATE's net crawled across Salem. Out here, outside the densest intersections, the Weave drew quieter but clearer.

Alex leaned against the wall opposite her, one heel propped back, arms folded tight across his chest. The lantern's light cut a narrow line along his jaw, his eyes dark and tired.

"You sure this is far enough?" he asked.

Maya closed her eyes for a moment and listened.

The node beneath the tunnel hummed, not as strong as Gallows Hill, but steady. A slow, patient note under the earth. Above and behind it, further toward the city, she felt the interference field ACHE against the lines, a constant low snarl. Here, that snarl was more like distant traffic.

"It's not perfect," she said, "but it's outside their direct grid. And the ridge pulls the lines together just enough to work with."

"Work with how?" he said.

She opened her eyes. "We need to know what we actually are together. Not just you grounding me on instinct. If HECATE is tracking my signature, and the Static is following every tear I make, we have to know what happens when we both lean into the field on purpose."

Alex uncrossed his arms and stepped closer. "So this is rehearsal. For whatever insane thing you're going to try next."

"Preparation," she corrected quietly. "Insane comes later."

He huffed a breath that could have been a laugh if he weren't so exhausted. "Alright. What do you need me to do?"

She patted the block beside her. "Sit."

He did, the concrete scraping under their combined weight. Their shoulders brushed. It was a small contact, but she felt his resonance respond immediately, aware and a little shy, like it knew she could hear it now.

"Give me your hand," she said.

He offered it without comment. His palm was rough and warm, a few calluses from climbing experiments and too many boxes of inventory at the shop. She wrapped her fingers around his and turned her attention inward.

First she found her own pitch. It rose in her chest like a familiar note, clear and focused. The Weave answered it, threads around them vibrating in recognition. Even tired, even frayed, her signature was precise. A blade of sound.

Then she listened for his.

It lived lower, closer to the belly than the throat. Warm, steady, not as bright but surprisingly strong. Where her tone cut, his held. She could feel how it wrapped around the lines of her signal, not smothering, just catching and anchoring them.

"That is you," she said softly. "This steady thing. I felt it in the woods, but out here it is... clearer."

He shifted, uneasy. "Feels like you are talking about my heartbeat."

"In a way I am," she said. "Only not the blood one. The Weave one."

"Okay," he said slowly. "So, how do we test this without breaking you again?"

She smiled a little. "We do not pull. We align."

He made a face. "You really have to stop making that sound like a yoga class."

"Shut up and breathe with me," she said.

He did, falling into her counted rhythm. In on four. Hold on two. Out on six. As their breathing synced, his resonance began to match her tempo without losing its own shape. Her sharp note and his warm one rose and fell together, separate but coordinated.

Maya lifted their joined hands slightly, palm to palm now, as if cupping something invisible between them.

"Listen to this," she whispered.

She nudged her tone a little higher. He kept his where it was. The field around them responded like a chord tuning itself. Threads in the tunnel walls shivered at both pitches, stones vibrating with a faint, unseen shimmer.

Then she did the careful thing. She shifted her note sideways, not up or down, until it sat in a precise interval with his. A fifth, her mind supplied automatically. Old music theory class surfacing from nowhere.

Between the two, something else woke.

A third frequency rose, not from her and not from him, but from the space where their harmonics overlapped. It filled the tunnel like a soft pressure change. The Static at the edges of her awareness tried to prick through, then flattened against it as if it had run into glass.

Alex sucked in a breath. "You feel that?"

"Yeah," she said, eyes wide. "That is us."

The third tone was different from anything she had encountered alone. It was not sharp. It was not warm. It was firm. A channel. A lane drawn clean through the field, narrow but extremely stable. Threads in the Weave bent around that lane instead of fraying at its edges.

She tested it with a thought, flicking a tiny blink-arc open at the far side of the tunnel, just large enough to move a pebble. Static stirred immediately, that familiar hungry hiss reaching for the stress.

Alex's grip tightened around her hand. He focused without asking how, his mind settling like a weight on the same shared note. The third frequency swelled.

The Static hit it and slid off, unable to catch.

Maya let the arc collapse and stared at their hands. "Two Walkers," she said slowly, "can create a stabilized lane. I tear things when I jump alone. We do it together, and the tear seals as we move through it."

"And that means?" he said.

"It means we are harder to corrupt," she said. "Harder to track. Whatever they are using to follow my signature, this will look different. Stronger. More complex. Like trying to trace a double helix instead of a straight line."

He let out a slow breath. "So, we confuse the bad guys and annoy the cosmic mold at the same time."

"That is one way to put it."

He watched her for a moment, eyes searching her face. The lantern flame flickered, sending shadows across the rough stone and his profile.

"Whatever comes next," he said quietly, "you are not facing it alone. I mean it, Maya. I am in this. I am your Shield, right? So let me be that."

The word settled between them like a promise. Shield. Her anchor. Her counter-harmonic.

The defenses she had been holding in her shoulders all night loosened just a little. She shifted closer, until their knees touched, and rested her forehead gently against his.

"Then we move as one," she whispered.

For a few breaths, there was nothing but the shared rhythm. Her sharp tone. His steady one. The third frequency holding them both. The tunnel felt less like a throat and more like a vessel, holding their sound, protecting it.

Somewhere under the ridge, the node answered, its own note aligning with theirs for a heartbeat. The field brightened. Their combined signature arced outward along the lines, not just up into Salem, but down and out, deeper into the undercity.

Maya felt it hit something.

Far below, beneath stone and water and old fire scars, a presence stirred. Not the jagged hunger of the Static, not the cold blank of the Residuum alone. Something older. Something that recognized the pattern of two notes woven into a third.

A pulse came back up the line. Slow. Measured. Like a massive heart considering its next beat.

Maya's eyes flew open.

"Did you feel that?" she breathed.

Alex nodded, jaw tight. "Yeah. Whatever that was, it noticed us."

Their joined hands remained steady, but the third note in the air took on a new weight. Out there, in the lattice beneath the world, someone or something had turned its attention toward their newly forged path.

The dyad had announced itself.

And the Weave was listening.

14

The Talisman Unbound

The descent into the earth ended with a metallic groan as the last of the anchors bit into stone. A narrow, artificially cut shaft yawned open above the ancient cavern. Dust sifted down like pale snow. Then came the first boots, heavy and disciplined, moving in tight formation as HECATE's assault unit climbed out of the shaft and fanned across the cavern floor.

Their harsh white floodlights flicked on at once. Blades of artificial light carved sharp angles into a world shaped by time, water, and the slow breathing of the Weave itself. The cavern did not welcome their presence. Its walls pulsed with pale blue veins, each one a living ley thread that throbbed in quiet, ancient rhythm. The bowl shaped chamber stretched wide around them, the floor dipping down toward the still black pool at its center.

Beneath that mirror-surface, the Talisman glowed like a submerged ember. Dull red, patient, and watching.

The generator came next, lowered on a humming winch. Its metal casing looked painfully modern against the stone. Cables slithered across the slick floor like roots searching for something to latch onto. The hum of the machine pressed at the air in a jarring, unnatural beat that immediately began to collide with the cavern's living resonance.

The Weave did not like it.

A deep vibration rolled along the stone like a growl.

Senator Victor Hargreaves descended last.

He stepped onto the cavern floor with the posture of a man arriving at a negotiation he'd already decided he would win. His suit had been swapped for tactical black, though the crisp precision of the cuffs gave away how out of place the attire was down here. He adjusted one glove, scanned the cavern, and allowed himself a single approving nod.

"This is it," he said quietly. Not reverently. Possessively.

Beside him, Dr. Corwin, the HECATE science lead, snapped open a hardened tablet. Two resonance technicians followed, each struggling under the weight of specialized scanners shaped like tuning forks mated with Tasers. Their LED panels flickered uncertainly in the living light of the cavern.

Hargreaves approached the edge of the pool. The Talisman's faint ember-glow reflected in his eyes.

"A point source harmonic anomaly," he said, savoring the phrase as if it were already his. "The heart of the problem."

Corwin cleared his throat and gestured toward the stone under the water. "It's more than that, Senator. This object is amplifying every Walker signature within the region. Our readings doubled on approach. It also appears to distort or choke those same signatures depending on environmental conditions. Think of it as a... field regulator."

"A regulator," Hargreaves repeated. "Which means an opportunity."

Corwin hesitated. His voice tightened. "Or a risk. We can't model all the variables yet. The artifact predates recorded history. It's interacting with our equipment in ways that don't follow harmonic physics."

Hargreaves turned to him. "Nuclear was the last century, Doctor. This century belongs to the people who own whatever that is."

He jabbed a finger toward the Talisman.

The cavern responded with another pulse, low and displeased. A line of ley-light flickered overhead, as if something unseen had stirred beneath the stone.

One of the resonance techs flinched. His scanner began to rattle, bouncing between readings like a broken compass. "Sir... the field is unstable. We're seeing Walker traces, but they're not static. They're moving. They're converging."

Hargreaves' expression tightened. "Then we'll take control before they get here."

Corwin tapped rapidly through data. "The Talisman is waking, Senator. We should consider containment before extraction."

"No," Hargreaves said, stepping closer to the water. "We're going to secure it and repurpose it. Properly tuned, it could neutralize a Walker or supercharge one. Either way, it stops being a threat. It becomes leverage."

The floodlights hissed as their power dipped for a moment. Behind them, the generator coughed, stuttered, and returned to life with a strained whine. The air in the cavern thickened. A cold draft curled around their ankles, rising from nowhere.

Corwin swallowed. "The cavern's reacting. Sir... this space is alive."

"Then it can listen," Hargreaves said.

But the cavern's hum had shifted. It no longer felt like passive displeasure. It had taken on a tone that vibrated in the bones. A warning, deep and ancient.

For the first time, Hargreaves hesitated. The faintest crease formed between his eyebrows as the pool's surface rippled without cause, rings spreading outward from the Talisman as if something down there had exhaled.

The Weave was responding to him.

Judging him.

And the judgment was not favorable.

A shiver of fear, small but unmistakable, passed through him before he forced it back down.

"We proceed," he said, voice harder than before.

But the cavern had already begun to wake.

And it was not on his side.

HECATE should never have found this place. No living map marked it, no surface structure hinted at the hollow beneath Salem. But after Maya and Alex escaped the mausoleum, they discovered that Hargreaves' teams had been analyzing every resonance anomaly created by Maya's jumps. One of those signatures had dipped too deep, brushed the edge of the cavern on her way back from the Deep.

It was a trace that should have vanished, a whisper in the lattice.

But HECATE had built technology to chase whispers.

Their satellite-linked scanners found the drop in harmonics, marked it, triangulated subterranean density, and flagged the anomaly as a "possible Walker den." Within hours, a strike team converged.

Maya sensed the moment they breached the cavern from a mile away. Something in the Weave shuddered, like a nerve she had not known was connected to her. Alex felt it too, a pressure behind his eyes, a wrongness in the air. They followed that feeling, slipping through old access tunnels and fissures in the stone until they reached a narrow tunnel overlooking the cavern through fractured rock. Close enough to see. Too close to intervene.

Now they watched from the shadows as Hargreaves' people worked.

HECATE had transformed the cavern's ancient heart into an operating theater. Portable floodlights cast cruel light across the walls. At the edge of the pool, technicians planted a ring of PIR rods, each one sprouting a thin antenna that quivered in the cold air. Cables ran from them to a control station where screens displayed scrolling harmonic graphs.

Two resonance cages waited nearby, metal arcs designed to trap a Walker the way Faraday cages trap lightning. Maya felt bile rise at the sight. Those cages were meant for her. For Alex. Maybe for others like them.

Hargreaves stood at the front of it all, hands clasped behind his back.

"Bring it online," he said.

The science team lowered a conductive probe into the water. A long cable fed out in slow coils as the device drifted closer to the submerged stone.

"Contact in three seconds," Dr. Corwin said. "Two. One. Contact."

At first, nothing happened.

Then everything did.

The screens erupted in phosphor green arcs. Graphs leapt violently, curves slashing upward in impossible spikes. Frequency labels flashed and vanished faster than they could be read.

FIELD AMPLIFICATION

PHASE SLIP DETECTED

UNMAPPED FREQUENCY

UNMAPPED FREQUENCY

UNMAPPED FREQUENCY

The technicians panicked, scrambling to reboot systems that no longer obeyed them.

"Pull the probe," someone barked.

"It's not responding."

"It's locked. It feels frozen."

Maya felt it too. The Weave tightened around the cavern like a net being drawn shut. Her chest constricted. Her breath hitched.

Alex touched the wall beside her. His fingers curled reflexively. "This alignment is wrong. Nothing about this feels natural."

The generator's hum stretched into an unsettling groan, as if time itself had thickened. The floodlights flickered once, twice, then died. Darkness swallowed the cavern. Only the faint blue ley glow remained, pulsing in slow intervals like the heartbeat of an ancient, sleeping beast.

Water dripped from the ceiling. A single drop fell into the pool.

It should have rippled.

It did not.

The surface swallowed it without disturbance, as if the water had turned to glass, or something deeper and heavier than water. Maya flinched.

The Talisman beneath the surface brightened to an ash-colored glow, a hue colder than red, darker than ember. There was no warmth to it. Only the suggestion of something waking.

One of Hargreaves' techs slapped the side of a dead monitor. Static smeared across the glass, then went pure white. All screens followed, washing the station in ghost-light before snapping to black.

Headsets squealed in a burst of feedback so sharp that several agents tore them off. After that, silence. No incoming comms. No signals escaping the cavern.

The PIR rods lit once with a single hard pulse. Ozone filled the air.

Then they went dark forever.

"Senator," Dr. Corwin whispered. "The Talisman is destabilizing our equipment. We need to withdraw."

Hargreaves did not move. His silhouette stood rigid against the faint glow rising from the pool. His breath steamed in the sudden cold. "No one pulls back," he said. "We hold position until we understand what we're dealing with."

"You already do," Maya whispered from her hiding place. "And you still think you can control it."

The cavern answered with a sound that was not sound.

A vibration felt in ribs, teeth, and the thin bones of the ears.

A warning.

A sentence.

A door opening in the dark.

Alex grabbed her wrist. His pulse hammered. "Maya... it is reacting to them. All of them together. And the Talisman. This is a perfect storm."

She knew he was right.

HECATE had clustered too much human machinery in a place built for myth. They had provoked the stone, the residue, the Weave, and something deeper.

Everything in the cavern was waking.

Everything in the dark was listening.

And nothing was under human control now.

Maya swallowed hard. "This is only the beginning."

Alex nodded, jaw tight. "Then we need to move before the beginning becomes the end."

The pool glowed brighter, like an eye opening.

The Static rose.

For a moment, the cavern holds its breath.

Then the walls begin to crack.

Not from pressure.

Not from movement.

From **something bending reality itself**.

Hairline fractures bloom across the stone ribs overhead. They spread in delicate branching lines, glowing faintly at first, then darkening into something matte and lightless. The cracks aren't empty. They're filled with an impossible black static, a crawling distortion that moves sideways like smoke trying to remember gravity.

It slips out of the fractures in slow, tendril-like curls.

The static doesn't float.

It **slides**, hugging the rock as if it's searching for a place to settle. Wherever it touches, color drains. Stone turns gray, then ghost-white. The green lights of HECATE's monitors desaturate to sickly frost. Even the blue veins of Weave-light dim under its approach.

Alex stiffens beside Maya, breath shallow. "That's it. That's what followed you after the purification ritual."

Maya can't answer. Every part of her is locked on the Talisman at the pool's center.

The stone pulses once.

Everything stops.

Sound doesn't fade. It **cuts out**, like a cord yanked from an instrument.

A falling water drop freezes midair, suspended above the pool.

Maya's lungs seize in her chest. She feels her own heartbeat lag, as if waiting for permission to go on.

The world holds still for a single, terrible beat.

Then the beat lands, and time rushes back like a gasp.

The technicians panic. Their voices collide in shouts, but none of it sounds right. One resonance specialist begins chanting the synchronization protocol, a practiced rhythm meant to dominate Walker energy fields.

At the third syllable, his voice shreds into noise.

The rest of the pattern disintegrates into a hiss like sand dragged across glass.

Maya watches his lips move, but no words escape, only grainy static that flickers in and out of sync with the shape of his mouth.

More static crawls from the walls, spreading across the cavern like a stain. The air vibrates with a sickening undertone, low and arrhythmic, a pitch that contradicts itself every second.

"Maya," Alex whispers, trembling. "Your after images are back."

She looks toward the pool and her breath catches.

She sees herself.

More than one.

Ten. Twelve. Twenty flickers.

Each a fragment of a past jump, each trailing her by half a heartbeat. Some look like the moment she blinked through the warehouse. Others look like versions from the Ipswich run, blurred by speed.

They layer around her like echoes of choices she never meant to leave behind.

Every after image vibrates with a faint jitter, a delay she recognizes as the residue tracing her pattern. They hover near the places where the Static is densest, reacting like iron filings drawn to a magnet.

"Don't look at them," Alex murmurs.

She can't help it. One flicker near the water seems to turn its head toward her, even though it's only an imprint. It's impossible, but she feels the attention like an eye pressed against the back of her skull.

A specialist rushes toward the pool with a scanner rod. He tries to step around a swirl of static, but misjudges the angle. The moment his boot crosses the tendril's edge, his outline smears.

His arm splits in two directions at once, as if time disagrees with where he should be standing. His face blurs in a sickening stretch, like someone dragged paint across a canvas.

Then reality snaps him back into one piece.

He stumbles, gagging, eyes swimming. "What... what was that?"

But Maya knows.

The Unmaking isn't attacking.

It's **unweaving**, testing the edges of form, loosening the threads holding matter together.

The Static is its presence made visible.

Her empath sense strains to interpret it, but everything is muffled. Emotions feel distant, like hearing through thick insulation. She can barely feel Alex even though he's pressed against her side. The Weave is muted in the cavern, swallowed by the distortion. Only the Static is clear, humming through her bones like an insect crawling under her skin.

"This isn't a creature," she murmurs, voice shaking. "It's a field. A force."

A correction to the Weave.

A hunger for equilibrium.

Alex grips her hand hard. "Can we run?"

Maya forces herself to breathe. The after images tighten around the pool like spectral guardians. HECATE's tech is collapsing. The Talisman is brightening.

She shakes her head.

"No," she says. "This won't stop if we run. It's not here for them. It's here for me."

The Static warps again, folding around the pool in a widening ring of distortion.

Time staggers.

Light bends.

Reality flinches.

And Maya realizes with a cold certainty that this is the first true manifestation of the Unmaking in the world above myths. It isn't a monster to fight. It's a **counterforce that erodes the shape of everything it touches**.

The world hums one beat out of tune.

Her jaw sets.

"This has to be answered," she whispers. "Not escaped."

The pool brightens again, as if the stone under the water agrees.

The Static moves before Maya does.

She feels it the moment she reaches for the Weave. The Current slides into her resonance, cold and slick, the same way it did during the failed jump back in the mausoleum. Her sigil flares hot, bright under her skin, then suddenly cools as if doused. The cold is worse than heat; it means the Unmaking has found the gaps between her pulses again.

Her breath stutters. She tries anyway.

If she can open even a short blink, she might drag Hargreaves away from the Talisman, or at least redirect the surge. The Weave is buckling. HECATE is losing control. Someone has to do something before the whole cavern becomes a dead zone.

She summons her pitch.

The Static beats her to it.

It surges along the same lane she reaches for, slipping into her resonance like a hand sliding into a glove. Pain detonates down her spine, sharp and icy, as if a needle of frozen metal has been driven straight into her nerves. Her vision blurs. Her nose starts to bleed instantly, hot and metallic on her upper lip.

The world tilts.

No. Not again. She will not let it ride her again.

"Maya!" Alex's voice is somewhere behind her, too far, too muffled. "Stop, you're pulling it in. Stop."

She cannot. It is already inside the cracks.

A hand slams against her sternum.

Another presses to the back of her neck.

Alex pulls her toward him, not physically but harmonically. The moment his palms touch her, something changes. He has done this once before by accident. This time he does it with all the focus he has left.

He finds her pitch.

She feels him do it. The recognition is immediate, like someone catching a falling instrument and correcting its vibration by instinct. He draws her resonance into alignment with his own, matching it beat by beat.

Then he adds his tone.

It is lower.

Steadier.

Broad where hers is sharp, open where hers is narrow.

Her breath jerks as if someone has plunged warm water through her chest. The Static inside her resonance shudders. It tries to cling to the gaps as before, but Alex's tone fills every space, a stabilizing pulse that spreads outward like a shield unfolding from her core.

The silence tries again.

It pushes.

It claws into the edges of her pitch.

Alex pushes back.

His head bows forward, jaw tight. A tremor runs through his hands. She can feel the strain tearing through him. His field ripples, dimpling in short bursts as the Static tries to punch through. It is looking for somewhere to go, some path to ride.

He refuses to give it one.

Maya gasps, shuddering as the invasive cold recedes from her pulse. The Static withdraws, pushed outward like smoke driven back by a sudden gust.

Her knees give out. Alex catches her before she hits the floor.

She stares at him, dizzy and breathless. "Alex," she whispers. "You are not just a Listener."

He shakes his head, still clenching his teeth. "I am not doing anything."

"You are doing everything."

The Static slams against their combined field one last time. Alex flinches, a low groan escaping him before he forces his rhythm steady again. His entire body is shaking. A pressure vein stands out in his forehead. He looks like he is holding back a thunderstorm with his bare hands.

But the Static cannot find her anymore.

Every crevice her resonance once left exposed is filled by his.

Her pitch is no longer alone. His surrounds it, protecting it. Anchoring it.

She cups his face with trembling fingers. "You are a Shield," she says, almost in awe. "You are the wall it cannot pass."

Alex draws in a shaking breath. "I am trying," he whispers. "I do not know how long I can hold it."

Fear crashes through her, sharp and immediate.

Not fear for herself.

Fear for him.

"Then we do this together," she says, anchoring her hands to his wrists as his pulse climbs. "I am not losing you. Not to this."

The Static curls back across the cavern, gathering like a storm waiting to break.

But for the first time...

It cannot reach her.

Not while Alex stands between her and the silence.

The cavern is chaos.

Floodlights lie shattered on the stone floor.

Hargreaves is shouting orders that no one is following.

HECATE techs scramble in broken formation while pockets of Static drift in slow, deliberate curls that ignore gravity.

And in the middle of it all, for one strange breath, Maya finds stillness.

Alex stands close, hands still shaking from shielding her. His presence steadies her pulse. But her mind is already reaching beyond the moment, pulling threads together faster than her fear can keep up.

Fragment XXVIII rises fully in her memory.

Not just the pieces she skimmed.

All of it.

"It is not meant to be wielded. It is meant to be endured."

"The Song that Builds cannot exist without the Silence that Waits."

"Those who carry the ash note carry its attention."

The phrases lock into place like tumblers turning in a lock.

She looks at the pool.

At the dull ember glow of the Talisman beneath the water.

At the way the stone vibrates, not violently but stubbornly, like something holding too much weight.

She suddenly understands.

"Hargreaves is feeding it garbage," she whispers.

Alex blinks, still catching his breath. "What?"

"It's a stabilizer." Her voice is quiet but solid. "The Talisman is supposed to absorb strain in the lattice. It's a brace, not a battery. And Hargreaves' tech is pushing misaligned patterns into it." She gestures to the dead rods and melted conduits. "He's forcing the Weave to deform around a stone that's supposed to keep it steady."

A fresh surge of Static ripples through the cavern, scattering a team of resonance specialists. One of them starts to scream as he is enveloped by the static and vanishes completely.

Maya barely flinches.

"This is why the Residue is spiking," she continues, mind racing forward. "Why it manifested so strongly. The Talisman can hold tension, but not like this. Not twisted and pulled in a dozen wrong directions."

Alex stares at her, understanding flickering behind his fear. "Then what do we do?"

She looks down at her hands.

At the faint green glow under her skin where her sigil hums.

At the fingers that have been tearing holes in the world every time she panics.

Her jumps bend the lattice. Her jumps create micro tears. Every movement is a distortion.

But distortions can be intentional. Tension can be shaped. Fabric can be mended if you know where the threads are thin.

She inhales deeply.

"If I jump along the grain," she says quietly, "I can pull the pattern back into alignment. I have been moving through the lattice without understanding what I was doing. But I can use that same movement to stitch it shut."

Alex's eyes widen. "Maya. That will put you right in the Current."

"It already knows me," she says softly. "It has my outline. My echo. My note. If I do nothing, the Talisman will rip Salem open."

He reaches for her hand. She catches his fingers and squeezes once.

She does not feel like a fugitive anymore.

Or a mistake.

Or a danger struggling to contain herself.

She feels like a Weaver.

"I am going to stitch this around the Talisman," she says, steady now. "And I am going to give it the right tension to hold."

Static slithers across the cavern floor, drawn to the stone's rising pulse.

Hargreaves yells something behind her.

She does not hear him.

Her fear quiets.

Resolve settles in its place.

"Alex," she says, lifting her gaze to the center of the pool, "stay with me. Whatever happens, do not let go of my pitch."

He nods, his breath trembling but sure. "I won't."

For the first time since the Weave broke open, Maya feels exactly where she belongs.

Not running.

Not hiding.

Not surviving.

Mending.

The Talisman pulses once, a low thrumming note that shivers through stone and bone.

Maya rises to meet it.

Maya knows there is no time left to debate or doubt. The cavern is coming apart in ways that have nothing to do with stone, and everything to do with the Weave being pushed past its limits.

She grabs Alex's wrist, pulls him close enough that her forehead nearly touches his, and says in one fast breath, "I jump to it. I take its note into mine. You hold the shield as long as you can."

Alex's inhalation stutters, but he nods. "I'm here. I'll catch whatever hits you."

"You catch me," she corrects softly. "Not the Static."

His jaw tightens. "I'll try."

"That's all I need."

She turns to the pool.

The water is black glass, the surface too still, too smooth, like a held breath. The Talisman glows beneath it, a dull ember in the center of the world.

Maya steps to the edge.

She does not reach through the water.

She reaches through the Weave.

She finds the Talisman's pitch, that deep ash note vibrating just beneath real sound, and sets her destination on resonance rather than coordinates. Her fingers lift and tremble slightly as she aligns herself to it.

The jump starts.

Her body flickers like a candle in a breeze.

The cavern drags behind her, lagging a half beat.

Shadows form around her feet, then ripple outward.

After images bloom around the chamber, faint outlines of her in poses she has not yet taken. All of them slightly off beat. All of them trying to sync.

Her breath stutters.

Then, in a flash of green-white, her hand closes on the Talisman in Weave space.

The shock is instant.

It shoots up her arm like she has grabbed a wire that carries both electricity and the entire history of the world's first breath. There is music in it. There is silence in it. And there is something else, something like a pulse that has been waiting too long to be heard.

Her resonance spikes.

Her head snaps back.

Light bursts from her sigil.

Alex shouts her name.

The Unmaking reacts before she can brace.

It surges into the same channel she is holding open.

Static lashes around her after images, giving them weight.

Some of them blink. One takes a half step toward her.

Reality trembles, not breaking, but bending too far.

Maya tries to hold the Talisman's note steady, but the pitch is too large, too old, too heavy. She feels her own hum stretching thin, like fabric pulled over a blade.

Then Alex's hands grab her from behind.

One on her sternum.

One on the back of her neck.

And his field slams into place.

He pushes a warm, low vibration into her, a counter harmonic that spreads sideways and fills the gaps the Static is trying to occupy. She feels him pulling part of the overload into his own body, siphoning it, grounding it, anchoring her in the storm.

"Alex, stop, you'll hurt yourself—"

"I'm not stopping," he gasps.

His veins stand out in his neck. His eyes water from the pressure. Every muscle shakes with the force of holding back the Current.

Still, the Static pushes harder.

Maya feels the fracture forming.

Not in the cavern.

Not in the Weave.

In herself.

The Talisman's note is beginning to fuse with her resonance, weaving itself into her hum with impossible precision. It is too much for any human body to contain.

Alex collapses to one knee behind her, hands slipping on her shoulders.

For half a second, the shield drops.

Just half a second.

And that half second is enough.

The Residue completes its trace of her pattern.

It follows the line she is holding.

It slides into the resonance she is binding to the stone.

The jump does not fully succeed.

The jump does not fully fail.

It fractures.

Maya screams as light pours from her sigil like molten glass.

Her knees buckle.

Her vision whites out.

Her body feels both too heavy and not there at all.

The nexus beneath Salem cracks wide open.

The Talisman's pulse hammers through her ribs.

Alex's voice echoes as if from the end of a tunnel.

Someone shouts Hargreaves' name.

Static sings like broken stars.

Then everything goes silent.

Everything goes white.

And Maya feels herself slipping free of her body, not into death, but into the Weave itself, into the lattice between moments, where breath and thought and gravity no longer mean anything.

The cavern, Hargreaves, HECATE, the Static, Alex's hands falling away from her shoulders...

All of it fades.

The Weave takes her.

<h1 style="text-align:center">15</h1>

The Five Threads Become One

There is no pain at first.
No sound.

No gravity.

Maya becomes aware of herself in stages, like someone waking inside a dream they were already walking through. She feels motion before she feels a body. She feels direction before she feels breath.

She is not lying on stone anymore.

She is not in the cavern.

She is not in her skin.

She is movement.

The Weave rises around her like a horizon made of light.

Threads stretch out in every direction, thousands upon thousands of luminous lines humming in slow, eternal chords. They converge and separate, bend and intersect, all of it alive with a rhythm she once only heard as hints and whispers. Now she is inside it, moving with it, part of its pulse.

Salem appears below her, not as a city but as a constellation.

Five nodes shine like lanterns in fog, each beating its own steady note.

Gallows Hill is the darkest, a deep indigo core shaped by centuries of grief.

The Harbor Knot glows in restless blue, water shaped into song.

The Old Burying Point throbs amber, ancient stories tangled through soil.

Naumkeag Stone Ridge radiates pale silver, cold and clean.

The Castle Hill rail tunnel pulses in a steady green, industrial and stubborn.

Five notes.

Five lights.

Five anchors in the pattern.

They feel like five voices calling her home.

She turns toward the first one without thinking, and her entire sense of self stretches into a comet trail. She becomes a streak of green white light, sliding along the thread that connects the nodes to one another.

As she crosses the first line, it brightens beneath her, like a string plucked by an unseen hand. The vibration runs through her, through everything that she is or remembers being. She feels that note fall into place, taut and aligned.

She moves again, faster this time.

Harbor Knot.

Old Burying Point.

Stone Ridge.

Rail tunnel.

Each time she passes through a node, the thread tightens behind her, snapping into symmetry. She is stitching the lattice together with her own motion, drawing it into order the way a seamstress pulls fabric smooth under tension.

The Weave warms around her, recognizing what she is doing, even guiding her toward what needs to be done next. She feels its approval like a breath of wind in a place that has no air.

The nodes begin to glow brighter.

Once.

Twice.

A third time.

Then they connect to one another.

Light leaps from one point to the next, forming sharp angles through Weave space, a star-shaped harmonic pattern blooming above the cavern where her body fell. As the star completes, a pulse rolls outward, deep and resonant, shaking everything in its path.

From within the Weave, it looks beautiful.

From the physical world, it looks impossible.

Streetlights flicker across Salem like someone is tracing a pentagon through the electrical grid.

Car alarms pulse in matching intervals.

HECATE instruments spike so perfectly it looks like a glitch in reality itself.

Maya feels it all in her bones, even though she no longer feels bone.

She hears herself think, but it is not a thought made with words. It is recognition.

I can do this.

The desperation that pushed her into the Weave dissolves.

It becomes something cleaner, something quieter.

Transcendence.

She streaks through the nodes again, faster, tightening them further. The star hums, threads adjusting themselves until every point resonates in perfect balance.

And at the center of the star, like a heart waiting for a beat, lies the cavern.

Lies the nexus.

Lies the Talisman.

Maya steadies herself, even as she feels her form blur at the edges, even as she feels her old sense of self thinning into something else.

She is the thread now.

She is the movement.

She is the one who will hold the pattern long enough to mend it.

And something deep beneath Salem feels her arrival.

It breathes.

Maya feels the star lock into place.

The five nodes around Salem hum in a balanced chord, light threads taut between them. At the center of that pattern the nexus flares, a point of pressure that wants to twist, to tear, to spill. She leans into it, not with muscles or breath, but with tension.

Something changes.

She realizes, with a sudden quiet shock, that she is no longer moving along the Weave.

She is the movement.

Her awareness stretches, thinning and lengthening until there is no clear difference between where she ends and the lattice begins. She feels her own presence as a single line running through the pattern, a thread of green white brightness woven through darker cords.

Pressure gathers along her length.

She is aware of distance not as miles, but as strain. Where the star pattern pulls hardest, the sense of herself tightens. Where there is slack, she feels the temptation of unraveling. Every slight adjustment in the lattice echoes through her like the pluck of a string.

She exists as tension.

On the far edge of her perception, something flickers.

A figure stands beyond the web of light, more suggestion than shape. At first she thinks it is a trick of the threads. Then she senses the outline clearly: a person standing outside the lattice, hands lifted as if pressed to an invisible surface.

Robes blur around narrow shoulders. Hair falls in silver streaks. The face is indistinct, but the bearing is unmistakable. Old. Tired. Watching.

Merlin.

He does not stand on a thread. He does not move with the currents. He hangs beyond them, in the thin space where matter and magic brush against each other without fully touching. To him, the Weave must look like stained glass looks to someone standing in a dark cathedral. Close. Brilliant. Untouchable.

His fingers brace against the unseen barrier. Not a wall, exactly. More like the skin of reality. He sees the lattice, but he cannot enter. His power was never in the currents themselves. It lived in the aura they cast.

A soft ache moves through her.

He did all of that, she thinks, and he never felt this under his feet.

The outline inclines its head, the faintest nod. For a heartbeat, she feels a scholar's curiosity pass through her, old and sharp. It is not her feeling. It is his, touching her through the barrier. Then the image blurs again, pressed back by a deeper chorus.

Voices rise in the Weave.

They are not voices in the human sense. There is no language, no syllables she could write down. They are pulses along the threads, changes in pitch and rhythm that her mind translates as intent.

One is rough and deep, like stone cracking under heat. It speaks in slow, heavy concepts. Weight. Balance. Consequence.

Beagron.

His presence does not localize to a single point. It folds along several thick strands at once, an old, familiar pattern imprinted into the lattice, more memory than active will. Whenever pressure gathers too sharply in one area, his note rumbles through, redistributing strain.

Others join him.

High, clear tones that arc between distant nodes. Low harmonies that sit under entire regions like buried drums. The sensation is like hearing a choir from the far end of a vast hall, each voice placed on a separate balcony, all singing the same song in different registers.

These are the ancient Guardians, the ones who walked the Weave before it sealed.

They do not speak her name. They do not instruct. They hold. They sing. Their work is constant adjustment, a quiet labor that has gone on for a very long time. As she listens, she realizes something that should have terrified her.

Several of those voices are thin.

Where the seal cut magic off from the mortal side, the Guardians could no longer recruit replacements. Some of the old patterns have frayed. Some threads hum at the very edge of breaking. The song is still there, but it carries more weight than it should.

Far away, beyond the cluster that is Salem, one note stands out.

Steady. Human-sized. Bright.

She turns toward it without moving, awareness stretching across a continent in a heartbeat. The Weave does not measure distance the way the map in her notebook did. It measures resonance. This beacon is strong enough to register through layers of other threads.

She cannot see the man himself. She sees his effect.

A column of intertwined light and shadow rises from a node somewhere in the interior of the country. Its tone is firm, neither sweet nor harsh, carrying the cadence of someone who has learned to bear things without bending. Shocks move through it at intervals, like aftershocks in a fault line, but it does not splinter.

Ethan.

She knows it as surely as if he had said his name.

His note does not feel like a mortal brushing the surface. It feels like someone who has already stepped halfway through the membrane between worlds. The light in his thread reaches deeper into the lattice than hers should at his age. A portion of him already hums with the same authority as the older Guardians. The rest anchors somewhere soft and familiar, in human time.

He did not die cleanly. He did not live cleanly either. He occupies that tough, necessary middle.

Maya feels a sob build in the part of herself that still remembers lungs. It does not reach her surface. There is no surface to reach. She lets the feeling pass through her like a small change in current.

Merlin outside.

Beagron and the old ones inside.

Ethan on the threshold.

Where does that leave her?

Her awareness folds back toward Salem.

The five-point star gleams, pulled tight. Beneath its center the nexus churns, a knot of stress where the Unmaking has gathered and the Talisman sits like a stone placed at the bottom of a whirlpool. Static curls in the gaps between threads, trying to widen them, to turn stretches of pattern into holes.

Understanding reaches her in a single, whole piece.

Weave Walkers are not simply people who learned tricks.

They are the parts of the system that notice damage and move toward it.

She feels it now as a function rather than a role. Where strain spikes, attention follows. Where threads fray, something in her leans in. If she ignored it, if she turned away, the pull would not stop. It would only hurt more.

They are the immune system of the world, waking one by one as the seal weakens.

Some, like Ethan, have already begun to cross over, their work lying partly in the Weave, partly on the mortal side. Others, like her, are still very new, their patterns untested, their limits unknown. Somewhere out there, the chaotic node in Miami flares and stutters. The steady one in Colorado hums like bedrock. Joe, Elara, Richard. Lines she has not yet touched, but will.

Her work is not to kill the Unmaking. That is not possible, and not even right. The Residue is part of the same equation the song belongs to. Her work is to keep it from overloading any one place, any one life, any one city, when the Weave opens fully again.

She is a hand on the dial, not a hammer.

The idea frightens her.

There is a version of herself that would have clung to the edges of her old life with both fists at this point, screaming internally that she is a person, not a system. That version still exists in her, very small and very loud.

You will vanish, it says. You will disappear into this. You will not come back.

Another part, just as honest, answers.

If you do not, all of this tears.

The Guardians do not quiet her fear. They do not soothe her. They simply continue their work, holding tension, balancing forces too large for human metaphors to contain.

One strand near Salem wavers.

Her attention goes to it at once, the way a medic scans for the worst bleeding first. The nexus wants to slip. The static pushes. The Talisman braces, but it was not meant to carry this much alone.

She realizes, in a calm that surprises her, that she knows what to do.

She lets her fear sit where it is. She does not push it away. She does not let it rule.

You are still Maya, she tells herself, as clearly as she can. You still love Alex. You still remember Isabel. You still care about shelves of books and dented kettles and stupid documentaries about haunted lighthouses.

You are also this.

Both things are true.

Her sense of self deepens rather than flattens. Mortal fear does not vanish. It becomes one thread among many, quieter in the presence of something larger that has finally found its name.

She is a Walker.

She is a stitcher of damaged lines.

She is part of the world's way of healing itself.

Mythic identity blooms in her, not as grandiosity, but as recognition of the scale of her task.

She feels the star tremble again. The center strains. The ash note in her own resonance waits, listening. The Talisman hums at the bottom of the pool, ready to take the right shape of tension if she can give it that.

Maya gathers herself along her entire length, thread bright, tone clear.

Then she begins to work.

The lattice flexes around her like a living thing.

Threads of light arc in every direction, tugging, quivering, humming in tones she can feel more than hear. At the deepest point sits the Talisman, and it does not look like a stone anymore. It looks like a dense, tangled knot where too many lines intersect without purpose. For a moment, she almost feels its panic. Too much tension. Too many crossings. No direction to send the strain.

Around that knot, the Shadow Current pools in thick, roiling static. Not smoke. Not shadow. Something like the foam that forms where ocean waves crush against each other in opposite directions. It churns without center, without intention, but with enormous weight.

Maya knows immediately what will happen if she touches that knot directly.

The lattice will tear.

And Salem will tear with it.

She steadies herself, a single glowing thread stretched between five luminous nodes. Her awareness widens until she feels the entire star shape she wove, every line under her guidance.

She does not push power into the Talisman. That was Hargreaves' mistake. She does not try to blast the knot or pull the stone free. Instead, she moves along the lines she controls, adjusting tension with the same instinct she used when sewing ripped backpacks in high school.

She pulls one node's thread tighter until it rings like a taut wire.
She loosens the next so it relaxes by a fraction.
She shifts the third, drawing its arc a degree closer to the center.
The fourth gets relieved, pressure siphoned away.
The fifth she coils slightly tighter, shaping a curve instead of a straight pull.

Each adjustment sends vibrations through her awareness. It is like playing a harp made of fault lines and moonlight. She feels the Talisman react, humming in short, pained tremors. The static around it surges and then recoils.

The pattern begins to change.

At first, it is subtle. A frayed line straightens. A sagging thread lifts. The star shape grows more precise. But the more she works, the clearer it becomes: she is closing a wound. The lattice bends toward order, toward something cleaner and stronger.

The Talisman starts to glow brighter at the center of the star.
A new pitch joins its old one.
Not pure Song. Not pure Silence.
Both. In balance.

She feels the Shadow Current shiver.

The static that had clustered around the knot begins to seep outward, thinning, losing density. It does not vanish. It simply redistributes, like fog dispersing into open air. What remains is the manageable background hum she has felt since the Deep, something the world can carry without breaking.

The crisis is passing.

But the cost hits her like a sudden drop through ice.

Holding this shape requires everything. Not strength. Not willpower. Identity.

Her sense of self begins to blur at the edges. She feels the part of her that is Maya Beaufort slipping backward, becoming quieter, thinner, as if she is being stretched across too many points. It does not hurt, exactly. It feels like being rewritten into something that no longer has a single center.

Her awareness of her body fades. Skin, breath, heartbeat, all of it becomes distant, dim, unimportant. She can tell she still has a body somewhere, in a cavern filled with terrified people and flickering lights, but she cannot feel it.

All that matters is the lattice.

She holds the pattern steady.

She keeps the tension right.

She keeps reality from tearing.

Then something shifts.

A deep, final alignment.

The Talisman sends out a low, full vibration that echoes through all five nodes. The lattice glows as if lit from within. She feels the star stabilize, its points locking into place with a quiet snap that resonates through her entire being.

The crisis is over.

The lattice settles, calmer and healthier than it has been in centuries.

A wave of peace moves through her. Not human peace. Not relief or gratitude or accomplishment. A structural peace, like the moment a broken bone sets correctly. She feels it radiate outward into the world.

And then she feels nothing.

In physical space, the cavern undergoes a violent, impossible shift.

A pressure drop sucks the air downward.

HECATE floodlights burst with sparks.

Every screen on every device whites out at once.

The generator coughs once and dies.

Hargreaves and his team are thrown to the stone floor as if someone dropped a massive invisible weight through the center of the room.

At the pool's edge, Maya's body collapses.

Her sigil flares once in a brilliant, searing pulse. Then the light dies down to a slow, faint throb under her skin.

She does not feel the fall.

She does not feel Alex shouting her name.

She does not feel the world.

Her last sensation before everything goes dark is the lattice humming under her like a living heartbeat, steady for the first time since the Weave began to fracture.

Agony dissolves.

Identity thins.

Peace takes her.

She is gone from her body before it hits the ground.

*****

The world comes back slowly.

It arrives first as a soft, steady beeping. Then the faint hiss of an oxygen line. A cool weight rests against the inside of her elbow, and something tugs gently at the skin of her hand. There is warmth too, human warmth, wrapped around her fingers.

Maya opens her eyes.

Dim hospital light filters through a curtain, turning everything gray and muted. Outside the window, Salem lies quiet, city lights blurred into stillness. The night looks strangely peaceful, like the world is catching its breath.

Alex sits beside the bed, slumped forward, both hands wrapped around hers. His knuckles are scraped raw. There is a bruise along one cheekbone. His eyes are half closed, exhausted beyond anything she has ever seen in him, but he is awake the moment she moves.

"Maya," he whispers, almost breaking on the name. He squeezes her hand, a short, desperate motion. "Hey. Hey, you're here. You're really here."

She wants to smile. Her lips barely move. Everything feels too heavy, too soft, like she is made of fog trying to remember how to hold shape.

Her gaze shifts past him.

On a metal tray beside the bed sits a shallow, heatproof container lined with sterile cloth. Inside it is a dusting of gray ash, fine as sand. All that remains of the Codex.

Beside the ash rests the Arcana of the Weave. Its cover is closed, but the leather trembles faintly, humming with low, patient resonance. The last pages inside it feel blank in a way that is not emptiness but expectation.

Maya lowers her eyes to her own hand, the one Alex is holding so tightly.

The sigil glows beneath the skin, soft as the pulse of a distant star. Light rises and falls in rhythm with her heartbeat, as if the Weave itself is breathing in her veins.

Alex laughs once, a quick, unsteady breath that sounds too much like relief on the edge of collapse. He brushes a tear off his cheek with the heel of his palm.

"You scared the hell out of me," he says quietly. "I thought I lost you."

Her throat aches, but she manages a whisper.

"Alex."

He leans in, eyes locked on hers, waiting for anything she can give him.

"Tell them..." Her voice cracks. She swallows, tries again. "Tell them the Weave is awake."

He freezes. A slow shiver runs through him, as if the words carry weight he can feel even without touching her field.

He nods once, fierce and certain.

"I will."

Maya lets her eyes drift closed again. She is not falling. Not fading. Just resting, anchored by his hand, the hum under her skin, and the quiet thrum of a living world outside the window.

She survived.

But she came back different.

And the Weave, for the first time in centuries, is listening.

16

The Fifth Covenant

Maya floated.

There was no weight, no temperature, no breath to keep track of. The distinction between inside and outside felt meaningless. She existed as awareness suspended in light, carried along by currents she no longer resisted. Her body lay in a hospital bed miles above this place, but here, in the luminous quiet between everything, she was more awake than she had ever been.

Threads stretched in every direction. They crossed, diverged, spiraled, and reconnected, forming a vast lattice that shimmered in colors she could not name. Some threads hummed with bright, clean tones. Others were soft and deep, like the echo of memory. Wherever the lines met, pulses of energy flowed, small bursts of light that rippled outward.

She realized she was seeing the Weave the way it saw itself.

As she drifted, a presence stirred at the edge of her awareness. Then another. Then a third. They arrived the way chords arrive in a song, each one entering at the moment the harmony needs it.

The first voice came from outside the lattice entirely. Measured. Curious. Analytical even in its reverence.

"Maya."

Merlin.

She turned, or the Weave turned her, toward a faint outline standing beyond the glowing threads. He looked like the depictions in old manuscripts: long coat, traveling boots, hair curling past his shoulders. But he was not inside the network of threads, only touching it with the barest suggestion of a hand.

He gave her a small nod, equal parts greeting and apology.

"I could only hear what the Weave allowed," he said gently. "You walk where I never did. Your path was closed to me long before you were born."

The second voice resonated like stone struck by a hammer. Low, ancient, carrying enormous weight without aggression.

"Child of light and ash," it said. "You held the knot when the pattern trembled."

Beagron.

His presence loomed far deeper in the Weave. He appeared not as a man but as a shape made of runes and memory, a kind of gravitational center that threads curled toward. When he spoke, the lines around them tightened, aligning to his tone. Approval radiated from him like warmth from a forge.

"You carried the Talisman correctly," he said. "You did not wield it. You endured it. That is why you are still here."

A third presence joined them, softer but more powerful than either.

Kemen. Her tone wrapped around her like warm hands over a frightened heart. Calm. Certain. A steadying pulse that had held the world together once before.

"The seal thins," she said. "The song rises again. And the Fifth Covenant begins."

Maya felt the words ripple through her pattern. Not as prophecy. As recognition.

She drifted closer to the threads. They responded to her presence with small flares of green white light. Her own note vibrated through them, unmistakable. She had left her mark on the Weave, or it had left its mark on her.

"What is the Fifth Covenant?" she asked.

Kemen's answer arrived like breath across still water.

"It is not a pact among gods," she said. "It is a bond among mortals who can walk the currents. Five threads. Five voices. Five who rise when the pattern demands guardianship."

Beagron rumbled in agreement.

"The Walkers."

The term echoed in her bones, settling into place.

Walkers.

Those who could step through lines the way others stepped across thresholds.

She was not alone.

The Weave answered her next question before she could voice it. Light swelled along several threads and then burst into images, not fully formed visions but impressions that carried emotion and movement.

First:

A cramped office cluttered with case files and half empty coffee cups. Joe Biggs, somewhere in the Midwest, lifted his head sharply. His brown scruffy curls fell into his eyes. For a heartbeat, he froze. His inner tone spiked in recognition. He whispered something under his breath and looked toward the door as if someone had just called his name.

Second:

A Miami rooftop at night. Heat rising in shimmering waves from tar and concrete. The chaotic Walker paused mid stride, firelight flickering along her arm. Elara's hair snapped in the wind, red brighter than the neon behind her. She blinked hard, as if seeing a flash of green white light in the corner of her vision.

Third:

Snow blown sideways across a mountain pass in Colorado. Richard

Barrett, tall and broad, stopped his trek through the drifts. Frost collected in his beard. The snow at his feet shifted shape, rippling under the force of his transfiguration signature. He turned slowly, sensing her. His note was steady, old, patient.

They all felt her.

And they all felt something else beneath her, a deeper pulse moving slowly through the network, ancient and powerful.

"The others hear you now," Merlin said softly. "Your awakening reaches them."

"The Walkers rise," Beagron repeated, his tone reverberating through the lattice. "Five lights against the dark."

Something tightened in Maya's chest.

Not fear.

Not loneliness.

Belonging.

A sense of being part of something larger than her own trauma, larger than Salem, larger than the crisis she had barely survived. A design older than any nation or doctrine. A pattern older than any spell.

"What happens now?" she asked.

The three voices answered together, not in unison but in harmony.

"You prepare," Merlin said.

"You learn the rhythm," Beagron added.

"You listen for the silence," Kemen finished. "And when it calls, you answer with light."

The threads around her shimmered, weaving themselves into a loose circle. She realized she was standing at the center of a nexus, newly stabilized by her work. The pulse that ran through it was strong and confident now, not frantic and tearing.

She drifted upward, the voices slowly receding.

The Weave dimmed, softening to the palest green white glow.

As consciousness pulled her back toward her physical body, Kemen's voice came once more, a whisper threading itself through the lattice.

"The Fifth Covenant forms."

Then silence.

Then breath.

Then hospital light.

And Maya opened her eyes.

John discovered storytelling as a child navigating foster care, where books became both refuge and inspiration. After serving twenty-four years in the U.S. Army with three combat deployments, He returned to writing, drawing on a lifetime of resilience, discipline, and imagination. He now lives in rural Tennessee, where he writes full-time and spends time with his family.